T0063218

THE STORY OF IAN

A rags to riches to rags tale
with a surprise ending

HYDEN STANDARDS

The Story of Ian
A rags to riches to rags tale with a surprise ending

iUniverse books may be ordered through booksellers or by contacting:

iUniverse LLC
1663 Liberty Drive
Bloomington, IN 47403
www.iuniverse.com
1-800-Authors (1-800-288-4677)

ISBN: 978-1-4502-8336-6 (sc)
ISBN: 978-1-4502-8337-3 (e)

Library of Congress Control Number: 2010918874

Printed in the United States of America

iUniverse rev. date: 05/31/2014

Other books by Hyden Standards are:
Dreamscapers & The Mirror of Life

A parody on finance, big government, the people governing-government, the government-governing people, destiny, and a bit of bad luck. The author knows firsthand that the issue of mental illness is just plain fate.

Dedicated to those who think it can't get any worse and to those who know it can. *And to my good friend, Louis Perrera, who, after overcoming so many of life's adversities, was sadly taken by life's one certainty.*

Also a shout out to my sons, David and Daniel (do your homework!) and a special thank you to Patti Stroh for arriving at the right time in my life to help me through the bumps in the road.

Part I

Cuba

"It's sometimes best to live alone than among bad company."

Chapter 1

"I chose telling you of Ian because he was the most interesting person to come my way in a while. Now, I'm not one to get caught up in issues of what's fair and unfair, uh-uh, that's not me; there are others for that. But in Ian's case, it would be unfair if I didn't first tell you about his mother and his grandparents. So here goes . . ."

The late '50's and early '60's

were a turbulent yet exciting time for Maria Suarez. The brutal years of the Batista reign were about to end and a new *change* was coming, a *change* that was supposed to make life better for all Cubans.

"It would be great to see that Batista bastard gone."

This was the sentiment shared by millions of Cubans who'd lived through the terror of Batista's police and death squads; squads that brutalized and tortured tens of thousands and left thousands more maimed. His death squads killed additional thousands during his second go around in Cuba.

"Oh yes, it would be nice to see that bastard gone."

Time would have many Cubans despising Fugencio Batista. But time would also show his replacement at not being much better, as Cuba's *change* would come at the hands of bearded rebels looking to add their own chapter to Cuba's turbulent history. But *change*, in and of itself, isn't always what it seems, nor . . . always for the best.

M aria Suarez was an extremely beautiful young lady and quite the charmer as a student at 'La Universidad de Havana.' She was a real head turner with a smile to match. She had stunning emerald eyes, luxurious long flowing black hair, and a Mediterranean tan befitting her Spanish heritage. (She had also been a teen Camagüen debutante.)

But if there was ever a flaw in Maria's personality, it was in her fiercely independent spirit. Being the only child of one of Cuba's wealthiest men had something to do with that.

Her father, Juan Suarez, had no reason to mistrust his daughter while she was away at college. He had no qualms in letting his only daughter live alone at the family apartment in Havana while she studied at la Universidad. Maria was even granted the luxury of a chauffeur for whenever wanting to visit the family estate in distant Camagüey. But time, again, would have Maria's freethinking spirit grow to rebel against visiting her family, thus causing her parents to despise her *new* free spirit thinking.

M aria had never taken to being a 'daddy's little girl' type. (That independent spirit thing again). She much preferred gaining her father's respect the old-fashioned way, by earning it. But she did love being at his side. It was at his side where she learned some of his business acumen.

Her mother, Elvira Suarez, wasn't too much into accepting their daughter's independent spirit though, especially when hearing of her joining up with 'Claro 13.'

Claro 13 was another of those radical student groups at La Universidad. Maria wasn't at college but a year when being swayed by the charismatically handsome and spirited Miguel Menendez, the 23-year-old leader of Claro 13. Miguel was in his third year of college when falling for Maria. As for his group, they were as disruptive, and destructive, as all the other radical upstarts on or off campus. (The moniker 'Claro 13' symbolized the 13 original members as being *supposedly* clear {claro} of mind.) Time would have Claro 13 grow to over a hundred headstrong members.

Maria's growing radicalism would force home several calls from school administrators wanting a word with her parents over her growing strong-mindedness and liberal ways. Losing her virginity to the ruggedly handsome Miguel had much to do with her growing defiance.

The day came when Claro 13, led by Miguel, decided to go toe-to-toe with the Batista authorities. By then, instead of being a soft-spoken debutante, Maria had become a shouter of brash words through bullhorns. (Claro 13 had begun resembling youth of today imitating gangsta lifestyle, though having nothing in common with the ilk.) But Maria would come to regret her mischievous and dangerous indiscretions, though during her school years her youthful indiscretions had been so much fun.

Claro 13 made it onto the Batista radar in August of '59. This was not a good thing, since they bit off more than they could chew when storming a Havana radio station and taking its disc jockey hostage. They were there to announce Batista's assassination, while a second group was to assassinate Batista. But the second group's assassination failed. Miguel and his compatriots were claiming victory on-air to Batista's death as the station was being surrounded by Batista's army.

Maria, who hadn't gone to the station because of a stomach bug that morning (butterflies?), had waited anxiously to hear from her fiancé, just as the station came under heavy gunfire from government troops. The firefight was so fierce that even the disc jockey was killed in the melee. While Maria tried calling the station, her fiancé's body, along with his dozen compatriots *and* the disc jockey, were being dragged from the station and piled onto the street. Miguel's death would send Maria more over the edge, with her fiercely independent spirit growing more ferociously radical after that.

Fugencio Batista fled from Cuba with his family on New Year's Eve 1959. With him went an estimated $200 million in cash. It was Fugencio's theft that helped push Havana into the hands of the arriving rebels. Cuba's peasantry class, who had for years been feeling betrayed, felt even more betrayed, but then relieved, when hearing that Batista was gone. Because of his fleeing, there had been little or no resistance by what was left of his Batistano army in stopping the ragged band of rebels entering Havana.

Maria waited until Fidel Castro was in complete control of Havana before showing her face in public again. It was then that she joined in with the hundreds of thousands of rabble-rousers hitting the streets to celebrate Batista's vanishing act. Next came the tearing apart of the elitist meccas, the casinos, cabarets, ballrooms, theaters, and hotels of the wealthy, except for one, which became the Fidelista headquarters.

The takeover by the bearded ones would've seemed passé, if not for the overzealous beatings, turned to excessive beat downs, which led to more torture and mayhem. The takeover of Cuba became just another in a line of socialist takeovers. Thousands upon thousands were wanting to flee Cuba then. (Cuba's takeover was just another of the many overkills that ended in overfilled graves during the 20th century.)

Maria even saw some of her father's associates get beaten senseless before taken to parts unknown. But she'd become so accustomed to violence during her college days, that hearing Che say, "el pueblo needs these beat downs" convinced her this was true. "These beatings are good for Cuba. Cuba needs a cleansing." But better or not, the beatings were pure brutality, taking hold of neighbors thinking themselves cheated by neighbors, and all backed by rhetoric telling the masses that violence was okay.

Still angered by the loss of her fiancé gave Maria even more reason for tossing in with the rebels. She wound up throwing her fair share of explosive fire bottles (Molotovs), which were filmed (and then later held as evidence against her wanting out of Cuba).

Not all of Cuba's provinces agreed with the violence. Many of the outlying provinces became alarmed when hearing of rebel bands coming to teach them about their *new* socialist freedoms (except for the province of the Sierras, from where the rebel movement had started).

It was in guessing correctly which side Cuba's bread was about to be buttered, that Maria was willing to jump into an even more scandalous relationship than the one she had with Miguel. Her next relationship again shocked her usually unshakeable father.

Juan Suarez erupted with anger when learning that Maria was in a relationship with Coronel Morales (soon to become the infamous Magico Morales). He was even more furious when learning the two were shacking up in the family apartment no less!

Col. Morales was 19 years older than Maria. He was also of the original Fidelistas who had sailed from Mexico on the Granma yacht with Fidel. It was his clout that got Maria running with a new circle of friends, Col. Morales's friends, who would keep her blind to places like el Paradon (while hundreds of thousands of Cubans were fleeing, with many more thousands wanting to flee, if not for the actual difficulty *of* fleeing). Maria would continue honing her rebel skills while on the arm of her older Col. Morales. But her being on the arm of such a high-ranking official also opened her up to scrutiny from members of the Party Directorate. This was not a good thing. But by then Morales had been taken in by Maria's beauty, wit, and charm, and cared nothing about what the Directorate, or even what her father thought of him or their being together.

"Pero Tito, mi amor," said Maria one night during their pillow talks, "there's got to be a better way of getting people onboard with La Revolucion without beating them senseless."

"Si, mi querida . . . but you wait; we rid ourselves of this Yanqui influence and you'll see a better Cuba; a Cuba that's moving forward. As for your idea of more schools and clinics . . . I'll pass that along to el Comandante myself."

No matter how history cares to record the Castro takeover, it was as old school as old school gets, and with pretty much the same results as dictators before him. The takeover replaced freedom with fear and . . . voilà.

Maria learned more of the selling points to La Revolución, but only after accepting her role as Cuba's Havana Jane. She aired La Revolución dogma from the same radio station where her fiancé had been shot. She actually didn't like that, but she was determined to do what she could for 'La Revolución' (or La Causa). While on-air she spoke only about La Revolución and about *change*. Many listeners grew to recognize her voice, and when seeing her in person, never forgot her face. This would work against her, as *change* in and of itself, would not, for a better life make, either.

Another positive that worked in Maria's favor was her near perfect English. (Because of her family's business dealings with the U.S., many of the Suarez ancestors spoke good English.) Maria practiced her English by reading her favorite English playwrights, which in the future she would read to her sons (including Ian). But her favorite books were always her dime store novels brought back to her by her father whenever on stateside business. (Her parents' passports and travel visas had already been taken from them.) The fact that Maria spoke such good English was seen as a good thing by the Fidelistas. But what was even better was her being the lone daughter of one of Cuba's wealthiest men, as she'd fallen in with the rebel cause. Her rejecting her wealth and upbringing played well with her Havana Jane persona. Maria, the rich girl turned rebel, became *the* perfect spokesperson for airing revolutionary (La Causa) rhetoric. The Fidelistas could have no better. Maria's voice became as familiar as the bearded one himself, though her rhetoric did break her parents' hearts.

Many Cubans were realizing the error of their ways by as early as 1965. But by then, the regime was fully dug in, and anyone speaking against La Revolución was dealt with harshly and severely. Castro's death squads did an even better job than Batista's squads at keeping dissension at bay.

Having ousted one tyrant for another, a confirmed communist no less, led many more Cubans to remove the blinders from their eyes and see La Revolución for what it was, a no 'light at the end of the tunnel' failing. (This failing has followed communism wherever it's gone; a failing in economic growth, setbacks, a rise in hunger, and all this shared among disgruntled communist masses.)

But Cuba's inner circle cared nothing about any of this. Cuba's non-elected officials saw what was happening in Cuba as right and proper . . . while profiting from right and proper.

Like most of humanity, Cubans, too, hated losing their freedoms over some pie in the sky 'share the wealth' nonsense.

Next to be lost was freedom to worship.

Then went free market capitalism. (*Free markets might sound oxymoronic, since no markets are ever free, but *freer* in western society, a society and culture that Fidel abhorred after admitting that capitalism was his nemesis. Any hope of dialogue between the U.S. and Cuba ended when Fidel claimed the U.S. as his nemesis also.)

To Maria, the early part of La Revolucion had been her 'best of times.' But by 1980, she was singing a different tune, as her best of times had become her 'worst of times.' By then, in her mid-thirties, with three sons, and having fallen out of favor with the Fidelistas, her worst of times had become her 'direst of times.' By 1980, she was freely admitting (to anyone who dared listen) that her fascination with La Revolución had been nothing more than her impressionable heart getting the best of her. But it didn't matter then, as her relationship with the father of two of her sons was over. Making public comments about "La Revolución being a straight up waste of time!" not only earned her a place in the State book, but also made it difficult for her to even think about leaving Cuba. The Interior Ministry (IM) had by then made it clear to her that fleeing would mean without her sons. This kept her holding her tongue, though barely, until finding a way to flee with her sons. Bad luck would thwart her efforts during the Mariel Boatlift. Another chance would come years after the boatlift.

Chapter 2

Maria's ancestral blood ran deep

in Cuba. The first of her ancestors to reach Cuba had been the Spanish explorer, Stefano Suarez. Stefano arrived in Cuba in 1502 and was so enamored with what he saw (of present-day Santa Clara) that instead of returning to Spain, he right away started building the first Suarez Estate. The Suarez estate in Santa Clara was where his son Fernando was born.

Fernando grew to resemble his father Stefano in manner and in spirit. He was also as bold as the old man, proven by his seeking out Hernán Cortés during the conquistador's stopover in Cuba. Fernando not only convinced Cortés to take him on his Azteca journey, but also warned Cortés about Cuban Governor Diego Velázquez de Cuéllar's plan of sending troops to the harbor to stop the Cortés ships from sailing to Azteca. Thanks to Fernando Suarez's warning, the Cortés ships had already sailed when de Cuéllar's troops reached the harbor.

Fernando would feel most fortunate to return to Cuba after the conquest of the City of Gold (which against popular belief wasn't as easy to conquer). It was upon his return in 1523 that he married Alicia Vazquez, a cousin to Milan bankers.

Alicia and Fernando had two sons they named Miguel and Antonio. Both boys would continue in the family tradition of banking, though the younger son, Antonio, was who delved into cigar and furniture making. It was Antonio Suarez who built the mill that became synonymous with the exquisite line of

Suarez furniture that would become known the world over. Antonio's other accomplishments was to become Governor of Cuba.

His father, Stefano, did not stay idle either, and at age 74, he again got busy building the much larger Suarez Estate in Camagüey. He would not see it completed. (Camagüey is a province the size of Rhode Island and Delaware combined.) It was in Camagüey where the future Suarez family members were born. Maria was the last to be born at the estate in Camagüey.

Maria had grown up seeing her father visited by people wanting to invest or buy into the Suarez businesses of cigars and fine furniture. (The Suarez banking interests had by then been handed off to a cousin named Miguel Vazquez, a man who would play a pivotal role later in Ian's life). But Maria's father was a go-it-alone type. He refused all offers from investors, and continued loving life with little pretentions, hating complications, and living by three simple rules: 1.) Family first. 2.) Keeping his workforce happy. 3.) Selling the best product possible.

Juan Suarez's self-effacing and humbleness was nearly to a fault, and when meeting him for the first time, one would've been hard pressed to guess his wealth, if not for his love of fine clothes (an obsession that Maria also had, as well as her future son Ian). Her father's unpretentious nature earned him many rewards though, to which his favorite was having one of the most loyal workforces in Cuba, a workforce of a thousand men and women who were on a first name basis with him.

But the good times ended when Havana ordered all businesses to be nationalized. For those refusing to nationalize, like Suarez's cigar and furniture factories, governmental strikes were ordered. More trouble brewed when the Suarez workforce refused to strike. In 1967, many businesses were fighting against nationalization. Maria's father was of the few who still managed a profit while fighting nationalization, albeit a small profit, but one that infuriated the Fidelistas when finding out about it. Juan Suarez's profits became a thorn-in-the-side to the regime. Having made it into the State book only made his dissention worse.

The Suarez estate was made up of 180-caballerìas (6,000+ acres). The property was broken into three, a third of the property planted in tobacco, a third in Middle Eastern hybrid trees (the wood that made the Suarez furniture so unique), and a third to house the wood mill and the cigar factory. The manor home sat upon 50 acres of beautifully landscaped land.

The Suarez workers were also among the few workers who were allowed to swap jobs, so long as they could get a fellow worker to agree to swap from between furniture and cigar making. It was a pleasant work environment on the Suarez estate.

The manor home was staffed by a dozen who did housecleaning, cooking, and cared for the gardening and the landscaping around the manor. All the staff were treated like family and not just hired help.

Juan Suarez was a town favorite and known on sight. But his being so well liked eventually worked against him, as snitches let Havana know how well things were going on his estate. Next, the Fidelistas wanted Juan Suarez's name besmirched, but the townspeople and his workers refused besmirching it. But the regime was fighting for its life in '67, and Havana wasn't going to toy with the likes of Juan Suarez.

The Fidelistas next created 'the Peasants' Revolt.' The revolt was to get the nationalizing process moving forward. It was also another way for getting the masses to rise up against their employers. But revolting wasn't in the cards at the Suarez estate, either. Snitches carried that news back to Havana as well. That's when the Fidelistas, who meant business, came onto the estate.

Meanwhile, on radio, Maria continued to rant about capitalism being a bad thing, that money was "the worst way to people's hearts." This baffled those accustomed to getting paid for their work. But it was best not to defy La Revolución.

Next came the land grabs. Fidel even seized his own mother's farmland and gave it away as proof to how serious he was about land reform. But land grabs, in and of themselves, did not, for a better life make, either. In time, Cuba's land reforms would prove a bust also.

Maria was always angling to build more trust between her and her Col. Morales. One night, after too much wine, she let slip that she thought her father might possibly be hiding money on the estate. This got the attention of Col. Morales. He had her draw him up a map of the estate and place 'x's where she thought her father's hiding spots might be. The map became a valuable tool for Col. Morales. He would later use this map for selecting an area among the Suarez hillside for placing a new missile site and bunker (a bunker that would bring him much trouble).

Morale's troops kept secret their reason for digging around the estate. But an angry Juan Suarez had his hunches. And while troops continued to dig, representatives from the Party Directorate also came causing trouble when wanting a head count to those who could be conscripted into military service. These same PD delegates were also the ones who ordered the furniture and tobacco factories closed. A near riot ensued when the Suarez's workers saw their livelihoods about to end.

It took a brigade of ill-trained soldiers to quell the workers' anger and send everyone home. Party leaders also had some of the Suarez land given away as a token gift from the government to the people. The first to be given land were Suarez's longest employed. But handing out land with no seed, tools, or serviceable farm equipment, made more land squatters than farmers out of people.

Once the gem of the Caribbean, Cuba had, by 1967, fallen far from gem status. There simply wasn't enough seed, reliable equipment, or replacement parts to help so many *new* farmers. (The regime wanted people to feed themselves, but that was impossible after having sold most everything to fund La Revolución.)

Cuba had become more third world than gem. But Juan Suarez wasn't about third world. He read well the writing on the wall and saw what was coming. Though humble and self-effacing, he still led people to protest at the town square. This, too, got written in the State book (from herein called the 'book or 'la libreta').

The troops ordered to be at the estate kept the Suarez workers from saving the tobacco fields and the hybrid trees (trees brought over as seedlings by the explorer Fernando Suarez.) Without care, the tobacco and hybrids began to wither. Workers still tried to sneak onto the fields at night to try fertilizing the fields, but the noise of their firing up tractors got them arrested.

Juan himself fired up a tractor one night and too, got fired upon by troops. He was desperate to save his trees by then, trees stronger than redwoods, becoming weaker as the months progressed. It was these trees that had given the Suarez furniture its unique grain, though trees soon to vanish.

Juan wound up suffering the loss of his trees and tobacco from his upstairs window. (A canker strain, similar to what would attack Florida citrus trees years later, wound up advancing the withering process.)

He was shot at a second time when trying to save his gifted Adirondack chairs from soldiers, drunk on wine stolen from his wine cellar, when seeing them trying to set his chairs on fire. (The chairs had been a gift from his banker cousin Miguel Vazquez.) The chairs had been under his favorite elm tree, where he liked to smoke his new leaf. The soldiers wound up destroying the chairs anyway.

Maria still continued to air more socialist print-to-broadcast viewpoints even while violence like what was going on at the estate continued against those refusing to nationalize. Hearing her socialist on-air talks made her father sick to his stomach. This was also when Maria tested her father's resolve about family coming first . . . when announcing she was with child.

Chapter 3

The fanaticism that took over

Cuba was the same fanaticism that has induced millions to serving hammer and sickle masters once the hammer falls on their heads. Napoleon, though not a communist per se, enjoyed an emperor-like status when getting his people to follow him into a losing battle. Stalin, a definite communist (and hero of Fidel) forced his people to do whatever he ordered. Hitler, Mussolini, and Mao were all dictators that arrived at the right time and place in history to enforce their will on others. Saddam, Idi, and Fidel were men with the barest of civility (or lack thereof) who also ruled with iron fists. Yet a bit of luck had played into the Castro takeover, to which Batista's vanishing act had been a big part of. But when Castro's cheering crowds got too rowdy and too loud, then all fanaticism had to stop, or else.

Maria's pregnancy saved her from seeing Cuba go into perpetual lockdown. It was while rubbing her growing belly and staring out her balcony window, and after herself just recently been shouting, "FIDEL! FIDEL! FIDEL," that she began to wonder why the regime was suddenly wanting people to quiet down. She knew the faltering peasants revolt had something to do with it *though why silence the people now?*

The regime got back to writing names in the book (la libreta) before starting to break heads again. Maria detested seeing the Fidelista squads beating people up; beatings she was ordered to downplay while on radio, though thankfully, her infant son (who she named Tito, after his father) would keep her busy enough to avoid having to see the discord that led to the '68 exodus.

Collateral damage . . . two words that helped Maria find sleep at night. She knew her Col. Morales was complicit in some of the collateral damage being seen on the streets. But her baby's colicky fits kept her from seeing more collateral damage being delivered on the streets.

It was during her '68 broadcasts (prerecorded from her apartment after the birth of her son) where she was forced to air braggocio guests who came on-air to tell the Cuban people that collateral damage was needed to further La Revolución.

Her Col. Morales fed her vanity more by hiring a nanny to help with their infant son, Tito. Feeding her vanity had been the way to go, since after her vanity was fed, Maria gladly broadcasted plenty of what her coronel and the regime wanted. But it wasn't just her coronel who was cashing in on her Havana Jane persona. The Fidelistas found the lone daughter of one of Cuba's wealthiest men speaking on-air against capitalism most refreshing.

Juan Suarez didn't think too kindly of his daughter speaking out against capitalism though, and he proved that by tossing the manor radio out the window!

Col. Morales was given command of several air defense stations in and around Havana. But though his new position brought him more power, it didn't bring him any higher rank, which irked him. It was while he was wasting time ranting at those in charge in Havana that Maria decided to visit her parents with her infant son. (Maria's parents couldn't come see her in Havana because Havana had become a dangerous place for them to visit.) It was while playing with their new infant grandson that her parents begged her to return to the estate. But her social status, popularity, and inner circle of friends kept Maria form wanting to move from Havana. Her parents' begging turned to hounding, and it was this that got her to leave early. It would be months before her parents would get to see little Tito again, and that time with his father Col. Morales in tow.

To Juan Suarez, seeing Col. Morales made for a definite grin-and-bear-it moment. Juan could barely contain himself when hearing Morales go on, ad-nauseam, about how good La Revolución was for Cuba, this while knowing of the beatings going on everywhere. It also hadn't gotten by Juan how much Col. Morales kept eyeing the possessions of the 200-year old manor.

That was when Maria's mom mentioned a church wedding.

"Now that you two have a son together, you should at least marry in the sight of God." But Morales wouldn't hear of it.

Juan could hardly contain himself when hearing Morales start in with the old communist dogma of "religion being the opiate of the people." It was all Juan could do to keep from going at Col. Morales!

Juan Suarez was happy to see Col. Morales's taillights fade in the darkness, but he was most unhappy to see his grandson and daughter leave with him. It would be many more months before Maria could visit again, though next time leaving her Col. Morales behind.

The Cuban government, since the Bay of Pigs, has always feared a U.S. invasion. This threat is what has kept Cuba's conscripted military drilling at all times. Maria thought it might be a military drill or a plane crash the day she saw from her balcony plumes of smoke coming from the airport. She had hurried to call her Col. Morales, who told her the smoke was coming from vehicles purposely left burning on the Havana Airport tarmac. More vehicles had been set ablaze and placed on other tarmacs in the surrounding provinces. The burning vehicles were for thwarting any attempt by journalist planes coming to cover a possible U.S. invasion. (This ruse was the brainchild of an exiled Miami radio disc jockey who for weeks had been airing about a top-secret U.S. beach landing that was coming. He fooled Cuba's high command into believing his ruse, and also into believing that cameras and crews were coming to film such a landing. What's left of these burnt-out vehicles today are covered in weeds.)

Only a few of the original members of the Granma crossing were still alive by 1968. Morales was one of those, and he was quick to point that out to high command when demanding his own star-filled sideboards. He stubbornly reiterated his sufferings during the days when the Batistano army had wanted at all of them while they were hidden in the mountains of the Sierra province. He got nowhere with his reiterations, so he next went to see Fidel. He got nowhere with Fidel, either. He then saw Raul. Had Che been alive, he would've visited with him, too, since none of the Castro brothers were giving him an ear. (*The Sierras was where most of Fidel's rebels learnt their guerrilla tactics when fleeing Batista's better equipped {thanks to the CIA} but poorly trained army.) But no star-filled sideboards ever came to Morales, who would continue to badger high command for them. (The Cuban military was already top-heavy with brass. Morales's continuing to badger for more rank would show him to be an impertinent stone in certain shoes.)

"I'm here reminded of Fidel's good friend, Idi Amin Dada. Uganda's dictator was another who loved star-filled sideboards. He wore so many self-professed battle ribbons and medals that he even had some hung on his vainglorious backside. Me, I was too busy gathering up Amin's handiwork to think much about his ribbons. Makes me laugh thinking about it now."

Col. Morales's badgering made him out to seem ungracious. Though he got more to command, he would never see any higher rank. Those busy with their own self-interests had no time to bother with Morales, whose 'Magico' moniker had started to work for him. (He was called el Magico because of his ability to make people disappear.) While Magico opted to be a thorn . . .

Maria again visited her parents in '68. It was here where she cried when seeing what the grounds had turned into since the last time she'd visited. Fields she'd once ridden horses in now lay in ruins. She cried plenty over the memory of her youth. It was then she thought to tell her parents to leave Cuba. Not her. Just them. She was still too high in popularity to want to leave Cuba. But seeing her parents playing adoringly with their grandson got her to forget talking about fleeing. Her father nagging her to quit her radio program and return to live with them is what angered her to leave early again and hence the reason her forgetting to mention their fleeing Cuba. Time would have her regret not having mentioned fleeing to her parents.

Her father had made it into the State book so many times that Maria knew trouble for him was imminent. Juan didn't help himself any by disobeying orders to stop holding his protest rallies. Yet no sooner had Cuban troops arrived to disperse his town rallies than he went to firing up the old printing press, which was also illegal. His new printing of 'La Mentida' (The Lie) newspaper found its way into many homes until found out. All La Mentida newspapers were ordered destroyed, with Juan Suarez being tagged a more dangerous revolutionary after that. He was ordered to cease and desist with his newspapers, which he did, but only to establish his own radio show called, conveniently enough, La Mentida. The State eventually jammed his signal and shut him down there, too. Back went Juan to the square, only this time with more black market speakers and a generator to power his microphone. He even called in favors with local musicians, entertainers, and dancers who he wanted entertaining the crowds during breaks in his rallies. He was written in the book for that, too.

"Papá, please!" Their phone connection was awful. "I'm begging you to stop with your square rallies. I'm hearing things." Maria had gotten the low down from friends about how her father's rallies were angering the hierarchy. "You gotta stop speaking against La Revolución."

"La Revolución? Ey hija, you got a lot of nerve. Where did you learn such disrespect? Must be from those fiends you call friends. Well, defend your fiends all you want, but I'm not buying into any of this 'Cuba is better' nonsense."

"Papá, please!" Maria hated thinking the phone might be tapped. "You know you're not supposed to say such things in public."

"Here we go again, with what we can and cannot say in public. Always with rules to shut us up. Hija, you of all people should know that no communist is ever going to shut *me* up." Juan toned his anger down a little. "Ey hija, I so hate arguing with you. Really I do. I just never thought I'd see the day when my little girl would come at me with such revolución nonsense. Nonsense that's getting us nowhere, by the way." Maria was really fearing tape was rolling then, so she changed the subject. "Papá, what if Tito and I came and stayed with you and mamá a few days? Just the two of us. No Morales. I know you two don't get along. Sound good?"

Maria put a lot of faith in baiting her father.

"Hija, you know Mamá and I would love that."

"Good. Then plan on us being there in the next day or so. But please, you gotta promise me you'll stop speaking in the square."

"Ah-ha! I knew it. Always with the conditions." Juan was back to being angry again. "Ey hija, you really need to stop hanging around them misfits you call friends. They've changed you so much that I hardly know you anymore. Just come home and get yourself back together."

"Misfits? Papá, *please*. The Fidelistas are no misfits. Quit calling them that. And quit talking against Cuba's right to equality."

"Equality? What equality?" His tone sobered. "Hija, tell me why you include yourself in all this nonsense, would you please? Don't mamá and I love you enough?" Maria didn't respond to that. "You can visit when you like. You know that. You know the door is always open to you. I'm not going to beg you anymore. You're a big girl. But quit telling me that Cuba's a better place, cause you know yourself it isn't. Your Havana brutes know it, too. They just can't accept the fact they're the ones who've ruined everything. You visit when you like. But remember, not you, not anyone, is going to change the way *I* feel about what's happening here. But if you do decide to come home, then I have something I want to discuss with you, and it includes the baby." Her skin prickled at thinking her father had just admitted to wanting to flee Cuba. She used misdirection again. "You know better than to call Tito a baby, Papá. Tito's almost four. He's no baby."

"Ey hija, I'm sure my little man will be quick to remind me of that when I see him, which I hope will be soon." Her baiting worked.

"Look Papá, I gotta run. I'm doing an interview with the Soviet Minister, and he just got here."

"Now there's more wasted time. And tell me hija, how does *your* illustrious leader intend to feed so many new soviet mouths, when we ourselves are starving, and that even with La Safra?"

"I'm not a little girl anymore Papá, so quit calling me that. Oh, and before I hang up, those new friends of yours? They're not friends, so quit thinking they are. Get it?"

"I'm way ahead of you, hija. I don't need you telling me about Havana's snitches trying to get one over on me. Shame on you losing faith in your old man. That's another thing this Revolución's done, made you lose your senses.

Ey hija, defend your cause all you want, but it won't change the misery I see everywhere."

"You're wrong, Papá. The people have a new voice now. A united voice. La Revolucion *is* Cuba. Cuba *has* a future now. You really need to get out more, Papá. Seeing is believing."

She heard her father take a deep breath before speaking again.

"It's because I love you so much that I'll forgive you that. But know this, hija; Cuba's no better off than East Germany or Russia. Why you think so many East Germans and Russians are coming here? I know you're not blind. Okay, so you're not a little girl, I'll give you that; and you have a handsome young son. I get it. But never forget, you'll always be *my* little girl, and *my* little girl is breaking *my* heart with her nonsense. And I speak for your mother, too. Well, I gotta run, too. I'm reminding people at the square today just how much *worse* Cuba is, not better."

"But Cuba *is* better, Papá!"

"Blah! There you go again. Better for your fiendish friends, you mean. *You* should be the one to get out more, hija. Go see if La Safra is *really* working. Go see how much *better* Cuba's harvest is. Oh, and while on the subject of starving, you want to tell me why Cubans haven't gotten the right to vote yet? What happened to *that* promise? Communism took that away too, huh?" He hated speaking down to her, but their conversation had led to it. "I know you're too smart to believe in all this *mierda*. Then again, I see so little of you, maybe you *do* believe in it. Who knows? But remember what I said, hija . . . so long as I have breath of life, and so long as your Comandante's in power, then I will speak my mind. Goes double for that fool you call a husband. You hear me, hija? Hija? MARIA!" The phone had gone dead due to another 'gran apagone' (rolling blackout), which was another of the things Cubans had grown accustomed to during Cuba's supposed better days.

Maria's radio microphone became everything for her. It had great pull during the '68 exodus, an exodus that took precedent over her visiting her parents. It wasn't until the exodus tapered off that Maria was granted time to see her parents.

While she was being driven back to Camagüey, her father was holding another rally.

"Hermanos y hermanas!" Two hundred people cheered as he spoke. "Our Cuba today resembles a fighter who has been sent to the mat one too many times." Cubans have always been big fans of boxing, so the analogy was not lost on them as they groaned, but approved. "Cuba has become nothing more than a neck to be stepped on." His generator and speakers carried the day. "We thought we knew corruption when we had Batista, but this tyrant today makes Batista look like a saint!" More cheers erupted as Juan took a moment to drink water and then point to his wife Elvira. "You all know my wife." The crowd politely applauded Elvira's presence. "You all know how deeply our family blood runs in Cuba. *Your* Cuba. *Our* Cuba. But what future do we have with a regime that steals our children's future? And for what? For this *mierda* called La Revolución? La Revolución, which has stolen our lands and our pride? Where will they put the rest of us, now that our jails are filled?" The crowd groaned until suddenly silenced by Juan yelling out, "But what did you expect from one who eats with his bare hands!" At first, the crowd was shocked by what he had just brazenly said, knowing there were snitches (chivatos) among them. But the crowd cheered anyway, cheering that turned into a crescendo of cheers, as 200 sounded like 2,000, minus a half dozen chivatos hurrying to call Havana.

Juan Suarez compared Fidel as corruption-to-holiness. He went as far as calling Fidel an anomaly in a nation once thought of as the gem of the Caribbean . . . but no longer. In response, Fidel ordered the arrest of several of Suarez's friends during the May Day celebration. One friend who was taken was his longtime neighbor, the pig farmer, Mr. Gutiérrez. Another forced to leave Cuba at gunpoint (after losing all to confiscation) was Miguel Vazquez, the banker, and his wife Delia. The Vazquez couple were put on a plane and sent to Miami on a no-return flight.

Juan responded to Fidel's threats by organizing the largest rally ever, and then ending his rally with a vigil for those arrested. This rally was where he sealed his fate when mimicking Fidel's favorite Stalin. "Nyet! Comrades . . . que pasa!" He even mimicked Stalin's walk and accent. "Nyet! Forget guns, amigos. It's shovels we need for digging ourselves from under this *mierda* Revolución!"

Again, chivatos headed for the phones.

"And these communists coming to teach us better ways? They can go to hell, too!" Juan waited out the applause before continuing.

"We were better off when the Yanquis were here. At least they didn't steal our food *and* our pride." Six hundred people cheered like never before. "But there is hope, my friends." He quit the Stalin impersonation as Elvira joined him. "There is always hope, my friends. Don't go letting this regime fool you into thinking that all hope is gone. It is not. Hope is what is bringing us together to resist this bullying. Use the Bolsheviks as an example. They, too, were a minority who fought off the yoke. So, too, was the United States in its early history." Suarez lowered his voice. "Granted, it's a sharp sickle at our throats these days. But faith, hope, and love, my friends. That's what cannot be denied us. Ever!" Again he had to wait on the crowd to settle. "Look at our Eastern Bloc friends coming to help us in La Safra. They've arrived even hungrier than us, and that's *after* getting here. I say enough already!"

"Enough!" was the same thing the Fidelistas were telling their snitches over the phone.

Those knowing Juan Suarez were stunned by his gaunt appearance. Anxiety over missing his grandson and daughter had taken off the weight. The torment to Cuba's future is what had given him his gaunt appearance. "Friends, stay on your guard against these roving bands of misfits. They are a danger that need watching."

Suarez suddenly fist pumped the air. Six hundred fists joined his.

"And stop calling those who are leaving us 'gusanos.' Remember, they leave behind their homes, too, and this thanks to el Comandante." Suarez mimicked puffing on a cigar, but then suddenly remembered something he'd forgotten to say. "Husbands and fathers, watch over your wives and daughters while these volunteers come to help us in La Safra. These volunteers have also come to help themselves." Suarez came to the edge of the stage.

"We've been had, my friends. You know it. I know it. Now we must get the world to know it. We need to take back what's ours and make things right. My blood boils, same as yours, at seeing what's happened to *our* Cuba." Six hundred fists pumped the air again.

Juan would've won an election that day if running.

He also purposely avoid his daughter's phone call later that night.

On a lighter note . . .

La Revolucion never did change Maria's love of dress. She would dress to the nines even if just lounging at home. Every function she attended, every speech, ceremony, and event, she was seen fashionably dressed. And there lied the rub. She was blessed to have kept her model's physique even after the birth of her son. She was still able to fit into almost all her designer dresses (a perk of being the lone daughter of a man of wealth). But by '68, lots of grumbling about her had begun from on high, from where the stinky stuff flows, grumblings from staid voices belonging to the high command's wives and mistresses who felt threatened by Maria's cultured ways and charm. They wanted her movie star looks that graced every party she attended, to be toned down. Her parents were dumbfounded when next seeing her sitting beside her Col. Morales, in his jeep, during a parade and review, and her being dressed in the same olive drab garb the regime had taken as its own.

Chapter 4

Juan Suarez had been wrong to
think that Cuba's Revolución would just simply fade in time. La Revolución's communist underbelly was no fad or a phase of simple necessity. La Revolución was based on a philosophy whose practice was to wear down its enemies, even if taking a hundred years and costing endless lives.

Maria had tried getting her father onboard the communist bandwagon. Instead, her father had been quick to remind her of her roots. "Ey hija; you and your damn communism! You can spew that mierda all you want, but that blood of yours you cannot deny. Your ancestors were all about heart. They were nothing like this fool who dresses like he's on safari. And I don't appreciate him smoking my cigars these days." Her father's health had also taken a toll. He did lots of coughing in between their chat.

"Papá, you sound awful."

"Don't worry about me. I'm fine. But I would be better if el Presidente and his thugs would just leave Cuba." Tape *was* rolling that day. "And needless to say, you bedding down with one of his thugs just tears at mine and your mother's heart."

"Oh Papá, will you stop? Morales and I have a son together, for crying out loud! You must respect that. And as for you saying these things about Fidel, please be careful. I don't want you getting into trouble for the things you say. Besides, Fidel's done a marvelous job of leading Cuba. His La Safra is having good results."

"You're kidding, right? All La Safra is doing is forcing what few educated people we still have left in Cuba to work fields they know nothing about working. And don't tell me again about being careful about what I say." Hearing that put fear in Maria's heart.

"Papá, please stop talking like that. You must change your attitude."

"My attitude is fine. It's this communist dogma that needs changing."

"Oh Papá."

"Ah, don't 'oh Papá' me. I hear you on radio; making this fiend out to look like he walks on water. But instead of raising the dead, he's more like overfilling our graves. You hear me hija? Hija?" Juan was left with a dead phone in his hands. This time, it was no 'gran apagone' moment that had shut off his phone, cause the lights were still on.

In making the rounds, Suarez's mill was discovered to have still plenty of uncut and unfinished lumber that the State could sell. Dozens of Suarez workers were forced back onto the estate so they could work the cut line. But no sooner had the saws begun cutting, than a series of mishaps started to shut down the lines. The Interior rep sent to inspect the mill blamed Juan for the breakdowns, and since the nationalizing process had made *his* businesses the State's businesses, Juan was charged with crimes against the State.

Juan didn't take too kindly to the allegations brought by the state rep standing at his door. So angered was he by the man's allegations that Juan grabbed at the man and then dragged him from the manor's rich mahogany door to the very end of the property, a good distance indeed!

"Too much blood, sweat, and toil went into this property for you to cause me so much trouble!" yelled Juan down at the man.

More charges came from his dragging the state rep off his property.

"An incorrigible old fool is that Mr. Suarez," had said the state rep through busted lips once back in Havana. "No changing the spots on that leopard."

And then there was the issue of Juan Suarez possibly hiding money. Maria had been right to think her father was hiding money. But it wasn't in burying that he hid his money. Instead, he sent $2 million in cash by way of a trusted courier to his banker cousin in Miami. (Juan's trusted Belgium pilot charged him a fee for hiding the $2 million aboard his twin engine Beechcraft in hidden compartments before taking off from Camaguey. The money went directly to Miguel Vazquez in Miami, money meant to help any Suarez family member if ever making it to the states.)

Maria had been too busy with the Bobby Kennedy assassination to know about the roundups occurring in central Cuba. This was where being an enemy of the State finally caught up to her father.

Juan Suarez was arrested and taken from his home in the middle of the night and jailed with hundreds of other known dissidents arrested that night. Once jailed, the boot stomping began, delivered by those hateful to capitalists like Juan Suarez, with hate enough to deliver more oomph with each kick. But the pain from his torture was nothing to the self-castigation he felt over not having at least attempted a coup to get rid of the bearded ones.

The beatings continued until guards no longer found them fun. Juan was then tossed into a dungeon-like cell with others waiting their fate. Little food and water was given to those numb from fear. The waiting was unbearable. Lack of food wasn't nearly as bad as lack of water, especially when guards purposely spilled water onto the ground so they could watch their captives lick it off the floor.

Juan was treated even worse once he was at el Paradon. But so determined was he to lock eyes with those committed to beating him that he stayed focused even through the beatings. Nevertheless, he suffered even more from knowing he would never get to see his wife, daughter, or precious grandson again. He thought of Col. Morales, who came to him even in his night terrors and tortured dreams. (Though knowing of the roundups, Col. Morales was purposely kept in the dark to the fate of these dissidents. He knew of Juan's arrest, but kept it quiet, while having Elvira Suarez's frantic calls rerouted away from the apartment.) Maria would miss out on surprising her father with news of being with child again.

"You cowards! Unshackle me and make this a fair fight!" But there was no fair fight coming from those brainwashed to believe that Suarez was an enemy of the State. Other prisoners were given the option of poison. Some took it. Not Juan. He was determined to go to the wall with his head held high. But he continued to lock horns with his jailers. He even made an attempt at an officer's gun. But he was so emaciated that he hadn't the strength to tackle both the officer and his aid. Juan was easily wrestled to the ground. El Paradon guards then laughed at him while pointing fingers and yelling "bang" as an example of what was to come.

The days of lying in feces not of his own making, while staring at faces hanging from cells begging for mercy (where no mercy would ever come) couldn't end soon enough for Juan. He witnessed one last reprehensible act before his turn at the wall. He saw an elderly business associate of his, who was but skin and bones, get sealed into his cell by a sheet of metal placed by guards sadistic enough to enjoy hearing the old man scream for water. Suarez would take to his grave the screams of his old friend dying from dehydration.

Next week, making the victory sign before 15 soldiers whose rifles were already hot from a day's workout, saw the seventh generational Suarez hold his head up high and shout, "Viva mi Cuba libré!" before 15 bullets silenced him forever. Juan was dead before hitting the ground. (His unknown burial site would cost Ian a small fortune to try finding. It was never found.)

I t took months for the state to come clean about Juan's arrest. They never did admit to his murder though. Maria refused to accept the charges that her father had destroyed property that was *his* to destroy. She was especially vocal about that. She also went on-air to refute claims that her father was planning a coup. She was disgusted by the IM's charges of her father being a traitor to La Revolución. Her badgering got G2 reps to stonewall her father's murder. They even made up a story about his having been seen boarding a raft that was headed to the U.S. "Probably lost at sea." Maria didn't buy that, either. She knew her father wouldn't have left without her mother.

Worse yet were the rumor mills.

Comforting her distraught mother was quite a chore, especially when Elvira Suarez refused to continue living at the estate without Juan. While Maria fought through her and her mother's tears, digging along the Suarez hillside continued. A company of Morales's men were now digging out his bunker.

Maria's mother needed more attention than her driving to confront her common law husband's men digging among the hills.

She decided to move her mother in with Mrs. Gutierrez, the pig farmer's wife, who was also still missing, before she headed back to Havana to confront her Col. Morales over her father.

"What do you mean you don't know what happened to my father? You command hundreds, but don't know what happened to my father?" Morales's non-committal attitude infuriated her. "What are you? A pendejo? And quit with that nonsense about his being seen on a raft, 'cause I'm not buying it, nor is my mother." Maria grabbed her bag and stormed from the apartment. At the door she yelled, "I guess I'll just have to get my answers from higher up." It angered Morales to hear her say that, but he still stayed quiet, knowing their inner circle of friends wouldn't dare give anything up.

Maria then refused to do any more radio programs "until I get answers to the whereabouts of my father." This caused great consternation among their inner circle of friends, in particular those working for State Security.

Maria waited an entire month before having a vigil for her father. A stone marker was placed over an empty grave in the Suarez cemetery that read: Here lies a friend to many.

Col. Morales created havoc when showing up to the graveside service wearing Cuba's newest battle regalia.

It was Mrs. Gutiérrez's pestering him for news about *her* husband that got him leaving the service early. As for those showing signs of resentment towards Cuba's new uniform, their names were written in the book, too.

Chapter 5

It was difficult for Maria to stay dutiful to La Revolución with her father gone. But it still didn't stop the Fidelistas from wanting her to go back on-air. Her second pregnancy and her staunch refusal to broadcast kept her off-air. It was difficult for her to maintain even a modicum of her old conforming self while her emotions were strung so high.

A knock at her door from a representative of the Ministry of Education came next. New educational tapes was being set to record for helping students and their Octobrist education. The ministry rep wanted Maria's familiar voice on those tapes. But Maria refused to do that also. (She actually despised *new* Cuba's Octobrist education, which was a steppingstone to conscription.) Her refusing to help with these recordings was added to her growing list of insubordinations.

The tension between her and Col. Morales eased once their second son was born. She named their son Juan, after her father, and got no argument from Col. Morales. She found it odd that Morales accepted her naming the baby Juan when he so disliked her father. She was soon to find out why Morales had been so distracted to care about any name. In the meantime . . .

Maria accepted a new posting with the Cuban Affairs office. Here she had even more status and better contacts than at her radio gig. (This also got her off the hook with the Education Minister.)

Using the same nanny that had helped with her first son, Tito, allowed Maria to focus on making an impression with the Charge-de-Affairs. Her crafty mind, good looks, manners, and her good English got her the position of assistant to the Charge-de-Affairs. As assistant, Maria was charged with hosting parties for foreign dignitaries visiting Havana (where she saw foreign dignitaries even poorer than Cubans).

That's when her Col. Morales's bunker came to light.

Instead of receiving sideboards, Col. Morales was suddenly facing a military tribunal, with the possibility of himself facing a firing squad!

Up until then, Morales had been an excellent field officer. He had been most proficient at keeping Cuba's western coastline secure. (It was his air defense station that had gotten a bead on Power's U-2 spy plane, which crashed in Russia, and got Powers two years of Russian prison time). But Morales's excellent track record was tossed aside when he was found guilty of black market dealings. The most unlikeliest of snitches was the star witness against him.

Maria had wondered why Morales was staying away from the apartment so often after their second son was born. She hadn't minded it, since he was getting on her nerves with his restlessness, but she still wondered about his absence. His charges, and the snitch that made those charges stick, would make his restlessness, and his recklessness, all too clear to Maria.

Morales' mistake had been in not filling his new bunker with ammo. It was under the guise of building an ammo bunker that he'd gotten permission to dig. Stopping his men short of stocking his bunker with ammo was a dead giveaway. But his biggest mistake had been in using his bunker as a lover's nest with his mistress.

Maria knew nothing of any mistress or bunker. News came of that as she was being driven back east to see her mother. She'd been granted a few days leave to see her mother, so long as she was back in time to accompany Cuba's finance minister to New York. (Cuba at the time was desperate for credit with the IMF. Canada and China in the future would find out just how uncreditworthy the Fidelista government really was in paying back loans.) Maria was kept from taking her sons with her on the New York trip for obvious reasons.

In New York, Cuba's finance minister asked Maria to deliver the IMF speech herself. (Her better English the reason.) She made a superb delivery, even adding in the promise of a more profitable Cuba, though arguing that Cuba's current monetary plight was the fault of the U.S. embargo (which is still in place today, though easing). But even though a superb speech by her, Cuba's wish for credit was denied. It was during the flight back home that Maria had wished her sons had been with her so they could all have defected.

It was when back on the Gutiérrez farm that Maria started planning the family's escape from Cuba. The problem would be in fleeing with the sons of such a high-ranking official as Col. Morales. (A similar scenario occurred with Elian Gonzalez in '99.) It was fear of raising flags that kept her from seeking exit visas for her and her sons. The backlash to the '68 exodus, where many of the educated had fled to the U.S. (to become cooks, dishwashers, grass cutters, care people, servers, hotel workers and housekeepers), made getting a visa nearly impossible. More so in Maria's case. (Those same stateside exiles are the ones who started the practice of sending much needed money back to their Cuban relatives.) As for La Safra . . .

Contrary to what Maria had reported during her on-air days about La Safra helping to raise crop yields, La Safra was actually proving a bust. Sugar, rice, and fruit, all once in abundance in Cuba, had all begun to decline because of lack of proper tilling and farming. Mandating people to work the fields for little pay only angered the masses more. (This was where stateside cash from 'gusanos' helped immensely.) By 1972, Fidel's speeches were sounding more like rants and hard to figure out. Fidel even went as far as blaming the Batista regime for Cuba's woes, even though Batista had been gone for over twelve years! Fidel's speeches were definitely getting harder to understand. With so much broken farm equipment and no available parts, with no seed or top soil for harvesting, with fertilizer being non-existent, with people working for little or no pay during La Safra, with hunger abounding, his speeches could only get the mandatory cheers, and not much else. That's when Fidel's red sickle was sharpened again. Maria by then would have gladly jumped aboard the dinkiest raft, if only her father had been captaining it. These were her solemn thoughts during her shameful moment days.

Chapter 6

Maria sought, and got approval,

for moving her mother back to the Suarez manor. Because she didn't want her mother living there alone, Maria hired a few of their staff to again live with her mother at the estate. But no sooner had her mother been back at the estate, than a group of women from the Provincial Affairs office came a-knocking. The group came bearing a gift. It was the worst gift ever for Elvira Suarez. There, in the group leader's smiling hands, was a portrait of Fidel, in his pensive pose, red star cap tilted to the side, and with a quite familiar cigar in his mouth. The portrait was for hanging in the house (a practice done in most communist countries). Elvira waited until she was handed the portrait of Fidel before flying into a rage. She stunned the group by breaking apart the frame to get at Fidel's picture. She next took from her apron a paring knife, which she used to cut to pieces Fidel's picture. Elvira's live-in staff were who separated her from the group leader, who was highly offended by Elvira Suarez's actions at ripping apart Fidel's picture.

"How dare you tear apart our el Presidente's picture?"

"And how dare *you* bring that dog to my house?"

The group leader was most taken by that.

"How dare *you* call *our* Presidente a dog?"

"He's *your* Presidente, not mine."

Elvira would not be calmed.

"We'll see about whose Presidente he is, Senora Suarez." Elvira's staff had to once again keep her from going at the woman.

Maria couldn't arrive fast enough to save her mother from getting ousted from the manor. Provincial Affairs made it illegal for Elvira Suarez to ever step foot on her estate again.

Maria wound up placing her mother back with Mrs. Gutiérrez, who didn't mind having her friend back. As soon as she was done with her mother, Maria went to search for the one responsible for getting her mother ousted from her home. She found who she was looking for right in town, standing on the steps of the Provincial Affairs office. The group leader was actually having a laugh with the town mayor over Elvira Suarez's ousting. But the woman's laughter was cut short when knocked to the ground by Maria!

It was Maria's military driver who had to jump in and save the woman from her beating. By then, a small crowd had gathered to cheer on their favorite town debutante. Maria's actions got her labeled as an agitator, which got added to her other labelings in the book.

In protest to how her mother was treated, Maria went back to wearing her Gallardo Paz, Holstein, Gucci, Volar, Ashland Caruthers, and other designer dresses. But she no longer had to worry about those once staid voices complaining about her cultured ways. Those women complainers now had their own troubles to deal with, as their husbands and boyfriends were also headed to jails around the island nation. The hierarchy had discovered international drug dealings going on among some within the inner circle. Several of those wearing star-filled sideboards had been found immersed in the drug trade. Fidel's firing squads were once again busy. This was a godsend for Morales, since news of the shakedown slowed his tribunal proceedings, which gave him a chance to put another of his Magico tricks to work.

Morales's earlier showering Maria with precious gifts (a way of ridding himself of some of his contraband) only angered her more. But it didn't stop her from selling what he gave her on the black market, after his jailing, that was. What money she made she hid with Mrs. Gutiérrez.

Trouble also brewed for Maria, as her son Tito had been conscripted, just as Angola was heating up.

Morales's ex-lover and aide-de-camp was by then finished with giving testimony against her lover's secreted loot. Minks, furs, fashionable clothing, precious gemstones, and cash couldn't keep her quiet. (She, too, had been wanting sideboards.)

But the Fidelistas really weren't all that concerned about Morales's infidelities. Heck, most of them had lovers on the side, too. His affair with his aide-de-camp was Maria's problem, not theirs. Their concern was his hiding so much loot. (Magico *really* wished he had the power to disappear after his ex-lover was done testifying.)

Maria, while waiting to hear about the tribunal's decision, saw her oldest son board a plane to Angola with Cuba's other boots on the ground. Her common-law husband's outrageous deeds were nothing compared to watching, through tear-filled eyes, her son leave Cuba. (Cuban troops would eventually number 535,000 boots on the ground in Angola.)

More bad news came the following morning when a hysterical Mrs. Gutiérrez called to say Elvira Suarez had died in her sleep.

While the tribunal had Morales on ice . . .

Maria missed having his shoulder to cry on.

While an ex-jilted lover testified against Morales . . .

Maria worried about their future together.

When most needing assurances to that future . . .

A possible death sentence could take it away.

While waiting on Morales's verdict . . .

Maria was granted permission to enter her estate grounds to bury her mother next to the empty grave of her father. In the background, among the hillside, was the infamous bunker.

After Elvira Suarez's burial service, a longtime friend of the family asked Maria, "How is it your mom, who was so strong, how is it she just upped and died?" Maria's answer was a simple one. "Times have gotten so bad here that it's killing people even in their sleep." This was when she proclaimed it had been a mistake to believe that Cuba's change would be for the better. Her insolence, too, got written in the book.

Chapter 7

Morales' aide-de-camp had been

the wife of a ranking member of the Party Directorate, which was bad news for Morales, but even worse for Maria, who after being embarrassed by Morales's illegal and deceitful actions, was then ostracized for being the common-law wife of a man who had just been found guilty of bucking La Revolución.

And that's when el Magico did his best ever trick, when going for broke, and revealing to certain members of the tribunal of his having other gemstones he would like to use as bribes. The bribery worked. But the payoff wasn't enough to get him completely exonerated. He was reduced to a lowly lieutenant and in addition, was also sent to Angola.

Before leaving, Morales tried one last time to get into Maria's good graces. He sent her a letter that arrived at the Gutiérrez farm where she was staying. In the letter he told her of a box he'd hidden behind the refrigerator in the Havana apartment. Maria ripped the letter to shreds when getting to the part about his wanting forgiveness. But she wasted no time in hurrying back to Havana to see about the box, where sure enough she found a cigarette packet sized box filled with precious gemstones and rare gold coins. This, too, she sold on the black market.

She made enough money from her black market gems and coins to buy an 88-seat bus, which she converted into a tourist bus. What money she had left she used for greasing the palms of those at the Ministry of Tourism. (They overlooked her blacklisting so long as her tours stayed trouble free and she kept greasing palms).

By 1972, Maria was making good money showing off central Cuba to her Eastern European and African tourists. It was while showing a group of tourists the Santa Clara police station (where Che went toe-to-toe with the Batista police) that all hell was breaking loose on the tiny island of St. Croix.

On Sept 6, 1972, five men wielding shotguns, handguns, and automatic weapons, invaded the Rockefeller-owned Fountain Valley Golf Clubhouse (today called Carambola). There they killed eight people, among them four tourists and two resort workers. Eight more people, mostly workers, were wounded as the five fled into the surrounding rainforest. U.S. Marshals scoured the island and within a week had arrested all five. Ten months later the 'Fountain Valley 5' stood trial and were found guilty of murder and multiple counts of assault and robbery. Each man got eight consecutive life sentences to be served at mainland prisons. Years later, FV5's ringleader, Is-ell Marsh (not his real name) was back in the Virgin Islands, this time in connection with a civil suit he'd brought against the courts. Is-ell was aboard a New York-bound American Airlines jet, flying on New Year's night, returning under heavy guard, when managing to obtain a gun hidden in the lavatory. Is-ell used the gun to hijack the jet to Cuba, where he would be safe from extradition. (The fact that Is-ell was a murderer and wanted by the FBI meant nothing to the Fidelistas, who considered Is-ell a victim of capitalism.)

And so it was that while on the FBI's most wanted list, Is-ell Marsh, drunk on rum, almost got run over by Maria as she drove her bus out of Santa Clara. (Is-ell had mistaken her bus for the regular city bus.) But Maria instantly recognized the notorious Is-ell and let him stumble aboard. He had gotten so much face time in Cuba that it was hard not to know who he was. Once on board and seated, he passed out. Maria let Is-ell sleep off his drunk while telling her group of tourists about the drunken criminal's exploits, exploits that instantly livened her bus tour. By the time Is-ell woke up, the bus was empty, except for Maria driving. It was then that she told him of her plans for him, plans that meant more drinking money for him, and a bonus for her tours. Is-ell was to board during her Santa Clara stops. Once aboard, she would show her group an FBI wanted poster with Is-ell's picture on it, and then let him go into his spiel.

"So yo see . . . I goes zee boom-boom with the AK 'cause I needs to puts some licks on zee white Mon, yo see. The white Mon, he eyes me funny 'cause I's black. But the white devil Mon, he vex me, yo know? I no breathe right, Yo understand me? So I go boom-boom and all good then, Yo feel me? I hijack plane to come here to my amigo, Fidel."

In the end, Is-ell's alcoholism won him over. He became more of a risk than an attraction for Maria, who then decided to change her route from central Cuba to be closer to Havana, which is where the money was anyway. What money she did make when having Is-ell onboard, she saved. She had plans for her and her youngest son Juan with that money. As for Is-ell, the Intel on him is that he either died in jail or was lost in Africa.

Chapter 8

La Safra (the time of the harvest)

became another source of anger for Cubans. La Safra was another pie-in-the-sky pipe dream, which annoyed more than helped. There was also the language barrier between those who had come to help in La Safra. The Soviets, in conjunction with Fidel, wanted for Cuba to lead the Caribbean in grain yields. But the Caribbean heat forced a lot of volunteers to go home, leaving their Cuban compatriots to deal with the increase in field accidents resulting from rotgut drinking. Angola was not going so well either, giving more reason for the drinking. What foreign volunteers were still left (several hundred were American Communist Party members) didn't mingle well with most Cubans. Teen Cubanitas were liking their new gringo friends a little too much, which triggered fights within their families. There was an increase in domestic violence attributed to this and the rotgut, with the dogma of 'unity first' ending with a rise in teen pregnancies. La Safra became a sour point with most Cubans.

Maria had her bus commandeered and rerouted for taking workers to the field, workers who carried their ration cards with them so they could get them signed by their field superiors before going home. A signed card entitled a person to the government run food stores, so long as there was stuff on the food store shelves. Even bare essentials were hard to keep stocked. (The same Miami disc jockey who had started the ruse about the U.S. landing, joked on-air about Haiti's Baby Doc doing a better job of feeding his people than Fidel.)

Fidel was never one to take blame for any of his misguided ideological ways. He continued to blame Cuba's woes on the U.S. embargo. He even tossed the Cuban people under the bus when blaming them for not doing more to fight the yoke of capitalist influence (missile crisis notwithstanding). He claimed the U.S. was holding a 99-mile leash on Cuba, while at the same time avoiding a sit down with President Carter over the war in Angola.

A troubling new report about a recording tape surfaced around this time, where Fidel was heard railing at soviet leader Khrushchev for denying him his missile moment. (This was probably where Khrushchev realized he was dealing with a madman. Relations between he and Fidel were strained after the soviet missiles were taken out of Cuba.)

The communist mantra of 'equality comes first' lost its luster when foreign visitors became crass to Cuban culture. Cubans wanted their foreign comrades to just leave, especially when seeing their visitors doing nothing to help grow Cuba's economy.

"Oye brother, these soviéticos are consuming everything in sight! Our children will have nothing. I've had it with this communist bullshit."

"Careful what you say, brother. You know Fidel has eyes and ears everywhere." By 1980, even chatting on the street by three or more people was considered unlawful. Fidel wasn't taking any chances. Even being in possession of more than one's food allotment could get a person jailed. Maria witnessed this firsthand when her neighbor was arrested for refusing to turn in his freshly caught tuna for the mandated government grunt fish. Her neighbor was in the middle of cutting up his tuna to share with family and friends when a neighborhood chivato led police right to his door. The old man was taken to jail first, and then his fish was sold to an area restaurant that catered to tourists.

Cuba was needing a new relief valve and that relief valve came in the form of: The Mariel Boatlift.

May 1, 1980 saw Maria using Embassy Row as a shortcut to getting to Havana. She was driving west to pick up another group of tourists when she was suddenly caught in a shootout!

Cuban guardsmen were firing upon an unarmed group of six men and women who had crashed their bus through the Peruvian embassy gates. (The group had taken up the Peruvian ambassador's offer of asylum for anyone wanting out of Cuba, and commandeering their bus had been their only option.) Maria was trying to steer clear of the shooting when one of the Cuban guardsmen fell dead against her bus after being shot in the crossfire.

Fidel charged the group for the murder of his guardsman and wanted them handed over to him. But the Peruvian ambassador refused to hand the group over. Instead, he gave the group and any others who wanted out of Cuba, asylum, which incensed Fidel. Troops were ordered to surround the embassy, which by then had 10,000 Cubans camped on the Peruvian embassy's grounds on this Easter morning.

In the Peruvian ambassador's asylum, Maria saw her and her son's chance to flee. But it meant having to unload of her stuff, including her bus, before returning to Havana with her 13-year-old son Juan to wait on escape. She wanted to take Mrs. Gutiérrez with her, but the old woman preferred staying at her farm. (Tito was still in Angola.) Once back in the Havana apartment was where Maria and Juan waited on their turn for freedom. It would be a long wait.

Communication from the embassy kept the world informed as to the happenings at Embassy Row. That's when news came of a flotilla of boats coming from Florida. The Peruvian grounds and the area around it was too small to hold the huge crowds that gathered, so Fidel begrudgingly gave permission for the harbor in Mariel to be open to the arriving flotilla. "Good riddance to all these gusanos wanting out," railed Fidel. His wheels were already spinning.

The flotilla was what Maria had been waiting for. With $8,000 taped to her thigh, she figured she'd enough to sustain her and her son until the right time came for them to hit the pier. She knew she'd be arrested on the spot, so she had to be careful picking her time to leave with so many roving patrols watching the harbor crowds.

When handed lemons, Fidel was a great lemonade maker. With the flotilla, he got the opportunity to rid himself of many of his dregs. These included dregs such as mental patients, gays and lesbians (who were housed as mental patients).

The Mariel boatlift lasted seven months. Once Fidel had most of his dregs gone, it was then time to close shop. (Some boat captains had been forced at gunpoint to take his dregs along with passengers.) The Mariel boatlift would eventually bring more than 127,000 people to freedom's shores.

Up until then, because of the security patrols watching the crowds, it had been difficult for Maria and her son to get near any of the boats. She even thought about her and her son leaving on a raft, but word was that rafts had become targets for Cuban gunboats.

Upon hearing that the flotilla was being shut down, Maria got her neighbor to drive them to the harbor. Once there, her son Juan actually outran her to the one ship left at the harbor, a tug named the Independence. But no sooner had they started to board the Independence, than she and Juan were forced off the tug by an officer who recognized her while rushing more of her chained prisoners onboard the tug before slapping handcuffs on Maria and son Juan.

Maria's last hope of escape went with the Independence. As for the woman officer who'd arrested her . . . she knew Maria from the photos on her ex-lover's desk.

Maria's plan of escape went for naught once put inside the same prisoner truck that had brought the chained prisoners to the wharf. She and Juan were taken to the same Villa Marista Detention Center where her father had last been seen before el Paradon.

But bad luck came in threes for Maria that day.

While holding tight to Juan's hand, her husband's ex-lover told her why she hadn't heard from either Morales or her son Tito. Maria had assumed she hadn't heard from her son or ex-husband because of war censoring. That's when she learned of the explosion of Cubana de Aviación flight CU-455. (The plane had exploded in mid-air eleven minutes after takeoff from Barbados's Seawell Airport. At 18,000 feet, two bombs had exploded aboard the plane, one in the rear lavatory, the other in the mid-section of the passenger cabin. Realizing an emergency landing was impossible, the Cubana airliner captain, after radioing the tower about the explosions, tried setting his plane down on the beach. But the attempt was nixed when seeing too many people on the beach. The plane then crashed into the ocean, killing all 73 passengers and five crewmembers onboard. Among those killed were 24 members of Cuba's fencing team, who had won gold at the Central American and Caribbean Championships, officials of the Cuban government, who might have been the target, an agent of the Interior, 11 Guyanese traveling to Cuba to study medicine, and the young wife of a Guyanese diplomat.) Also seated on the plane had been Tito and his father Morales. Maria was numb to her jailer's taunts after that.

Chapter 9

Maria might have been numb

when knowing of her son's Tito's death, but she wasn't blind to her jailers having stolen her money. She seethed at seeing them take her hard-earned cash. But she did have to settle her anger once charges were brought against her. Her lone consolation was in holding her only son to her.

At her trial, she was given a year's house arrest for trying to flee. Her son Juan was taken from her and sent to finish his Komsomol studies before Octobrist. (She seethed at that, too.) She begged the courts to allow her to do her house arrest at the Gutiérrez farm. She could care for the old woman, plus be near her son's Komsomol School in the Camagüen district. Her request was granted. (Cuba's Octobrist schooling is based on the Bolshevik revolution of 1917. Juan had already finished his Pioneer stage in Cuba's educational system. Komsomol was next before Octobrist. His late brother Tito had been conscripted right after completing Octobrist.)

Maria put on hold her next plan of escape until having her son with her. It was while at the farm that she learned of other attacks against Cuban interests. There was the bombing in 1976 of a soviet freighter near Cuban waters. This was followed by the attack on two government-fishing vessels in 1977. A bomb explosion at the Cuban Embassy in Lisbon killed two Cuban diplomats. (Even the radio jockey in Miami lost his legs to a car explosion.) Then came the most violent Cuban exile of all, Orlando Bosch. Bosch started his own wave of attacks by launching into Cuban airline facilities overseas, starting in Jamaica, moving on to Barbados, and then working his way to Panama. Bosch's second visit to Barbados, while accompanied by friends (who later were found to be members of the CIA), was when the Cubana airliner exploded. (These attacks gave Fidel the impetus to rant at the U.N. for endless hours about what was happening to Cuba's interests abroad. He continued to blame the U.S. for harboring all these "criminales." But upon the U.S. ambassador's demands for criminales like Is-ell Marsh to be returned to the U.S. for trial, Fidel went deaf. But there was one more dangerous than all of Cuba's harbored criminals who was already headed to Cuba.

Special Alliance/London, a branch of Interpol and MI6, entrusted specifically to deal with the growing wave of home terror groups, had dubbed him the 'Wolfe.' His full name was Ian Red Wolfe. The Wolfe was one of the most prolific bomb makers outside of the Middle East. His skills were known throughout the terror world. It was the Fidelistas wanting success with their 'Operación Tiburón' that got them interested in the Wolfe. But the Wolfe would be in need of an interpreter. That's where Maria came in. She was given early release from her house arrest so she could accept her new G2 posting as translator to the as yet unseen Wolfe.

Special Alliance agents had gotten wind that the Wolfe was headed to Cuba by way of French agents. S/A London's Chief Brady was hot for Wolfe after his bomb had just killed eight British soldiers plus the son of a Parliamentarian magistrate serving as an observer at a Castlereagh checkpoint. Other agencies, including the CIA, were also wanting at the Wolfe. But S/A's Chief Brady had first dibs on the Wolfe. But the Wolfe heading to Cuba made him a tough target to arrest, so orders were given to board the freighter he was on. But by then, the freighter had already reached Havana. Operación Tiburón (Operation Shark) was waiting for his expertise in bomb making. Maria is who would keep the Wolfe in Cuba.

It was his grandmother, Rebecca Murphy, who had named him Red and that because of his flaming red hair. But it was more than just red hair that startled Maria when first seeing the Wolfe. His formidable 6-foot 4-inch 270-pound frame, to her petite 5-foot 4-inches and 130-pounds, was quite imposing. But she kept the intimidation factor to herself as she quickly took control and set the rules for Red's stay in Cuba. Nevertheless, there was something about his lone wolf persona that attracted her.

In Maria, Red saw a quintessential beauty. The G2 agents spying through the mirrored glass cared nothing about all that. In Wolfe, Maria saw a new ticket to freedom, if playing her cards right. She had no idea how much of a ticket he really was.

The Wolfe's increase in violence began when seeing police beat to death his uncle during the '72 Derry Massacre. He made his mark after that, making and setting bombs off in Ireland and beyond. His need for escape from the Castlereagh bombing was a given. Brains, brawn, and money is what kept him from being captured at the Dublin docks when being sought by Dublin police. A Nigerian freighter bound for France is what got him out of Ireland. Once in Paris, the Wolfe paid the underground to hide him until he could decide on Libya or Cuba as his next home. The choice was made easy by the Cuban consulate who spoke on behalf of el Jefe himself, who then promised the Wolfe safe passage aboard a Cuban freighter to Havana.

But Red was no fool. His bomb making skills carried assurances, and his main assurance was money. Paying Red for skills needed was no problem from a government wanting its own try at terror abroad. (Red's choice was also made easy when knowing that the Brits wouldn't be taking him to any jail if caught.) A Cuban freighter it was.

Red's arrival in Cuba coincided with Maria still struggling with her demons over the death of her son Tito, and then worse when Juan was taken by conscription. In the Wolfe she saw an opportunity to change all that. She refused to put in much effort in her translations without being assured that her son Juan would be exempt from service. She was already struggling with the Wolfe's thick Irish brogue when G2 agents agreed to her demands. SIM and G2 wanted the big Irishman to deliver on the goods, to teach their shark teams how to properly wire and detonate his self-designed tote bombs before Hamas and the Brotherhood stole the terror limelight. Maria made do with what she could, even teaching the Wolfe (el Lobo) a good bit of Spanish during translation, and in the process, learned a thing or two about bomb making herself.

The Wolfe was the maker of a thin-coated aluminum explosive tote bag that could bring down a wall, blow up a bus, stop a train, or bring down a plane. His particular brand of boom was reason enough for Special Alliance to want to liquidate him. The CIA also came into the mix when his totes were found being used in the Middle East. Hiding in Cuba is what kept him alive.

Maria had an epiphany moment while working linguistics and drawing up charts and schematics per the Wolfe's instructions. It was when turning in his recent ideas that she suggested the Wolfe move into her apartment. SIM and G2 headquarters was within walking distance of the apartment, so agents wouldn't have that tough a time keeping them watched. Her epiphany moment also led her to demand more living expense money, and to have her son Juan returned to her. Both requests were granted, including having her son working for SIM in Havana.

Her son Juan, at first, had plenty of trouble understanding the Wolfe. But time would see them both getting along just fine once the language thing was worked through. After that, he and the Wolfe were often spotted at the Malecón seawall, with Red's pale skin, height, and bright red hair easily spotted when standing their staring out at the waves. Juan is who taught the Wolfe how to read Spanish, while his mother attempted to make their unit a family, which at first felt strange, since she and the Wolfe weren't a thing . . . yet.

But time did what it does.

Their relationship wasn't all peaches and cream, Red's brogue notwithstanding. Red's rough-edged mannerisms grated on Maria, who had to first play psychological nursemaid to his dysfunctional upbringing.

Red had been fiddling with bombs as early as age 12. By 24, he had clients as far away as London buying his explosive devises. A London-based terror cell named 'The Wind' was his best client. The Wind was made up of mostly Palestinian youths led by a thirty-something fanatical cleric steeped in sharia law wanting his group to establish itself in the terror business. Four members of the group came to Red's door one morning looking to buy product. But Red's ability to read body language told him the Arabs were meaning to rip him off and possibly even to kill him. He was good about things like that.

Red had never been much into fanatical causes, religious or otherwise. His deep-seeded hatred was geared more towards the British government and the memory of his uncle on Bloody Sunday. But he knew in the four Arabs he had trouble, so he played as if being a big fan of their cause, while at the same time needing to use the bathroom before sealing their bomb deal. A few minutes later he returned with his favorite whopping stick in hand, a 34-ounce Wrigley bat with knife blades set into the wood. He delivered a painful beat down with his bat, playing batter-up with the four Arabs, though letting the youngest Arab limp away, so as to warn the Wind never to try fooling with him again. The three Arabs left behind were never seen again.

Those in the terror business got the gist of the Wolfe's bloody hand of justice (and this was probably another reason why he chose Havana over Tripoli, even though Kaddafi's people offered him more money for his bomb making skills).

The Wolfe's mother was Sarah Ray Murphy. Sarah had been a plain and shy girl when meeting Red's father, Günter Wolfe. Günter was an expatriated German field officer who had a difficult time living down the fatherland's defeat in the war to end all wars. Günter Wolfe avoided going home after the eleventh hour of the eleventh day of the eleventh month when hearing how some of his townspeople were beating, and even killing, some of the returning soldiers for failing the Kaiser. Günter, who had found a map to County Donegal inside the backpack of a dead Irishman fighting for British infantry, instead used the map to get him to Ireland. Along with the map were letters and a year's wages, which didn't amount to much, but enough to furnish Günter a small cabin among the hills of Donegal. It was here where he met Sarah, and where the two became two peas in an imperfect pod. Their union brought them their son Red, who brought them much misery and grief, particularly Günter, who never heard his son call him dad after his son became a teen. *Some kids are just born evil that way* thought Günter, whose son loved his mum, but seemed to hate him.

Günter blamed his son's dysfunctional attitude on his maternal grandmother, Rebecca Murphy. Rebecca had been involved in the Dublin General Post Office uprising of 1916. She was cousin to Padraic Pearse, leader of that day's uprising. But before the uprising, their group had to wait out a 13-day deluge. It was during the deluge that Rebecca got to write in her journal about how worried her cousin Pearse was, when saying, "We're going like sheep to the slaughter." A second member of their group, a man named O'Rahilly, who left behind an inherited fortune, a successful business, and a devoted family, commiserated with Padraic, saying, "Yeah, but Pearse, old boy, sheep or not, if we wound this clock, we might as well hear it strike." The Brits would oblige them of that. (The slaughter of almost their entire group did better-organize the future IRA.)

Rebecca, too, had gotten shot during the Post Office uprising. She would have died of her wounds, if not for getting quick medical attention. She did a spell in prison, was eventually pardoned, got married, and had her daughter, Sarah.

Red loved his grandmamma as much as his mother Sarah. But his world was turned upside down when his mother died of the consumption in '46. Worse was when his grandmamma Rebecca died of the same consumption a year later. He received hardly any comfort from Günter, who at age 60 was a shell of a man by then, of fewer words than when he first arrived in county Donegal. That's when Ian Red Wolfe, at age 18, decided to strike out on his own. But not before sitting atop his favorite hill and waiting on his next bomb to explode, a bomb that ripped apart his house, and his father, who was napping at the time.

Chapter 10

Chances of there being a Wolfe

junior ended the moment Ian was born. He had none of his father's features (though he later in life credited his father for giving him his 5'11" stature). Ian was born with nearly all his mother's features, including her Mediterranean tan, shiny black hair, and even her emerald green eyes. He even had her finely chiseled nose. But his father Wolfe cared nothing about that when holding his infant son in his arms. It was the first time Maria ever saw Red cry.

It was Maria who named their son Ian, though making it sound more like 'Eon' when she said it. She also gave Ian the middle name Red, same as his father. But it was Wolfe who stopped her from writing Wolfe on the birth certificate. Maria understood the concern over that. "Best just write in your Suarez name," Wolfe said. The precaution was a sound one. But a name change wouldn't be enough to hide the sins of this particular father.

The Wolfe was taken aback when hearing that all seven Tiburón teams had been arrested. To the agencies investigating the arrests, there was no denying whose bombs the teams had been carrying, plus one of the Cubans arrested in Madrid gave up the Wolfe for a lesser sentence. This confirmed to those looking for Wolfe his exact location, to which Havana vehemently denied knowing any Wolfe or any Operation Tiburón. "Common defector talk," was

Havana's answer to the world. The Wolfe's liquidation orders were put into play once again when knowing he was in Havana. He was the first ever to be run through age recognition software, which spit out a very good likeness of him at age 45.

Once done with his commitment to bomb making, the Wolfe was offered a position on Cuba's elite security detail. This is the detail of men and women that surround Fidel whenever he travels abroad. (Cuba's security detail is even larger than the U.S. ambassador's security detail!) Fidel had purposely kept himself surrounded with these many security people for fear of being arrested by U.S. Marshals while visiting the U.N. in New York.

October 23, 1983 saw Red take his first trip out of Cuba. It was during his flight to Spain that the U.S. Marine barracks was attacked in Beirut. The attack gave Fidel lots to talk about during the flight. But the flight back 72 hours later wasn't as lively when knowing of U.S. Rangers crushing Cuban troops on the island of Granada. One could've heard a pin drop on that flight. But the only thing SA/London cared about was the Wolfe. Spotters had sighted him boarding the Cubana airliner in Havana to Madrid. Chief Brady was sure the Wolfe would travel again, which would give Chief the chance he'd been waiting for years on.

While the Wolfe got more involved with the Fidelistas, Maria, at age 37, got more involved with her youngest Ian's upbringing. She was astonished at Ian's affinity for math. By age six, Ian was doing double digit addition and subtraction. By age seven, he was doing triple multiplication.

Maria assumed her young son's phenomenal gift with numbers had come from her side of the family. After all, numbers had always played a big part in the Suarez household. Ian would continue to use math to his advantage, where at age 9, by using math, he built himself a perfectly symmetrical bridge out of Popsicle sticks!

Maria was impressed. Not so his Octobrist teachers.

"Why waste so much glue and sticks, young Suarez? And what of your studies? Best spend your time on your pioneering studies and less on this foolish bridge building."

Later that same night . . .

"You go ahead and cry, hijo." Maria held her bawling nine-year-old close. "You're so far ahead of the curve you even intimidate your teachers. Probably got that from your grandfather." Ian asked about his grandfather. His mom told him only of the good things, not about the painful memories she held inside.

"You be yourself, hijo. That's what your grandfather would've wanted. Be yourself."

It was days later when the Wolfe surprised Maria with a startling announcement. "I want us to leave Cuba." Maria was sought of joyful when hearing that. "Soon as I'm back from New York, we're gone."

"But why?" she asked.

"I'm tired of this socialist crap!" Red answered. "We've got enough money to live in Budapest. Ian will get better educated there. Just start packing for when I get back. We're gone soon as I'm back." Red kissed her and kissed his sleeping son Ian. He saw the stick bridge and smiled. "Some bridge, huh?"

"Our Ian loves challenges."

Maria's son Juan stood at the door offering his hand to Wolfe and wishing him safe passage.

"You're the man of the house until I get back, Juan. Keep everyone safe."

"Yes sir. I will."

The Wolfe felt duty-bound to serve on Cuba's security detail because the Fidelistas had taken him in. But he, too, had had enough of the rhetoric. His thoughts were so in tune to leaving Cuba once back that he failed to notice the man snapping pictures of him while boarding the plane to New York, pictures that would confirm his getting on the plane.

Chief Brady immediately sent Team Charles One (TC1) hurrying to board a military jet cargo plane headed out of Dover to New York. The plane was to land in New York right behind the Cuban delegation. Once there, a U.S. Customs chopper ferried TC1 to WTC7 where another Customs van drove them to the gates of the U.N.

Back at Kennedy airport . . . protestors slowed the Cuban buses down with protest signs slamming against the windows, giving TC1 more time to set up.

Prior to the Cubans arriving in New York . . . in flight, all Fidel could talk about was a new suit he was having tailored by a loyalist to La Revolución once in New York. But the placards slamming against glass and shouts of "Murderer" cut short the talk of any new suit. (*Protests today are done blocks away from the U.N. gates, making protesting a moot point.)

S/A's Chief Brady's assistant, Marshall Evans, an expert on the new neon-carbon fiber Max Luker-240 sniper rifle, had also joined TC1. It was Evans who had ingeniously disguised the short-barreled rifle to look like a long lens camera on a tripod. All members of the TC1 team, including Evans, carried impeccable credentials to show police in case police wondered about them. The Wolfe trap was set soon as the buses appeared.

Red was given time to settle in before being asked to accompany a fellow agent to lower Manhattan to bring back Fidel's tailor. (This tailor, along with dozens of other provocateur/infiltrators, was later rounded up in a major sting operation begun in South Florida. The man's shop was discovered as a site for laundering money from Cuba's nationalizing process. Most of these agent provocateurs were sent back to Cuba by way of Guantanamo.)

Evans was who tapped TC1's sniper on the head when seeing the Wolfe's flaming red hair. A slight squeeze on the CO2 powered trigger sent a dumdum round traveling 3260fps and striking the Wolfe in the head. The high-placed round cut through brain matter like a hot knife through butter, shattering the upper portion of the brain stem before exiting. Red fell to the ground and bled out.

Chief Brady broke out the good stuff when news came of the shooting. On the tellie behind him was Fidel spewing out his usual rant from the U.N. podium, claiming more wrongs being done to his Cuba, while outside the Wolfe breathed his last. (Fidel would later claim the bullet had been meant for him.) Sharing in Chief Brady's 25-year-old scotch were several agents from multiple agencies. It was the CIA agent, after downing his tumbler of scotch, who gave Fidel's tellie image the finger. (The CIA had long since stopped planning Fidel's takedown after President Kennedy's 'do not disturb' order.)

The Wolfe takedown made for a giddy moment all around at London's S/A tracking station (a station house intentionally made to look decrepit where even its building address was missing. No mail was ever delivered there. Every window was boarded to ward off vagrants. But inside the four-story brick structure was found the most sophisticated station this side of Langley, with its basement joists removed to accommodate the massive electronic tracking map used for tracking cell groups in Europe. Staffers used an underground corridor found though a neighboring tube station for getting to work).

Collateral damage . . . it was all she could think about. But what annoyed Maria most, and what she would carry forever in her heart was *why kill my Red and not Fidel?* This question would haunt her to her last day.

Ian bawled over knowing his dad wasn't ever coming home.

Even 19-year-old Juan cried over Wolfe.

Maria did her crying in the dark, never allowing her sons to see her crying or suffering. The financial burden to the Wolfe being gone came later. But on that day, while Maria stared up at the sky with tear-filled eyes, she wondered what the strange cloud formation in the sky meant. She thought it might be a sign that her Wolfe had gone to heaven. She would later learn that she had just witnessed the Challenger disaster.

Chapter 11

There was no widower's fund,
supplemental income, or indemnity insurance to help Maria with her loss, and even G2 agents came sniffing around for what money the Wolfe might've stashed in the apartment. Maria had expected their visit. She had already hidden Red's $7,000 inside empty tin cans, which she shoved inside her household trash each day in the event of a surprise visit by G2 agents.

But $7,000 only worked out to less than $3 a day, in a city more expensive to live in than when on the Gutiérrez farm. But with Mrs. Gutiérrez's passing, her farm had gone to the State, so the farm was now off limits to Maria.

She was still looking to flee. But fleeing would take another eight years before President Clinton's additional 20,000 new entry visas would give her a shot. (These were the visas the Cuban Ministry made extremely difficult to get without paying a small fortune for them.) Once news came of the U.S. allowing rafters to stay if reaching U.S. shores, more rafts got started. (Elian Gonzalez's mother drowned while trying to make it to Florida in 1999.) But Maria still feared leaving by raft. Rafts had always been sport for Cuban gunboats.

But fate had a different exit strategy for Maria. It began the day she rushed in from the rain, carrying bags of black market goods, and barreling over a man kneeling to tie his shoelaces. Down they both went when she ran into him. From her bags spilled cakes and bread, which she hurried to hide from the Harbor Authority uniform. Her worry grew more when seeing the man playing blind to seeing her black market goods. Wanting to make peace, she offered the Harbor Authority officer coffee in her apartment. "And one of these cakes to go with it." The offer was accepted. It was over coffee and cake that she found out that she and the Chief of Harbor Operations had something in common, and that was . . . they both wanted out of Cuba.

Not only was he Chief of Harbor Operations, but he was also the captain of a Japanese tugboat named the 13-de-Marzo. But before the World War II era tug could be used for their escape, it would need an engine overhaul. This was where being chief of harbor operations worked to his favor. The 13-de-Marzo's boat captain managed to procure an engine overhaul, done quickly, and thus allowing them to set their escape date for July 13, 1994.

July 13 was a nail-biter for Maria, Juan, and Ian. It was hard for the three to contain their nervous excitement at leaving. Maria had to remind her sons numerous times to keep their excitement in check or they would give away their escape.

The night took forever to come, and when it did, they had to wait out the roving patrols going by. Once clear, the three were hurried to the harbor by their neighbor. The moonlight was strong that night, giving them the ability to see the harbor, and once at the harbor, seeing the crowd of people hurrying aboard the 13-de-Marzo!

Maria almost decided to go back right then. But she was given little time for thinking as the boat captain wanted everyone onboard so he could start getting the tug going.

Ian was the only one who noticed lights coming on inside the other neighboring tugs. He mentioned this to his mother, but she was too wound up and nervous to do much more than shush him. Ian worried about the lights on these other tugs.

The plan was to head to an area of the ocean known to anglers as the 'toilet.' Once past the toilet it would be a straight shot to the Florida Straits. The hope was to see land by sun-up. But again, the best-laid plans don't always go according to plan. Tensions eased as the 72 people aboard the tug heard the engine begin to throttle up. It was then that people began to greet each other.

That's when the Polargo 5 rammed them head-on.

Polargo 3 came in quick and rammed them broadside, an impact so hard that it shattered the rear railing of the 13-de-Marzo.

The Polargo 2 gunboat tried cutting them off.

Knowing what the penalty would be for stealing the 13-de-Marzo is what forced their captain to slam the throttle forward. Polargo 2 had to move out of the way when seeing the 13-de-Marzo chugging onward.

But no matter how good an engine overhaul, the 13-de-Marzo still wasn't fast enough to outrun the quicker gunboats. The additional weight of 72 people and the tactics used by the gunboats made outrunning the Polargo gunboats impossible.

The next 40-minutes were spent in a cat and mouse chase that took them well into international waters. That's when the gunboats opened up with their water cannons, knocking people into the ocean, including 10 children. Orders were to sink the 13-de-Marzo. The commander of the gunboats was intending to do his commanded duty.

The water cannons tore apart the deck of the 13-de-Marzo, which sent more people into the water. Among those sent overboard was a 5-month-old infant ripped from its mother's arms.

Orders were orders.

Polargo 5 crashed through the hull of the 13-de-Marzo, splitting the tug in two. It was here where mothers, husbands, wives, sisters, brothers, cousins, neighbors, all went into the ocean.

Ian had just cleared the surface of the water when seeing the section of the tug his mother and brother were trapped in go under.

And still the gunboats kept coming, trying to develop a whirlpool in which to drown everyone.

The crew of a passing freighter were who filmed the attack of the 13-de-Marzo. They also filmed the gunboats trying to create their whirlpool. This would cause great consternation with Amnesty International and Human Watch. Sharks didn't care about any of that though.

Ian dived back underwater and tried catching up to the sinking tug. But the inky blackness won out. His last gut wrenching action was to yell out his mother's name while underwater, which almost drowned him. He returned topside to catch his breath and watch the fins start tearing into lifeless bodies. And still the gunboats came. A blast from a fast approaching U.S. naval frigate is what finally got the attackers to depart.

Fearing an international incident is what forced the commander of the gunboats to pluck from the ocean those lucky enough to still be alive and head back to Cuba. Thirty seven people were left dead in the ocean, among them 13 children and the infant.

The fins terrified Ian. They'd tasted flesh and wanted more. Gunshots from a fast approaching Zodiac kept the fins away from him.

It was just as Ian was being pulled from the water that the first half of the 13-de-Marzo came to rest on the ocean floor. His mother's eyes were staring directly up at him as he was lifted out of the water.

Several more Zodiacs shot at sharks while retrieving bodies, while in the distance was heard the quickly departing gunboats.

Once back in Cuba, the women and children survivors were released, but the men were jailed. As for the U.S. wanting Cuba to recover the bodies from the ocean . . . Fidel's response was that Cuba didn't have enough trained divers for such a deep-water recovery.

"I am reminded of a woman who lost her mother, brother, and nephew in the 13-de-Marzo attack. This woman would again try for freedom and make it while atop a truck inner tube. There was another ingenious group of rafters who floated to Florida in a panel truck that had its engine propelling them forward. I also saw a number of Haitian rafts attempting at freedom. Theirs was a longer and harder crossing. But what annoyed me most was seeing folks reaching freedom's shores. It just made my job tougher."

AP/Miami/Feb. 24, 1996:

Cuban MIG fighter jets shot down two 'Brothers to the Rescue' planes early yesterday. The attack occurred 10 miles outside of Cuban waters. The unarmed BTTR planes were all piloted by Cuban American pilots searching for rafters when they were fired upon. American fighter jets were scrambled from several bases in Florida, but there is no word as to whether U.S. fighters had orders to engage. The attack comes less than 2 years after Cuban gunboats sank the 13-de-Marzo tugboat. In that attack, 37 people including 13 children were drowned. An intercepted radio transmission heard between the MIG pilots has them taking their shoot down orders from an air defense station located on an estate in the province of Camagüey. Reason for the attack is still unclear. The BTTR planes, which were all retired USAF Cessna Skymasters, may have been mistaken for real USAF planes. In the attack, four Cuban-American pilots are feared dead. The BTTR planes left Opa-Locka Airport yesterday morning. It was when nearing Cuba that the lead pilot radioed that missiles were being fired at them. It is believed this downed pilot is who sent the first distress beacon. The lone surviving plane used evasive maneuvering to avoid being shot down. Pilot Jose . . . (Continued on page 6)

Part
II

Banking

"Of all of life's absolutes, the thing that makes most sense to me is that there are *no* absolutes."

Part of Ian's valedictorian speech.

The hungering to achieve is what makes achieving possible.

Author

Chapter 12

"Maria may have known of Ian's tenacity for living, but what lay ahead for him would have probably killed her of a broken heart anyway."

Ian suffered greatly the loss of

his mother and brother. He suffered their loss in an odd way though, staying quiet, not speaking to anyone, not even to investigators wanting to know more about the attack on the 13-de-Marzo. A youth counselor was sent to visit Ian at the Krome Detention Center, but he didn't speak to her, either.

A month went by before Ian finally got to try his English on someone, and that someone was an older gentleman claiming to be his kin.

"So, who are you again?" Ian asked of the older gentleman standing outside his cell.

"I told you already, I'm Miguel Vazquez. I am your grandfather's cousin, well, while he was alive, at least. But we can talk about all that on the way home." Miguel Vazquez had come directly from an INS hearing to take Ian home.

"Home? Whose home?"

"Well, yours, if you like," said Vazquez.

"But I have no home here in America."

"You do now."

Ian perked up at that. "Really? How so?"

"Because that's how family works, Ian. Family helps their kin when in need, and you, my boy, are in definite need. But come on, get your things. We can talk about all that on the way home."

Ian's trust in Miguel Vazquez was because of how much the man knew of his mother. Ian was also happy to be leaving the Krome Detention Center (which is more a holding center than a nice place to stay). Ian wanted out of Krome and Vazquez was his ticket out.

At 14, he considered himself a good enough judge of character to know that in Vazquez he had nothing to fear. Riding in Vazquez's late model Cadillac also helped to calm some of his anxieties. The sights rolling past on I-95 helped to calm more his anxieties.

It was during the drive that Ian learned about the kinship between him, Miguel, and Delia Vazquez. But it was difficult concentrating on their talks with so many new cars and sights going by.

Pulling up to what seemed a palatial home to Ian made him want to pinch himself to make sure he wasn't dreaming. Having Delia Vazquez at his door to greet him home proved it wasn't a dream.

That night's dinner was memorable also. It started with salad, yucca with garlic and olive oil, rice and black beans, breaded steak, and ended with flan (custard).

Ian learned to absolutely love Delia's cooking from then on.

After dinner, it was cafecitos in the living room, where Ian's feel-good moment ended when seeing the grainy film of the 13-de-Marzo attack playing on Vazquez's television set.

Vazquez, in wanting to know more about the attack, had gotten a prerecorded VHS tape from a friend working at the Spanish television station, which he'd slapped into his VHS machine to watch. Ian right away hurried to find the off button. "No, Vazquez, please!" (As a sign of respect, Cuban culture allows for males to call their elder by their last name.) "Please Vazquez, I beg you . . . I don't ever want to see that tape again." Vazquez felt so bad about what he'd done that he right away burned the tape with gasoline. (Other news events would quickly replace the 13-de-Marzo attack anyway.)

Vazquez waited a few weeks for Ian to settle into their home before having a house party in his honor. He wanted to introduce Ian to his associates at the bank. A house party was the best way of doing that.

Ian did not at first get the laughter associated with his Ian Red Suarez initials. (He would later in life understand all too well the significance of IRS.)

The night of the party, Ian had to respectfully remind Vazquez, away from prying ears of course, that it was already difficult enough for him to attempt blending into society without having to constantly hear about his miraculous rescue at sea, that which had cost the life of his mother and brother. Vazquez actually blushed from embarrassment when Ian told him that. "Oh Ian, my boy, I'm so sorry. And you are right. I have been going on a little too much about you and the 13-de-Marzo lately, haven't I? Seems I'm all mouth when it comes to talking about you. Please forgive me. Seems like I'm apologizing to you a lot lately; first the tape, and now this."

But Ian just smiled. "No harm, no foul, Vazquez. Isn't that what they say in baseball?" Much like in Cuba, baseball fever was already taking hold of Ian. (The fact that Miami had a new ball team to root for was fueling most of Miami's baseball fever.) Vazquez's passion, however, was golf, a sport Ian would learn to love also.

Their next celebratory moment came when INS gave Ian permanent resident status in the Vazquez home. It was after piling into the family Deville and heading home that Ian finally felt rooted.

But not all went as smoothly for Ian as his being rescued or taken in. His first year in Miami saw him go through a lot of difficult hurdles. One was the challenge of learning a new city. The other was his new school, where a film crew actually followed him around his first day at Hialeah Miami Lakes High. The looks from students seeing him followed by a camera made him feel creepy.

Ian had always been more on the quiet side, and as the quiet type, his first days at HML made him feel shell-shocked. The noise level was especially shocking . . . until time did what time does. But his fear of being singled out for being Cuban, ended when seeing that the majority of the student body was Spanish. He settled in pretty well after that.

Ian's good looks had already gotten the attention of lots of the girls, in particular one very attractive blonde, blue-eyed, tomboyish sophomore named Cathy Hancock. It was Cathy who became his girlfriend and helped to root him more.

Ian's affinity for math was quickly noticed by his math teachers. But his introverted nature made it difficult for him to accept the gifted programs being offered him. But once understanding the advantage of being so gifted, his attitude changed. He suddenly went from being introverted to being more outgoing. It was then that he started asking the right, and not so right questions, and getting the right, and not so right answers (public education being what it is).

Nonetheless, Ian caught on fast.

His mental idiosyncrasies, on the other hand, those main anxiety issues that were manifesting into bi-polar, were another matter. But his continuing hard study habits would keep him achieving and overachieving, where within a few years he even bettered his English to near impeccable.

But it was his math skills that kept him noticed and at the front of the class while at HML. He even helped his friends with their math, including Cathy, who in turn helped with his anxiety issues, until . . . breaking his heart.

Friends came easier for Ian in Miami than in Cuba. His having had a dissident and non-conforming mother, plus an Irish father, had made him a target among his Cuban classmates and teachers. But he had nothing to worry about in that regard at HML. Walking arm-in-arm with the prettiest girl in school also helped to keep his head high.

Then came the bullying.

Ian was at his locker one day when the worst of the lot, a black kid named Rashid, came a-knocking. "Yo, man; best check your pockets, ya feel me, bro? Hand me some money, or I'll begin to bust up that bastard Cuban head of yours."

It was the word 'bastard' that angered Ian.

"Que? Whada you say?" Ian's wheels were spinning. "Me no speaky the Ingles so well."

Rashid grew angrier when hearing that. "Motherfucker! Listen you spic; you want a piece of me?" Flexing did not intimidate Ian.

Soon as Rashid came closer, Ian threw his books on the floor and went at Rashid! "No, Negro; I don't want just a piece of you; I want the whole thing!" A flurry of well-placed punches put Rashid on the ground.

Word got around fast that day about Ian. He had no more trouble with bullying after that (though in time, a different sort of bullying would challenge him). Ian saw bullying as the antithesis to his surviving the ocean and seeing another day. In the meantime . . .

Ian had a grand time between studies and playing ball. His grand time did include lots of time with Cathy, plus filling his room with awards, which included two 'Student of the Year' awards, the 'Presidential Award,' and ending with 'Valedictorian' in his senior year.

He and Cathy rode many of the metro buses together. This was his way of learning the city, plus without a driver's license, the buses were the only way of getting to the beach, which the two loved.

But Mr. Hancock, Cathy's father (her mother had died a year earlier) had a problem with his daughter spending so much time with Ian. He liked that Ian had an Irish first name, but hated the fact he was Cuban.

Mr. Hancock was the type of racist who befriended before sticking his knife in a person's back. "Oh, come on, Cath. Yours is just some stupid puppy love, is all. Get rid of the Cuban and find yourself a nice *white* boy to wait on you hand and foot."

"But Ian already does that."

"Cathy," his tone became more serious, "you know you can't trust these Cuban boys."

"Oh, dad, you're incorrigible. Ian's not like that." But it didn't matter. While Cathy continued dating Ian, her father got to planning.

Ian eventually had to resort to climbing onto Cathy's second floor balcony to see her at night. But the neighbor's kid, a teen also wanting to date Cathy, was always watching for Ian so he could rat him out to Mr. Hancock.

Mr. Hancock was a long haul operator. He wasn't going to stand for his daughter disobeying him while he was away on his long haul trips. He decided to move himself and his daughter to North Florida, claiming the move would help his trucking business. The move came with little warning for Cathy and even less for Ian (who thought the kid next door reminded him of the snitches {chivatos} back in Cuba).

Cathy's father had to use bribery to get her onboard with his moving plan. Though his trucking income couldn't afford them such a rapid move, his late wife's insurance money could. (Mrs. Hancock had died of salmonella poisoning the day prior to Ian being rescued at sea.) With the money, Cathy's father not only bought them a new house in North Florida, but he also promised Cathy a master bedroom (the home had two master bedrooms), a new Apple computer (becoming the rage), a flat screen TV, and a bright red convertible to drive to school. But bribery came at a price. She had to cut all communications with Ian.

It was a lot of bribery. But she would still miss Ian.

It was three days of not knowing where Cathy was that finally got Ian driving over to her house. Seeing the realtor sign sent a chill down his back. Finding the house completely empty really did him in.

Even driving in Vazquez's new Cadillac couldn't calm the hurt Ian felt from Cathy's moving betrayal.

But seventeen's an age where bouncing back is easy. Ian did just that by taking as his new girlfriend Cathy's best friend in school. But he never did forget Cathy.

Ian earned side money by tutoring friends prior to them taking their college entrance exams. He himself was undecided as to what major to choose. This gave him time to major in a new study . . . golf.

Vazquez is who got him started in golfing.

Ian's OCD is what got him perfecting his swing, and a pretty good swing at that.

His saving his tutoring money is what got him his first great set of clubs.

Vazquez was a good golfer and gave Ian stiff competition when on the course. But once Ian got good, it was hard to beat him once past the front nine. By then, Ian had developed one heck of a swing, which got him competing in the Dade Youth Regionals.

It was while driving home with the '98 regional trophy in the backseat that Vazquez mentioned his wanting Ian to work at his bank.

Ian had arrived in Miami just as the dot.com bubble burst. He didn't know enough about finances *then* to make sense of the Asian debt crisis of '97, though Vazquez explained it best he could. But he did get a good heads up to the Russian debt crisis that came next, (which led to the Russian default of '98). Vazquez by then had taught him enough about finances for Ian to understand the undercurrent to Russia's financial crisis. Numbers and financial math continued to excite Ian.

Vazquez next got to explaining the Long Term Capital Management (LTCM) debacle of the late 80's, which Ian wanted to know everything about. Ian liked comparing past and present regulatory changes with the financial math that was fascinating him. Seeing simple startups, by using math, becoming giants in industry, awed Ian.

Thanks to Vazquez, Ian also learned to properly read the markets. He took to understanding cycles, and getting a feel for the rise and fall in cyclical financial history. He also liked studying recession history.

The start of the new millennium brought greater math challenges for Ian. Vazquez created a breakfast wager based on the morning's Dow readings. Ian was to pick choice gainers for a chance to win their money pot. This was where he learned to use the earlier rising Nikkei index to help him make his picks. Vazquez would simply just read his paper while Ian made his calculations. Ian's compulsion for winning earned him the pot nearly every time (OCD being what it is). But the real winner was Vazquez, for he had been testing to see if Ian was fluke or real. To test his theory, Vazquez suggested that Ian try investing in one of *his* choices. Ian took Vazquez's advice and invested $2,500 in Novell. Within two months' time, Ian's $2,500 became $11,000 ($28,000 in today's market). Vazquez had his answer then. Ian was no fluke. And that's when he suggested Ian go for an MBA degree "from a highly accredited college, of course." But Ian had something else in mind before an MBA. He wanted to become a U.S. citizen.

"Okay then, Ian," he had surprised Vazquez with that, "I'll set up your citizenship test while you pick a college. Fair enough?"

"You bet." While they had been talking, Ian had been busy getting ready for the prom. "Oh, and Vazquez, I'd like to take my citizenship test on my mother's birthday."

He surprised Vazquez even more with that. "Alright, Ian. Sounds good. Highly commendable of you. Your mom's birthday it is then. Now . . ."

Vazquez helped Ian with his bow tie. Vazquez put on his famous smirk when asking, "So Ian; what's your take on derivatives math?" Vazquez was back to testing theories again.

"Derivatives math?" Ian loved it when they talked shop. "Now that's one *crazy* math, I can tell you that. But it's a math I like. I'll want some of that math once I come back from college, Pop." Vazquez loved it when Ian called him Pop. He also liked what he was hearing.

"Well then Ian; you get cracking on that MBA and I'll promise you I'll have a desk waiting for you at my bank. You can handle all the derivative math you want then."

"Best be careful there, Pop."

"Why?"

"Because that's some freaky math."

"Well, if anyone can figure out freaky math, it's you, Ian. Now, you start college . . ."

"Citizenship test first, Pop, remember?"

"Yes, Ian, of course." Vazquez stepped aside so Delia could hand Ian his girlfriend's corsage right as the prom limo blew its horn.

Vazquez handed Ian two-one hundred dollar bills.

"Wow! $200 bucks, eh Pop?"

"Now that's a derivative you can bank on, kid."

"You got that right, Pop." Ian kissed Delia on the cheek. "Thanks for the flowers." Vazquez really loved it when Ian acted like a son to them.

Investments. Financial derivatives. Over-the-Counters. Managing hedge funds. All these fields held a math that Ian obsessed over, an obsession coursing through his veins while swearing allegiance to the flag and becoming a U.S. citizen.

There were still tears in all their eyes when making for a celebratory dinner at the Forge (where a cake shaped and decorated as the U.S. flag waited for Ian, courtesy of Delia and Miguel Vazquez). It was upon their return home that they found the Wharton letter in the mail.

Delia, when coming to say goodnight to Ian, and to congratulate him more on his Wharton letter, found him teary-eyed. "Hey, I thought we were all through with the tears tonight, hijo?" Ian was like the son Delia had never had, that's why she called him hijo. He didn't mind. But she was mistaken about the tears being over the Wharton letter. When finding out that his tears were over missing his mother and brother, Delia cried, too.

As a way for getting Ian to focus more on school and less on his mother, Vazquez started the 'Maria Suarez Charity Fund.' He started the fund with $500,000 of his own money, which would be managed through his Bank (and eventually by Ian). The Maria Fund would also include various golf tournaments. "So I can win back some of that money I keep losing to you on the field, Ian," joked Vazquez on the day Ian was packing. This selfless act by Vazquez put him more over the top for Ian.

Ian continued to deal with his manic modes in the best way he knew how, by expelling as much of his ramped-up energy by playing golf. His mood swings were another matter though, and much harder to hide, especially when depression set in. That's when Ian would stay locked in his room until his depressive mood was over.

Ian fought his depressive demons alone and in silence. Looking forward to the new math he would learn about in college did help to calm his depression when it set in. Golf also helped. An additional obsession would be computers, once computers became more user-friendly. Ian's love for computers would become another obsession that would make him quite savvy on the keys. This would help him at Wharton and beyond.

Something else that helped ease his depressive solitude was Vazquez wanting to adopt him. For Ian, that was like icing on the cake. (Adding the Vazquez name would in the future help alleviate any hassles with inheritance law.) His accepting to be adopted by the Vazquezs' put a little more pep in his adoptive parents' steps. The elderly couple was quite happy to have Ian as a permanent part of their family.

A phase of extreme manic mode took hold of Ian the morning of his train ride to Pennsylvania. The night before he'd exacerbated his mood by speaking to an apparition he thought was his mother, an apparition that spoke to him nearly all night. Next morning, just before it was time to board the train, Ian drove Vazquez crazy with more questions about his mother and her early years in Cuba. Vazquez, seeing where Ian's questions were headed, chose telling him only of Maria's good times, and avoided telling him of her failures due to her rebel spirit.

Taking him to the train could not come soon enough.

Vazquez had one last thing to give Ian, which he gave him after loading the last of Ian's bags in the car. It was a leather portfolio with 'Family Bank' embossed on the front. What Vazquez handed Ian was his grandfather's two million dollars with 30 years of accrued interest totaling . . . "Am I reading this right, Pop? $5.2 million? You're kidding, right?"

"*You* know how to read a spreadsheet. Those numbers aren't dummy numbers. You have in your hands *real* money to invest now."

Though shocked by what he held in his hands, it's what Ian did next with the portfolio that shocked Vazquez.

"Why are you handing this back to me, Ian?"

"Because I want you to deposit it in my mother's charity fund."

"*What!* Now wait a second, Ian; you sure you want to do that? I mean, that is *your* money to do with as you please, you know."

"Yes. So I want it in my mother's fund."

"All of it?"

"Sure. Why not?"

Vazquez needed a quick drink from the den bar for that.

It was getting time to leave for the Amtrak station. "Listen, Ian, why don't you just take some time to think about this; go get settled in your new school, and *then* decide what you want to do with *your* money. I can put *some* of it in your mom's fund . . ." he caught Ian's look. "Really? All of it?"

"Pop, I'm headed to where I'm going to learn about how to make money. You handing me that large an amount makes me feel more like a lotto winner who gets handed what they don't know how to handle. Just put *all* the money in my mother's fund. If it makes you feel any better, double up on the golfing tournaments, so I can win some of it back when I'm here on break."

"So, all of it?"

"Yes, all of it, Pop. Besides, I'm seeing plenty of rafters drifting up on shore these days. Lots of them are Haitians, too. Make sure they get some of that charity money, too, will you?"

"So none for yourself?"

"Well, I could always use a little for a car at school. But I guess we can talk about that later."

"Don't worry about a car. Delia and I already took care of that for you."

"You *did*? Wow, you guys are the best!"

"We? It's *you* who just gave away $5.2 million! And you think *we're* the best?"

"I see why my grandfather trusted you so much, Pop. But I'd still rather see my mother's money go to helping the rafters. It's not like they get what I got."

"Oh? And what's that?"

"You and Delia taking me in, for one, making me feel like family. And remember, you did say you would have a seat waiting for me at Family."

"Sound more like your grandfather every day, you do. Now, let's go."

"I sure wish I'd gotten to know my grandfather. But hey, you've done great by me, too, you know; feeding and clothing me the way you have; giving me this great house to live in. Heck, you even pay for my friends whenever we go out! What's that all about? It should be *me* paying for my friends, not *you*. Anyway, the money goes to charity, okay?"

"You got it, kid. Now let's go, before the train leaves without you."

"Hey Pop, if you get to add in more tournaments, then know that I like that Doral course a whole lot."

"Doral it is then. Now let's go. And when you're settled at Penn, let us know, so we can have your car delivered."

"Wow. I can't wait to see what car it is."

"Well, it's nothing compared to what you just gave away, I can tell you that." *And something your mom wouldn't have approved of, I'm sure* thought Vazquez as he stepped on the gas and got them headed to the Hialeah train station. (A week later, a cherry red mint condition 1968 Chevy RS convertible was delivered right to Ian's dorm. In the trunk was a new set of clubs.)

Ian continued being an exceptional student at college. He was studious enough to impress his first year teachers. His hungering to achieve was obvious and pronounced. He took to the challenges of a more lucrative math while learning to speculate in another fast rising speculative market. He loaded up on so much extra credit work that he literally gained enough credit points to graduate early if wanting to. His teachers understood his rushing through his studies because of the bank seat that waited for him back home.

Ian made friends easy at Wharton, just like he did at high school. He and his friends golfed together to break the monotony of their hard studies. But his mental issues continued being a problem, dealing with his issues on his own, working through his haunted visions and voices, though never letting his issues slow him down.

Meanwhile, in Miami, and true to his word, Vazquez *was* preparing Ian a place at Family Bank, just as the largest speculative market in history was starting to grow.

Chapter 13

Ian could've just as easily

majored in any of the sciences, history, or even drama (he'd done such a good job at playing the lead in Man of La Mancha in high school). But the dot.com and its math is what drove him crazy enough to want to know more about finances. Having an adoptive father who owned a bank made getting an MBA from Wharton the absolute right choice. Wall Street math continued being a challenge that Ian wanted to tackle. It kept him up late at night studying trends, more so than even some of his professors.

For Vazquez's 72nd birthday, Ian drove home in his classic RS. In his travel bag was a beautiful handcrafted bracelet to give Vazquez with his name engraved on it.

Delia again had his favorite combo of rice, beans, and breaded steak waiting for him once he showered and changed. It was after their late lunch that Vazquez took him into the den to tell him of another surprise.

"What? Are you kidding, Pop? You want *me* to take *your* chair at the Bank?"

"Well, not right away, of course. You'll have to train first. But no, I'm not kidding."

"What's the catch?"

Vazquez had his reasons for wanting Ian to take over at Family. He wasn't about to share his reasons quite yet, though. "Ian, you of all people should know that when it comes to the bank, I don't kid."

That's when Ian noticed the weight loss on his adoptive father.

"You doing alright, Pop? You look like you're not getting enough sleep. You actually look like hell."

"Yeah, well worrying about you driving all night made me this way. But nah, I'm alright. Lots going on at the bank to keep me busy is all. But hey, you're home now, so I'm good. Now, what about a round of golf? Give me a chance to win back that $200 you won from me last time."

"I hope it's not a grudge you're holding." Ian smiled when coming to hug Vazquez. "So you really think I can run your bank?"

"Can't think of anyone better to run it. You just get that MBA, so we can frame it and hang it on the wall in *your* office."

"That won't be long from now, Pop. Now I'm so excited, I can't *wait* to get back to school. My friends are going to freak when I tell them what you're planning for me at your bank. I also got a professor who's going to want to give me plenty of advice for when I start working for you."

"Well, that's good. Take all the advice you can get, cause with this market today, you'll need all of it."

"If you think Wall Street's crazy now, wait till Bush takes over."

"Supreme Court will be deciding that soon."

"Oh, you know he's going to win. I just can't believe Florida gets to decide who becomes president."

"There's lots more happening in Florida than just deciding presidents."

"Funny you should say that, Pop, cause our last class discussion was about this rollercoaster ride on Wall Street."

"Mark my words, Ian; this new housing bubble is going to take us for more than just a ride. You best get finished at Penn and get back here quick."

"Hear you loud and clear, Pop. Now, about that golfing bet?"

"You got two Benjis in your pocket?"

"Sure do, Pop."

"Well, then let's go."

But try as he might, Vazquez just couldn't get past the front nine. He lost his $200 by default.

You want a Cuba Libré, Ian?" They'd gone to the den for an after dinner drink and chat. Vazquez was asking Ian if he wanted a rum and coke. But Ian never did like drinking. He was just happy to chat with the old man about more money stories. "You know I don't like that stuff, Pop."

"You're such a light weight, Ian. Join me."

"Nah."

Vazquez downed his first Cuba Libré before picking up where they'd left off at dinner. "So you're saying this securitization craze, this credit swap craze, is something your professors think is worthy to invest in? And what of OTCs?" Vazquez went to fix him another while listening to Ian answer.

"Over-the-Counters are the way to go, Pop."

"That's how they're reading it at Wharton?"

"That's how they're reading it everywhere. Some of my professors are skeptical. But you gotta go big to win in investing, Pop, and OTCs are a big money winner. Of course, you got to put in *big* money to see *big* returns."

"I hear more deregulations are coming."

"You know Bush and Greenspan are all about the wild ride. But you've got accountants. What do they say?"

"Our people in accounting are too swamped with mortgage loan apps to stay abreast of all this credit swap stuff. Accounting's got their heads buried in the sand, so to speak, and that's why I need you here. That math of yours will do us a whole lot of good once you're here. Street's scaring a lot of folks, me included. But I'd like to get at a slice of that OTC pie. I think this new administration will be good for Wall Street."

"Investing in OTCs is like running with the big dogs, Pop. You *should* get Family into securitizations."

Vazquez downed his second Cuba Libré (mentidita).

He was using the alcohol to numb his pain.

"Sounds like you're a natural at giving orders, Ian."

"Times are booming and markets are booming too, Pop. Construction here in South Florida is going gangbusters. You're crazy not to take advantage of what Greenspan is offering. Chop your rates and watch your loan packages double. You'll be running with the big dogs then."

"You need to finish school and save your dog analogy for when you return." Vazquez went for another mentidita (little lie).

"Say Pop; you're going at those rather quick, don't you think?"

"You worry about getting finished at school and let me worry about my drinking. Oh, and while on the subject of *big* dogs . . . what do your professors think about all these AAA ratings of late?"

"Healthy markets bring healthy returns."

"Blah. I sense a cycle. And I think some of these AAAs are flawed. I can't believe with all this hedging and no one's carrying red. I don't believe it. I think Street's hiding something. And you gotta watch out for Goldman Sachs." With that, Vazquez downed his final drink of the night.

"I bet you're feeling pretty good right about now, eh Pop? And quit worrying about the markets. You're not that heavily invested, so why worry. But once I come work for you, we *will* be heavily invested, I can assure you."

"No, *you* watch. This $5 trillion of daily trading is going to come back and bite us on the ass."

"How you figure?"

"Because too many are holding too much skin in this game, is how I figure. The market is growing way too fast. This can't be all from honest trading. I'm telling you now, lots of people are going to get hurt when this cycle ends. *You* watch."

"That's your Cuba Librés talking, Pop. Besides, John Maynard Keynes begs to differ."

"Oh, quit with all that Keynesian stuff. Living for the moment is no way to live."

"You can't take it with you, Pop."

"Yeah, but you don't have to take it all and leave nothing for anyone else. People got to leave something behind for their loved ones. At least *you* have your mother's charity fund."

"That's different, Pop. My mother's fund isn't affected by the Dow."

"That's *your* youth talking, Ian, and you're missing the point. For starters, at Family, we're swamped with loan apps wanting *my* money to pay off *other* banks' loans. That's not a good sign. Too much easy credit is going to ruin people. I'm telling you Ian, this live-for-the-moment nonsense is no way to live, nor is it a way to grow an honest economy. No one is saving money anymore. Ben Franklin must be turning in his grave." Vazquez caught Ian's confused look. "What? You didn't know Franklin was a master of frugality?"

"Master of frugality?"

"Or as your Keynesian math would say, a cheapskate. But Franklin lived frugality like an art form, though it's sad to think of him being called a cheapskate nowadays." Vazquez stood and stretched. He thought of another drink, but decided to go to bed instead. "Just remember the tulip days of yore, Ian. I know you've studied that at school."

"We have."

"Funny, now even the Dutch have started to forget their own history, now that *their* markets are so healthy. All Europe is buying into this speculative nonsense."

"It's not nonsense, Pop."

"Mark my words, Ian, what goes up . . ."

"Geez, after this talk, I think I'll go hide my money in my mattress, thank you very much."

"Might be the only way to save it. But don't be so apathetic. It's just that numbers rise and fall, Ian. Cycles come and go. But with these numbers today, when it comes time for the fall, the fall's going to hurt this entire economic structure that will be felt the world over."

"That's the rum talking."

"Whatever."

"Pop, you're wrong, just like people were wrong during the panic of '73."

"What panic in 1973?"

"Not 1973 . . . 1873! When Jay Cooke & Co. went under. You know, right after the Civil War."

"I wasn't around back then."

"Oh, don't be so facetious."

"Oh, well, now that *might* be the rum talking. So what about Jay Cooke and 1873?"

"A big recession that turned gains-crazy once it was over."

"I'll have to go read up on that one. But a recession isn't like a depression, son. Especially for those barely making it. Words are just words to those struggling to feed their families. And that's what has me bothered. But let's leave it at that for now. Go rest, cause tomorrow we're at the Lakes, where I intend to win back my money."

"The Lakes is open?"

"Renovations were finished last week. We'll be one of the first to try out their new greens. Tomorrow at noon."

"Tomorrow at noon it is."

But the following day, Vazquez would do no better, and would again default his $200 after quitting at hole #8.

It came time for Ian to graduate from Wharton. He did, with high honors earned through a high GMAT score and a completion of Wharton's INSEAD Fountainebleau program. He even did a stint at Wharton's Singapore campus before graduating.

He was brimming with pride when coming through the front door of the Lakes house after his final drive from Penn. In his hand was his MBA degree, already framed, when handing it to Vazquez.

"I'm home to stay now, Pop."

"Glad to have you back, hijo. Now go show this to Delia."

Ian woke Delia from her nap to surprise her of his being home. Her happiness at seeing him there woke her right up. "Ey Ian; I don't think Miguel has anyone at the bank with an MBA from such a coveted school. Ey, hijo, an MBA from Wharton; so impressive."

Vazquez entered the bedroom and said, "I'd take him right to the bank to hang that degree, if it weren't for it being Sunday." They shared a laugh and then prepared for lunch. A few hours later and Ian and Vazquez were on the links. It was on the links where they continued their bank talk.

*   *   *

Ian began his career at Family much like he'd done everything else in his young life, being focused, studying hard, and taking it all in, so he could develop a savvy in banking that would help drive him forward.

But there was a drawback to his investment strategy for Family, a drawback that slowed his pace considerably. First, there was his age. Then, as private banks go, Family was nowhere near in the league of the bigger South Florida banks, so that squelched his investment strategy. He did get to at least hear Vazquez say to his staff how happy he was for having made the right choice in bringing Ian onboard. But right choice or not, his nit-picking is what put Ian's plans on hold for investing, so long as Vazquez held tight to the Family reins and its $200 million coffer. Ian needed leeway with that.

Vazquez's investment decisions for Family were keeping them from hitting the markets with gusto. His decisions were grindingly slow, far, and in-between, and based on weak or late performers. Ian had better ideas for better profits. His wanting his share of the derivatives market kept him tinkering at his desk in search of an investment strategy that would gain Family more money, and all this from a 21-year-old who knew higher risks meant more profits from riskier OTCs. What Ian planned next would need several Cuba Librés before Vazquez would even think to loosen Family's purse strings.

But Ian's math showed profits right away. His study of the dot.com implosion had taught him to be cautious enough to make gains in the larger speculative markets, where Visa, MasterCard, AMEX, and sister cards were all setting record swipes at the credit machines. Ian's math also helped move Family through the derivatives maze frenzy being sold on Wall Street. In time, Family's share of derivatives earnings would bring huge returns and all thanks to a spirited 21-year-old who was *still* learning the profit and share game.

After the dot.com implosion, the mere mention of investing in anything computer related would bring laughter, more so from Ian's classmates, who most wound up working as Wall Street analysts. But their laughter ended when seeing the companies Ian started investing in. Though not household names yet, Google and YouTube were on the rise. Ian got kudos from his friends when reading those investments dead-on. But then came trouble.

Ian, as youngest CFO ever at Family, was stung by his mentor's decision to override a $12 million loan decline to friends of his, who Ian thought couldn't pay back their loan. The money was needed for a construction startup. These men were friends from Vazquez's old neighborhood in Cuba. They were among many seeking loans at the time. They had even been at Ian's house party years back. But their math looked like trouble to Ian, so Ian said no. Vazquez still overrode his decline though, and went ahead and gave his personal approval for the $12 million. Ian's gut instinct told him there would be trouble. His gut instinct was right. But by then, the blueprinted Ponzi scheme had taken hold. Vazquez had seen it otherwise, "they being from the old neighborhood and all," but it was still a Ponzi. It made for many heated arguments at home, with Ian reminding Vazquez of his own words, "to never mix friendship with business!" To Ian, the loan was a definite no-no, but it no longer mattered, as the $12 million vanished without a single dollar paid back. (The scheme would eventually send two of Vazquez's four friends to prison. Worse would be having the loan scrutinized by federal regulators who came hard at Vazquez in '01.) Vazquez's error in judgment not only cost Family $12 million, it also cost them points, penalties, and fees by regulators who flagged Family for the loan.

Ian felt like he'd been sent back on the porch to lie with little dogs after that, which irked him plenty. He didn't wait for Vazquez to down any more Cuba Librés before demanding Family go public!

"Ian, are you crazy? Look hijo, we'll get through this."

"No we won't, Vazquez. Those regulators aren't leaving the bank until our 't's' are crossed and our 'i's' dotted."

"Come on, Ian. It's not all that."

"Oh, it's all that and more. I said no to that loan. Now two of your four friends can't even be found." Ian hated when they argued, but there was no avoiding it this time. "Look Pop; this isn't why you brought me to Family. You never before blew off my advice until your friends came around. Now we got federal auditors going through our books. This is no good, Pop. We've already been fined. If more of our customers find out, we'll lose our credibility as a bank! We gotta go IPO. There's no other choice. We've *got* to go public. It's the only way to fix this, or we lose Family, or rather *you* lose Family." Ian sounded as if he'd been sitting years as a Chief Financial Officer. Banking had taken a good hold of him. His banking bloodline was showing. "You can kiss Family goodbye if we don't go IPO, Pop. Simple as that."

"We'll find another way, Ian. I promise."

"No, we won't. Look, you were always telling me to stay focused. Well I'm focused now. Public is our only option."

"Just put on your thinking cap! Come up with some other idea besides IPO. Use that damn math of yours, will ya? I don't want us going public. That would mean bringing in a Board, and I'm the only one my bank needs."

"Not anymore, Pop. You loaning money to those thieves just made you out to look like a criminal, or why you think we got regulators looking through our books? Forgive me for that, Pop, but it's true. We got 20,000 account holders we stand to lose if we don't make this right. I know those scoundrels were your friends. At least they *were* your friends until now. Mistakes happen. I got it. But we're doomed if we don't make right with these regulators. I guarantee things will get back to normal the moment we mention going IPO." But Ian could sense Vazquez wasn't buying it. "You've already lost your shirt. Pop. You want to lose your pants, too?" He gave Vazquez his most determined CFO look. "We go public or bust. It's your call, Pop. It will always be your call, so long as we have a bank. I don't think I need to spell it any clearer." Ian stood. "With that, I'm going to the links. You're welcome to join me, but I think you got some thinking to do, so I'll leave you with your thoughts."

"Damn that analytical mind of yours, Ian."

"Hey, you were the one who went against your own advice, and mine."

"You, who can sell ice to Eskimos, I sure hope you can get a board of directors to invest in a bank that's been flagged."

"You just make the announcement. I'll make the pitch. No sweat. But you best be ready to modify Family's future. And we're going to need to open up a whole new department just for studying this credit craze that's going on. We're falling behind the curve on these *stratospheric* credit numbers. Might even need to come up with our own credit card, if you catch my drift."

"Is that because deregulation's on the rise?"

"You got it." Ian smiled. "Now, how's that for a starting pitch?"

"Oh yes, Ian could've easily majored in drama, alright. But it didn't matter. He still couldn't stop the inevitable."

Ian's pitch was good enough to get a dozen new directors to invest in Family's new strategic future. The new Board members agreed to keep Vazquez on as CEO, but their eyes were on Ian (with one member even calling Ian the Youngblood of banking). Ian got the new Board to infuse Family with $500 million on the promise of a 15% return within twelve quarters. That's also when Family Bank became the *New* Family Bank *of* Florida.

Ian may have convinced the Board members that he was as financially ruthless as they were (his already having several million dollars in his portfolio at just 21), but he was wrong to think he could keep his heart out of banking. He wasn't like the new Board members. He was too caring to be heartless.

Ian geared up for another run with the big dogs during the housing bubble craze. It had come time to beat the clock on ARM loans making home customers giddy. But the fact that most of their customers were immigrants, some even having arrived in Florida by way of raft, brought out more of Ian's heart. President Bush didn't help things when tweaking ex-President's Clinton's first-time homebuyer program, which was the start to putting folks into homes they wouldn't be able to keep current once job losses started. Ian would have way too much heart in the game by then.

Try as he might, Vazquez hadn't the stomach for Family going public. He burnt out quick once the Board took over. He hadn't Ian's moxie for keeping up with the ever-changing options market, or the housing craze that the Board was looking to grow on. But the South Florida housing boom also brought as many headaches as gains. Vazquez had had enough of it by September.

Ian's financial wizardry kept things going at a steady pace. Vazquez however, suddenly wanted to keep the family separate from Family business, so bank talk was kept to a minimum at the house.

"Say Vazquez," started in Ian one day, "why don't you and Delia do like you planned; take a trip and go see the world. You certainly have the money for it. Go take one of those long cruises, you know?"

Vazquez's pride was still toying with him, and so, too, was his vanity. But he couldn't deny that Ian had Family growing, and it was thanks to Ian that the bank's numbers were showing a conceivable 15% return on the Board's $500 million. Family's future was looking brighter each day that Ian went to work.

But the $12 million loan kept rearing its ugly head. This was nothing though compared to the cooking of the books that eight of the twelve in accounting were doing once regulators were gone. It wasn't just the Board cashing in on the good times anymore.

Vazquez's loan transgression had the Board fearing his error in judgment might lead to future repercussions, or even worse, criminal charges, if he was still-sitting CEO. Ian's math came to the rescue again.

"Listen, Pop," they were in the den, this time with both of them drinking little lies. "I have a way of clearing the books of that loan mess, but it entails you hanging up your spurs."

"Couldn't come at a better time."

"I thought so. Look Pop, you got plenty of stock in your portfolio, so I know you're solid."

"Don't forget who has seniority here."

"Easy, Pop. I'm just worried about who gets voted in as new CEO. I need your vote if I stand a chance of getting voted in before you retire." Vazquez hated the word 'retire' but knew it was the thing to do. "Yes, but Ian, I'm just one vote. This was why I didn't want us going public. I'm not so sure the Board's going to vote you in, with you being so young and all."

"Don't worry about me. I got something for the Board that'll get them to see the light of me becoming CEO." Vazquez didn't doubt it. He'd come to know that Ian could usually back up what he said.

The next morning, Ian searched out Vazquez's lousy loan document, placed his name alongside his mentor's, and then transferred $13.2 million from his portfolio to cover the loan plus penalties. He'd already paid $3 million in fines while the $12 million still hung in the balance. But no more. Ian got the charge-off proceedings stopped, which got the regulator vultures to quit circling Vazquez. Ian was broke but happy, and his heart felt happy, too.

Ian's fast 'charge out of the gates' was stopped the morning of September 11, 2001. The bank, like most banks that day, lost a little of its moxie.

After establishing a charity for the victims of 9/11, Ian got the bank's quarterly earnings to outpace the recession that came after the attacks. Construction slowed after the attacks, but then got started again, allowing Ian to buy up more AAA bundled derivatives offered by Street's big five.

Ian was so busy producing dollars even through the '01 slowdown that he barely had time to go through all the daily spread sheets, good spread and bogus, before sending his numbers to accounting. It was more sign and go to keep his desk from cluttering. Big mistake there. But a call to accounting usually got his chief accountants giving him the correct answers. Big mistake there, too. But by then, Ian had 27 Family branch offices to deal with, with a 28th office opening up right down the street from the State Capitol in Tallahassee. Too much activity at the bank was another reason why Ian failed to see what eight of the twelve in accounting were doing.

Ian had been quite studious when picking the right LDOs, CDOs, and their tranches (selected slices within packaged derivatives). It was a challenge to him to continue as savvy as he was in making the right financial choices, though not as criminally savvy as the likes of Madoff, Sanford, and Prince.

Ian's best profits came from the riskier securitization bundles. In this he caught some big dogs napping. He managed to piggyback on a particular CDO package that was sold to Iceland, though taking his gains right before Iceland took on debt it couldn't chew. (Iceland would soon enough be in a financial tailspin of its own doing.)

Ian's method to buying and investing got noticed by multi-billion dollar hedge fund groups like Johnson & Galleon, Sanford, and others. It was this that he used for selling the Board to his becoming the next CEO. Ian needed to be sitting CEO if Family had any chance of making mergers with these giant hedge funds.

"Time's come for that vote, Pop."

"You know you already got my vote."

Vazquez was busy looking at a travel brochure and studying a map on his desk while speaking. "It's the rest of the Board that needs to vote you in. I told you before I don't see that happening with you being just 22."

"I guess I'll take the Johnson & Galleon offer then."

"Be real, Ian. And I hope that's not bitterness talking."

"Not bitterness, Pop. I'm just sick and tired of waiting. But I am serious. I hate leaving Family, but me taking over the Johnson office in Charlotte . . ."

"Charlotte?"

"They're handling billions there, Pop." Ian flashed ten fingers in the air. "Like *ten* billion in cash flow alone, Pop."

"Well imagine that; selling out Family for money."

"So long as I don't sell out *our* family. But come on, Pop; Galleon's merger with Capital alone netted them $3.6 billion. That's *B* for billion, Pop. You know those are numbers I love. It'll be no skin off my nose if the Board decides to vote someone else in as CEO." That was a lie and Vazquez knew it by Ian's tone. He didn't say anything though. He just got on the phone and made the meeting happen.

Soon as he hung up, he looked at Ian and said, "I know there's no one more motivated to protecting our assets, and our asses, than you. I would like nothing better than to see you in my chair. But it was you who wanted us going public. Let's just hope it doesn't backfire on us."

Ian's power play came the next day.

The vote continued tough all morning. It was like picking the Pope. Three times the Board was deadlocked. Lunch had to be called in after the third tie.

The problem was that the members didn't want to rock the boat. They were in line to receive their payout in less than a year, and having Vazquez until then, albeit as just a fill-in CEO, was fine by them. That's when Ian reminded them that the Johnson deal wouldn't be on the table forever. Nor would the Prince Sanford Group deal, either. Both were looking for merger opportunities.

So tough were the Board proceedings, that Ian had no time for a sit down with Albert Morella, a close family friend, who was needing his take on some funky math that had been submitted to him by the same Sanford Group that was courting Ian. Morella Investments would go it alone with the Sanford group (and pay dearly for it without Ian's advice).

The final vote was called late in the afternoon. By then, four calls from Albert Morella had gone unanswered.

The tiebreaker came on Vazquez's vote.

And that's how Ian became the youngest bank CEO ever.

Then he blew off the Galleon Group.

He also blew off the Sanford Group (who by then had run off with Albert Morella's money).

Ian's future plans had nothing to do with any mergers. At least not with any group outside of Family. His first order of business, after officially becoming the head of Family, was to start 'Red Market Funds.' RMF was a sister flagship to Family, and would run on startup capital borrowed from the Family coffers. The upside to having RMF in the building was that it was easier to handle the 300 vested accounts that were started the first day of RMF business. The downside was having all those profits run through the (corrupted) Family accounting department.

Miami . . . the gateway to Central and South America . . . and *the* perfect place for a diversified bank like Family to draw from its Spanish pool of customers, especially with jingles like 'Let *our* Family help *your* family into its first home.' Jingles like this helped to bring in over $1 billion in new mortgages.

The local newspaper took notice of Ian, too. They did a spread on Ian in the local section, claiming him to be a financial guru who had found his own financial fountain of youth. (His age played a little there.) The local paper wrote him up as having a Midas touch in banking. His philanthropy through his mother's charity was mentioned also. Little, however, was mentioned of his newly formed profit-sharing program for his 1,100 employees. But his employees didn't mind, and that's all that mattered to him. His heart again.

Ian also bought the Brickell building that Family had been in for years. The building became Family headquarters.

Ian had so much going on, he barely had time to eat a proper meal before hurrying upstairs to glue himself to his monitor, cellphone, and touch screen pad in his RMF office. (He was one of the first to have wireless online service installed in his Cadillac, this before the smartphone.) He continued staying so busy trading that he hadn't time to even sense the swindling shenanigans going on in accounting. (The low man on accounting's totem pole had been fired for trying to get a heads up email to Ian.)

More merger opportunities presented themselves. The Stoddert Group was next to court Ian. But much like Prince, Johnson, and the Galleon math, Stoddert's math didn't make a whole hell of a lot of sense to Ian, either. (*Both Stoddert and Prince would go down in flames, leaving taxpayers to clean up their mess to the tune of $100 billion plus. Sir Prince himself wound up in prison.)

RMF was Ian's baby, while having Family running smooth and making money, which made the Board happy. His RMF team he housed on the 12th & 14th floors, a team that resembled a ball club with a heck of a bullpen. (Baseball analogy again.)

Street, too, ramped it up a bit, once the Dow started doing the wave. Some numbers on speculative securitizations did get fudged, which would lead AIG to assume more risk than it could handle (OTCs in and of themselves showing signs of credit sloppiness). But so long as the Dow continued to rise, so long as spending money on money not yet earned continued, most were happy with the madness.

Chapter 14

Ian had things running so well at the bank that he could afford spending more time on the RMF floors. But it was while being bogged down with RMF business that his chief accountant continued to fool him into believing that all the bank's spreadsheets were telling an honest tale. The criminal shenanigans hadn't yet affected Family's credit worthiness. In fact, accounting's erroneous numbers grew *more* their credit worthiness, but at the expense of getting them back on radar. In the meantime . . .

Ian's computer compulsion led him to buy a premium custom-built computer that was designed and installed for his office, whenever he got around to choosing a permanent office in the building. Also with his computer came a mobile device that kept him wired to his PC no matter where in the building he might be. This was so he could stay abreast of all of RMF's dealings, buy orders, and Put options. Any purchases of derivatives or OTCs that needed his approval were done by electronic signature. A click of a mouse and he was done.

While it was the practice of most managing hedge fund groups to keep their operations and dealings a closely guarded secret, Ian purposely ran RMF as a client-friendly environment. It was an open door policy with any of RMF's clients wanting to know RMF business. They could visit RMF anytime. Ian didn't want any of his investors to think any surreptitious dealings were going on at RMF.

Because of this practice, RMF saw, in '04, their accounts grow from 19,000, to over 30,000, which brought in an additional $650 million in buy orders. Word spread quickly about Ian's savvy in profitable margin calls outdoing losses 16 to 1.

"Let the good times roll!" was his favorite motto.

His chief accountant used the housing bubble (craze) to hide the illegalities in accounting. While those numbers tasked the bank, Ian's diversionary tactic to hiding the Vazquez loan from view got FDIC regulators snooping. Regulators did not want to see another Enron/Anderson scam (though on a much smaller scale).

In fairness to Ian, accounting did get him to scratch his head a time or two to their math. *But why rock the boat* had been his thinking.

The fact that most of those working in accounting had been personally hired by Vazquez is what kept Ian thinking they were the right people to handle the books during Family's most profitable times. But by '05, it was hard for Ian not to see some of the discrepancies in their daily tally sheets. But his chasing after a slice of Wall Street's daily $7 trillion pie kept him too busy to do anything more than take a cursory look into accounting's numbers.

Ian didn't want anything to distract him from running with the big dogs. There weren't enough hours in the day for distractions. His was a sign-and-go attitude, while trusting his accountants (his mentor's choices) to following the guidelines of bank law. Time would show that this was inept thinking.

Family falling below the cash threshold is what brought the first set of federal regulators to the door. No longer could Ian trust his math to work out the kinks generated by illegally worked-up balance sheets. Those he called the 'crew' (the accounting dept.) had been found with their hand in the cookie jar, with four of the eight who'd stolen most of the missing money suddenly buying plane tickets to the Caribbean islands the moment regulators started the coffee brewing. None would answer their phones. Ian had no choice but to reroute Family's money back into RMF, which was a bad thing, too, since market trading was beginning to show its wear.

It got to where Ian was constantly at his computer, studying sideboards, graphs, checking the direction of his competition, using the earlier rising

Asian markets to gauge his financial decisions. But his financial fountain of youth had begun to run dry in '07; his speculating Street in advance of itself had become a hit-or-miss prospect that went counter to his wizardry math. The housing bubble was showing stress too, lots of stress, but a stress professionally hidden by math that had far more wizardry than Ian's. Everything was based on the good times never ending. But being steeped in worthless paper like the Mae's (Fannie & Freddie would eventually be led into conservatorship) with more worthless paper collapsing the loan giant IndyMac (fourth largest failure in U.S. bank history) should've been sign enough for Ian to get out of the derivatives market. But he was kept so busy with RMF dealings that he failed to see the sign.

S outh Florida wasn't the only region poisoned by the madness to mortgage-crazed markets. Arizona, Illinois, California, and New York had all bitten of the fruit. The number of Joneses buying, then flipping homes they could ill-afford in the first place, grew exponentially once lending rules eased and deregulation took hold. (Arizona saw a record number of subdivisions built literally overnight, which gave Florida a run for its money.) A phenomenal upsurge in home prices, especially in South Florida, continued even while the Iraqi war was going on.

Newly arrived immigrants, knowing of the housing program, clamored for first-time homebuyer status. It was this program, tweaked by Bush (then tweaked more by Obama) is what got most of the newly arrived folks into their first homes, also.

Hugo Chavez even wound up growing the Family coffers more. Chasing many of his people out of Venezuela helped to bring in an additional $450 million in home loans to Family. Regardless of how risky home loans might have been, so long as the Maes were promising to cover, almost all loans got an approval stamp.

Next to burst was the equity bubble, but not before people spent billions of their equity dollars on frills that made them feel good. This helped fuel the flipping craze, a craze that was being taught around the country in seminars resembling tent revivals.

MacMansions got flipped. Condos got flipped. Mobile homes got flipped. A tree house would flip, so long as the land the tree stood on was sellable.

Even unsellable tracts of land were suddenly showing signs of a profit margin. Folks lucky enough to own small swatches of land in the Keys were suddenly sitting on a gold mine.

The equity bubble got folks spending billions on new cars, trucks, and boats. Most homes in South Florida had four and five cars parked out front. It wasn't long before South Florida took first place in traffic gridlock over L.A.

But it was still the loan markets that kept Family firing on all cylinders. It's also what kept the Board members smiling. The loan-through-credit craze had allowed people to think credit was the same as cash. And while the majors continued approving and sending out their own embossed plastic, the U.S. growth-to-debt ratio, in 2012, went from an already staggering 34% of household income to an unsustainable 100% of GDP. (This now accounts for the burdening $50,000 per every man, woman, and child in America.) History was no longer repeating itself. It was being re-written.

"We're taking on the world and all that's in it!" It was his lousiest Tony Montana impersonation, but it suited Ian just fine during the Family Christmas party of '07. It was rare seeing him drink booze, but he had much to celebrate, starting with his personal wealth exceeding $38 million, plus another record year in profits, and this during wartime and a downturn in the economy.

RMF had been the major contributor to that year's profits.

No mention was made of the eight chairs sitting empty at accounting's table, nor of the four in accounting already arrested.

"Banco Familia . . . tu familia . . . tu casa." Ian held up keys and jingled them. This was to be the new jingle to run that year, a jingle that brought applauses from the 1,100 plus at the Christmas party. (This jingle would run as far south as Argentina, where Argentines would net Family another $300 million in mortgages by next year's end.) But $13 billion in Family assets could not change fate. (Even the jingle commercial would return to haunt Ian in the form of jingle mail once the meltdown started.)

It came time for Ian to choose his permanent office. He wanted an office to rival any of Street's biggest named financiers. He hired an architect to design a floor plan for the 3,200 square feet he'd chosen on the ninth floor.

"But Ian, the *whole* ninth floor?" Vazquez sounded incredulous when hearing of Ian's plans.

"Not the *whole* floor, Pop. Acquisitions & Estates will still be near the elevators. It's the rest of the floor that I want." Ian was talking while watching the sheetrockers roll their scaffold around while hanging up his new sheetrock.

"Well, I don't see how the Board's going to approve you such an extravagance."

"You don't have to worry about that, Pop. I've already made it clear that I was footing the entire bill. I'm paying for all the renovation myself. Not to worry. But hey, I even have a golf closet being put in for us. And wait till you see our bathroom."

"Our bathroom?"

"For those days when we come in from the field all sweaty."

"Thought of everything, haven't you, son?"

"Kitchen and entertainment area too, Pop. I really can't wait for the office to be finished." Ian got so excited talking about it, that it triggered his pacing. Vazquez hated it when Ian got to pacing.

"Oh, Ian; please don't start that pacing thing of yours again." He had to step aside while saying that. "You really need to see a doctor about all that hyperactivity of yours, you know that?" Had Ian known about the downgrades going on upstairs, about the bleed-out that had started at RMF, he might've paced forever. Instead, his suit jacket got caught in the sheetrockers' scaffold while pacing. In pulling his coat away from the scaffold, he knocked the sheetrockers' radio off the scaffold. The radio crashed to the ground and broke.

"See there, Ian?" Vazquez was already reaching for his wallet. "See what your hyperactivity gets you?" The workers were confused by the older gentleman speaking down to Ian, who they knew to be the boss. "Come on Ian," said Vazquez, after handing over a $100 for a new radio. "Let's go eat. I'm hungry. And you may want to call your contractor and offer him more money to get your office finished quicker."

"Hey! That's an idea, Pop. And what say after lunch, we go take in a few holes? I got my clubs in the car."

"You always have your clubs in your car."

"Hey, they were your gift to me, remember?"

"Oh yeah, that's right. Well, I'm not really up to swinging today. Maybe tomorrow." Vazquez was feeling a bit off that day.

"Wow, now that's a first for ya, Pop. No golfing?"

Upstairs, RMF was taking in more downgrades. By the time they were done with lunch, the downgrades had settled. But the coming weeks would force Ian to be more at his desk and less on the links.

Four months later, his office was ready and it was as imposing as any of Wall Street's heavy hitters. He now had his own espresso station built among marble countertops in a kitchen with all new Sub Zero appliances and pickle-stained cabinets. The bathroom was of custom design also. It housed a changing room, a dressing room, two huge closets, two large shower stalls, and a metal tub whirlpool. All the walls of the office were done in faux marbleize, with a 110-foot strand of vertical Mylar, which was remotely operated, and could closed off the bright morning sunlight reflecting off the bay in minutes. In the ceiling and walls were the best-money-could-buy music speakers. At the far end of the office was a 12-seat mahogany conference table with drop-in laptops at each seat. A billiard table, with table ends resembling the front and rear bumper of a '57 Chevy, which at a push of a button could convert to a domino or poker table, was situated near the windows. Collector furniture was used throughout the office. From the local art college, Ian had purchased a dozen quality works of art done by local art students. Custom track lighting, plus two large flat-screen TVs for following the daily markets and the Dow, complimented his office.

But the crème de la crème came in Vazquez's gift.

Vazquez had found two of Ian's grandfather's millworkers owning their own woodshop in Hialeah. He hired the men to replicate Suarez's old manor desk. The custom-built desk was delivered just as Ian was settling into his new office. Ian was shocked to see it took six men to deliver his gifted desk, a desk of exquisite design and craftsmanship. The $24,000 desk was breathtaking. The desk also came with a $1,200 ergonomic chair.

Vazquez's other surprise wasn't as charming. He waited until Ian's computer tech was done hardwiring Ian's PC to the desk before dropping the bombshell of cancer eating away at his insides. Suddenly, the desk, chair, even money itself, meant nothing to Ian. Finding out about Vazquez's cancer was like having to relive the 13-de-Marzo all over again.

Chapter 15

Vazquez hadn't gone through all

of what he'd gone through in life so that cancer could just steal him away. Vazquez was no quitter, and he proved that by booking a four-month cruise for him and Delia, a cruise that would invariantly keep him from witnessing the growing troubles at the bank.

Ian did miss the camaraderie he and Vazquez had developed over the years. He also let it be known he would spend his last dollar if it meant bettering Vazquez's health. But there's only so much that money can do.

Ian suggested a few fishing trips for him and Vazquez right before leaving on the cruise. They even tried a few rounds of golf. But the sun was too much for Vazquez to handle while on his chemo medication.

Then Vazquez did something crazy. He upped and refused to take his chemo or radiation. This shocked his doctors, who were already upset because of his fishing and golfing excursions. What Vazquez did next really shocked them when he upped and fired them!

Vazquez decided to take a more holistic approach to his treatments. It was his new holistic doctors that thought it fine his going on a four-month cruise. They were even fine with his fishing and golfing. But even the best-money-could-buy healthcare couldn't stop the inevitable, as stage four was meaning to eventually break down Vazquez's body. But he was going to enjoy life while he could.

Ian's portfolio nearly doubled in '08, to almost $50 million in personal wealth. But then came September 18 and wham . . . 40% of his income was lost.

September 18 was, for many, where the good times ended.

The fact the local media had aired a documentary of how young Ian was when amassing his wealth, at the cusp of record layoffs, made his success story a bit hard to swallow to those affected by the sudden economic meltdown. (Like his grandfather, one would've been hard pressed to know of Ian's wealth, if not for the way he dressed. He was friendly to most, with a down-home attitude that went with his friendliness. His vices were expensive watches and his RS, plus another beautifully restored '76 convertible Eldorado {last year Cadillac made a convertible}, which he liked driving to the links. He also bought the Vazquezs' an easier-to-drive Mercedes and kept Vazquez's Presidential Cadillac parked in the garage. All these items would in time be confiscated by federal authorities.)

Dating had not gone so well since the days of Cathy. He'd dated a few girls in college, but no one worthy enough to bring home to meet his adoptive parents.

His unsuccessful dating was due mostly to his OCD mannerisms. He didn't like traveling by plane or ship (hating the thought of there being an ocean beneath him), and this ruined any vacation possibilities with any girls he dated. He did like hiking, but the girls he was dating weren't into driving for hours just to hike forest trails. His girlfriends wanted him to be more of a jet setter, which he refused to do. Later, he dated some of the women at the bank, but here again, his homebody lifestyle grated on his dates. He was tagged an eccentric by one of the women at the bank. The moniker stuck. None of his dates cared for fishing or golfing, and most disliked watching movies in his home theater. There'd been a time or two when the right buttons had been pushed for a sneak upstairs. But having sex in the same house in which his elders slept (thinking a 10,000 sq. ft. home not large enough to hide the moaning) made Ian feel weird. There was a five-star hotel not too far from the Lakes house that was better suited for those rendezvous. But even after hours of great sex, Ian still wanted to be back home, proving that his was a quintessential homebody lifestyle. "Shame he's so damn handsome," said his last girlfriend to friends at the bank. Ian didn't care. His memories always ended with Cathy, who had been good to him while in school. He had even tried finding her through facebook (but an abusive boyfriend had forced her to delete her page before Ian could find her). But no matter his failings in the love world, it was his tenacity to correct his losses that kept him achieving wherever possible, though working through the '08 meltdown was tough enough.

Wall Street continued hiring quants straight from college, most strapped to large student loans, to help sift through its weakening numbers to find the answer to its decline. The reasons were obvious. But reeling in the good times was anathema.

For Ian, across the board losses continued to chip away at both RMF and Family's assets. It was during a round of golf (he'd had it with sitting at his desk that day) when the first bundle of jingle mail reached the bank. Jingle mail would soon overfill the Family mailroom.

Even Ian's sleep pattern was altered by the disruptions caused by the OTC markets sliding to near nothing, and making it all too clear that Street's finely honed math was fraught with blatant errors.

Vazquez had to cut his trip short because of his weakening condition. He took to bed as soon as he was home.

It was during his adoptive parents' first night back from their cruise that Ian, in passing their room, heard laughter coming from it. He knocked, then entered and found that instead of resting, Vazquez was sharing a laugh with Delia over photographs from an old shoebox. Ian was invited to join his elders in their reminiscing moment. He was handed photos that told many tales. But not all the tales were good tales. But there was one photo that immediately caught his attention. The similarity of the man in the photo to his mother was uncanny. "Let me guess. This is my grandfather, right?"

"Juan Suarez himself," answered Vazquez, who winched while pointing at Ian's grandfather. Delia handed her husband a pain pill to alleviate the winching.

In Ian's hand was a photo of his grandfather with arms around a much younger Vazquez. Both men were laughing in the photo.

"So, what was so funny?" Ian just had to know.

Vazquez was slow to respond because of his pain. "Huh? Oh, us laughing you mean? Well, you see, Ian . . . that was the day your grandfather sabotaged his cut lines."

"Sabotaged his cut lines?"

"Oh, he caused a ruckus that day, sabotaging the line and keeping the State people from getting his wood. The cut lines and their mysterious breakdowns caused quite a stir." Vazquez pointed at the photo. "We were laughing because Fidel's people couldn't figure out how to get the lines started again. Of course we had to wait for the troops to leave before we could laugh. But that was one crafty devil, your grandfather was." Vazquez started to laugh when remembering the day, until pain forced him to shut his eyes and wait until the pain eased.

"Pop, you need another pill?"

"Ey hijo, I could take a hundred pills and it wouldn't help."

A tear suddenly fell from Vazquez's eye.

"The pain that bad, Pop?"

"Ey, hijo, my tears aren't over the pain; they're from thinking of your crazy mother and what she was trying to do with the two of you. Ey, que loca, trying to cross the way she did."

More tears came then, forcing Delia to hand her husband the tissue box and say, "Stop it, Miguelito. It does no good to let Ian see you suffer like this."

"But Delia . . ."

"But nothing. It does no good you carrying on about Maria." She turned to Ian and said, "He's been doing this all day, thinking of your mother."

"But imagine how happy she would be, Delia, if she were alive to see what her Ian has accomplished." Vazquez's words made him winch more. Delia was right in saying it did no good suffering the past. "She is still with us in spirit, Miguel," said Delia while pulling the comforter up to her husband's chin. "Maria took her chances like everyone else that day. Doesn't do any good to bring all that up now, dear."

"I guess you're right, Delia." His voice was starting to sound medicated while he struggled to sit up. "Ay, Ian," Vazquez rolled back some of the comforter while trying to sit. "And here I thought I'd get to see a *free* Cuba before I died. Instead, those bearded bastards are *still* in power. Ooh . . ." the pain dizzied Vazquez a moment, ". . . I guess this is what they mean by selling your soul to the devil."

"Please Pop, take it easy."

"Why couldn't we have been more like the French?"

Even through the medication haze, Vazquez was still able to catch Ian's look of confusion. "Yes Ian, the French. They overturned an entire monarchy with just pitchforks and rocks. And what did we get? We got the Bay of Pigs, thank you very much."

Vazquez lost his train of thought when being offered water by Delia. He looked to Ian to remind him where he'd left off.

"Uh, Bay of Pigs, Pop."

"Oh yeah, la Bayana de Cochinos. What a disaster. Hell Ian, even the British had the cojones to withstand 12,000 rocket attacks by the Nazis, and this when the Nazis *knew* they were going to lose the war. Hell, the Brits even fought off the Spanish Armada with just a few fire ships. Conyo Ian, even the Contras got to run off the Sandinistas with just machetes and clubs."

"Yeah, after being helped with Reagan's weapons. Don't forget that. And the fiasco that was the Iranian weapons exchange."

"Yeah, but you can't compare all that to a tiny beach landing, which is what we got. Kennedy sure dropped the ball that day. No air support. No artillery. Nothing but wanting to save face with the bearded one. Promising to never bother Fidel again is what got him assassinated. Ooh . . ." the pain again stole Vazquez's breath away. Delia helped her husband to lie back down.

While waiting for Delia to finish making Vazquez more comfortable, Ian went to remembering the last time he and Vazquez had gone fishing in the bay. They were in their 17-foot skiff when out of the blue, with a faraway look in his eye, Vazquez had begun to talk about the days he would hang near the Malecón. Ian was certain that had he not been in the boat with Vazquez, Vazquez would've probably tried taking the skiff to Cuba.

"Hello? Earth to Ian." Delia broke Ian of his reverie. "A little help here?"

Ian was helping Delia with the comforter when Vazquez suddenly grabbed his arm. "Promise me you'll never forget Cuba."

"What the hell, Pop?"

Vazquez purposely avoided Delia's stern look.

"Never forget where you came from, Ian."

"Of course not, Pop. I never will. You know that."

"Seems most of us have become too Americanized to remember Cuba."

"That's not true."

"Yes it is. But it doesn't matter. You just keep your mother's charity going, you got that, Ian?"

"I got it, Pop. I got it. But you're not going anywhere anytime soon, so quit your blathering and go to sleep."

"You came into our lives at just the right time, you know that, Ian? Delia and I have been thanking God for you ever since." Ian fought through the tightening in his chest, a tightening that came with knowing that Vazquez's time was drawing near. It was then that Vazquez handed Ian the picture of him and Suarez together. "You keep that, Ian; that way you'll have the two of us watching over you."

But Ian had something more he wanted to ask, and he didn't want Vazquez to drop off into his fog without asking. "Say Pop, one last thing, and please don't take this the wrong way; but can you tell me a little more about my biological father? I mean, please don't think me ungrateful; you've been the best father ever," he looked at Delia, "and you as a mom, too." He set his eyes back on Vazquez. "But if there's maybe something you haven't told me about him? Anything?" But it was too late. The fog had come quicker than expected.

It was Delia who answered for Vazquez, and in not so nice a tone. "Ey Ian, you really should leave that part of your life alone. We were gone from Cuba when your mom met your father. What little we know of him is not good. Just leave it alone. Continue to live your life in the memory of her, not him." Ian had earlier Google searched his father, so he could understand Delia's concern. It was also here where he discovered that certain agencies, including agents with Special Alliance in London, were still keeping the Wolfe file open, which included the possibility of eavesdropping on his son. Ian knew to be careful.

Delia handed him another photo from the shoebox.

"We had our own issues to deal with once we got to Miami."

Ian was now holding a photo of a 'Keep Out' sign taped to one of the hotel windows on Miami Beach. Ian looked to Delia for an explanation.

"You could cut with a knife the racism that met us here, Ian. Forgive me for saying this, but we didn't have time to worry about what your mother was doing back in Cuba. Sorry." She handed Ian another photo. In this one, she and Vazquez were holding hands in front of Miami's Cielito Lindo (Freedom Tower). "We tried seeing a brighter future here, regardless of how people acted towards us." Ian handed back the photo, which Delia put back in the box before returning the box to the closet. She had to raise her voice from inside the closet to be heard. "We also had to ride in the back of the bus, and the blacks didn't much like us there, either. It took Johnson's Great Society moment to make things a little better. But it took a while for the civil rights movement to take hold down here, though you wouldn't know it by the racism that's still prevalent today." She came from the closet and waved Ian to follow her downstairs. "I think I'll go for a little sherry. Care to join me?"

"Not for a drink, but I'll help with the lights and the alarm."

"Good."

Delia continued to speak while going downstairs.

"Signs in windows weren't as bad as the hoops Miguelito had to jump through before getting Family Bank started." Delia made for the bar in the den while Ian went to set the alarm. They met back at the stairs.

"You know, we almost made Ybor City our home before coming to see this house." She finished her sherry and set the empty glass on the foyer table. "Of course the house didn't look anything like it does today. We added the den and made the kitchen larger. Would you believe, back in the day, Senator Graham's cows used to drink from our pool?" Ian laughed when hearing that.

"Wow! Imagine that. Well, you don't need to worry about any cows these days, eh Delia?"

"Oh, we didn't mind the cows. What I mind now is the traffic." Delia had already had a few fender-benders since living at the Lakes.

They started back up the stairs with Delia saying, "It's been a real blessing you taking over Family. I don't think Miguelito could've taken much more of this new bank craze that's going on."

"So you know about this bank craze?"

"I learned quite a lot about banking from Miguelito, my dear. When he first started Family, his main worry was about your grandfather's money."

"Why?"

"Because he wound up needing that money to make the minimum cash threshold needed for starting even a little bank like his. I know about the revenue requirements also."

"So why didn't Vazquez, knowing so many people, why didn't he just partner up back then?"

"Come on, Ian. You know the answer to that. You come from the same stock as he. Problem back then wasn't starting a bank; it was us being exiles and having an additional $2 million to start a bank with." They made it to the top of the stairs, where one final flick of the switch made the downstairs dark. "But don't kid yourself, Ian; nothing's as bad as today's deregulations causing so many defaults. And there's always those cash transfer receipts you have to worry about."

"Oh, so you know about CTRs too, huh?"

Delia made a face. "I know plenty about CTRs. Oh, and I forgot to mention that back when Family was started, Miguelito was erroneously coded a 6103 by Revenue."

"Oh wow, now that's trouble." (*Code 6103 was the same revenue code that President Nixon used for getting the low down on his political enemies while he was President.)

"Ian, you see the patio furniture outside? We used that as our furniture for the first few years here in the house."

"You didn't! But what of all the entertaining you all did?"

"Didn't do much entertaining back in the early years of Family. It was all touch-and-go and hope for the best back then with us."

"But you now have what, like $800,000 in insurable household stuff?"

"We've come a long way since then, Ian; a long way since Miguelito drove a beat up V W Bug to work."

"A Bug? Oh, please do tell." Ian was amazed at what he was hearing.

"That VW used to stall whenever it rained." Delia was having just as much fun remembering as in the telling. "Some type of short circuit thing. But soon as Family was up and running, Miguelito took out his first car loan to himself. Once that was paid for, he made out a furniture loan to himself. That's when the entertaining started. Yep, for a while there, Miguelito was his own best bank customer." Delia laughed at that, too. "But on a more serious note, and I almost forgot to mention this, but I have something that came in the mail that I need you to look at." He waited at her bedroom door while she went to get a letter from her night table, which she handed to him.

Ian's eyes widened when seeing the letterhead.

"But Delia, this is a Revenue letter."

"Duh. I know it's a Revenue letter, Ian. It's what it says about our personal finances, where we owe back taxes, which I need you to look into. Maybe have somebody in accounting look into this? I really don't want Miguelito to know about this. He has enough to deal with."

Ian was already handling a big Revenue worry at the bank. There was the possibility that fraud charges due to accounting's mishandling of each employee's withholdings might bring Revenue's own coded horrors to Family's 1,100 plus employees. (Arrears and penalties on owed Federal, State, and Local taxes, plus Social Security and Medicare taxes, were already amassing in the millions of dollars in fines against Family. Auditing agents were already on their way to Family.)

"Uh, Delia," Ian hated to think that accounting's mishandling of his adoptive parents' funds would also bring more trouble, "accounting's so bogged down with training our new people that I might have to have someone in town look into this."

"Do what's best, dear. Just get someone reliable."

"You bet."

"What ever happened to Royce and Turner, anyway? Why'd they turn on us?" Delia knew all about the bank's accounting fiasco.

"Uh, don't worry about any of that." Ian didn't want to worry Delia with any more of the legal ramifications to accounting's fiasco. "I'll get yours, and my numbers right. I got a meeting scheduled with the Feds soon as they bring Royce and Turner back from the Caymans. Maybe then I can figure out why they turned on us."

(Royce and Turner were headed back to Miami in handcuffs.)

Ian kept quiet about his having received his own Revenue letter.

Ian surprised Delia right as she started to close her bedroom door with, "So, no more on my biological father?"

Delia was surprised by the question and sounded it. "You really aren't letting this go, are you? I thought the subject was closed." The grandfather clock's sudden chime of midnight broke the angry moment. "Oh my, Ian, midnight already. Where *does* the time go?"

But Ian wasn't letting up so easily. "So how it is you and Pop knew about me, if you weren't staying in contact with my mother?"

Delia took his hands and looked directly into his eyes. "Since you're not going to give this up, and remember you asked; do you remember us telling you about your grandparents' good friend, Mrs. Gutierrez?"

"The pig farmer's wife?"

"That's the one. Well, that's how we kept up with you in Cuba. When Mrs. Gutiérrez passed on, her nephew, who lived in Havana, he's the one who kept us up to date with you, your brother, and your mom."

"Hey, I think I remember him. Eduardo, right?"

"That's who told us about your father Red. So long as we kept sending him money, Eduardo would keep sending us info on all of you. Eduardo is who told us of your birth. He was too scared to interact with your father though. Seems many people were scared of the Wolfe. That's what they called him, the Wolfe, by the way. But you already know that, I'm sure. Now can I get some sleep?"

Ian still had one more question. "So how is it that Castro's sister got out, but not my mother?"

"Still with the questions, eh?" Delia breathed deep before answering. "Juanita Castro didn't know half of what your mother knew about the regime. That alone made it impossible for her to leave Cuba. Time will tell whether Juanita Castro did work for the CIA or not. Won't matter if she did though. Your mother, she just knew too many of the wrong people. That's what cost her in the end."

"My brother, too."

"Sadly, yes. But you know what, Ian?" Delia pointed at her sleeping husband. "Miguelito has been carrying the stigma of your brother and mother's death like a stone around his neck. He couldn't get to Krome quick enough to bring you home when hearing you were there." Delia reached out and grabbed Ian's hands in hers. "Focus on the future and forget the past. You keep poking a snake in the eye and it will bite you. Plus, none of it really matters. You know why?"

"Why?"

"Because in the end, it was your mother's love for your father that brought you into this world. And that's *all* that matters." Delia smiled when giving Ian a goodnight kiss before releasing his hands and closing the door behind her. From there, Ian hurried to his room to do one last Google search. What he found there about Delia amazed him.

Delia had never been the stay-at-home type. She had gotten involved with the Peter Pan flights soon as she and Miguel settled in the Lakes. (*Operación Pedro Pan was a coordinated effort by the U.S. State Department, the CIA, the Miami Roman Catholic Archdiocese, and several prominent Cuban families who all joined together to help bring 14,000 Cuban children to America, whose parents were opposed to the Castro takeover. Operación Pedro Pan later included children whose parents fought to keep their children from being sent to Soviet bloc schools and work camps. All the newly arrived children went to relatives living in the U.S., or to friends of the family, or placed in-group homes found in 35 states. Delia and Miguel Vazquez had donated a home in South Broward to the Pedro Pan children.)

Ian put his computer to sleep, then took from his wallet the photo of his grandfather and Vazquez together. He leaned the photo against his reading lamp and went to reading a favorite book of his titled: <u>Terrorism in a World of Terrorists</u> By Dr. Dana Warrick

Ian gave the photograph one last stare before turning out his light and hoping for sleep. But less than an hour into dreamscape, his enemy mind had him back out in the ocean again. He was back with the fins and the floating bodies. He tried screaming, but only got an imaginary mouthful of saltwater for his troubles. He was nearing the point of giving up his spirit when the sunlight woke him.

But it wasn't the harsh sunlight streaming in through blinds he'd forgotten to close, or of his favorite author's book hitting the floor that had awakened him, but Delia's grief-stricken sobs telling him Vazquez was gone.

Chapter 16

While packing her husband's clothes, Delia got to thinking about just how short their vacation had been. Meanwhile, at the bank, Ian was furiously pacing in his office. He was fighting his own demons that came with Vazquez's loss. He hated to even look over at Vazquez's golf bag. It was difficult dealing with his mentor's passing. Even the failings that were going on upstairs at RMF, with losses nearing 40% in ARM mortgages alone, couldn't distract him of his suffering.

Ian next called home with an offer to Delia. He offered her a new home if wanting to move from the Lakes. He offered her a beach condo or a Gables estate. Anywhere else, any home, to avoid the memories the Lakes house held. But it was precisely *because* of the memories in the house that Delia wanted to stay put. But not Ian. He opted for staying in his office, upwards of 16 hours a day, sleeping on the sofa, just to keep from going home. Delia figured him out. She guessed he was using work as a way to dull the pain of losing Vazquez. She had no way of knowing that he was also dealing with voices in his head that were becoming louder because of the loss. There was also the Revenue issue she didn't know about. Regulators were once again camped downstairs in the Family book room.

A new Revenue letter, more threatening than the first, was waiting for Delia in her mailbox once she was back home from giving Vazquez's clothes to charity. The new Revenue letter demanded payment on tangible tax arrears amounting to $2.1 million upon receipt of the letter.

Ian had too much on his plate to resolve Delia's Revenue issue, so he set it aside for later. He was knee-deep in handling the fire sale going on upstairs at RMF. In the mailroom, jingle mail continued to grow due to record layoffs that would continue throughout 2010 and into 2011, which would by then collapse the mortgage market.

Ian's math continued showing an ugly truth.

Having federal auditors in the bank didn't help.

The sentencing phase of Royce, Turner, and the 6 others did nothing to cheer him, though it made for quite a news story, which also made plenty of trouble for the bank. The coffee pot was put on indefinitely by auditors and federal agents then.

Dozens of fraud charges on misdirected funds, including state and federal withholdings on 1,100 employee filings were found in arrears at Family, causing chaos with Family's new accountants. Delia's tax issue had itself brought liens against the Lakes property.

There was little time for Ian to establish a course of action with the fire sale going on at RMF. Family was starting to resemble a sinking ship. Ian's signature loan that he used for paying off Vazquez's troubling loan to his chums was also flagged by auditors. Falling below cash threshold again was another red-flag item to deal with. This was when Revenue's Criminal Investigative Division (CID) came into the picture.

The OJI heading Atlanta's CID office was a stick-in-the-mud named R. Terrence. He was not only overseeing the Atlanta office, he was also leading it during a year of ratings, reviews, and performances.

The OJI already had a desk full of audit files and a monitor screen loaded with names of people being investigated with large bank and investment holdings. He had his investigators working overtime in examining what they considered illegal handling of hedge funds and taxes due on such funds. OJI Terrence was already angry with his workload when finding Ian's name added to his list after coming from using the bathroom. Fresh coffee gave him the impetus to review the criminal charges being sought by Florida's FDIC and FERC agents, in particular charges against RMF during a slowdown that was seeing deficit spending near crisis level. (Ian's IRS initials gave OJI Terrence a 'WTF' moment.) Agent Terrence had been doing Revenue collection for over

28 years. His attitude was that he was sworn to enforce collections to right the national kitty. Ian was no exception.

Ian was forced to use his own money to help staunch the bleed-out at RMF while Street continued to reinvent itself. But his $100 million only proved to be a Band-Aid against the growing losses from those walking away from their ARM loan mortgages once due. (Total foreclosure rates would eventually come one every seven minutes.) But those who had become deaf, dumb, and blind to nothing but spending money not yet earned were starting to feel the repercussions from spending so much of that not yet earned money. Credit was needing constant feeding even if just minimum payments. Feeding the beast was President Bush's way of encouraging people to "spend money or the terrorists win." A small stimulus of $300 was worked into that year's tax refunds for people to spend as they wished (a minuscule amount compared to what was being stolen on Wall Street). But instead of $300 in purchasing power, most folks used their paltry refund for paying down credit card debt. (The $300 was deducted from the following year's refunds anyway.)

Those in the know (the 1%) were the first to read the writing-on-the-wall. Heck, most of them had written what was on the wall. As Street began to melt, the 1% within the 1% refueled, retooled, reloaded, and extended their vacations when knowing where securitization and derivatives were headed. The hoarding of profits had already begun prior to the downgrades leading to the meltdown that would take generations to fix.

Family ended 2008 steeped in losses brought on by the foreclosure debacle. As for RMF and its bundled securitization packages, those packages with their wonderful tranches (selective packaging within packaged derivatives) could no longer be sold once the Maes went into conservatorship and the meltdown continued. As for the housing market, the only houses selling were those being plucked by capitalist vultures paying pennies on the dollar for foreclosed homes.

Ian realized too late that he'd allowed Family too many Adjustable Rate Mortgages, plus too many packaged collateral debt obligations (CDOs), handled through RMF to keep Family from suffering through the brunt of the housing collapse. His restructuring gimmicks no longer worked for him. Worse fallout came when news of Family's downgrade, because of their accounting fiasco, went public. This got more Family customers withdrawing their money from Family and thus forcing a fourth regulatory fine for falling below threshold a third time and this *while* regulators were in the building. This was the final straw that forced Ian to start closing some of the branch offices, starting with the Tallahassee office. The rest of their branches went by way of domino effect.

When needing to play his cards close to the vest and hide what was happening at Family, Ian played his cards face up.

It was when the Dow dropped 1,800 points in just days (during a time of unsustainable debt-to-GDP levels, which was double the gilded age and the roaring twenties combined) when the public finally opened its eyes.

Quantitative experts compared fund market growth as cake the 1% fed on, until there was no cake left. The buddy system, which is what got deregulation to happen, is what vanished even the crumbs from the American taxpayer.

The meltdown of '08 saw an additional $11 trillion from federal, state, and local obligations, plus another $37 trillion in future obligations get added to a bill that couldn't be accounted for. (When Alan Greenspan became the Fed Chairman in 1987, public and private debt totaled $10.5 trillion. When he retired in 2006, the market debt alone had shot past $43 trillion!)

Credit venders, mortgage bondholders, and the architects of asset-backed securities (ABSs are the anomalous Structured Investment Vehicles {SIVs} that took billions from the markets once those in the know smelled smoke) vanished in droves when seeing the markets show its true color.

"A billion here and a billion there and pretty soon you'll be talking *real* money," joked one senator from the floor during a session of endless debacle, a senator whose lifestyle differed from the 99%. (*Author's note: It takes 17½ days to count a million seconds. It takes 32 years to count a billion. You'll not live long enough to count a trillion.)

Deregulation allowed the wolves to guard the henhouse, the wolves being the investment banks after having merged with commercial banks. (This was a no-no written into law for reasons that were obvious during the Great Depression.) But the buddy system made that happen, which gave the newly merged banks an opportunity to nearly monopolize America's banking system (though having been deemed criminal when Microsoft, Enron, Synergy, and Reliant tried monopolizing their own respective markets). Mergers like Citi, Chase, Morgan, BoA, Wells Fargo, and others made for strange bedfellows. The Federal Reserve (which is neither federal nor have anything in reserve) continued to purposely hide its head in the sand while the financial party was on. Tons of plastic cards embossed with 21st century robber baron names were approved in minutes. Michael Milken's elixir math, which had shown hedging to be an art form (to the tune of a $400 million fine and his being put in prisoned until 1993) apparently wasn't enough of a warning sign to keep runaway investors from continuing to invest in misbehaving derivatives that had forced the '87 crash. What had been a few dozen managing groups in the '80's had, by '06, become thousands of hedge fund groups, with RMF being one of them. By '09, even RMF was carrying enough badly disguised SIVs to wallpaper the interior of the Family building!

Volatility was created by exponential results from an outrageously *new* way of making money on money not yet earned (and with AIG the biggest insurer to such speculative nonsense). Next with too much skin in the game was Congress. But Washington couldn't reel it in fast enough, as first-tiered accounts made up for half the day's market trading, at a time when foreclosures were becoming a pandemic. Those promising to do the people's business had conveniently forgotten what the people's business was.

The average American household was too busy trying to put food on the table to notice, or do much about, the burgeoning debt crisis. After all, that's what voting for a sane congress was all about, to help bring down the national debt. Instead, what the taxpayers got was the 'Troubled Asset Relief Program.'

TARP was Washington's answer to the 'too big to fail' banks. Unfortunately for Ian and Family Bank, *they* were not among the too big to fail.

His classmates working at Sachs wouldn't return his calls. They were too busy serving the long line at Sachs of those needing immediate cash infusions. (*It had gotten to where the bigger banks simply refused to loan the smaller banks money, and instead of using the bailout money for making loans as promised by congressional fiat, most of the majors, after the meltdown, just hoarded what they got from TARP, with some even going right back to investing in derivatives!)

Washington bureaucrats next slapped taxpayers in the face by trying to pass a bill that would make filing for bankruptcy much harder, this as

396 tons of cash went missing in Iraq. (Lewis Paul Bremer III, head of the CPA in Iraq, hadn't much to say on that.) Closer to home, Orange County, California's public trust, and public pension funds went belly up. The city of Stockton, California was added to the list of cities heading to bankruptcy (and could've surely used some of that vanishing Iraqi cash).

It was hard for a manic-depressive like Ian to admit he'd misread the markets during his days of managing $3 billion plus through his Red Market Funds. September 18, 2008 proved he had.

The killjoy started with Shearson-Lehman declaring bankruptcy. Another example of world market impropriety was Barclays Bank underreporting its borrowing costs to avoid showing its financial weakness. Because of this illegal impropriety, Barclays had to pay some $450 million to settle charges by U.S. and British authorities for its underreporting borrowing costs during the meltdown. (Their underreporting hid higher costs that had helped certain traders.) Next was Bear Stearns on the ropes.

An additional scandal involved London's Interbank Offered Rate. The LIBOR had reported unsecured loans from banks like Citibank, Bank of America, JPMorgan/Chase, and Barclays, who typically report morning borrowing rates to the British Banker's Association. But their reports were lies. LIBOR reported rates that weren't actual costs, and this manipulated rates. (*Why this matters is because LIBOR, like the prime rate, uses a set interest rate to track trillions in consumer loans such as ARMs. Nearly half of prime-borrowers, plus a majority of sub-prime borrower accounts, are linked to the LIBOR rate.) This kind of manipulation resulted in higher borrowing rates for many consumers and homeowners. This affected RMF's borrowing from Goldman Sachs, their primary lender of choice when in trouble, which by '09 saw RMF losses outpacing gains 6 to 1.

Dropping below threshold (the death knell to over 2,000 banks during the Great Depression) was an embarrassment for Ian. A late night Skype session with a classmate working at Northern Rock telling of Rock's financial woes didn't lighten Ian's mood, but he listened otherwise, right after signing to pay another threshold fine.

"Ian, your troubles don't even compare to what we got going on here at N-Rock. I wish it were just fines we had to worry about. We're sweating the big drops over here, bud. Hell, there's even talk of us sinking. Can you believe that?"

"The historical Northern Rock? I can't believe it."

"Believe it." Northern didn't sink, though it did stay in a financial tailspin for a while. The Royal Bank of Scotland was spinning, too.

Fearing the markets might drop further got Ian to transfer what money he had left (some $22 million) into his mother's charity fund. His actions, too, got flagged.

Family was deep in the red when 44,000 of their mortgages went into default and headed to foreclosure. While CEOs from Lehman, Solomon, Bear, and Countrywide were all jumping ship, Ian, in 2010, was still trying to right the Family boat. But it was like bailing water with a teacup.

While Bear Sterns teetered and fell . . . Ian kept RMF and Family floating.

After the Solomon merger failed . . . Ian still kept RMF afloat.

After Lynch managed to hide its $33 billion in losses from Bank of America (who then needed the Treasury to help pay some of its merger costs) . . . Ian still kept RMF afloat.

But it wasn't meant to be.

The financial tsunami had already sunken many ships. (Irony of the Lynch group, headed by Thain and cohorts, after the release of TARP money to help BoA buy out Lynch stock, had Thain demand an insulting $6.7 billion in severance for his group before relinquishing the reins at Lynch. This merger would in time cost CEO Lewis his job at BoA for a merger he hadn't wanted in the first place!)

More culpable were Moody and Poors giving AAA ratings to less than AAA rated accounts. No sooner had the ratings houses come clean than they audaciously downgraded America's *own* rating!

Gone were the easy pickings and skyrocketing profits of years past. SIVs and derivatives were nothing more than paper fooling investors into believing that home prices would continue to go up.

Salt to the wound was the Dow hitting nearly 15,000 points before the meltdown erased 2,000 points in a matter of days. The time for humbling had passed, with some investors not wanting to humble at all. Ian was not one of these, but in 2009, the media portrayed him as one.

Family had at one time been one of the very best banks for Floridians to park their money in. But having RMF made it impossible to show capital gains after 2009. The Family Board had by then conveniently forgotten that it had been *they* who had wanted Ian to go balls-to-the-wall in investing their money (and proving why greed leads the seven deadly sins). Smiles and good times ended once profits soured. Frowns and yelling came next.

By 2010, Ian was stuck behind a closed door, still searching for a way to right his sinking ship. His last hoorah was trying a new jingle . . . "carry our card in your wallet and you won't need any other card." It didn't work. Customers still kept withdrawing their money.

The start of 2011 showed Family with an additional half billion in losses from defaulted loans, though paltry when compared to losses at Lynch (merged with BoA), Wachovia (taken over by Wells Fargo), Citi (merged), and Countrywide (defunct). But Family's losses were enough to end Ian's reign as youngest CEO.

Though a nibbler compared to schemers like Madoff and Prince, Ian had still, through RMF, let the markets and his accountants get away with a financial windfall. Charging hard out of the gates when handed the baton by Vazquez saw it all go for naught by 2011. The Over-the-Counters had not only done in Ian, but it had returned him back to the porch to lie with beaten dogs. His getting flagged for transferring his entire portfolio to charity got him a hefty FERC fine of $20 million. The fact he evaded transfer receipts, which carried millions in penalties, made him out to be purposely hiding money in his mother's charity fund. He wound up having to use some of the money to pay off his $20 million fine, which made him feel like a heel, but it did avoid him court time. He would try and survive on stocks and Put options.

He kept digressing at his computer, thinking, hoping, trying to guess when things would get better; watching his monitor so much his eyes couldn't take the strain; going through eyewash like it was water while waiting for numbers to rise.

It was on a night when his blinds were closed and his office was pitch dark that he saw the apparition of Vazquez sitting on the sofa. It was when attempting to have a conversation with his mentor's ghost that Ian knew it was time for his own vacation. He knew the hammer would fall soon, *so why wait any longer?* (The night rover logged in that he'd seen Ian talking to himself while waiting for the elevator to take him to his car.)

OJI Terrence had by then tacked an additional $3 million in fines to Ian's tangible assets and to Delia's personal finances. Confiscations were around the corner. As if not bad enough, the fourth quarter of 2011 saw RMF vanish with a click of a mouse. It was then that Ian booked passage for he and Delia aboard the Valor, the only cruise ship offering onboard golf. It was as the ship was leaving the port that the Board voted him out of Family.

W hile getting better at swinging his clubs aboard the Valor . . . Family's Board began merger talks with Banco Sinn S.A.

As his ball plopped into the ocean from an over swing . . . the Board voted unanimously to deny paying his severance.

Delia went shopping at their first port of call, Charlotte Amalie, and wasn't there to see Ian toss his cell in the water when hearing that his Put options had sold short, making him money, but then having his moneyed account locked down by CID/Atlanta. He couldn't unload his personal LDOs quick enough to keep auditors from taking that, too. But instead of talking about that over dinner, he and Delia got to talking about how well their Baked Alaska was . . . until Delia started complaining about chest pains before collapsing in her dessert.

Delia slipped into a coma from which she never recovered. She was 78-years-old when pronounced dead at the St. Thomas hospital.

Delia's death was another tragedy that knocked Ian for a loop. But he kept his wits about him while renting a G-4 jet to fly he and Delia's body back to Miami. He interred Delia next to her husband in the family mausoleum in West Dade. From the cemetery, Ian went directly to the bank, but was kept from entering his office by security guards. He drove back to the Lakes house where he finally got to mourn in peace. But there were still other bitter pills to swallow.

Chapter 17

Ian hated being back in the spotlight again. All the media wanted to talk about was his 'flame out at 31.' The local media especially made his life a living hell. What got fingers flying across keypads was his losing millions in the game of investment banking. Much was written about his losses. No longer did his giving to charity matter. Even the prison sentences given to those guilty in accounting didn't get the attention his losing control of over $8 billion in banking assets did.

'Miracle banker loses control after going hog wild in the speculative market.'

'From nearly drowning in the ocean to drowning in the derivatives market.'

Even worse was written about him.

It was the C-Span coverage of Alan Greenspan's congressional hearings (where the Maestro claimed he too had been duped by Street; the Maestro, whose bulky briefcase had always been considered filled with monetary wisdom, when in fact it was his actual lunch he was carrying), finally got the attention drawn away from Ian. But C-Span wasn't there to cover how the new Family/Sinn Board had decided to refuse his contractual $2 million severance pay. This led to his next court filing.

He was just returning from the county clerk's office when finding Revenue agents parked in front of the Lakes house. At first he thought they were media people until showing him their CID badges. There were no handshakes or coffee after that.

"Mr. Suarez, the OJI has sent us to make a list of your possessions. So if you would kindly show us in." Once in the house, agents immediately went to listing everything of value. A call from the OJI to his lead agent told him the OJI was in route to Miami.

Soon as the listing was completed, a signature was needed.

"Mr. Suarez, you are not to remove anything we've listed until your audit investigation is over. The OJI has also ordered you not to make any more contributions into your mother's charity fund until your case is closed." Revenue was not playing games with Ian.

Ian was both stunned and angered by the agent's callous tone.

"You're kidding, right? You're telling me I can't do with my money as I please?"

"That's the OJI's orders."

"You know, with what I've paid into the system, and with me just having paid a $20 million fine, I would think it would be Revenue giving *me* money!" This actually made the lead agent laugh.

"Not in this lifetime, Mr. Suarez." The lead agent's face-hardened. "Now back to serious again . . . I need to know if you have any money in the house."

"Like I would tell you that."

"You're under a Revenue audit, Mr. Suarez. It's a crime if you're hiding money while owing taxes. That's why first order of business is to keep you from giving to charity from what might be due us."

It was hard for Ian to hide his anger. "Save your gestapo tactics for someone else. I know it's not *illegal* for me to give to charity what I want."

"It is when you're under audit, Mr. Suarez; plus we do a better job than the gestapo when it comes to getting you to pay up. Now sign here so we can clear out. And remember, what's on this list stays on this list until a judge hears your case."

"Bad enough I already have a severance issue . . ."

"You'll be seeing a tax judge a whole lot sooner than any judge handling your severance issue. The OJI assures you of that."

"What is this? More scare tactics? And what of my $20 million fine? You think that kind of money grows on trees or something?"

The lead agent motioned his people back to their cars. "They don't usually fine a person such an amount if not having done something wrong, get my drift?"

"Glad to see you're leaving, agent."

"Get snippy all you want, Mr. Suarez," animosity rose in the man's tone, "but I would advise you to get yourself a good tax lawyer. Better yet, just come clean when the OJI gets here and make things right. Avoid going to prison over this."

"More scare tactics I see. Now it's prison for someone who's flat broke. Give me a break, will ya? Besides, you guys have a history of making more mistakes than I ever could, so save your intimidation tactics."

"Mr. Suarez, whatever you're hiding, we're gonna find it. You can bank on that, pardon the pun. But you'll get no pity from us in the meantime, and you certainly won't get any from the OJI over your money transfers. You're also on record to inherit your adoptive parents' money soon, aren't you?"

"That's what I'll be living on."

"Not if you haven't settled with us, you won't. If your parents' portfolio clears before this investigation's over, than I would highly recommend you use *that* money to settle your debt with us."

"Yeah, right. Like anyone does that."

Ian didn't let on that he already had plans for the $4.4 million portfolio.

"You brought this upon yourself, Mr. Suarez."

"I thought you were leaving."

"I'm leaving alright. And by the way, those initials of yours? That a joke or something?"

"In Cuba there's no IRS, so no; it was pure coincidence on my parents part. Now, are you done?"

"Remember the OJI's not coming here on vacation, Mr. Suarez."

"With what I've paid into the system, he might as well be having a vacation on me."

"I'll let him know you said that."

"Please do." Ian was happy to see the agents leave.

Later that day, try as he might, Ian still couldn't get the visit from agents from affecting his golf swing during practice for an upcoming tournament. He landed in sand three times and ended with a lousy 94. He drove home with one less club in his bag after tossing his 4-iron in the Lauderhill drink.

The only reprieve he had left was his nightly online chats with new friends, the author, Dr. Dana Warrick, whose books he liked so much, and Mike St. Donovan, founder of the Liberty website and Press. It was with Mike and Dr. Warrick that he discussed his Revenue and banking horror story.

The new Board members of Family/Sinn were contesting Ian's severance on the grounds that he was the one responsible for the near collapse of Family because of his RMF dealings. Though his severance wasn't near the likes of Mozilo's $360 million severance (prior to Countrywide folding), Sullivan's $25 million (plus $153,000 for car and parking fees), Fuld's $350 million, Mudd's $28 million (and this after the Feds took over his company), or O'Neal's $161 million (prior to the BoA takeover), Ian still needed his severance if getting a shot at the markets once Street settled. In the meantime, the St. Augustine invitational beckoned him on after giving his severance lawyer a $10,000 retainer to fight for him in court while he was gone.

Whack!

For one long moment he lost sight of his ball . . . until it finally dropped from the sky and fell onto the green just 30-yards shy of the 18-cup. He had been making shots like that all day. Two shots later and Ian was in the cup and winning the St. Augustine prize money . . . just as the mail carrier was placing in his mailbox another Revenue demand letter for immediate payment of $336,000. At the same time that his Revenue letter was being delivered, his attorney was being argued down over his severance. (Unbeknownst to Ian's attorney, the judge ruling against Ian had been a customer of Family and was angry over Family's travails.) Ian knew none of this while driving back home in his Eldo, with the top down, his cell phone turned off, the prized trophy in back, and the $50,000 first prize money in his pocket. Back in Miami . . .

OJI Terrence was hopping mad when learning of Ian's new charity: The Family Employee Relief Fund. Because of the Sinn buyout of Family, most of the 1,100 employees of Family had been laid off due to restructuring (and lower waged workers. Sinn didn't want to deal with the backlog with their withholdings). Ian had felt guilty about the job losses due to his mishandling of Family business, which included his oversight with accounting. The subsequent loss of so many jobs troubled his conscience and got him kicking in with the recently awarded Vazquez portfolio. Since the state was taking its sweet time with kicking in unemployment compensation, Ian decided the $4.4 million would help those ex-employees until finding jobs. (One majority shareholder had thought the layoffs a good thing for new Family/Sinn. "After all," she'd exclaimed, "they're just bank employees, for crying out loud!")

Ian was feeling pretty good about himself when pulling up to the Lakes house. He arrived smiling over his having outsmarted Revenue by using his Wolfe name for cashing his winnings. But hiding behind the Wolfe name wouldn't keep confiscations from happening.

* * *

Contrary to popular belief, trading and hedging were not the major causes to the '08 meltdown. Street's massive losses stemmed largely from firms creating mortgage bonds and other complex investment vehicles that created a math that left even Ian scratching his head. His chance to right the Family ship ended when his first lender of choice, Goldman Sachs, refused to loan Family short-term loans when most needing them. Being flagged by both the FDIC and SEC hadn't helped.

But no bleed-out was as severe as AIG's, whose near death spiral had threatened to take down more than just Street. By then, Ian's financial ruin was a certainty.

Lobbying vultures used smoke and mirrors to run off with an additional $100 billion from pension funds swapped for more of Street's worthless paper. The securitization market by then was near worthless, as found out by Ian when trying to unload his once highly touted OTC packages that RMF could no longer sell off.

The South Florida housing market had earned its phenomenal rise in pricing mainly because of the changes in the capital gains tax to one's primary residence. The public no longer cared about the loose lending standards making loopholes easy to climb through; loopholes making background checks near obsolete by the time the housing bubble burst.

But Family's loose lending standards were a far cry from the likes of Ameriquest, First Alliance, Long Beach, and Quality. It was among these financial giants where Re-Fis and ARMs credit went crazy.

Too many customers were allowed far too much home on too little income during a time of 'normalcy bias' (normalcy bias is what kept the Jews living in Nazi Germany even after Kristallnacht and the Polish invasion. Normalcy bias is the *duh* that convinces people all is good, when it's not).

It wasn't by coincidence that public storage went from a $2 billion a year industry to a $38 billion a year industry, which by 2010 had way too many garage and yard sales failing to help people unload themselves of their stuff before bolting. Jingle mail had by then become the norm.

As for those rules that had been set in place to at least allow consumers a moment of common sense discipline before signing on the dotted line . . . those rules got axed and were replaced with looser lending standards. Wide was the path to financial ruin when credit became the norm. Commissioned-based brokers and agents saw to it that the public got its skin's worth of credit.

Those who had gotten to believe that their homes were their best investment learned quick that no home was exempt during the meltdown, especially when the ARM teaser loans came due. It wasn't by coincidence that 3.3 million bankruptcies were filed in 2009 alone.

Flipping and the equity craze . . . two trains of thought that stole more of people's sensibilities. And how could it not, when flipping seminars resembled tent revivals instead of teaching seminars. Lots of Kool-Aid was drunk then.

The forbidden fruit of easy credit, increased lines of credit, maxed-out lines of credit, minimum payment lines of credit (a bank's favorite customer) was deeply bitten into. Added to this was the securitization and speculative 'apple on a stick' that had, by 2009, grown rotten to the core.

Millions of people spent billions of dollars living a multi-trillion dollar lifestyle, which they could no longer afford by 2011. Live for the moment overrode common sense. The largest generation of retirees in history, the baby boomers, simply refused to reel it in or make any effort to teach financial constraint to their children (who would bear the brunt of the current debt crisis). Most retirees already living beyond their supplemental means continued using credit as buying power to letting the good times roll. Once reverse mortgages came to light, reverse mortgages got used up, too.

It took a 1,440-point drop in one day to get people to finally check their pockets. Instead of frugality and thriftiness, live for the moment had left most pockets empty, and all thanks to easy credit.

"Better to go to sleep hungry than to awaken in debt." These had been the words of Ben Franklin, words that ran counter to John Maynard Keynes's 'Paradox of Thrift,' where it was argued that thrift, in and of itself, undermined prosperity. There it was again, the 'live-for-the-moment and forget-about-tomorrow' nonsense that had locked every man, woman, and child into a bludgeoning debt crisis.

Thrift, once an esteemed virtue that had taught people to at least save for a rainy day, by the time of the meltdown, found most of Middle America without even a financial umbrella to stave off raining debt. Thrift and savings had become two words loathed by the public, but words suddenly wished for. The time of easy credit, that which had made people giddy when receiving their plastic cards, no longer made anyone giddy when it came time to pay up. In ARM loans alone, over a trillion dollars was lost, which then brought construction to a halt.

Ian felt he'd a right to feel angry when hearing of Fannie and Freddie getting theirs, while BoA used *its* bailout money to make the Lynch takeover happen. WaMu, AIG, GM, and Chrysler (whose majority shareholder was Fiat) all got theirs. AIG alone needed bailout to the tune of $118 billion, and this after their CFO, Joe Cassano, had mentioned at a quarterly meeting that "without being flippant, it would be hard for us here at AIG to lose a single dollar in any of our swap transactions." He was off by a mere $441 billion! (AIG would later insult the taxpayer further when their top-level execs were found lounging at a stress-free spa environment paid for by bailout money.)

But it wasn't just CEOs, CFOs, COOs, share directors, top-tiered managers, or presidents of companies wanting a piece of the bailout pie. Multi-nationals that had merged with American corporations wanted at the American taxpayer pie also. (Another drop-the-ball moment was when the government decided to buy up GM stock at $53 a share and then unload the same 500 million shares a few years later for $33 a share, a net loss to the taxpayer of $6 billion.) Next up was appointing a pay czar (a socialist title if there ever was one) for overseeing the $787 billion in TARP money that was offered to the too big to fails.

But some banks didn't want their books scrutinized. These were the banks that quickly repaid their loans with interest so they wouldn't have to open their books. (Some banks claimed they were forced to take bailout money, but still kept their books closed.) All this and more was going through Ian's head while waiting for his cup-a-soup to boil. That morning he had taken his $50,000 winnings and added it to his other monies from stocks and shoved everything inside his four bathroom plungers. He had just gotten off the phone with a friend at a Montserrat bank. Instructions on wiring his money to her would be forthcoming . . . just as his doorbell rang. Those ringing the bell caused Ian to even forget his soup.

Chapter 18

The tax judge who ruled on

Ian's case had been particularly interested in Ian's rise and fall from financial grace. But OJI Terrence wasn't interested in any of that.

"Your honor, please; this man would know every trick in the book for hiding money. He almost brought down his own bank because of his money dealings!" This wasn't true, but it did sway the judge who bought into the OJI's feigned look of impatience. "Your honor, please; I would like another shot at his house before he goes hiding his money."

"Yes, well I've taken that into consideration, agent Terrence. But Mr. Suarez here claims he has no money. So can I continue with my questioning him? To see what he *does* have?"

"Sorry judge."

"No need to be sorry, agent Terrence. But I do think I have a pretty good grasp of things here today though."

"Yes sir."

Ian couldn't believe what he was hearing, and because of it, he couldn't contain himself from saying, "Sounds more like a frat party among friends in here today." He faked saying this to his attorney, but he angered the judge with that.

"That will be enough, Mr. Suarez."

"I thought we were here about an auditing error." Ian's attorney tried getting him to quiet.

"Auditing error?" The OJI shouted while standing. "There's no auditing error here. And don't even think I'm buying into you being broke either, Mr. Suarez. Don't even go there. You got money stashed somewhere and we're going to find it."

The judge banged his gavel. "Gentlemen, please, kindly redirect your attention to me and not to yourselves." It was the judge's turn to feign impatience. "I've got plenty of other cases to rule on today before going home, so if you two would kindly listen."

"Just rule against him, your honor," said OJI Terrence. "So I can have my people at his house this afternoon."

This just gave Ian more reason to shout. "Are you kidding? My house? You've already been at my house. What more do you want?" Ian pointed at the two auditing agents sitting beside OJI Terrence who were busy rifling through paperwork. "Those two there have already been to my house and listed my things. What more you want? And what part of broke don't you understand?"

Nope. Never pays to get snippy.

"You're not broke," started in Terrence. "You probably got money stashed in some offshore account somewhere."

This got the judge's attention. "Um, Mr. Suarez, do you *have* an offshore account?"

"No sir, I do not." Ian knew he was perjuring himself, but he felt like he had no choice. He just couldn't rightly give away the last of his money, at least not without a fight.

"Well, Mr. Suarez," continued the judge while putting on his glasses to read, "I still have a problem with you *not* filing your golf earnings these past few years, and using the last name of Wolfe to hide your earnings. That in itself borders on the illegal." Having no social security number to match the Wolfe name had caught up to Ian. Tracing deposits back to his Suarez account is what had gotten him tagged. "Hiding money under an alias," continued the judge "is money you could use for paying down your tax debt."

"But I don't *have* a tax debt, your honor." Ian's attorney could no longer get him to sit. "And an alias isn't correct. Wolfe *is* my last name."

"But your social security number is issued to Suarez. And you also have the hyphen of Vazquez added to your Suarez name. Explain that one, Mr. *Suarez*?" The judge's patronizing tone irked Ian.

"The Vazquez name I've had to drop because of all the trouble it's causing me with the house. As for Wolfe, it *was* my father's name." Ian's attorney jumped in with, "Your honor, please, whether he's Suarez, Vazquez, Wolfe, or Ching-Chang-Choo, we're not here about names; we're here on a preposterous tax bill, and I do mean preposterous! As for his golf earnings, it is what my client lives on. I also might add that golf season *is* over."

Ian's attorney tried keeping Ian from saying more, but couldn't.

"So what's this court want from me, blood?"

"Uh, your honor," Ian's attorney tried saving face. He'd been paid a good amount of money and needed to show himself at least earning it. "I've been doing tax law for a lot of years," his voice was already sounding defeated, "but I've never seen anything like what agent Terrence here is trying to pull today. We've already presented proof that the IRS auditing numbers are bogus." Ian's attorney looked over at the CID auditors and added, "But if Revenue wants to maybe rework their numbers, then we might . . ."

"Rework numbers hell!" shouted OJI Terrence.

Ian shouted too with, "I'm good enough with numbers to know your math is *absolutely* off!"

The OJI jumped to his feet at that.

"Don't even try, Mr. Suarez. Don't *even* try. I didn't come all the way here today to bargain with you." Agent Terrence looked directly at the judge. "We have him on $3 million plus. It's time to collect. We're not here to bargain." Terrence ended his spiel with a smirk right as the gavel sounded.

"Enough!" It was the judge's turn to shout. "Enough already with you two."

But there was no stopping Ian from getting in the last word.

"Your honor, Revenue makes mistakes all the time. You know that. Or why this courtroom? But these bullying tactics are beyond belief. And I also want to go on record as saying I'm *not* going to be easily bullied. And what of my $20 million fine? Doesn't that count against such erroneous tax errors?"

"Your $20 million fine has nothing to do with your tax issues, Mr. Suarez," said the judge. Ian sighted right in on the judge.

"I'm flat broke, your honor. I have my golf earnings to live on. That's it." He could tell right then that his words had no effect on the judge. Seeing that, he ended with . . . "Where does this all end, eh your honor?"

"That's enough, Mr. Suarez." With that, the court reporter straightened and prepared to take down the judge's ruling. "If there's nothing else . . . I'll ask everyone to stand." The judge's tone told Ian his had been a losing cause from the get go.

Every year, the Internal Revenue Service sets 800,000 liens, 3.2 million levies, and executes over 12,500 seizures. Though many are of clear legal standing, some people do become victims of a system that shows its flaws especially during a time of ratings and performances. Ian had been tossed under the bus during a year of ratings and performances. Though living a hermit's life in 2014 (albeit in a 10,000 sq. ft. home) didn't stop the tax judge from ordering his possessions to be seized. CID agents were at his door that very afternoon, just like the OJI wanted. Agents re-inventoried his stuff before it all went to auction. Agents also videotaped the entire interior of the house while Lakes police stood by in case Ian tried stopping agents from doing their duty. But there would be no disruption. Ian just took the intrusive visit in stride.

Though the judge had lowered his arrears by $200,000, this still made for an implemented settlement of $2.9 million, which, without his severance, he could not pay. (*With power exceeding all state and local authorities, federal collection agents can pretty much do as they darn well please once having their district director's signature on their confiscation orders. Not even the Supreme Court can stop collection agents doing their job.)

Revenue's Criminal Investigative Division (CID) is known as the 'giant killers' division. The division is made up of roughly 3,800 men and women. At the time, OJI Terrence was leading the largest CID group out of Atlanta. As the recently appointed OJI, Terrence felt it was his sworn duty to knock giants to their knees. Ian was just such a giant, though not looking so in court, or when handing over the keys to his cars. But as agents were about to leave, a lone agent, while checking out the den, shouted that he'd found something.

Ian wondered why it had taken them so long.

Agents came on the run to find a safe hidden behind the Pellegrino horse painting in the den. Ian's dummy stash of $3,800 made the lead agent giddy about finding more, but there was no more cash to find. The real stash was still wadded up inside Ian's four plungers. (Ian had yet to transfer his money offshore. He hadn't wanted to set off any flags by transferring his money until after his revenue issue was over.) None of the agents had cared to even handle any of the slightly used plungers, let alone look up inside them. Had they, they would have found a total of $180,000, the last of Ian's money, wadded up inside them.

The intrusive visit ended with agents even taking Ian's golf club bag from the foyer closet (a bag he would replace soon enough).

*An example to Revenue's powers can be found in the stories of Senators James Couzens of Michigan, and John Williams of Delaware. Senator Couzens was one of the first legislators to investigate charges of graft and corruption at Revenue. Senator Couzens believed that widespread corruption within Revenue was destroying the integrity of the Service to collect taxes. Senator Couzen's concerns led him to chair a select committee, which looked into the allegations. A year into his investigation, the tenacious senator Couzens was summoned off the senate floor by Internal Revenue Commissioner, David Blair, and one of Blair's associates. The Revenue Commissioner had the audacity to hand Senator Couzens a bill demanding immediate payment of $11 million in back taxes. But the intimidation tactics failed. After a long, bitter, and costly struggle, it was discovered that Revenue actually owed Senator Couzens $1 million.

In Senator John Williams case, the senator was able to break through the powers of retaliation that Revenue wielded over people. Less than a year after taking office, the man Delawareans called Honest John, went to the Senate floor with startling accusations that proved Revenue employees in Wilmington were embezzling money from tax payments. Approximately 2,000 transactions had been manipulated in an effort to cover up stolen and misappropriated tax payments, including embezzling from Senator Williams' own personal account! Revenue headquarters made every effort to stop Honest John in his tracks. But senator Honest John's stubbornness against being sidetracked or stonewalled is what brought Revenue's scandal to light, a scandal that ended the career of hundreds of agents, and brought lengthy prison sentences to bureau collectors in Boston, San Francisco, New York, and St. Louis. (Even Bureau Chief Schoeneman had to resign, along with his predecessor, Joseph Newman, later convicted of tax evasion also.)

But the devil was in the woodwork the day agents left the Lakes house, for right after they left another knock came to Ian's door, bringing the County tax collector. The county wanted payment on the overdue property taxes, which had been accruing interest and arrears for over four years, totaling $26,000. "I'm sorry Mr. Suarez, but the grandfathering of this property ended the day Mr. Vazquez died. And no, I can't take a painting as payment, though that is a lovely horse painting." Ian would never understand why a $54,000 horse painting could not be traded on a tax bill.

Ian's situation was made worse when OJI Terrence went ahead and coded him a potential #148. Coded as an illegal tax protestor sped up the process of auctioning his things and going after the house. The government auction happened within weeks of inventory, which thereafter left him sleeping on a queen-sized air mattress in a near empty house (which reminded him of when finding Cathy's house empty). Next came the order to vacate, so the house could be sold at auction. By then, Ian had wired his money to his friend's Kroneisse Bank in Montserrat. The offshore interest-bearing account would net him a small monthly stipend, and though in an economy that was sucking people dry, it was a stipend nonetheless. He kept some money to buy a used car, plus to rent himself a small one-bedroom apartment off Flagler, buy used furniture to furnish it, and put his remaining $8,000 under bags of frozen peas. It was frugal living after that, with the need for stocking up on cup-a-soup and wheat crackers a given while trying to stay off the government radar, this at a time when the once mighty dollar had dropped to just 7¢ of buying power from 25 years ago. That's when his Montserrat account got flagged.

His offshore account was miniscule when compared to what runaway investors like Brunei, Thayer, Eisner, and Ribald were hiding in the islands. But that didn't stop his account from getting flagged. His was the first transfer caught by Homeland's new digi-routing software. The agent pulling duty that day almost let his transfer slide, if not for it being a year of review for DHS also. And that's how Ian's name returned to the OJI's desk.

OJI Terrence did a double take when seeing Ian's name pop up on his screen again. He seethed, but then his anger was replaced with a smile. *I got you now little squirrel* thought Terrence while calling the Miami Revenue office (during a time when the daily interest alone on the nation's deficit was a whopping $3 billion. Even granny's worn pocketbook was in danger of being rifled through by Revenue's new 36,000 hires.) It was to one of these new hires that the OJI spoke to in Miami. "Now listen here, what was your name again?"

"My name's Knight, sir. Ms. Emily Knight."

"Right. Well Knight, I want you to stop what you're doing and find me this Ian Suarez fellow ASAP, agent uh . . ."

"Agent Knight, sir." Emily Knight was nervous and at the same time mad that her boss's boss had forgotten her name so quickly.

"Well, Ms. Knight; here's your chance to shine for me."

"Yes, sir."

"I've already coded him a #148. That should bring you up to speed on this man, you hear me, Ms. Knight?"

"Yes, sir."

"Even if he's living under a rock, I want you to find him, you hear me, uh, your name again?"

"Ms. Knight, sir. That's K-n-i . . ."

"Forget that. Just go find me this Ian fellow. And find me whatever money he's got stashed with him."

Ms. Knight sounded unsure of herself. "So do we arrest him? Is that what you want?"

"You got it."

"But any idea where I can find him? The address in his file says it's not current."

"Check that lawyer he used in court. I bet he knows where this bastard's hiding. And hurry, cause I want this Ian flagged, tagged, and bagged before reviews are up. Shit, I might even help you by boosting him to #168." (Code #168 is a potentially dangerous taxpayer.)

"Yes, sir, #168 would help, but, so that I'm clear, you know my boss here has me bogged down with cases."

"I'll be talking to your boss next, Mrs. Knight."

"It's *Ms.* Knight, sir. So you want me putting aside all my files for this one guy?" But Ms. Knight was talking to an empty phone. (*Code 168 is what gets agents stopping cars, breaking down doors, boarding yachts, and even commandeering planes. A person that's coded #168 is never taken off the potentially dangerous roll, even if paying faithfully into the system for years.)

Ms. Knight figured Ian for a big deal when coded #168. She did find it strange though that he was added to her list right after the OJI spoke to her. But hers was not to ask why, just to find Ian, who at the time was headed to the Doral golf course.

Ian was competing in another season opener sponsored by his mother's charity fund. First prize money to this event was a phenomenal $250,000, an event that coincidentally occurred on tax day, 15 April. But ordeals like fines, levies, forfeitures, confiscations, severance, a flagged offshore account, and Ian's being tossed from his Lakes house, wouldn't compare to the life-changing event that was about to happen to him, an event that began with the darkening clouds arriving from down south.

Chapter 19

Those who know South Florida

know how erratic the weather is there. Currents from both the east and west make for the perfect conditions for developing storms, besides the hurricanes and the occasional tornado or waterspout that the area sees each year. But knowing this didn't stop Ian from teeing off at hole-#1, even with the approaching storm clouds. He made himself deaf to the distant rumblings within the clouds.

South Florida is all about weather. A person can be standing on one side of the street, sun shining bright, while on the other side it could be pouring down rain. Ian had seen this same anomalous weather when as a boy in Cuba, where mudslides and flooding are common.

This still didn't stop him from teeing off amidst the rumbling from down south. He'd already set his mind on his swing after eyeing his name on the electronic scoreboard. Ian was not about to let the storm ruin his concentration. But this was no ordinary storm.

His first shot off tee was a great one.

His second shot was a phenomenal rip that landed just 15 yards shy of the #1-cup, where he finished hole-#1 at 2-under par.

He hurried to zip up his jacket before driving his cart to hole-#2, where again he had another marvelous first shot . . . a shot that went high into the sky, losing his ball in the thickening dark clouds a moment, until seeing it drop past the downfield markers.

He ended #2 at two-under par also.

Ian was on a roll as more thunder rumbled from down south.

He drove his cart quickly to hole-#3.

One of the tournament rules was that if a player got to finish the front nine holes before a wash out, then he or she could carry their score into the next day's round, which to Ian, after going 2-under at his first two holes, meant carrying a great score. He did however notice players who playing ahead of him, decide to forego playing any further, and instead head back to the clubhouse for liquid libations. Ian wasn't for any of that.

Ian had no sooner set his ball down on the #3 tee than he gave it a tremendous whack and sent that ball sailing too. He gauged the wind correctly and used it to stretch his shot for longer distance. Those inside the clubhouse, while watching the jumbotron, prayed the storm would arrive so it could ruin Ian's score. That's when they saw Ian's best shot yet. The storm was taking its sweet time to arrive.

Ian went birdie on #3.

He happily holstered his club cowboy-style like he'd seen his favorite pro do years back before hurrying to #4.

Homestead Air Reserve Station began blowing its warning claxon right as Ian teed off at #4. Radar was showing a potential for a twister. A skeleton crew of airmen rushed to tie down jets and choppers right as the wind began to pick up. Rain was imminent. So too was the possibility of a twister. Homestead residents were familiar with this weather pattern though. They'd grown accustomed to seeing twisters touch down in the Everglades.

Ian had again used the strengthening winds to his advantage, waiting to strike his ball at just the right moment, waiting his time before sending his opening shot sailing 280 yards downfield. His swing was getting better, not worse as he went.

He ended with birdie at Hole-#4.

The scoreboard now had him in first place.

Ian thought his incredible game was being directed by God himself. *Maybe for all the trouble I've been through.* That's what his mind made him think anyway. On this day he could do no wrong with a club. He compared himself to a pitcher throwing a no-hitter during a series game. That's how his mind played him when hurrying to hole-#5.

Ian was needing to stay focused if he wanted to reach hole-#9. Sensing the $250,000 prize money within his grasp got him focused enough . . . and blind to the distant lightning.

His miraculous game continued after hole #5 where he sat at 4-under. He was now focused on breaking Doral's amateur club record.

But hole-#6 brought reality. He had a difficult time keeping his ball on the tee at #6. But with no storm warning horn sounding yet, he went for broke and sent his #6 ball sailing high into the sky. He paid the price though for over swinging and landed on his butt, but not before watching his ball arch into a curve that dropped 40-yards shy of the #6-cup, but . . . in sand!

Ugh! Not now!

Ian threw his club on the ground and yelled directly at the darkening sky. "Not today, you don't!" He brushed off his pants, grabbed his clubs, and jumped in his cart to hurry to the #6 sand trap, where he spent several minutes studying his shot while more thunder rumbled.

Two miles east of Doral, on the Palmetto Expressway, a single bolt of lightning suddenly struck the 36 Street overpass. Those in bumper-to-bumper traffic near 36 Street were startled by the lightning striking the concrete barrier. Motorists started blowing their horns right then.

Ian felt a slight vibration underfoot from the strike that hit two miles away. But it still didn't detour him from his quest of getting in nine holes. He used a chip shot to get him out of the sand and two shots later to get into the #6 cup for even par.

From his cart he could see the #7 flag taunting him.

But isn't seven supposed to be a lucky number?

Thoughts like this is what got him committing to hole-#7, just as a cart approached.

Steve was head of grounds keeping and also a friend of Ian's. He'd known Ian since back in the day when he and Vazquez would play Doral.

Steve was similar to Ian in that he, too, had earned his stripes the old fashion way, by working hard and sacrificing. It showed in how well the award-winning course looked. Steve had also gotten his first mortgage through Family, and that was thanks to Ian's help, so theirs was more than just a casual field acquaintance.

Ian was happy to see his friend pull up. Just not right then.

"Oh, hey there, Steve." Ian was ready to get his cart going to #7.

"I sure hope you didn't ride all the way out here to try and get me inside. I haven't heard the horn yet, you know."

"You're right, but you will. I wouldn't think of ruining your game though."

"Good, cause I got to go."

"Ian, I know you got a great score and all, but look above you, man. You know the bosses are gonna call it any minute now."

"So then quit holding me up."

Steve pointed at the darkening clouds. "Hate saying this Ian, but I got a *bad* feeling about you being out here alone."

"There you go jinxing me again."

Steve exited his cart to approach Ian. "Not jinxing you, bro. Just wanting you to be safe. Look, take my cart. It's gas powered. It'll get you to #7 quicker than your slow ass battery cart. But you gotta hurry if you're thinking of making nine before this storm hits."

Ian was thrilled at the offer and looked it. "Hey, that's great, Steve." Ian quickly hooked his bag to Steve's cart. "I really do appreciate this, Steve."

"I know you do. But don't go trying your luck with this weather. You know good and well this stuff isn't no fly by. Heck, I don't know why you just don't call it a day and get at these guys tomorrow. You're good enough to be swinging with the pros anyway."

"You don't just give up a score like this, Steve. You know that. You're still holding me up though."

"You're right. Go. Go!" Steve jumped out of the way, but still yelled, "Ian, you see lightning, you get your ass inside. I'll try stalling the bosses long as I can for you."

Steve had seen his share of bad storms during his years of working at Doral. But this particular storm had him worried. The air had begun to thin, which in and of itself was a bad sign, especially when the winds suddenly died down and the air got warm, a danger sign for sure, as more lightning flashed and webbed throughout the clouds above. All indications were that one bad rainstorm was about to unleash itself of some serious water. (Storms like the one Ian was challenging kill an average of 90 people in the U.S. a year. Though the odds of being struck by lightning are 1 in 28,500, it's still an average of 90 per year, with Wyoming leading in lightning deaths. Golfers *are* the number one victims of lightning.)

But the #7 flag was too much of a taunt for Ian to just pack it in. "Don't worry, Steve," he yelled back, "if I see lightning, I'll run. And thanks again for the cart." Ian was already nearing the #7 bridge as he yelled back. Minutes later he was setting up his tee at #7.

Steve claimed it was an inner voice that told him to turn around when he did. Clairvoyance, sixth sense, spiritual awakening, call it what you will, Steve would forever remember what he saw next. Two bolts of lightning struck the ground near Ian. One bolt of lightning hit the pond, which absorbed most of the electrical charge, though the remainder of the charge found Ian's feet. It was the second bolt that got Ian, though first striking an old cypress tree near Ian before knocking him to the ground.

Ian at first felt a tingling sensation run through his body and end in his back. He also found his club too hot to hold anymore. Fifty thousand volts of raw power had just surged from tree to ground to ravage Ian's body. So massive was the jolt that it even set the cypress tree on fire and even made Ian's teeth hot!

This was what Steve saw.

Steve was mortified to witness what he saw. He spun his cart around as quickly as he could, but when stepping down on the pedal, found the cart going slower instead of faster. The batteries were dying out. Steve jumped from the cart and went racing to his downed friend. It was when reaching Ian that the deluge started.

Ian had never felt pain like this before. It was indescribable what he felt. His worst fear was not being able to breathe. Melded skin in his air passages was making it difficult to breathe. But he could still somehow smell the burning cypress and the burnt meaty smell of his flesh. His gums ached and so did his teeth. He looked up and saw Steve, but he couldn't raise his hand to him. He could see Steve yelling down at him, but he couldn't hear Steve, nor could he feel a muscle in his body, just the feeling of choking, which frightened him.

Steve kneeled to his wheezing friend. He went to open Ian's windbreaker, thinking it would help get him to breathe, but found parts of Ian's jacket had melded to his skin. Even the elastic in Ian's socks had melded to his ankles. His metal buckle, too, had become soft metal.

The sizzling sound that Ian heard was the rain making contact with his singed hair, which was still smoking when Steve dialed 911. Ian by then had begun looking for his quiet place.

Rescue #1019 was just nearing the 36th street exit when getting the call on Ian. Rescue #1019's driver got the truck's triple air horn blowing and its lights flashing to get traffic to clear. It was with its siren and horns blaring that #1019 managed to reach the gates of Doral in record time. A guard waved them through and a second guard pointed them down the fairway. Steve's frantic waving and a pop-up flare from the cart showed the way for #1019.

But the deluge had softened the ground to the point where #1019's wheels got bogged down. Hearing the tires spinning is what got the EMTs jumping from in back and hurrying with a gurney between them. The pair rushed to Ian in the rain.

The third member of the team, Kendra, was the newest member to #1019. She stayed behind to prepare for what she hoped would be a rescue and not a recovery of Ian.

Ian was deep into his quiet place when being roughly lifted off the ground and taken back to rescue #1019. A shot of adrenaline later and he felt like he might make it . . . while across the Atlantic, a new storm was brewing, a storm of a different sort, but one that was as dangerous as any storm to strike Ian.

London's Special Alliance agents were just then discussing the 'Ian issue' in a building that hadn't changed much since the days of his father's kill order. Some of the original equipment was still there, but much had been modernized, making S/A's London operational building as sophisticated as any of Langley's substations. A small fortune had been spent on modernizing the S/A building, which included a more modern electronic map that MI5, MI6, Interpol, CIA, and some FBI agents stationed abroad would use when tracking Europe's growing list of terror cells.

"So, this Ian Wolfe fellow . . ." Chief Brady was interrupted by his assistant Marshall Evans. "Not Wolfe, sir. He's name is Ian Suarez." Across from Chief Brady sat the newest member to S/A London, a Royal Guardsman named Landers Ferguson, who had thus far stayed quiet.

"Once a Wolfe always a Wolfe, Evans, so quit." The Chief was angry at being interrupted while reading Ian's file, where it said Ian had been using his Wolfe name to hide behind. Chief Brady cared nothing about Ian's golf earnings. What he cared most about was Ian's rags-to-riches-to-rags tale. "This Ian's just like his old man."

"How you figure, Chief?" asked Evans. "He's nothing *like* his old man. He's a banker. Well, was a banker, while his old man was a bomb maker."

"There I beg to differ with ya, Evans," said the Chief. "I bet junior's more radical than even his old man was. You see them fines and confiscations he just went through? None of that happens without a reason. I bet he ratchets his anger up by putting to good use whatever his Pa and Ma learnt him while back in Cuba. Nope, Evans, once a Wolfe always a Wolfe."

"Come on, Chief," cut in Evans. "This bloke was a wee lad when we offed his old man." Outside the Chief's glass partitioned office were dozens of field agents busy eavesdropping, translating, dictating, and updating the huge electronic map on the wall.

Chief Brady went back to reading Ian's file. "Fuck's sake Evans, lad or not, his mum was Wolfe's eyes and ears. Come on man, Ian's the Wolfe's spawn, for Christ sake! I'm telling you now, you stay in this game long as I have, and you get to sensing things, and I sense something bad in this Ian bloke. I'm telling you, Evans, junior knows a thing or two about bomb making." Evans was only half listening. He went back to taking in Ferguson, who was still sitting staunchly in his seat without saying a word. *Chief sure knows how to pick 'em* thought Evans. *This Ferguson looks like one stone cold killer.*

Ferguson was tall, well-proportioned, and sported body language that warned to be 'best not be mess with.' He had come to the Chief's attention right after being awarded the Royal Victorian Order for special service to the Crown (for services kept secret).

"Fuck's sake Evans, there you go again," the Chief was railing at his assistant now, "you suddenly becoming this bloke's solicitor or something? What are you, a blooming sentimentalist all of a sudden? You've read the cub's file. You know about his fortune. And golfing my arse! Golfing's a front.

Something's not right about this Wolfe cub. And the yanks are too busy with this cyber terror nonsense to notice. I'm telling you, Wolfe's kid is a *trained* troublemaker." This got Ferguson's attention as Chief looked directly at him. "And that's where you come in, big fella. I need you to be my eyes and ears in the states on this Ian Wolfe fella."

Evans again interrupted with, "It's Ian Red Suarez, chief. The file says Suarez. I don't know why you keep calling him Wolfe. He was also going by his adoptive parent's name, Vazquez, but I think he dropped that. Could be Ian Red Suarez-Vazquez. I'm not sure."

"Bloody hell, Evans; Ian Red whatever. I don't care whether he's Vazquez, Suarez, or whatever else; to me, he's still a Wolfe. He can hide behind as many bloody name changes as he wants; he's *still* a Wolfe to me!" The Chief didn't wait for a response from Evans while pointing at Ferguson and saying, "You, I need in Miami, like yesterday." Chief stood and went to fetch his coat from the coat rack near the door. "I'm headed for me afternoon pint, and then I'm going home." Chief was known for more than just a pint before going home. "You suit up for travel, Ferguson, Evans will help you."

"Chief, do you really want to do this?" asked Evans.

Ferguson suddenly broke in with a few questions of his own. In a deep resonating voice he asked, "So what goods does this bloke have that I need to watch him?" Ferguson waited for his answer while watching the Chief finish wrapping his scarf.

"I don't know the goods nor his expertise, but I figure him to know lots of people. I still want him offed at some point. Use his father's sin if you have to, but I want him dropped."

Evans quickly jumped in with, "But Chief, you're forgetting this guy's a survivor of that Cuban gunboat attack in '94, remember? And he *is* living in Miami." Evans turned quickly to Ferguson. "I'll get you suited up with the right paperwork for checking in with Homeland. But Ian's a Cuban living in Miami, so shooting him in cold blood isn't going to go down too well." Evans turned to the Chief. "And he's got those charity funds working for him, plus that workers' fund he's created with his adoptive parents money, so he is a most likable fellow with folks in Miami."

"So why the kill order, chief?" asked Ferguson. "I don't usually get sent to kill someone over losing their money. What gives? This Ian got some top-secret stuff that we need to extract?"

"For fucks sake, not you too?" The Chief was beside himself now. "Are you two purposely forgetting who gives the bloody orders around here? Yours is to do as ordered, not become another bloody barrister!" But the Chief's anger lasted but a moment.

"Listen here, Ferguson; this bloke's old man blew up *his* old man while the poor slob slept! How's that for a gene pool? This bombing shit runs in the family blood, and if we let this Ian fellow detonate, then we're screwed. I'm thinking sleeper. Lots of sleepers have come from Cuba; you know that, so yes, my kill order stands. It's gonna take careful planning on your part to take him out though. But your Victorian Cross tells me you can do it. But you might have years to wait. This fella's smart though. Don't go letting him know you're onto him. Money's there to keep you trailing him until I give the word to off him."

"No need to tell me twice," said Ferguson while standing. "I just need me weapons before boarding the plane. I'll bring ya a Wolfe, a cub, a bear, a bloody rhino if you want, but I need me weapons."

Chief Brady made a face. "Don't worry about all that, you clog. You'll have your weapons with you on the plane. But I'm warning you; don't take this Wolfe fellow lightly. And when you're in Miami, you need to check-in with my friends at Homeland. I don't want them booting your arse back to me because you didn't share information. My boot, your arse, you understand?" Chief was a big enough fellow to follow through with his threat. He had his own history of dastardly deeds before becoming Chief of S/A London.

"So does this assignment have a name?" asked Ferguson.

Chief was at the door and ready to bolt. "Yes it does. This operation is called 'Eye for an Eye.' Oh, and don't go confusing this mission with any of your other Middle Eastern romps. This is stateside stuff we're talking about. Everything begins and ends with Homeland." With that, Chief Brady hit the door, and moments later was walking through a tube passage that led to his car. His favorite pub, where his pub mates were waiting to wager on soccer, was just a mile away.

Ferguson looked over at Evans and facetiously asked, "So Eye for an Eye, huh? Not very damn original, is it?"

"It's appropriate, believe it or not."

"How so?" Evans closed the door to prying ears.

"You remember the Castlereagh bombing?"

"Barely."

"The check station that got blown up by the Wolfe back in the eighties?"

"Bloody bad business going on back in them days."

"Yeah, eight paratroopers, plus a judge's son were killed in that blast."

"So what's that got to do with this Ian fellow?"

"That judge's son just happens to be the Chief's nephew. His brother wound up taking his life over losing his boy."

"Oh, well, now that *does* make a wee bit of difference. But where does this Ian fellow fit in all that?"

"Eye for an eye, remember? Chief wants to close the Wolfe file permanently before retiring. Eye for an Eye is his last hoorah before making the Wolfe file disappear, so don't screw up." Ferguson's smiling face said that he was more than happy to oblige.

"And don't go blabbering to the Yanks what you heard here, Ferguson. They got their plate full of stuff that needs disappearing. Just do as the Chief ordered and *do* think before pulling the trigger. But hey, I envy you going to that warm Florida sun, while we're all stuck here with our bloody weather." But Ferguson wasn't thinking anything about weather. He was just thinking how best to carry his silenced sidepiece under his new Seville Row jacket when boarding the plane to Miami.

Part
III

The COL

"People tend to believe what they wish to be true."

Francis Bacon

Chapter 20

Ian's voices in his head had grown louder. Male voices. Female voices. Young and old voices. Voices having conversation inside his own subconscious. But there was one voice among the many that was louder than all, a male voice that guided Ian towards the light. "Go with the flow, Ian. Go for the light and awaken." He did as told and awoke to find a day nurse injecting his thigh with insulin.

His eyes popping open, after being in a coma for 40-days, startled the day nurse into knocking over her syringe tray!

It was in attempting to say he was sorry for startling her that Ian discovered he had lost his ability to move or to speak.

It took two nurses to sit him up so that doctors could exam him. Tests had already shown that the lightning had not only damaged some of his spinal receptors and neurons, but that his brain stem had been affected also, and was probably the cause of his losing muscle function. The voices in his head were a substitute for his losing his ability to talk.

Ian never did let on about his voices, not even when working through the grueling rehab that eventually got him back on his feet and walking again. By then he'd gone through some exhausting skin grafts and laser fusion surgery that helped re-establish his motor skills. That was when the real fun began . . . physical therapy.

Most patients in Ian's condition could not have met the challenge of such exhausting rehab. But Ian was not like most patients. He worked hard to get his motor functions back working again, which included strength training in a swimming pool, from which he had to be saved a time or two after passing out in the water from sheer exhaustion.

Speech therapy was just as tasking.

It was little reward when after years of rehab and he still couldn't talk. He was at the Center of Life (COL) by then and continuing his rehab.

But when will my voice return?

Speaking was all he could think about. He wrote about his wanting to speak in his journal. He was using a pen and a writing pad to communicate with everyone including his speech therapist. His therapist is who assured him that time would bring back his voice.

The COL was a 14-bed, level II monitoring facility that dealt mostly with Near Death Experience patients. Staff at the COL were trained specifically for getting NDE patients back on their feet and living independent lives again (though half of all COL patients never did see independent living again, due to either health complications or death). But staff at the COL saw in Ian a tremendous survivor and fighter. He worked hard during his 4 years of rehab, with barely a whimper, though hurting immensely while his body healed. That did not include his voices though.

Ian had to be taught to walk again, and that was as challenging as all his therapy combined. Because of his disability, he was in line for a disability hearing with a disability judge to establish his SSI/disability income. But there were still the inner voices to deal with; voices tormenting him by saying he'd been released from the dark for a 'special' purpose in life.

S taff wrote him up as a miracle. So did the media. They called Ian the 'Miracle Man'. (A staff member even tried getting Ian to pick some lotto numbers for her. She didn't win.) Ian continued communicating the only way he knew how, by using his pad and pen for everything. Once he'd settled into his routine of rehabbing, he asked about his mother's charity fund, and his ex-employees' workers fund. He discovered the workers fund had run out of money, and his mother's fund had gone by way of forfeitures and fines. He didn't ask about his golf earnings or about any upcoming tournaments because he was done with golf. *"You're beyond golf,"* his voices told him, *"you were picked for a special purpose. Don't forget it."* How could he, when they kept reminding him.

His voices continued trying to charm him, which in itself was troubling. He almost let on about his troubling mental conversations, but then decided it best not to share such secrets with staff. He was nearing independent living status by then, and telling of his voices would mess that up. The voices had already assured him of a positive future, *"so why rock the boat, Ian?"* He really hated it when they called him by name. Had he mentioned his voices, he would've been put on more serious medications, not that he wasn't on some serious meds already, but adding anti-psychotics to the list of meds he was already on would've made it harder to getting back into the real world. Taking large amounts of anti-psychotics usually meant needing to live in an assisted living facility. He sure didn't want that.

Ian was afraid of staff finding his 'Mind' journals and reading through them. In his 'Mind' journals was where he wrote about his growing psychotic events, written down after each of his harrowing mental events. He kept his Mind journals buried inside a backpack he bought at a local dollar store. His Mind journals held his night terror experiences, experiences occurring more frequent as his disability hearing neared. The voices that had already warned him about his night terrors, increased, and he was never really *that* ready for such tormenting. It was staff, after seeing his condition and the condition of his room one morning (after one of his events) who suggested he go on Seroquel and Depakote. That had been a month ago. He still hadn't gotten used to the Seroquel, hated it really, but he stayed medically compliant, a prerequisite to living at the COL. He'd written about all that in his Mind Journals. Four years of writings were in his Mind journals.

"I assure you, your voice *will* return to you, Ian."

"But I . . . want . . . to speak . . . now!" It was all the words he could get out, at the cost of a coughing bout, which then hurt his throat more.

"Easy does it, Ian. Don't get yourself all worked up."

Easy for you to say he wrote on his pad **you have your voice. But me, after 4 years . . .**

She stopped him from writing any more. "An injury like yours takes time to heal, Ian. You just have to wait. Continue to gargle and do more of your humming exercises and you watch, your voice will return. I promise."

"Knock it off, Ian" cut in one of his voices. *"Quit giving her a hard time. You're going to mess things up for your hearing. Remember you're outta here once they know you're getting a check."*

He really hated it when they called him by name.

Yet his psychotic episodes would continue to leave him drained.

The only episode that ever made sense, and it was during his 40-day coma, was the one where he walked towards the light during his 40-day sojourn. That's when the man's voice had shown him the way out. That was also the voice that had told him he was about to be tested by fire. Ian didn't know what all that meant, nor did he dare mention it to staff or to his doctors, knowing a lifetime of meds would come from mentioning something so crazy. The mention of being tested by fire did worry him though. His solace continued to be in writing in his Mind journals, a half-dozen filled by then. More would be filled before leaving the COL.

His other solace was in driving. He was of the rare few NDE patients who got to take his driving test again and passing, and thus being granted his driving privileges. But it had taken four long years to be able to sit behind the wheel of a car again.

Doctors thought his untreated diabetes may have been what woke him of his coma, albeit after 40 days. But Ian knew better. He knew the real reason why he'd been brought back from his trail of despair. It had nothing to do with diabetes. But he kept that a secret, too.

He hadn't wanted to enter the light, since the dark hadn't been all that frightening. His hadn't been a scary dark coma, but more like a restful sleep in the dark. In the dark he'd felt no worries nor hassles from tax agents, judges, or financial losses. But the voices continued being a problem, turning into full conversations in his head while in the dark. He was still hearing conversations, though none were loud enough for him to make out what the voices were saying. These head conversations were a part of him now . . . while stuck in the worst bumper-to-bumper traffic ever!

Horns blared from everywhere. Sweat poured down his face, during a heat wave, and with no working a/c in his car. *So is this why I was brought back? This is my testing by fire?*

"*No, Ian. Your reality is you being late again for your psychiatric appointment.*" He really hated it when they called him by name.

Chapter 21

Ian was headed to what he hoped

would be his last visit with his psychiatrist, Dr. Langston. On this visit, he was hoping to get his medical file signed off, so the disability judge could make a final ruling. It was with his disability income that Ian intended to live on. But traffic was making it impossible for him to inch closer to his doctor.

July is a tough month for traffic in Miami with so many new summer tourists visiting South Florida. It was worse for Ian, as the sweltering heat brought out more of his moodiness and brought out more side effects to his meds. He even saw wisps of oily smoke rise from the highway's overheated asphalt. The traffic gridlock seemed to go on forever. Horns blared all around him from angry motorists either late for work or late for boarding cruise ships. The driver behind him suddenly hit his horn to get Ian moving.

Ian saw his exit, an exit that seemed miles away, though it was just past the upcoming tollbooth. He took from his change cup the ten quarters needed for the toll, wiped sweat from his brow, and waited for his turn at the change bucket. *Seems like I'm late for everything these days.* A new fear began about his being late possibly messing things up in his file. He *so* wanted to be back on his own, and wanted nothing to hamper the disability judge's decision to granting him his monthly income. Blaring horns broke him of his thoughts and reminded him to go. One angry motorist even cut in front of him in route to the change bucket. *So is this what I woke up for? To deal with morons like this?* A cacophony of horns and shouts were his answer.

It had been just a few months earlier, right after getting his license, that he bought his first clunker. The one he was driving now was his second clunker, as his first he smashed against a tree while hurry back to the COL to make curfew. (He told police he'd been sideswiped, when in fact he'd fallen asleep at the wheel because of some medication side effects.) *This traffic's too damn awful!* It was his turn to hit his horn, a weak sounding horn at that, but an additional horn nonetheless.

He had rushed from the COL earlier than usual that morning, even avoided breakfast, so he could get a start at traffic. But it didn't work. Traffic was already bad by the time he reached the Palmetto. Worse was trying to reach the Dolphin Expressway, where thousands of extra tourist vehicles added to the gridlock. The Dolphin was a madhouse this morning, and the heat wave that had been lingering over the city going on three days made the madness worse. *No a/c and late again for my appointment. Just great.* Ian hit the wheel in frustration.

He'd chosen driving over riding the buses. He was done with riding the cramped and overcrowded buses, especially the #38 out of Homestead. He was also tired of riding the Metrorail.

There was another advantage to driving, although definitely not in this traffic, and that was that driving proved he was ready for independent living. But being late for his scheduled appointment didn't help.

Once at the change bucket, Ian angrily tossed in his $2.50. *Used to be just 75 cents before I got struck by lightning. Must be the county needs more money to steal?* He hit the gas and went for the home stretch . . . until feeling his Lithium/Ativan/Wellbutrin mix start to kick in. The meds were always messing him up. *Makes me sweat.* His sweating caused wrinkles to his clothes, clothes that had taken an hour to iron and starch. He reached for his backpack and struggled to get a towel to wipe himself dry with. He happened to catch the time on his cheap wristwatch just as horns blared because of his erratic lane change prior to exiting off the freeway.

His next adventure would be in finding parking. But he first had to wait on the Civic Center light before finding a building to park in.

While at the light, he absentmindedly rubbed at the raw spot on the back of his head. The fist-sized spot would never see hair grow there again. Doctors said the spot had been the exit point to the lightning. Along his back were diamond shaped scars caused by flash burns. The flats of his feet also had burn marks, which doctors said were the entry point to the lightning. He'd lost a bit of feeling in his toes, which is what gave him his slight gait. He had other scars on his neck and hands (some of those made by the EMS crew and doctors). But Ian wasn't complaining. He would be the first to admit that all in all, his battle scars were a small price to pay for still being alive. But he still had kept his good looks, and every once in a while he got the women turning their heads.

But there was still the issue of what was going on inside his head.

"Calm yourself, Ian." There they were again, the voices, knowing him better than he knew himself. *"You won't find parking if you don't slow down."* *"Quit getting yourself all worked up. Dr. Langston will read through your anger."* *"He wrote you up last time for your anger, remember? That's why you're on Xanax, remember?"* *"Say bye to independent living, if you mess things up."* Yep. Knew him better than he knew himself.

He'd been getting lots of instruction from his voices of late. *"Prepare to receive."* *"Strengthen your resolve."* *"Your journey begins soon."* Stuff like that. He didn't know what his voices meant, his daily grind being what it was. An example to his daily grind was living with the cost-of-living horror that most of society was having to live with, a horror that was stealing his monthly stipend of $480, which he was still receiving from his offshore account. Trying to stretch every single dollar had taken precedent over most of his issues, while his voices continued to taunt. He still needed to find a parking space, where his anger continued when seeing the price of $14 for parking. *Why's everything so damn expensive these days? I got no idea how people make it these days.*

One of the causes to the rupturing economy was gas prices having shot past $7 a gallon. The blocking of the Hormuz Straits by Iranian gunboats had put barrel prices at an all-time high again; this while fracking in the northwest had been halted by the present administration's wanting to follow the past administration's policies. The U.S. Navy was doing what it could to clear the Straits, while the U.N. tangled with issues in the Middle East, where riots had put 72% of the world's petrol supply in jeopardy. Commodities, too, had skyrocketed because of petrol prices. *Riots are going to start happening here if we don't do something to curtail this rampant economy.*

Ian dried himself with his towel while waiting for the parking attendant to make change. He frowned when staring down at his wrinkled shirt. *I went to a lot of trouble to get my shirt and pants just right, and this 100° heat has just ruined that. Damn it! If it wasn't for those damn confiscations, I'd be driving my Cad with its sweet a/c.* The memory made him pound the wheel again.

"Here you go sir, $18, $19, and $20, and your receipt. By the way, the only parking left is topside." *Ugh.* Topside meant having to go back into the sun again. But at least he was across the street from where he needed to be, JMH Mental Health.

Had he arrived a few hours back, he could have just as easily raised the parking bar himself and gotten in. He'd done it before. *If it hadn't been for traffic today, I could've done that today* just as he popped back out into the bristling sun. *Ooh, I hate this heat!*

He found his spot and parked.

He didn't bother to lock his car once off. *What for?*

In his rush to reach for his backpack, he accidentally hit his horn and scared an elderly couple walking by. "Oops. Sorry folks. Didn't mean to scare you." The couple made as if he didn't exist while hurrying to the elevator. *Geez, the paranoia these days.* Instead of joining them, Ian decided to take the stairs. He hit the stairs running, two at a time, while at the same time tightening the straps to his backpack. It was a miracle he didn't slip and break his neck. But he had other things on his mind, like trying to avoid Nurse Chang (who reminded him of Nurse Ratchet from 'One Flew over the Cuckoo's Nest') who would give him hell for being late.

"Oye loco!" It was the elderly couple coming from the elevator that yelled at him when he startled them when running past. But he was in full manic mode by then, running as if in a track meet, so there was no time for an apology from him. He was wanting to beat the walk light before traffic started again. He was too late.

Ian bounced from leg to leg while waiting impatiently for the crossing light to turn green. Once it was green, Ian started to run, but was nearly run over by a late turning cab. But manic mode gave him the reflexes to juke past the cab's hood in one fluid motion, making the cabbie yell out, "Hey! You crazy mother . . . ." but Ian was already on the other side of the street by then. Seconds later he was charging through the glass doors of the Mental Health building and seconds after that he was banging on the elevator buttons. (The cabbie was left staring at the JMH building and thinking it was the right place for the crazy white fool that had slid across his hood.)

Come on. Come on! It was all Ian could do to keep from yelling for the elevator to arrive. He happened to check his watch just as the doors opened. *Damn it! So late! And look at this junk watch. What a far cry from my old Cartier.* Once in the elevator, he started banging at the up button prior to getting out his prewrite journal. His prewrite journal was where he wrote the stuff his doctors and therapists liked to read. His prewrite journal was full of positive thinking stuff, though some of it was pure fabrication. That's how Ian played his doctors, giving them what they wanted to hear, especially Dr. Langston who was a fan of his prewrite journal.

Besides his prewrite journal, underneath his towel and his portable CD player, past his collection of CDs and a spare pair of shoes, were his Mind journals, his real journals, the journals that really needed to stay hidden. *Any of my doctors ever read those and I can really forget independent living.* Ian made sure his pack was closed before exiting the elevator into chaos.

Not only was the waiting area full of patients, but it was Nurse Chang herself who was doing the sign-in sheet. *Oh-no.*

"Robinson! Lopez! Rosario!" yelled Nurse Chang, with her American born though slight Asian accent. *Oh good, she's busy.* Ian tried getting to the end of the hall without her seeing him. He wanted to play it as if he hadn't heard his name called.

"Come on people. We haven't got all day," yelled Chang. Ian's ploy did not work, as Chang eyeballed him right away. "Well, well, well, if it isn't our Mr. Suarez." Chang made a beeline straight for him.

"I don't know why we even bother to give you an appointment, Mr. Suarez." Ian tried to write *traffic* on his pad, but Chang stopped him. "Forget all that writing today. Just find a seat and listen up for your name." Chang went from Ian to reprimanding a black fellow coming from the restroom. "Ah, Mr. Robinson. There you are. Maybe we should be also testing your hearing today."

"But I was just washing my . . ." Chang waved him off, too.

"Just get in there and see Margaret. She's waiting on you, and she hasn't got all day." Ian and Mr. Robinson shared a WTF glance.

The waiting area had four long couches. Every spot was taken except for an end spot on the farthest couch, which was near the courtesy phone. He would have rather not been so close to the courtesy phone, but he wanted to sit, so he begrudgingly made for the spot, but not sitting until trying to smooth out the wrinkles on his shirt and pants, hating what the sweat had done to his appearance, then finger combing his hair while sitting. Though he felt a mess, he was still one of the better groomed in the room. Many folks in the room were untidy, and that mostly due to their medications.

While waiting for his name to be called, he took that morning's newspaper from his pack. The newspaper had been given to him by the COL staff prior to his rushing out. Staff knew he liked to keep up with the baseball scores, plus he was of the few who could actually concentrate on what he was reading (unlike those heavily sedated), so the paper was his. Just before starting on the front pages though, he looked around and saw where he wasn't the only one hearing voices.

Chapter 22

Ian wasn't at all bothered by

the elderly man sitting beside him wrapped in a dirty Mickey Mouse blanket, nor was he troubled by the woman sitting next to him and talking to herself. There was a man who suddenly started slapping himself, as if on fire, across from Ian. That didn't bother him, either. He had gotten so used to such behavior at the COL that he'd grown accustomed to it here at Mental Health. Even the old homeless woman sitting at the end of the couch and combing her scraggily hair with an imaginary hairbrush didn't bother him. But what did get his attention was the slapper who suddenly jumped to his feet and left the room. *Wow! Medication overload for sure.*

Ian spied the newer patients waiting to see doctors. There was one who had his father sitting next to him. Two homeless patients had social workers sitting beside them.

More patients arrived, and with the new arrivals came one that Ian really worried about, a woman he'd gotten to know all too well, arriving ready with a scowl on her face.

Hope Chang and staff are ready to handle this one.

He had named her Lady Schizo. He didn't know her real name, but Lady Schizo was appropriate enough. A month before, Lady Schizo had gotten angry over losing her seat to another lady. In the process of going at the woman, Lady Schizo actually spit at Ian when he tried stopping them from fighting. Both women wound up on the floor before Chang and staff could grab Lady Schizo. They Baker-acted lady Schizo that day for spitting, pulling hair, and making the woman bleed from her bites. *And today she doesn't look so fine, either,* thought Ian. *Her scowl could mean trouble.* The woman who took the seat where the slapper had been began fumbling through her purse for makeup. The result to her makeup was to look like a clown.

The old fellow with the Mickey Mouse blanket suddenly dropped to the floor and sat Indian style with his blanket wrapped around him. None of the regular patients thought this odd, though Ian could tell the new patients were bothered by the old man's odd behavior. He'd seen the man do similar stuff before, so that didn't bother him, either as he hid behind his newspaper.

Arriving in the room was one of the liveliest patients yet. His name was Jay Johnson, an overly flirtatious ex-jock who liked to be called Jay-Jay, in anticipation of his sex change operation. But J. Johnson's doctors weren't yet ready to sign for Johnson's transgender operation quite yet. They were still treating him with hormones before eventually allowing him to become Joanna. *Lots of identity crises these days* thought Ian before beginning to tackle the day's news.

Though he felt sweaty and disheveled, Ian was still, compared to most in the room, looking above board. His condition was also more of a controlled insanity. But he was in the right place alright. He was needing as much help as any of the others who were waiting their turn to see doctors. His voices said so.

The patient talking on the courtesy phone behind him suddenly got louder. The man was actually trying to set up a drug buy for after seeing his doctor.

Now how in the hell can a person waste $200 on dope in an economy like today's? This was the never-ending question with Ian, the economy and what it was doing to people. *But this guy wasting $200 on dope is absurd.* He tried not to stare, which was a good thing, since the junkie's tone meant trouble. Ian went back to trying to concentrate on his paper until suddenly having Nurse Chang in his face again.

"Earth to Ian Suarez; is anyone there?" Chang was back to annoying him. "First you're late, and now you're deaf." Ian began writing on his pad as Chang spoke. "Maybe we should just let everyone else here go ahead of you, eh Mr. Suarez? You know, let them see their doctors, let you see yours last? I guarantee you won't leave here until about 10 o'clock tonight." Ian hated her annoying tone and looked it. He attempted to write ***forgive*** but got stopped again.

"Just go in and see Margaret. She's waiting to take your vitals."

Margaret was one of the many techs training in the Mental Health facility. A few months of working in Mental Health had turned Margaret into a pro. She quickly took his blood pressure and pricked his finger to get a sugar reading in one smooth motion. But she saw trouble right away in Ian's glucose reading. She walked over and showed his reading to Nurse Chang. This brought Chang over. "So, you're almost at 400. What did you have for breakfast, ice cream?" Ian shook his head no. "You looking to have a diabetic seizure today?" Margaret got busy writing Ian's 400 into his file as he wrote on his pad ***this would be the best place for a seizure, don't you think?***

"Oh, funny that, eh?" He got Chang's goat with that one, which he regretted right after writing it. "You think 400's a joke, Mr. Suarez?" It was too late to take back what he'd written, so he just sat back and meekly waited for Margaret to finish writing. "Get back to your seat and *do* listen for your name next time," said Chang in her authoritative voice.

Ian hurried back to the couch, where ironically enough the old man on the floor had saved his spot for him. For doing him that favor, Ian offered to buy the man a soda, to which the old man nodded yes. "You gotta still watch my seat, okay old timer?" The old man nodded his head yes again, as Ian went off to buy his soda with his backpack slung over his shoulder. But when Ian reached the machines, he found that soda prices had gone up since the last time he was at Mental Health. He angrily paid the $2.50 for his old friend, but for himself he chose to drink from the water fountain.

Once back, he handed the old man his soda with a friendly pat on the shoulder, then sat back in his seat to continue reading the paper.

The junkie was in a more agitated state than before. Ian heard the junkie slam down the phone and make right for Nurse Chang to complain about his long wait. Chang didn't take his complaining too lightly. She grabbed the man by his shirt and escorted him right to the elevators.

The regulars like Ian had seen stuff like this before.

Ah, she's probably doing him a favor anyway, thought Ian. After that he got deep into reading about the new Venezuelan oil crisis. *Now Venezuela too? I guess this must be why I just paid $120 to fill up my car.* The news got worse on page two, with China's petrol grabs causing more friction around the world. *Making war at the pumps, more like it.*

Page 3 carried more on the saga of the current administration's blame game against the past administration's handling of the economy. *Madam President sure likes to blame everything on the past, though she's been in office going on four years now. Blah! No wonder her popularity's dropped to 32%.* It had been years since any president had gotten better than 40% of popularity during their remaining time in office.

The local section of the paper didn't carry much better news either. The city council was proposing a new jobs creation bill, similar to the government's, which was supposed to help local commerce with hiring people. Part of the county's jobs bill dealt with new construction, *which anyone can see isn't happening. Just another bells and whistles jobs bill. Construction isn't happening and banks aren't loaning any money for construction. Hoarding money is what they're doing, the bastards!* Disgusted with the news, Ian turned to the financial page. News there wasn't much better, with the bleakest holiday sales numbers leading financial news. *And another million workers headed for unemployment after their part-time jobs run out. Great. I really don't know how people are making it these days. Some jobs creation bill!*

Even though he was still living at the COL, Ian, too, was feeling the pinch from the economy. Madam President's current spin was that there was "always light after dark." Ian thought it pure political bunk while turning to the only section that made any sense anymore, the sports section. News there was bad also. *Damn it! Marlins lose another one.* He got to thinking about Madam President's light after dark spin. *Pure nonsense. Anyone can just check their pockets and see there isn't any light left. Light on the horizon my ass!* Finished with sports, he turned to the final section of the paper, the editorials.

Opinions. Everyone had one. Losing one's job did that. Now there was talk of more increases in insurances, taxes, fees, and this while the dismantling of the Affordable Healthcare Act was taking longer than expected. Small business America was already on the ropes, as 95,000 small businesses had already closed shop due to over-regulation, excess codes, and stricter (for money's sake) fines. The fact that traffic cameras had just been recently shown to actually cause more accidents (12% increases) hadn't done anything to change the 31% increases in ticket fines. *Oh, small business America is done alright. Anyone owning a small business today is living a pipe dream. Today's money is in victimization. Feel victimized and bling-bling, you're in the money. Meanwhile, this talk of new tax increases should make people even madder.*

He read an editorial piece written by a company exec who wrote using a pen name. The exec wanted people to know that his company was fighting tooth and nail to keep their people working, but that 319 government agencies were doing *their* part to keep *their* people working also. The dream of entrepreneurship was on life support. The future was looking bleak *and bound to get worse if China continues at its petrol grabs.* There was also trouble with Canada's oil supply. 'Hope and change' had refused to upgrade the Alberta pipeline, a pipeline that had brought in 2.7 million barrels of oil a day to the U.S. Now that oil had been grabbed by the Chinese. China built a whole new pipeline that went directly to waiting tankers after injecting Canada with a much needed $4.4 billion boost. Added to that was the missed opportunities with the Dakota shale fields, where drilling and natural gas rights had been hindered by environmental and bureaucratic concerns. "IAN SUAREZ!" Nurse Chang's yelling almost made him drop his paper!

"Again you refuse to listen up for your name. What's with you today?"

Ian hurried to write in his pad, but Chang just yelled, "Go! Dr. Langston's waiting to see you. Go! Go!" But before leaving the room, Ian took one last look around and thought *I hope to never see this place again.* He hurried to make that happen.

Ian had done a great job of hiding his symptoms from his doctors. But as much as he thought he'd fooled his COL therapist, it was she who had sent him to see a psychiatrist. It had to do with the COL staff reporting his nightly behavior of late. But patient overload at Mental Health meant time was of the essence. *I just need Dr. Langston to sign me off and I'm done. Then I never need to come back here anymore.* Ian's racing thoughts were replaced by the sound of his loud squeaking sneakers on the linoleum floor while walking to Dr. Langston's office.

But Nurse Chang had been wrong about Dr. Langston waiting to see him. The office was empty when Ian got there. This still didn't stop him from walking in and sitting down to wait. He prepped for his visit by laying out his pad, pen, and his prewrite journal. He laid everything out right next to Dr. Langston's prescription pad. Ian noticed his name was already filled out on the top script.

Right then his bipolar mania got the best of him. It started with his feet tapping the floor, to a twitch in his feet, to then crossing his legs and kicking out when suddenly hearing from the overhead speakers: ***CODE RED! CODE RED! DISTURBANCE AT THE SECOND FLOOR WAITING AREA. THIS FACILITY IS NOW IN LOCK DOWN UNTIL FURTHER NOTICE.***

The warning repeated itself.

This was the absolute last thing Ian wanted to hear, on a day when he was least wanting to here it. The facility in lockdown meant he would have to stay longer than he wanted to. *I knew that bitch's scowl meant trouble!* His thinking was interrupted by a loud chirping sound that came through the speakers.

Ian felt like a prisoner. This was not a good thing while in manic mode. He felt like getting up and running, but he didn't know where to run to. A window would've been nice, but the jump would've hurt him. (That's why all windows in the building were locked.) He began to pace anyway, in an office barely big enough for a desk and two chairs, when hearing a familiar voice say, "Easy there, Ian. This lockdown will be over soon." Dr. Langston had returned. "Relax and sit. Put those breathing exercises they teach you at the COL to good use." The soda in Dr. Langston's hand was why he'd been absent from his office.

In closing the door behind him, Dr. Langston shut out some of the warning alarm sounding in the hall. Ian was deep into his breathing reps, but could still hear the alarm, this while taking in Dr. Langston's more noticeable gait. Ian's breathing reps settled him enough to write ***why you limping doc?*** Ian was referring to Dr. Langston's artificial leg, a replacement to the one he lost overseas.

"Oh that." Dr. Langston settled heavily into his chair. "I got fitted for a new thigh cover yesterday and the damn thing's been rubbing me raw. That's why I brought my cane today. But I'll manage." Seeing Ian's journal got Langston's attention. "Don't worry about me, cause today is *your* day, Ian. Now, let's see what you got for me to read today." Loud yelling came from the waiting area.

"You know about any of that going on out there, Ian? Do you know why she went off? I imagine they'll be Baker-acting her as we speak." Ian shook his head no. He didn't much care at this point.

Dr. Langston busied himself with Ian's writings. He smiled at something he read, which made Ian think *now him smiling's got to be a good sign.* Langston sneaked a peek at Ian.

"Don't worry about the alarm, Ian. I'll let you out the back if the lockdown's still in place when we're through." Ian gave Dr. Langston a thumb up for that. Langston's smile suddenly turned to a frown when reading something in Ian's prewrite. "You wrote here that you had a sit down with the head of Metrorail's maintenance. Is that true?" Ian shook his head yes.

"Well, please do tell." Langston knew Ian wasn't a liar. He put down the journal and waited for Ian to write out his explanation.

Ian wrote **fountain**.

"Fountain? I don't get it," said Langston.

Ian scribbled on his pad as quick as he could before sliding it over. **Read more of my journal entry.**

Dr. Langston turned the page and read aloud. "I was thirsty. I got off at Dadeland to drink from the water fountain and found it was out of order. I got off at the next stop. Found the water fountain there out of order, too. I rode to the next stop. Fountain there was broken also. I then rode out the entire rail line and found eight fountains out of order. I went the next day to maintenance in downtown. I saw the head of maintenance. Did my speaking with my pad of course. Now all fountains work."

Langston looked at Ian. "The head of maintenance? Really?"

Ian wrote **he knew about me. Used to be a Family Bank customer.** Langston gave his desk a slap while laughing.

"That damn brains of yours could serve its purpose well right here in this community. You should run for City Council, Ian. You probably would do a better job than the wackos sitting on it now, I imagine."

Thanks doc, but you must be crazy. No politicking for me.

Something else in Ian's journal caught Langston's attention. "So tell me of this house you're wanting to buy? And is there a support group for you in North Central Florida?" The house was something Ian had found online. "And why so far north?"

Ian quickly wrote **traffic here is awful and this city's too noisy. I want to go where it's quiet.**

"Well I can't argue with you there, Ian. Heck, if I had a choice, I'd follow you north, too." That's when Dr. Langston started signing off on Ian's file. It was Ian's turn to smile. *Now that's what I'm talking about!*

"Well Ian, I don't see any reason why you shouldn't be getting your disability income soon enough." Ian gave him another thumbs up.

Langston handed Ian his medical file as soon as he was done signing. "Now you be careful with that file, Ian. Give it right to staff when you get to the COL. And remember to stay medically compliant while at the COL." Next came the refill scripts.

Langston got to his feet, grabbed his cane, and motioned Ian to the door. "Get the door for me, will ya? I'm going to get me another soda before my next patient, so come on; I'll walk with you to the elevators. If this lockdown's still on, I'll go down with you and let you out the back. So let's go." Ian liked the sound of that and hurried to get the door.

"I'll miss those journals of yours, Ian." Ian was surprised by that and wrote **thanks, doc. I'll miss you being my doc.**

"If you do move north, make sure you have your new doctor read your journals, okay? It'll help with your treatment. You have a gift with that pen of yours. Any doctor will enjoy reading your stuff."

Thanks doc.

Suddenly, from the speakers came: ***LOCKDOWN IS NOW OVER. YOU ARE FREE TO LEAVE THE BUILDING.***

"Well now . . . that couldn't have been timed any better, eh Ian?"

Ian was right then thinking he was really going to miss his sessions with Dr. Langston. The man had always been straight up with him since their first visit. Dr. Langston had been plain spoken and a man of good intention, if not for patient overload. That was the downside to working at such a large facility like JMH. Dr. Langston was also a sports fan, which Ian liked, though liking more his basketball to Ian's baseball and golf. But Ian's thoughts were suddenly interrupted by a new inner voice, one he'd never heard before, a nasty sounding voice with a slight evil bent to it, that said, *"I dare you to show Dr. Langston one of your real journals, Ian."* The voice scared Ian a little, especially with its abrupt laugh.

"*Focus Ian,*" said the calming voice of reason. "*Just concentrate on getting out of here. Get back to the COL. Turn in your file. You were warned about voices like his coming to bother you. Settle down and breathe. Think good thoughts.*"

Easier said than done Ian mentally answered back.

"Are you okay, Ian?" Ian had forgotten about Dr. Langston being beside him. A look of concern was written on Dr. Langston's face. "You blanked out on me there a moment. You okay? I read in your file about your 400-sugar reading. You want I should order Nurse Chang to give you insulin before leaving?" Ian was saved from answering by an onrush of patients when seeing Dr. Langston enter the waiting area.

"Whoa there folks! Just settle down." Dr. Langston used his cane to keep people from knocking him over. "Please, all of you take your seats. I promise to get to each of you in due time." Langston looked at Ian and said, "I think we should make a run for it, don't you?" Ian smiled at that and wrote **you lead, I'll follow.**

Dr. Langston smiled also. "I guess I'll just say goodbye here. Don't forget the pharmacy. Remember what happened the last time you forgot to pick up your refills." Ian would have preferred not to have been reminded of the night he crashed his car into the tree. "Oh and Ian, if you hear thunder while on the links . . ." but by then Ian had started for the elevators. *My golfing days are over, doc.* Minutes later, he was at the pharmacy and picking up his scripts. Minutes after that, he was stuck in traffic again. *UGH!*

A woman in a black Hummer made as if he didn't exist. She literally forced him into the emergency lane, where he then had to cut in front of a Mini Cooper to get back on the freeway. *Sorry bub, but size does count.* Ian was looking for payback on the Hummer, but traffic wouldn't help him. The Hummer was already five cars ahead, which made paying her back difficult. From where he was, he could see the woman in the Hummer fiddling with her radio and envying the way her a/c blew her hair back.

That's when he noticed his gas gauge.

What the hell? How could I have burned through a quarter tank of gas already? It was painful to watch his car burn gas so quickly. He hadn't noticed, but he was creeping up closer to the Hummer. That's when he spotted the woman's gold and diamond bracelet. *Wearing ten grand in jewelry and still cutting me off. Bitch!* Ian pulled his backpack closer and took from it his bag of pills. He also took out his towel and a water bottle. He had a heck of a time uncapping the water bottle, and a worse time uncapping the safety cap to his Ativan. The water bottle he dropped because of sweaty palms. He had to dry swallow his two 1-milligram Ativan pills, which left a terrible aftertaste in his mouth. The Ativan was for calming his anxieties. The Lithium was for stabilizing his moods. The Seroquel was for the voices. None of it worked when at the mercy of a realm of his own making.

He'd been tagged an insomniac by the COL staff. But since he never caused any trouble after lights out, the staff had allowed him to watch his late night sports roundup on TV, so long as it didn't disturb any of the other 13 resident patients. Baseball is what he most watched. Late night sitcoms came next. Late night sitcoms came next and anything after that, anything to keep him from falling asleep in his room. His latest night terrors were the cause of his staying away from his bed. He also had, of late, some color change issues. He would be walking through grass and bam, the grass would suddenly change hue. Stuff like that. He'd written about it in his Mind journals. But it was remembering the previous night's apparitional visitor that had him white knuckling his steering wheel. The voices had told him hers had been a premonitory visit, *but to what premonition?* He was about to find out.

Chapter 23

The fact the COL was a facility

of just seven rooms with two beds to each room worked well for Ian. He shared a room with a highly sedated patient named Harold. Harold was kept sedated because of his seizures after his boating accident. Harold was found floating face down in the bay after having knocked himself out when hitting his head against the gunnel of his skiff before it capsized. Rescuers estimated that Harold had been in the water about eight minutes before they got to him. EMTs revived him, but that's when his seizing started. Doctors were forced to induce Harold's coma as a way to control his seizing until a time when the right medications could help him. Phenobarbitals were keeping Harold sedated, and that made him *the* perfect roommate for when Ian had his psychotic episode moments like . . . the Night of Snakes.

The Night of Snakes had occurred a month prior to his being stuck in traffic. It was much like all his other psychotic events, seemingly real, vivid, and frightening. No sooner had he shut his reading lamp off and made his room dark than his pillow began squirming. Something in his pillow had wanted out *bad*. As soon as he unzipped his pillowcase, two large black snakes slithered out onto his bed. Immediately after kicking them off his bed, two more snakes popped from the pillow, then two after that, and two more until his whole bed was covered in snakes!

His snake episode had been a tough one to deal with, especially when having no voice to yell with, which in the end was a good thing. He almost made the mistake of hitting the room alarm, but stopped himself when thinking what trouble he would cause himself if staff found him battling something he knew wasn't real. Night of Snakes was tough, much like all his other episodic night terrors, all handled in silence once accepting them to be hallucinations. Only his voices had kept him company, telling him his events were part of his soldiering process, and a way to strengthen his faith for other upcoming life events. He had a tough time buying that one, but sheer exhaustion always won out in the end. Staff was shocked to find his room in such disarray after that event, his known for being so neat and tidy. He was sent to see the COL supervisor right away, who suggested he write what he thought he saw in his journals as a way to deal with his hallucinations. Ian instead beefed up his prewrite journals and let all who needed to read them, read them. Night of Snakes went in a Mind journal where it belonged. He ended the Night of Snakes entry with a description of how scary it was hearing the snakes hissing at him.

Then there'd been the Night of the Tactical Assault.

On that night, he had no sooner made his room dark than he heard rotor wash outside. He looked out his window and saw a black chopper landing right outside the COL fence. Under a three-quarter moon he saw a team of black clad operatives jump from the chopper and make for the fence. Ian's psychotic event did not allow him to figure out how they could've jumped the fence so fast. He even heard safeties click off their guns as they hurried towards his window. (Commonsense reasoning would have told him that the team would've simply knocked at the front door if wanting him.) Hearing the window being jimmied (a breeze making a tree limb scratch the glass) got Ian hurrying into his closet and piling his freshly starched and ironed clothes atop him as camouflage. Hearing his name called out from the window was the worst of that night's terror. Fear and exhaustion wore him out that night, too. Morning staff were shocked to find him asleep underneath his piled up clothes. (The COL supervisor made the determination that his newly prescribed Seroquel and his watching the movie 'Black Hawk Down,' was probably the reason for his hallucination.) But it was the prior night's visitor that had him white knuckling the wheel of his car.

She had been coming to him in dreams of late. But never had she appeared to him like the previous night. He awoke to seeing her apparition sitting at the foot of his bed, a most unsettling sight, to say the least. She was just sitting there, staring at him, his having no idea why, or how long she'd been sitting there staring. Her appearance was a hell of a thing to wake up to. Her not answering him when asking her why she was there forced him to sit up. She just kept staring, not saying a word, not even conversing in their usual dream talk. Nothing. Just her stare bearing the look of bad news, like the day she'd told him about his father never coming back. Her contemplative stare worried him enough to try touching her, but her apparitional hand shooed his hand away. "So why *are* you here?" he had asked. She unnerved him by not responding. The worry lines on her starkly white wrinkled face wrinkled some more, which also bothered him. She faded slowly from sight before he could ask about his brother. That made her visit even more ominous. The rumble of a loud V-8 roaring past him broke him of his reverie.

It was a miracle he hadn't wrecked, since he hadn't been paying much attention to the traffic. He had been driving by instinct when seeing he'd finally reached the 874 split-off, where he really needed to concentrate on his driving and less on daydreaming. A second horsepower aficionado zoomed past him, which made him grip his wheel tighter. The lady in the Hummer went roaring past next.

Ian couldn't keep up with the faster moving traffic. He stayed in the right lane while listening to his valves knocking once past 60mph. He didn't want his clunker to blow up, so he eased off the gas pedal, which annoyed the driver in a classic Shelby that was behind him, who roared by also. Next to zoom by was a driver fiddling with his radio while doing 70mph, just as a late model ZR1 went chasing after the Shelby. Ian noticed the ZR1's driver was actually watching a movie on his in-dash screen while trying to catch the Shelby. Next to go by was a late model Lincoln whose driver was turning pages in a book strapped to a dash-mounted book holder. Ian missed seeing the driver behind him texting while driving. *Damn if these drivers aren't crazier than us at the COL!*

And that's when his premonitory moment came into focus.

Ian began stepping down on his brake because of a slow moving Town Car ahead. His brakes made their usual worn-rotor squeal as he hit his horn to the slow moving relic of a Lincoln (same type that President Kennedy was assassinated in.) His horn did nothing to get the Lincoln's driver to speed up. Ian flashed his lights. Nothing. The Lincoln stayed stuck at just under 50mph on a stretch of the 'pike where 70mph was the norm.

Ian tried a lane change, but faster moving traffic wouldn't let him pass. He saw his needle dip below 45mph, which then made him worry about possibly getting rear-ended. There was no chance of getting around the suicide door Lincoln.

The Lincoln had an inch-thick coat of grime on the body and windows. Ian wondered how a person could allow a car to get so dirty. That's when he spotted the driver's window go down and an arm extend to wave him on.

The 2-mile sign announcing the COL went by on his right.

He was still focused on the arm waving him by, a woman's wrinkly arm at that. That's also when he noticed her bumper sticker, the only thing clean on the car. The sticker was made of bright red lettering on a white background, which read: **Ian . . .**

Quit Your Bitching and Start the Revolution!

He did a double take when seeing *his* name on *her* sticker!

Quit Your Bitching and Start the Revolution!

Now his name was gone. *What the hell?*

It was all he could do to stifle his fears while watching the woman's arm waving him on, an arm that seemed strangely familiar. But it was the sticker that had all of his attention, and no longer one sticker, but a whole slew of stickers covering the entire bumper!

Quit Your Bitching and Start the Revolution!
Quit Your Bitching and Start the Revolution!
Quit Your Bitching and Start the Revolution!
Quit Your Bitching and Start the Revolution!
Quit Your Bitching and Start the Revolution!

Ian couldn't believe what he was seeing.

"Ian!" A new voice shouted from within his own psyche. The voice sounded like the man who had walked with him during his 40-day sojourn. Goose bumps popped out on his arm as the voice said, *"Your marching orders are there before you, Ian."* The man's voice was replaced by a gaggle of voices, and all wanting to add something. *"Start the revolution!"* He and the Lincoln were suddenly the only two cars on the 'pike. *"Your destiny calls you." "Accept your calling. Why you think you were brought back from the dark?" "Your path*

in life is now here." The wrinkled arm still waved him on. *Something about that arm.*

"Your messenger wishes you to pass, Ian. Don't keep her waiting." This time it was the man who commanded him to pass. Ian did so, and when changing lanes and stepping on the gas, noticed that the bumper only had the one original sticker.

Ian absentmindedly left his turn signal on while approaching the driver's window and seeing the driver. He wished he hadn't. It was her matted wet hair that gave her away. *Oh my god!*

It was a good thing there hadn't been any traffic, or he probably would have wrecked right then. He let off the gas and slid back behind the Lincoln. *But why her, dear God, tell me, why her? And why now?*

The red lettering on the sticker began to run as if like blood running off the plastic as the Lincoln started to pull away.

Quit Your Bitching was running red like blood.

Why in hell did I have to take so much Ativan?

"All prophets have received their messages in much the same way, Ian."

Quit calling me by name.

"Some messages come in dreams," said a new voice. *"Just be grateful you received yours here today."*

But what does quit my bitching mean? I mean, really, please, just stop.

"There's no stopping destiny, Ian. Unless you want to go back to the dark." *"It is what it is, Ian."*

Stop it! I want no more of this; I'm begging you!

"No time for that now, Ian." It was the man again. *"And expect to be lied to, scorned, and ridiculed. You already know about pain, so more pain shouldn't bother you."*

But why more pain? Haven't I gone through enough already?

"No prophet ever delivers messages without feeling the brunt from their deliveries. You are now like the prophets of old." Ian gave thought to just crashing his car and be done with it. *"Remove thoughts like that from your head, Ian. That is the devil toying with you. You are destined for great things, so accept your calling."* He could swear it was his brother Juan talking. *Is that you, brother? Oh, my god, I've lost my mind!*

"Your mind's fine," said his brother's voice.

The Lincoln was almost out of sight by then.

"Strengthen your faith, Ian." The man again. *"It's all you have left now. Faith for healing and seeing your mission through."*

What mission? And what's so important about faith? I don't even know if I even have any faith.

"Oh, you have faith alright, or why you think we brought you back? Faith is important because it will see you through." His exit coming up is what got him to focus again.

Minutes later he was back at the COL, rushing to hand in his file and pills, to then hurry to his room and spend the remainder of the day writing in his journals about his experience. He spent hours writing. After dinner, he spent more hours at the computer, searching for a webmaster to start his new website titled: Quit Your Bitching and Start the Revolution! (Herein known as QYB).

He wound up filling two whole Mind journals with thoughts and ideas for his QYB site. Money is what he most needed next, not just his disability money, but his retro, which he was counting on for making the down payment on the North Central Florida home and to start QYB. He ended the evening by writing in his journal about how well his mother drove the Lincoln.

Chapter 24

Ian had been so frazzled by

seeing his mother driving with a bumper sticker that told of his life's quest, that the next morning, the morning of his disability hearing, he overslept. Staff hurried to wake him, where he wound up missing breakfast for court. He was ravenous when stuck in traffic again, and more ravenous when roaming the halls of the court building while waiting his turn with the judge. He had already been called, so he had to wait to be called in again. That wasn't until the afternoon.

Ian almost fell asleep while waiting on the judge to render his verdict after reading through his medical file. Thankfully his sleepy behavior didn't hinder the judge's decision to rule him both physically and mentally disabled (ruling physical over mental). Didn't matter to Ian though. He was just happy knowing his COL days were over. A four-year retro check was also coming.

He made it back to the COL in time for dinner, where he told of the good news. Right after dinner, he went directly to the computer, where he spent hours clicking and typing until it was time for bed. (He was the only one among the 14 patients who could also navigate a computer without med interference.) He emailed his webmaster, wanting to know the progress to his QYB site, before emailing his banker at Diamond Bank/North Florida. It was Richard 'Dick' Weaver who held the paper to the house in North Central Florida. An attachment email came in while he was emailing his banker. The attachment was from his webmaster showing samples pages to the new

QYB site, its blog and chat pages, plus the home page. The blog and chat pages were where Ian intended to tag the latest revolutionary gossip to. His postings would pertain mostly to banking and investing issues. But the QYB website would not come cheap. His QYB homepage would have 'Quit Your Bitching and Start the Revolution!' as a header at the top of the page. Even his Wharton schoolmates working on Street would get to chime in with thoughts and opinions. A click of the mouse sent $500 to his webmaster, and another click sent $1,000 as a binder between him and Dick Weaver.

Richard 'Dick' Weaver not only held the majority of the deeds at Dream Harvest Estate, he was also DHE's Association President. It was as Association President that he got Ian voted into the 55-plus community of Dream Harvest Estate. It was Ian's special circumstances such as his disability, his being single with no children or pets, plus a life story that played to his favor that helped get him voted in. As President of the Association, Dick Weaver held a lot of sway on the Board. As President of Diamond Bank, he also could seal deals at DHE with just a stroke of his pen. Having Ian's $1,000 binder, along with his monthly supplemental income direct deposited into Diamond Bank, plus Ian's last $25,000 from his offshore account, a prerequisite to approving his mortgage, made the contract on 34 Starling Circle a done deal.

Everything was looking up for Ian.

Too bad that Dick Weaver had his own agenda running.

But Ian was too focused on designing his new website and moving into his new home to worry about anything but starting a new life for himself. His head was starting to clear thanks to having hurdled the challenge of independent living again.

The negative was having his $25,000 transfer from Monserrat flagged for lack of Cash Transaction Receipts, thus causing his name to return to OJI Terrence's computer, who seethed when discovering Ian's latest endeavor. *Lightning strike my ass! This guy thinks his disability's gonna save him, he's sadly mistaken* thought agent Terrence while getting Miami on the horn. *I'm going to tag and bag this guy myself this time.*

Ian had a rough time with manic mode the day of his moving from the COL. His compulsive disorder was seismic enough to frustratingly force him to pack, unpack, and repack his bags and boxes several times, just so his mind could be happy that every square inch of space in his car had been used properly. That's how his OCD played him. It took the COL supervisor to remove him from his room and *she* pack his things, for him to leave that day.

Once the car was finally packed, it was time for the hard goodbyes. Four years of tough memories, from his being on the brink of death to walking again, brought many tears to staff and himself. But he kept control of his tears until being in the car, where through teary eyes he saw in his rear view mirror some of the staff still crying while waving goodbye. This brought more tears to his eyes while pulling away and noticing among staff a few patients also standing there waving in their fog of medication as some had no idea why they were even waving. But once on the road, it was time to focus.

In his pocket was $500 cash (his debit card was waiting for him at Weaver's bank). He figured $500 was more than enough for the 330-mile trip north, a trip that began at the local filling station before jumping on the 'pike. Gasoline, snacks, drinks, 2 quarts of oil, and a couple of jugs of water (in case his clunker heated up) cost him his first $100. Oil and water he placed in the trunk alongside a new microwave and microwavable goodies that he'd purchased days earlier. On the seat next to him was his backpack with bottles of water, a new hand towel, a fresh pack of tee shirts, and his dozen journals. On the floor of the car was a new pair of sneakers and a box of a 1,000 count printed QYB stickers, same as the one on his mother's car. The 1,000 stickers were for his first 1,000 QYB subscribers. Also in his backpack were his meds, his Glipizide, Metformin, his benzos, mood stabilizers, and pain meds (100 Oxycodones that he'd never taken), which he then carried to the canal at the rear of the station. He dumped all his meds into the briny water and watched all his pills dissolve before heading back to the car. The containers of pills he tossed in the dumpster. He slapped two QYB stickers on the fuel pump and drove off.

He sped up the onramp a little too fast, which forced him to lean on his brakes. His new house keys jingled on the keychain as he made the turn. The sound of the keys made him smile. *If all goes according to plan, I should be in my new house before dark.* But even best laid plans . . .

Palmetto traffic was once again horrendous that day. It took 45 minutes just to get to Doral and another 45 minutes to reach I-95. While driving in stop and go traffic he saw dry lightning flash across the Everglades. The sight of lightning brought a chill to his spine.

Once beyond the big curve in Hialeah, traffic began to move, not much, but enough to keep him off the brake until reaching the I-95 junction. It was slow going after that, with traffic jammed solid all the way into Broward. But once reaching North Lauderdale, traffic finally started to flow. But no sooner had he gotten up to speed, than his temperature gauge began to rise. This forced him into the emergency lane, where he had to wait 15-minutes for the car to cool down before pouring water into the radiator. He stayed in the slow lane after that.

Lantana was where he decided to take his first bathroom break. But as soon as he got off I-95, bang, his right front tire blew out. Worse than that was finding his spare tire flat, too. He'd no choice but to ride the rim all the way to the nearest service station, which wasn't that near. Once he pulled into the service bay, he found he'd ridden his rim too long, bent it, which made it impossible to put a tire on it. Several calls were made to area junkyards before the right rim was found. Tire and rim cost him $100.

His troubles were far from over.

Ian's temperature gauge started to rise the moment he crossed into St. Lucie County. He had to again pull into the emergency lane and let his clunker cool down before pouring the last jug of water into the radiator before noticing that his water pump was leaking like a sieve. Luck had him a compatible water pump waiting for him at the Port St. Lucie Service Plaza, except there were no service bays available until after dark. It was 9 o'clock when he finally got driving again. Water pump and labor cost him $200.

Traffic had built up exponentially by then, especially big rig traffic, which made driving with his windows down a hassle. Every time a big rig went roaring by, the stuff in his car, especially his stickers, all got blown everywhere. Ian decided it was best to just take an early food break and hope that the big rig traffic would die down. It was coming up on 10pm when he drove into a Cape Canaveral eatery, where he filled up on pancakes and coffee. But when looking out at I-95 traffic, instead of truck traffic dying down, it had actually increased, slowing traffic more. He asked the restaurant manager if it was okay for him to catch a few hours of sleep in his car. The man said it was alright, so long as he parked away from the entrance to the 24/7 restaurant.

Ian wound up sleeping until dawn.

It was when turning the key that he found his battery was dead.

The same shift manager gave him a jump, which got him back on the road, a good thing, since a battery would have taken all his money and he still needed gas. But best laid plans . . .

When in Daytona, Ian, while turning onto SR 40 West, heard a hissing sound right before his left front tire blew!

So angry was he at his car that he would've easily poured gas on it and set it on fire, if having had the spare gas to do it with. But luck again brought him another Samaritan, who gave him a lift back to Daytona where . . . a used tire cost him $20, another $10 for the station nerd to drive him back to his car, and another $10 for the jerk to air-ratchet-tight his lugs. It was a 'grin and bear it' moment for sure, with just $48 left in his pocket and a car nearly empty of gas, with still some 60 odd miles to go before reaching Dream Harvest Estate. Ian did the only logical thing he could do; he prayed a foxhole prayer before spending the last of his money on gas.

His foxhole prayer was answered though, when a little over an hour later, with his car heating up again, he *finally* got to park underneath his new carport. He breathed a sigh of relief when shutting his car off and saying out loud, "Thank you, Lord."

First thing he took in before entering the house, was the silence from the neighboring forest. Last time he'd seen such a forest was in Cuba.

It was while getting out of the hissing car and stretching that his DTs began. The shakes from his withdrawals (and no doubt nerves) went from subtle to rigorous, which then had him worried that he might not be able to unload his car before the big shakes began. Added to that was it started to rain.

He had to run from car to house in the rain several times to get most of his stuff inside. All of the DHE homes were manufactured homes set in a wooded community neighboring the national forest, which in itself was Ian's new medication. But his growing tremors left little time for enjoying the sights right then. The last thing he brought in was his new air mattress.

But even while drenched, Ian still took the time to take in the wildlife that was enjoying the retention pond behind his house. He actually walked downhill in the rain to visit the pond, where he saw deer, foxes, and raccoons mingling together. The sight made him sad when wishing his brother and mother were there to see the sights with him. Then he remembered he still had his new microwave in the car. He hurried back uphill, the shakes getting worse, grabbed the boxed microwave from the trunk, almost dropping it, and missed seeing his new neighbor staring at him from her kitchen window.

Ms. Brown was about to educate Ian in what a real nemesis was.

Part IV

Life

Show your walk daily and if need be use words.

Said during a blog with JennaCal412
prior to his arrest.

Chapter 25

Ms. Brown wasn't known as the

resident witch-bitch for nothing. Hers was more snoop than curiosity over the man she'd seen shaking while stumbling in the rain with a new microwave in his hands. *I wonder if he stole it* was her thinking.

Ms. Brown had kept at her window for days when trying to catch a glimpse at her new neighbor. She had to wait a week for that to happen, which at that point she simply thought Ian had died in the house. Stuff like that happened from time to time in the 55-plus community. Yet there was Ian, still suffering from slight withdrawals, but at least able to walk to his mailbox. It was his disheveled appearance that got Ms. Brown calling Weaver at the bank.

Ian suffered through his withdrawals much like he'd suffered throughout everything in life, in silence, and on his own. He was still suffering from dry heaves and dizziness when finally walking outside. But dry heaves or not, the fresh air did him a world of good by just standing there taking in the breeze from the neighboring forest. He noticed the swinging of his neighbor's kitchen curtains, wondering if his neighbor had been watching him on the sly.

Inside Ms. Brown's house, her interest was more on giving Weaver a piece of her mind, and less on her curtains. "Who's this idiot you moved in next door to me, Dick?"

"Your new neighbor is who that is, and no one you need to worry about, Emily." Weaver wanted nothing getting in the way of his agenda.

Most homebuyers would have found 34 Starling Circle a nice enough house just the way it was. But to an OCDer like Ian, it still needed repairs and additions. The carport needed some repairs. A couple of kitchen cabinets needed replacing. The stainless steel sink had a few dings in it. The carpet was worn. It was nothing for any homeowner to lose sleep over. But Ian was no ordinary homeowner. As an obsessive-compulsive, these, and other repairs, were major hassles for him.

To Ian, it was 'out with the old and in with the new' at 34 Starling Circle. And thus began his to-do list, a list that would bring him much trouble at Dream Harvest Estate.

DHE was a community of 176 homes set among 90 acres that bordered the national forest. Unlike in South Florida, where canals govern the flow of storm water runoff, at DHE, 12 retention ponds handled the above ground overflow. This not only helped to control flooding, it also kept the retention ponds full, which thus kept the ponds teeming with wildlife. The pond behind Ian's house seemed to be the animals' favorite.

First order of business for Ian was to buy himself a wooden bench from the local hardware store, on which to sit alongside the pond to watch the wildlife enjoying the surroundings. He even saw the occasional black bear come to sit and eat the tall reedy stalks along the bank of the pond. Since Ian neither was no hunter, the animals didn't fear him. A number of different birds also made their home at the pond. A pair of Michigan sand cranes did however peck at him when he got too close to them. Birds from as far north as Canada and as far south as Chile made DHE their home. This was where the DHE streets got their names. (DHE was also a registered bird sanctuary.) But the tranquil moments ended at the sound of hunters' rifles. That's when the animals would scatter, which then made them easier targets once back in the forest. The fact that DHE had 'No Trespassing' and 'No Hunting' signs posted everywhere, plus private road signs, still didn't keep hunters from wanting at what the ponds had to offer. Ian abhorred hunting and its results. To him, hunting was the one negative to living so close to the forest. In time, the two-legged species, the only species on the Earth who know and recognize death, would bring more negatives to Ian's peace and quiet. But first there was his to-do list.

Starling Circle was a cul-de-sac made up of seven homes. Ian's was the middle home among the seven. All the homes at DHE were of a pitch-set design, which put them level to the ground. They were unlike most mobile homes, in that they had either level garages or carports.

First thing Ian wrote on his list was wanting to paint the metal flashing of his carport a bright red. He liked red, and because he liked red, he also wanted to add red mortar and bricks to the four support columns. Unbeknownst to him though, red paint and bricks to support columns were against DHE code. Ian didn't think to check the DHE handbook, since he'd forgotten to get one from the office, so he went ahead and bought red paint, bricks, and mortar.

His home was a three-bedroom design with a screened-in porch at the side of the house that made up the 1,500 square foot layout. The home was a far cry from the 10,000 plus square foot Lakes home, confiscated years back, but at least 34 Starling Circle was his . . . well, his and the bank's anyway.

Next thing on his to-do list was to buy the 'best money could buy computer' for his QYB website. He went to the bank and withdrew $15,000, a large sum to be sure, but one that he figured would buy him everything he needed on his to-do list, with money left over for re-depositing. While at the bank, he decided to stop in and say hello to Weaver, who he felt was at least a social friend, but was told by his head teller, Helen, that he was out of town.

Weaver was dealing with his own closet full of skeletons.

Ian got home and immediately took down his shutters and prepped them for painting, which got Ms. Brown making another phone call to Weaver's voicemail. By the time she was done complaining, Ian had the first shutter stripped and painted. Painting the shutters red was a no-no also.

Ian next went to tearing out all his old screening from the windows and framed patio including the patio door. He got all the metal frames cleaned and prepped for re-screening. These projects of his would take days to complete, but the weather turned foul, so he couldn't complete any of what he started.

To Ms. Brown, his house looked a mess. She complained about that too on Weaver's voicemail. (By then, Weaver's shady investment dealings had caught up to him too, which kept him from returning to North Florida. If he had been around, he might have kept Ian from opening up the can of worms he was about to open with the DHE Board over his to-do list.) But he was so excited about his to-do list, and especially his new fence, that he thought nothing of seeing no other fences at DHE when hiring a fence company to put up 120 feet of fence. The drizzling rain did little to hinder that, especially when paying cash. Fences were against DHE policy.

Now, besides the violations for red paint, bricks, and a fence, Ian went to tilling a large section of his backyard for planting a spice garden and pumpkin patch. The spice garden was okay, per se, but not the pumpkin patch. That, too, was a violation.

Ms. Brown was beside herself when unable to get Weaver to return her calls. "You asshole," she yelled into the phone, "You moved a farmer next door!" She called the DHE property manager, but he just told her to wait on Weaver. Ian was Weaver's problem. As for the property manager, he'd already filled out several fines and violations on Ian's property. By then, Ian had set himself up a workshop underneath his carport, where he could size and cut his newly bought rolls of screen. He also bought buckets of roof paint for sealing his roof the moment he got a chance. He also bought a pallet of 30-pound steppingstones that he placed at intervals from his home to his bench at the pond. Bench and stones were against code also. Ian wasn't done though.

He visited the electronic box store in town and bought what was touted to be *the* best money-could-buy computer. He also bought all the goodies that went with it, including wireless printer, keypad and surround sound speakers, an upgrade for listening to music while writing online. The sale was just shy of $4,000, which was a shocker to Ian, but one he figured Quit Your Bitching would make up. He still had to talk himself into handing over the $4,000 in cash.

While in town, he made his first mortgage payment. Future circumstances would make this the only payment he made on time.

Once home with his computer and after setting up all his wireless drivers and booting up, his PC crashed! A glitch in the software got him rushing back to the store. But since his PC was the only one in stock, he had to leave it for repair. Back home, a call to his webmaster got him jotting down setup procedures for when finally having his QYB computer back. It was after saying goodbye to his webmaster to go check his mailbox that he found the first of the violations in his mailbox.

His enemy mind kept him at his list, which then included ripping out his old carpet for new vinyl flooring. What he hadn't figured on was how expensive vinyl flooring would be thanks to the increase in petrol prices. Ian had to re-install some of the old carpet and settle for only half of the vinyl he'd intended. In the meantime, he'd created an eyesore of a trash pile outside. The pile was made up of empty vinyl flooring boxes, rolls of old screening, ripped out carpet and padding, the old kitchen doors, the sink, a busted mirror (which shattered when tossed on the pile), and last but not least, bags of household trash. This was a big mistake with bears in the area. But Ian was under the impression that DHE provided trash pickup. Trash pickup came with a charge and needed a setup fee payable before pickup, so trash pickup wasn't free. He wondered why it was taking so long for his trash to get hauled away, but he didn't worry about it enough to keep from piling up more trash. The bears appreciated it. One morning, Starling Circle woke up to trash scattered everywhere on the cul-de-sac, which angered Ian's neighbors plenty.

Ian, after picking up all the trash and piling it up *again* (still wondering why no pickup, but figuring it would at some point get hauled away), got too busy working on other projects to care much about how his neighbors and his trash pile. He got busy acid washing and pressure washing his driveway in preparation for new staining. The previous owner of 34 Starling Circle hadn't done much upkeep to the exterior of the house, and it showed by the inches-thick mildew on the driveway and walkways. Once all the concrete was clean, Ian re-stained it terracotta red. This was another no-no, since all driveways at DHE were supposed to be Seagull Gray. But Ian really liked red. The DHE Board was *seeing* red, same as Ms. Brown, who was breathing fire over Ian's muriatic acid cloud prior to staining his driveway red. Red was the last straw for both Ms. Brown and the Board. But Weaver hadn't yet returned from his Big Apple trip, so complaints had to be put on hold until then. Ms. Brown did seek out and hound the DHE Board treasurer, Mr. Green, about getting Ian to stop any more of his projects. Green, who had a thing for Ms. Brown though still being married to his wife, didn't find Ian home when driving by. All he could do was report all the finable offenses and take them to the Board.

Ian's one silver lining while at DHE was making friends with Nancy and Willard Smith. The Smiths not only lived at DHE, but they also owned the hardware store in town where he rented the pressure washer and sprayer he used for painting the driveway. The Smiths did not sell him the terracotta. They had assumed he was getting the proper gray from Mr. Green's paint store. The Smiths warned him afterwards about the staining being wrong, but Ian loved how the staining had turned out. Another $500 fine came for the driveway, and another $500 for his trash pile. These he shoved in his kitchen drawer with the rest of his fines.

His lone moment of comfort came when enjoying his new startup website surpassing its first thousand subscribers. His take on quantitative easing four (QE4) got many of the 1,000 wanting more. Some of his classmates, now working on Wall Street, chimed in with also wanting more of his take. His postings had made light of what printing money for money's sake would do to the economy. He was correct, and his financial knowhow also got his 'Posted for Discussion' (PFD) page humming. It was PFD that would bring thousands more subscribers to the QYB fold. He then needed another 1000-count box of stickers for mailing. But the stickers were expensive to make and troublesome to mail. He thought selling them at $5 apiece would make up the expense, though not wanting an electronic trail through PayPal or credit cards meant having to use the honor system to pay for stickers at a time when finances were overriding honor. The honor system simply was not the way to pay for stickers, and it showed in Ian's dwindling account. But he did make friends with the print shop owner in town, who not only liked making the QYB stickers, but also became a fan of QYB. He allowed Ian credit in his shop, even took over mailing duties, so long as Ian paid the bill. But the bill was hard to pay with yet another fine reaching his box over the pumpkin patch.

Ian woke one morning in sheer manic mode and needed to expend energy on something. He expended his energy raking leaves. He also had writer's block, so in thinking of writing and expending energy, he raked up one heck of a pile of leaves, a huge pile to be exact, which he then set on fire.

It was Ms. Brown herself who guided the Fire Marshal right to Ian's backyard. Ian knew nothing of needing a burn permit for burning leaves. But the fact they'd been under dry conditions, with no rain in sight, plus being so close to the forest, made the Fire Marshal's $500 fine a given. This fine he could not so easily put aside. If not paid within 30 days, a county lien would be placed on his house, which would then certainly create trouble with the bank. Ian had to begrudgingly pay the Fire fine. By then, QYB had surpassed 5,000 viewers, with most wanting stickers, which gave Ian a reason to be happy, until the print shop bill came due. His insightfulness into America's continuing woes in finance was nothing to his own financial woes. He did get to see two QYB stickers in town, which made him happy, but he still had to tell his print shop buddy to wait until his supplemental income came in so he could pay the man. Ian was one of 58 million needing their supplemental income to make ends meet.

His writing style continued to unfurl as he continued to write about financial subjects that definitely hit home with most people. It was his take on whatever current financial topic was making the rounds that grew his site more. While a winter chill took hold of North Central Florida, he wrote. While rain came with the first sign of winter, he wrote. While the nightly chill tried to find its way in, he wrote. But he did have his occasional bouts with writer's block, and when that happened, he found stuff to do, like borrowing the Smiths' company truck for removing his trash pile and hauling it to the county landfill where it cost him $200 to dump. He wrote about that too.

When he arrived back at his home from dropping off the Smiths' truck, he heard Ms. Brown yelling "Dick!" into her phone while standing by her car. Ian headed down to the pond and avoided her stare.

Dick Weaver had just returned from a sit-down with federal prosecutors in New York when hearing of Ms. Brown's travails.

Weaver wished he'd let Ms. Brown's rant go to voicemail. He had already heard some of Ian's drilling and hammering in the background on some of her other messages. Ian was deep into his to-do list by then (building flower boxes at the time). The eight unstained boxes (weather made it impossible to stain them) were something else to annoy Ms. Brown.

After the boxes, Ian got started with rescreening. He rolled out his rolls on his worktable and cut to size what he needed. He had a radio playing loud while working, so loud rock music also annoyed Ms. Brown's classical music listening time, especially with the aluminum carport making the radio reverberate.

Ian, seeing as how it had stayed sunny for a few days straight, broke from re-screening to climb atop his roof and pour out some roof coating. While he still had his roller in roof paint, he decided to recoat the carport roof. But before applying the paint, he had to repair some panel seams with caulk. It was when running a bead of caulk down the middle seam that his work boot got stuck between hip and seam. In attempting to loosen his steel-toed boot from the seam, the center seam buckled and sent him crashing atop his car!

The relief of not getting hurt (just a small cut to his hand was all) got him laughing. It was his laughter that woke Ms. Brown from her nap, as she'd fallen asleep on her patio chair while watching him. She was still rubbing sleep from her eyes when catching Weaver on the phone to complain about the damage Ian had done to the carport. Weaver didn't need to be reminded he was still the owner of 34 Starling Circle. He was too busy getting his numbers straight for another sit down with auditors to have time to read Ian the riot act. He sent Mr. Green to do it, except Mr. Green was in the middle of a nap also. By the time Green did get by Ian's house, Ian was gone. But Green took in the damaged carport, which he reported along with the carport columns being mortared and bricked, along with the unapproved eight flower boxes, and the driveway still being red. Green's report hastened Ian's troubles with the Board.

$\mathbf{H}$e still had glitches with his website that needed his webmaster's help. The four turn pages to his website were always in need of updating. Forty thousand subscribers in under five months would also require a bit of security tweaking. Updates were causing more trouble than helping, so Ian agreed to pay extra to just get his webmaster to finish the tweaking needed. (Ian would in time become as savvy at troubleshooting and fixing glitches as his webmaster.) But troubleshooting a faulty PC was another matter, as his PC crashed yet again, and this *while* his webmaster was updating QYB!

Not only did this new crash force Ian back to the store, it also forced him to use a library computer to keep his postings updated while his PC was in repair. But without his home computer running QYB 24/7, Ian needed his webmaster to carry QYB on *his* server, and that brought an additional charge. His one bright spot that day was seeing another thousand subscribers tuning on to QYB.

It was his blistering off-the-cuff, by the seat-of-his-pants and witty commentaries that kept QYB growing . . . growing enough to make the 'Start the Revolution!' a banner heading, which also got red flagged by Homeland agents while checking the Net. Dr. Langston's words had rung true, about Ian having the gift to entice readers to keep reading his off-the-cuff postings, in which he ridiculed those in power and went after the 1%, which is what the 99% (since history has abounded) really wanted.

Knowing of Street's daily daring-dos got Ian noticed by not only those hurt by the economy, but also by those doing the hurting. Ian's angle to posting did make the 1% a bit uncomfortable. It was more than his in-depth explanation to the cause and effect of the '08 meltdown that got him noticed, since by then the '08 meltdown was old news. The Dow had since reached 20,000 points, and that meant everything was going up. He wrote about that, too.

It was the writing of a *new* meltdown looming, one that if not stopped, would make the '08 meltdown seem trivial, which brought more QYBers to the fold. Three thousand dollars in Association fines couldn't deter Ian from telling of what the future might hold, as a staggering 50% unemployment rate could be looming also, with no future growth to speak of. Writer's block didn't hit him then, but it did hit the next morning, sending him to paint his eight flower boxes a bright yellow, a color that infuriated Ms. Brown enough to hound Weaver again. Weaver was himself infuriated at Ian for having blown off his scheduled Board meeting.

Ian got a kick out of seeing a 'Help Wanted' sign on the lobby door of Diamond Bank. It was the first time he'd ever seen a help wanted sign posted on a bank. He was still smiling at that when entering Weaver's office. But his smile faded when seeing Weaver's face. The anger in the man's eyes kept Ian from sitting.

"Mr. Suarez, did *not* seeing *any* fences at DHE *not* tell ya something?" Ian got busy writing on his pad while Weaver talked. "Thanks to *your* fence, I got all of DHE on my back, including that damn neighbor of yours, Ms. Brown. You must take that fence down ASAP." ***Why no fence?***

"Still can't talk, eh? And why no fence? Because it's against the rules, is why. We decided early on when developing DHE that it would be more cost effective without fences. It plays better to the look of the place, you know, nature and all. So no fences. That's why we don't allow any pets. You got enough squirrels out there to keep you company. Besides, no fences is in your deed restrictions."

Deed restrictions? "In your handbook." ***Handbook?***

"Please don't play coy with me, Mr. Suarez. Handbooks are in the manager's office. I remember telling you to pick one up when you moved there." ***I don't remember you saying that.***

Weaver looked down at his desk calendar to see what more he'd written on Ian. Weaver didn't live at DHE, so whether he knew of Ian grabbing a rules handbook or not wasn't on him. His concern was the two-thirds mortgages his bank held on DHE homeowners. He didn't want any more defaulting mortgages to occur, especially when getting ready to cut out once unloading himself of his pocket mortgages, which he hoped would be soon. But in the meantime, Weaver needed to keep the peace at DHE in order to continue living peacefully in his luxurious sprawl of a ranch home outside of town.

"And Mr. Suarez, what's this about your driveway still being red?" ***Call me Ian.*** "So what's this about a red driveway, *Ian?*"

Its terracotta. Not red. "Whatever; terracotta, white, blue, pink, it's gotta be Seagull Gray. You gotta re-stain it, and you gotta do it quick. The Board's hounding me about that, too, which, by the way . . ." ***I was too busy with my site for any meeting.***

Weaver let out an exasperated sigh when reading that. "I can't believe how many people you're pissing off out there, in what, like only five months of living at DHE?" Ian started to write, but Weaver stopped him. "Forget all that writing nonsense. Just get to making things right out there. Go see our Board Treasurer, Mr. Green. He's the first house past the rec area pool. He owns the store in town where you can get the right color for your driveway. You can also start by getting him on your good side. Or his good side. Whatever. See Helen before you leave for Mr. Green's number."

Ian's anger led him to attempt speaking his first words since leaving the COL. "But I . . . like my . . . driveway red." He regretted it immediately after doing it, the pain it caused his throat being that bad.

"Sounds like you best stick to writing, Mr. Suarez, I mean, Ian."

Ian at that point would rather have had Weaver just go back to calling him Mr. Suarez.

"By the way Ian, blowing off our meeting was not a smart thing to do." Weaver feigned impatience by looking at his watch. "Well, I got no more time for this now. I got a closing in an hour and I need to get ready for that. You also need to pay your fines. We're not erasing them from our books, so don't think we are. And pissing off the Fire Marshal wasn't a smart thing either." Weaver stood to put on his suit. "I can't waste any more time with you. Just don't forget our talk." *I never thought I'd get fined for burning leaves.*

"You might have trouble speaking, but you're not blind. You do know about forest fires, don't you?" Weaver humphed while putting on his suit. "I'm surprised the Marshal didn't arrest you right then for burning without a permit." Ian hated Weaver's patronizing tone and it showed in his face. "Look, just start to make things right with your neighbors, will ya, Ian? Get your driveway back to gray, take down your fence, and quit annoying people, *especially* Ms. Brown. Got it?"

Can't re-stain in this weather we're having.

"Okay, I'll give you that. But soon as the weather clears, you get on it. Go get your stain from Mr. Green. That'll help. In the meantime, take down your fence." *Critters will get at my pumpkin patch.* "Oh, I'm glad you mentioned that, cause I'd almost forgotten; flowers are okay, but not a pumpkin patch. I mean, what is it with you and growing vegetables? Is it something to do with you being Cuban or something? You don't live in a farming community, you know. Simple gardening's okay, but that's it."

Ian wrote nothing after that. He didn't want to let on about his having just bought a red paneled shed for the yard, red to match his driveway and window shutters.

"Just check with me first about anything you might still have up your sleeve, Mr. Suarez, uh, I mean, Ian. Okay?" Weaver held the door open for Ian. "And don't forget to go see Mr. Green, and that doesn't mean paint something else green." Weaver chuckled at his own jest while walking alongside Ian to the lobby, where he made sure Ian got Green's number.

But Ian was determined not to re-stain or re-paint anything. He liked the work he'd done, getting his driveway to look so uniform, and his house *was* starting to shape up *his* way. Plus spending an additional $600 on more stain was out of the question. *"Start the revolution, remember Ian?"* This was of the rare times when he agreed with his voices.

"**W**hat were you thinking when moving this *nut* next door to me, Dick?" Weaver had been more friends with Ms. Brown's late husband than with her, and he hated the way she said Dick. He tolerated her calls, but was at his wits end with her constant texts, especially while standing in line to board another plane to New York. Weaver could still remember the time Ms. Brown had been voted off the Board for causing trouble among Board members. It was obvious she still hadn't learned to deal with people.

"And he acts crazy, Dick."

Weaver was brought from his reverie by her shouting.

"You ask me, he's on some kind of drugs, is what he is. Maybe he's making drugs in the house, Dick."

Good thing no one's asking you, Emily.

"A walking liability is what you got living next door to me, Dick. And how in the hell did you get him approved for living here anyway? He's too young for living here."

Weaver couldn't take it anymore. "Listen Emily; your neighbor's a done deal, so please, just bake a pie and go over and give it as a gift or something. You can do that, can't you Emily?"

"Bullshit to that, Dick. And from now on, its Ms. Brown to you, not Emily; at least not until you clear *your* mess, *Dick!* You either lay down the law on *your* boy, or so help me, I'll find someone in town who will, and you know I will. I mean, just look at the fiasco he started with burning them leaves. What's next? He starts another fire and takes my house with it? Bullshit to that. Remember the rules, Dick. You sold him the place. Remember the rules."

Weaver didn't doubt that Ms. Brown would cause trouble. She wasn't known as witch-bitch for nothing. But Weaver had too much on his plate to bother with her troubles. *Plus the man's disabled.* "Look Emily, Ms. Brown, whatever you want me to call you these days; I'll have a serious heart-to-heart with Mr. Suarez once I get back. But right now I gotta go. It's my turn at check-in before I board."

"Fix your mess, Dick." Emily Brown just wouldn't quit.

"For crying out loud, Emily; will ya give it a rest already? Why not try that neighborly love I just told you about?"

"Neighborly love my ass."

"He's already been fined. What more you want?"

"Screw neighborly love, and screw you, Dick! I'm going ahead and seeing someone in town over this. I got your ass with his driveway still being red."

"The weather's been bad these days, Emily. The guy can't paint in this weather. You know that. Look, I got airport security looking at me funny. I'll talk with Mr. Suarez soon as I'm back. Promise."

"So Suarez, huh? Is he Mexican or something?"

"You really gotta stop, Emily"

"You're a sorrowful piece of work, you know that, Dick? Moving a damn Mexican next door to me!"

"Will you cut that out? And he's not Mexican. He's Irish and Cuban."

"Different slice of the same turd."

"I'm hanging up now, Emily. Deal with it."

"Ms. Brown to you, remember that, *Dick*."

"Whatever." Weaver left Ms. Emily Brown steaming in her racist juices.

The upside for Ian in those days was his QYB website continuing to grow. The downside was that Starling Circle had started to lose some of its luster. At least stickers sales had grown, but payment on stickers was still dismal. The honor system continued to show its flaws. But he still refused to set up PayPal or take plastic as payment. He saw using $5 credit to pay stickers as an antithesis to what QYB stood for, or so his enemy mind made him believe. But printing and mailing charges were still running him an average of $3,500 a month and he was already behind a month for starting the New Year. His print shop buddy was a godsend though, floating him what he needed to get people their stickers. But it still took imploring QYBers to follow through on paying. Ian wrote the following on his PFD webpage . . .

IRSuarez@QYB.com: Ian here. Say listen folks, stickers are running low again and I can't continue to print and mail them on *my* dime. I hate to sound like *I'm* bitching, but do remember, we all have a *revolution* to grow.

The message did help. People began sending in more money, with some folks even sending in extra as a donation to QYB, which also got flagged by Homeland and sent directly to Revenue.

Ian's computer crashed again after his 'help with sticker sales' message. It was the fourth crash in as many months. Now his computer was past 90-day warranty. The repair cost was $200 (a defragging issue) plus an additional

$200 for his webmaster to carry QYB again. It was back to the library in the meantime. But at least January brought an additional 20,000 new subscribers, which helped ease the suffering from a best money could buy computer.

It was when having coffee with his friend Nancy Smith that he learned about DHE being a bird sanctuary. *Makes sense to me. I was wondering why all the streets had bird-names.*

"I noticed you haven't repainted your driveway yet, Ian."

And I'm not going to. He didn't stick around to argue the point with his friend. He had other stuff to do.

He headed to town where he bought a large birdbath at auction for $500. He had the triple-tiered bath, weighing in excess of a thousand pounds, delivered to the house. The bath also came with circulating pump and a light kit. As soon as he had it delivered, he went to digging a trench for burying his piping and lights. But while digging, he accidentally nicked his main water line, which caused his yard to flood. Ms. Brown couldn't get on the phone quick enough to holler at Weaver about Ian's birdbath, while also telling of his flooding the yard. In the meantime, Ian got a plumber to fix his leak and while the man worked, Ian finished laying out his piping and wiring his bath. Ian filled in the trench as soon as the plumber was done. He hit a switch and voilà . . . pump and lights worked beautifully.

The fines for no permits on electrical and plumbing came the following week. He looked forward to shoving those fines in the drawer when seeing how many birds had started to gather in his new birdbath. *After all, it is a bird sanctuary, isn't it?*

This and everything he'd done thus far seemed logical enough to him, just not to the Board, or to the constantly complaining Ms. Brown, who continued to leave angry messages on Weaver's voicemail. (She did get to snicker when seeing how angry Ian became when getting more fines for his birdbath.) This was also when the DHE grounds keepers stacked Ian's steppingstones back onto his property. This brought a labor charge, which technically was a fine, $250 for labor, which too got shoved in the drawer. It didn't bother Ian any that the stones were back in his yard. He just wound up using them to enlarge the base of his birdbath.

Having birds around gave Ian reason for continuing his humming exercises. He was humming along with the Jays, Bluebirds, Robins, Yellows, Reds, and all sorts of South American go-betweens while rescreening when Weaver showed up. With Weaver came the rain.

Chapter 26

Ian's vocal cords weren't quite up to full strength when Weaver showed up, but they were strong enough to allow him a few words without needing his writing pad. It was a good thing he could talk a little, cause it didn't look like Weaver would have allowed him much time to write. Weaver walked up while Ian was busy putting in the lower half of the screen door.

Ian noticed Ms. Brown smiling smugly from her window while partaking in what she hoped would be a total reaming by Weaver.

"So I see you're still causing trouble out here, eh Mr. Suarez?"

"Ian . . . remember?" His voice was weak, but at least heard.

"So finally you speak."

Ian pinched his fingers together as to say a little.

"Well that's good, Ian; so now you can explain to me why your fence is still up, without me waiting for you to write." Weaver's tone was insultingly stern.

"My . . . fence?" Ian played dumb.

"What, from voice, to deaf now? You heard me Ian. Yes, your fence."

"Please . . . I really . . . got no time . . . for this today." Ian pointed at the gathering storm clouds. "Weather's . . . coming." Ian had to take a moment to massage his throat. "Plus . . . my fence . . . I have . . . to sell . . . on eBay. Now . . . can I finish? Before . . . it rains?" Ian *so* wanted to speak, but it was tough with his throat already sore.

Weaver took notice of Ms. Brown coming from her house to sit on one of her patio chairs. He waved to her, but she didn't wave back. He turned back to Ian and said, "Can we go inside and talk?"

"Uh . . . I'd rather . . . we didn't."

Weaver was surprised at Ian not allowing him into his house.

"Well, okay then; I guess I'll just say what I came to say out here."

"No . . . you don't . . . understand. It's not . . . that I don't . . ."

"Forget I asked, Mr. Suarez. Just listen."

"Please . . . Ian. Remember?" The reason Ian didn't want Weaver going inside was because, much like his adoptive parents, he too was using patio furniture as house furniture. He made quick work of installing his lower screen by expertly using his rolling tool while Weaver talked. "I still got plenty of residents complaining about you here, Ian."

"Complaining?"

Weaver pointed at all the building material stacked underneath the carport. "For starters, most folks here would've just gotten the maintenance guys to do their screening." Weaver pointed at Ian's fence. "But *that's* your biggest problem right now. I thought I was clear when saying I wanted your fence gone by the time I got back from my trip."

Ian gave the lower half of his screen door a final squeeze with his tool before answering. "You just . . . heard me say . . . I got to sell it . . . on eBay." Ian massaged his throat while pointing at the clouds. Rain had already begun. "Storm . . . coming."

This got Weaver angry. "Your fence needs to go *now*."

Ian thought to allow his banker in the house, but it was embarrassing enough watching his friend Nancy, whenever she came for coffee, struggling to stay seated comfortably in his plastic chairs. He was counting on sticker sales one day to afford him furniture, but thus far sticker sales hadn't made him any money.

The sprinkling of rain got heavier.

"And there's also your fines, which you have to pay," said Weaver.

Ian took from his work apron a rag to wipe clean his hands, before saying, "Is this . . . where I . . . pucker up?"

"Pucker up? Oh, you'll be doing more than puckering up, if you don't start making things right out here. And Mr. Green says he hasn't seen you at his store yet. What's with you? First your fence. Then your driveway. Now you got this huge ass birdbath pissing people off. Really; what's with you? Now do you see why you're getting so many fines?"

"I can't . . . afford . . . any fines."

"That's not *my* fault." Weaver's tone stayed angry. "And it's also not *my* fault, you continuing to blow off our Board meetings, when we're only trying to help." Instead of responding to that, Ian surprised Weaver by pointing at Ms. Brown and asking, "Is she . . . a member . . . of your Board?"

"No."

"Good. Cause she's . . . a lousy enough . . . neighbor." Ian's voice was near hoarse now.

"Funny that, Ian, cause Ms. Brown says pretty much the same about you." Weaver looked over to Ms. Brown and waved at her again. She still didn't wave back. *What a bitch* thought Weaver while turning back to Ian. "Your neighbor's not the issue here, Ian. You are." The rain was starting to turn heavy, wetting Weaver's suit, which he hated. He took out his key fob and started his car remotely.

"You're making me to regret having sold you this house."

"You had . . . no problem . . . taking my money . . . for this house." Ian was then needing to squeeze his throat to get the words out. "So don't . . . give me that. And I am no fool. This . . . isn't . . . about . . . some fence . . . or paint . . . so what gives?"

Weaver instead took that as his cue to leave. Ian had hit a little too close to home for Weaver's liking, who spoke while heading to his car, with Ian in tow. "Too many complaints about you, Ian. And you had also best start getting right with the Board, or your troubles are going to grow." Ian turned to Ms. Brown and gave her an exaggerated wave. Weaver had started getting into his car by then. He was a big man, so it took a moment to get comfortable. "Ian, please leave that woman alone. She's enough trouble already without you stirring her up. Be more friendly."

"No . . . being friendly . . . with that woman."

Weaver hadn't heard him over the rumble of his V-12.

"What did you say? Oh never mind; look, just best start with taking down them bricks around your columns. You should have never done that in the first place. My insurance guy would go apeshit if seeing them bricks on your columns."

"Why?"

"*Why?* Because he'd consider them as projectiles, is why. Storms, Mr. Suarez. You know the drill. And I hear the grounds people had to lift *your* steppingstones from the pond? I believe a labor bill is due on that also."

"Already . . . got it."

"Then makes things right by paying it." Weaver had his car in reverse when saying, "And do something about them flower boxes of yours. That yellow's hideous. And don't forget . . ." he hit the gas, "to pay your fines!"

But Ian was too shocked to answer because right then he saw Weaver's diamond cluster ring. *It can't be!* Ian wanted so badly to get another look at Weaver's ring, *pouring rain be damned,* but Weaver was already hydroplaning out of Starling Circle. The ring would lead Ian to Google search Weaver, and in the process, found out a little too much about Weaver's dealings with members of the Prince Sanford Group. Prior to Ian going back inside, he took from his car a QYB sticker and went and stuck it on Ms. Brown's Cadillac.

*   *   *

Ian started the year steeped in debt, which by February was even worse. Sticker and mailing fees alone were costing him $7,000 a month. This, along with his near $3,000 monthly living expenses was making life tough. Sticker sales *had* increased, but not enough to help him financially. His print shop buddy allowed him extra time to pay his bill without incurring a fee, but it still troubled Ian enough to remind his QYBers to please pay for their stickers. It was thanks to his buddy that the stickers were getting mailed, and so he started his posting by thanking his print shop buddy by name. Eighty thousand QYBers read his post, which at the start of March was nearing 100,000 subscribers. He was back to showing the fallacies of the honor system, on a night when he was required to show up for another DHE Board meeting.

His posting read:

IRSuarez@QYB.com: So now you know who is responsible for mailing you my stickers. But my print shop buddy and his family have to eat also. So while you think on that, I have it on good authority that the powers that be have also noticed my stickers, which I believe are a great way for breaking our great society of its lethargy ingrained by the G and the conglomerate media. Quit Your Bitching and Start the Revolution is all about breaking rank, and 80,000 of you seem to agree. So how about it? Can you *please* send in your

$5 pledges for the stickers so that I can continue to print more? Money order and checks are fine. Heck, cash is fine, too, if you can find a way of keeping your money from being scanned by the USPS. I'm Ian and I'm *OUT!*

His posting worked. It even got an additional 30 bloggers to help with his online blogging chats, and to help spread more the message of QYB.

It was his off-the-cuff, by the seat-of-his-pants, risqué, in your face writing that continued to gain him attention. His readers were not of the low-information voter kind, but mostly those who had either lost their jobs, were about to lose their jobs, or were living from paycheck to paycheck as part-time workers trying to keep up with full-time bills. These were the perfect folks for wanting a revolution, any revolution, so long as it brought food to the table and some monetary gains. It had been a while since people had been able to save any money. But Homeland saw it differently. In Ian they saw a militant, especially when teaming up with sites like Rage.com, Militantstrike.com, and Liberty.com. Liberty's owner and publisher, Mike St. Donovan, became good online friends with Ian, which was a bad thing for Ian, since all three radical sites, including Mike's, were already on Homeland's watch list.

It continued being Ian's knowledge of banking and his history in finance, albeit a disaster in the end, plus his spot-on estimation of where Wall Street was headed (some of that learned during his early morning wagering days with Vazquez) that continued to work in his favor. His countering the pundits' glass-half-full promises to a nation bordering on financial ruin made his message clear: To overflow the glass, changes had to be made. His classmates still working on Street helped him to deliver his message, but most had to do it on the sly, since Ian had become persona-non-grata to most of Street's 1%.

Ian was always about people-speak. His Posted for Discussion page proved he was all about people-speak, while his home page he kept loaded with topics of discussion. But he was still irked, to the point of sometimes ruining his concentration while writing, about the $4,000 in fines that were lying in his kitchen drawer. The stress from that alone kept his voices humming . . . until shouting on the day his mortgage bill came with a late fee. Ian couldn't get to the phone quick enough to complain to Weaver.

"Oh, so *now* you want to talk, eh Mr. Suarez? And yes, that's a late fee for last month's payment."

"But I . . . made the payment."

"Yeah, but it was late, *duh!* It's funny though, you blowing off our meetings, but now find time to call me. Well, the bad news is, it is what it is."

"I won't . . . pay the late fee."

"Then my bank will continue to add interest and penalties. See where I'm going with this?" Weaver's voice turned even more threatening. "This is what happens when you don't play by the rules, Mr. Suarez. And while on the subject of money, this year's homeowners fee is due. Best not think to blow that off too, or you'll be seeing a lien on your house."

"But I paid . . . last year's fee. I moved here . . . in June . . . I should have . . . a six month credit."

"Oh, so now you want a credit, eh? You're a hoot; you know that, Mr. Suarez? You make like our fines are fantasy, and still expect what, favors? I think that lightning strike that hit you fried your noggin."

"I'm not . . . asking for favors. I'm not . . . asking for credit. I'm asking . . . to be left alone."

"Sounds to me like you ruined that already, Mr. Suarez."

Ian was about to mention the ring, but thought it best to keep that as a hidden weapon of knowledge. As for Weaver . . .

Weaver had his own agenda involving Ian. He didn't want to let on about the two liens already working their way against 34 Starling Circle, or his mother-in-law who had already shown interest in 34 Starling Circle as payment for the loan she'd made him when he had to hurry back to Florida with her daughter.

"The DHE Board wants their fines paid, Mr. Suarez. You caused enough trouble earning them, so it's time you paid them."

"So, is this . . . you cheating me . . . out of *more* of my money?"

"What the hell, Mr. Suarez; you're a trip, you know that? If you're talking about the homeowner's fee, everyone has to pay. You're no exception. Besides, you've already pissed off our Treasurer, Mr. Green, so you can't expect any extension there. Whatever money you have over on last year's fee, will be applied to your fines. End of story. And by the way, Green says he still hasn't seen you in his store."

"And he's *not* . . . going to see me . . . in his store. And if . . . you're trying . . . to make this . . . a Peter stealing . . . to pay Paul . . ."

"Ha! A real trip, you are. And steal you must, if you consider me Paul." That's when Ian hung up. He'd had enough of Weaver for one day. For lots of days, in fact.

His one bright spot that day was finding his P.O. Box in town loaded with payments on stickers; $2,000 worth in money orders, checks, and several hundred dollars in cash (people had slipped cash in between folded print paper to avoid scanners). Ian was ecstatic at seeing both the money and the wanting of more stickers. He rushed right over to his print shop buddy and handed him the $2,000, which made his buddy happy, since his bills were piling up, too, and the money helped with that.

But Ian's bright spot moment vanished when finding another fine in his mailbox for the eight flower boxes and their unapproved yellow color. The second envelop had the new homeowners fee in it, and it too, had an increase of $200 over last year. Ian was back to grinning and bearing it.

Hindsight would show that Ian should've broken his thinking here, regardless of his differences with Weaver as his banker and holder of his mortgage, or that as Association President, that Weaver had his back. But Weaver wasn't about having anyone's back but his own. That's how Weaver rolled. Ian should've known this, especially after knowing of Weaver's ring (though not yet knowing of Weaver's matching lapel pin). Ian was still under the impression that his future at DHE would brighten once QYB made him a profit. Hindsight also would prove that Ian should have overruled that thinking, but didn't.

Ian managed to get from some of his old classmates the sales numbers to the previous year's Christmas shopping season; numbers so dismal that major shareholders and government pundits would have rather not had Ian made them known to the public. But made public the numbers were, thanks to Ian and QYB. He followed that up with the dismal shopping numbers of the Valentine's Day sales also. Major retailers were showing a definite decline in sales, though one wouldn't know it by the Dow index.

IRSuarez: It just goes to show you that the Dow no longer speaks for the common man. Middle America continues taking it on the chin, and instead of moving forward, this economy looks like it's moving sideways. (This post brought another 40,000 to the fold.)

The media, at the behest of the current administration, continued their 'rose colored glasses' spiel to a future that wasn't so rosy. Ian kept it real though, as much as people hated to read about it, and it was his real-spiel that grew QYB to 200,000 in March. He missed seeing it go past 200,001 because his best money could buy computer right then crashed again!

Another repair and server bill came next. But at least from the library he got to see QYB go past 250,000 subscribers with most having or wanting stickers. He was now making just enough to pay his repair and server bill. That's also around the time Ms. Jenna Davis came into the picture.

He could never figure out, as computer savvy as he was, how Ms. Jenna Davis got his personal email account. But he was glad that she did. Jenna's attached photos are what did it. Her first email to him came with a straightforward message of wanting to know more personal things about him and with the possibility of meeting sometime in the near future. Then came the photos. Wow! It was all Ian could say before being left speechless because of her provocative pictures. It was hard to believe she was 40 with a body like hers.

Ian tossed caution to the wind once Jenna promised that all things were possible if they hooked up. But she, too, had her agenda. She was sweet with the words, sounding sweeter still upon their first phone chat. Her British accent had been a bit difficult to work through, her high-pitched voice at times sounding sort of metallic, which made reading her tone difficult. But Ian had her pictures to stare at while talking and that made up for it.

"But I still don't understand why it sounds like you're talking though a can." Jenna noticed the low battery indicator on her device, which explained why Ian was hearing a can echo.

"Look love, I'm in London, which isn't right around the corner from Florida, you know." She would call him 'love' a lot, which he liked, and it was her mentioning of Google searching his real father in wanting to know more about Ian that he liked also.

Though she had definitely baited Ian with hook, line, and sinker, Jenna was careful not to let on about her agenda. Playing the part of a liberated woman, with no kids, though enticing Ian into believing there might be kids with him, if their relationship ever got that far, got her hooks deeper into him. Jenna had already told Ian she was the owner of a multimillion-dollar software company based in England, which bore her name. Ian had already checked to confirm that and found the Davis company website to be quite impressive.

Ian pleaded to meet her in London. But her busy schedule was her excuse for keeping her distance. At least for a while, anyway.

Jenna had figured Ian to Google search her, and that's why she used the Betty Boop cartoon caricature as her profile pic. Ian asked, "Why Betty Boop?" Jenna explained that it was a privacy issue.

JennaCal412: While on the subject of privacy, as a belated birthday gift to you, my love, I am sending you something in the mail.

What she sent which arrived first class and quickly, was a laptop with a card that read: To my sweet Ian, this is for those times when your nasty PC breaks down again. The tracer software installed in the laptop was concealed by a Union Jack icon in the taskbar. Also, Jenna's attachments sidetracked Ian from following her attached URL address. Had he followed the URL, he would have found the pictures all originated from a brothel in Amsterdam. But he had an admirer who played as if after his heart, and that was good enough for him.

Chapter 27

He'd driven by the Mega furniture

store dozens of times before finally deciding to go inside and browse. While he was parking, he noticed store employees replacing the previous month's huge 'Valentine's Day Sales' banner with a new 'March Madness Sales' banner. *Anything to get sales these days* thought Ian.

February's and thus far March's QYB stickers sales had afforded him a little pocket money for buying a few pieces of furniture. Not much, but some. He *so* wanted to at least replace his air mattress with a *real* bed, an entire bedroom set if he could swing it. *A sofa would be nice, too,* he thought, while checking his to-do list as he entered the store. But checking store prices quickly showed him that his $3,000 pocket money wasn't going to buy him much. A memory of his friend Nancy struggling to sit comfortably on his hard plastic chairs made him also wanting chairs, so he looked at dining room chairs, along with an array of nice dining tables. *I could easily put my computer on a dining table like these here.* His current worry was having his plastic table collapse with his recently repaired PC still on it. That got him looking at new desks, too. But the prices of the desks told him he would have to wait until a few months for a desk. *Nothing like my custom desk from years back, but good enough.*

Walking into one of the largest chain of furniture stores, while holding a list, was like a target for the store's commission-based salespeople, of which the leading salesperson, a woman named Melanie, was already on her way to

Ian. She'd spotted him since parking his car. She saw his list and asked for it to better show him around the *entire* store. Melanie was in no time chatting him up as if they were old friends, with *his* list still in *her* hands.

Melanie wasn't tops in sales for nothing. She had started out in cars sales, so the routine of closing sales was a key trait of hers. She also had her store manager, Frank, watching her back, so all bases were covered. Frank was already at the second floor banister waiting for the signal to move in with the freebies that would usually get people to buy. Frank's store wasn't the regional top selling store by luck, either.

Melanie went right for the jugular when knowing of Ian's $3,000. That's when she started in with the store's 'buy now/pay later' mantra, and . . . telling him he could keep his money, "so long as you pay the taxes on your purchase today. You keep the rest and have no payments for 12 months." Ian told her how he felt about credit, but his was a *long* furniture list. "Plus the bedroom set you want alone is $3,000, uh, Mr. Suarez, right?" She had a way of batting her eyes.

"Call me Ian."

"Okay then Ian, but our 'buy now/pay later' credit plan is perfect if you want everything now. All I would need is to run your credit." She ended her spiel by batting her eyes again.

By then they were at sofas.

"Remember Ian, you can have all that's on your list and even have it delivered to your home in just days, if your credit's approved. You know that, right?"

"Sure I know that, uh, what was your name again? Sorry."

"It's Melanie." She did the eye thing again, but inside was pissed at Ian for having forgotten her name already. *Not a good sign.* Sales was all that mattered to Melanie. Ian could tell by her game face. He'd seen the same look on some of his RMF people back in the day.

"Heck Ian, I might even get my manager Frank to okay maybe a delivery by as early as tomorrow, if we have all you want in stock. How's that for quick?" They were at dining room sets then.

His falling in love with a pickle-stained dining table with matching chairs is what got him thinking about 'buy now/pay later'. Melanie had already gotten some of his info, but would need more to run his paperwork through for approval. She bid her time for that, not wanting to ruin her chance at a sweet commission. She let the furniture do the talking, while working numbers in her head. Next was the desk department. Ian was now up to $10,000, which included a living room set.

Ian was slowly sold on the fact that he could furnish nearly his entire house if getting his credit approved, so he gave Melanie all the information needed for running his credit. *Though it's $10,000, I should be able to pay it off with sticker money before the first payment's due. Unless of course, I get declined.* He had no worries there, as Melanie was already returning with a smile on her face. "Well guess what, Ian?" She didn't wait for him to answer. "You've been approved for your entire purchase!"

"My *entire* purchase? But I haven't decided to buy anything yet. How about I go home and think about it, then I call you maybe tomorrow?"

"Hey, no sweat. But if you're looking to beat me up a little, I can go see my manager and see if I can get him to knock off 10% for you being a new customer and all. How's that? But you gotta sign today." Ian was still fighting his inner conscience when Melanie went in for the kill. "Heck, you know what, Ian? I see my manager right over there; I'll go talk to him and see what else I can toss in with your purchase. Who knows, maybe we can even get some of your pieces to you tonight. Don't go away." Ian still wanted time, and even thought of leaving right then, but a voice reminded him it was a *whole lot of nice furniture.* Melanie returned moments later with an even bigger smile on her face. She was already thinking of spending her near $400 commission from Ian's sale. "Guess what?"

"Oh no, that's how you started when telling me I was approved." His reply was simple lighthearted facetiousness. "Okay, Melanie, go ahead and tell me."

"Not only is everything on your list in stock, but Frank says we can have you delivered tomorrow." Ian still had slightly cold feet.

"I don't know, Melanie. It's still ten grand, you know. Look, how about I just buy the bedroom set today, which is something I *can* afford, and I'll come back in a week or two and see you again."

But there was no way Melanie was letting Ian walk out the door that easily. "Ian, you got a year to make your first payment. What? You don't like keeping your money? Keep the cash in your pocket. You're already approved. Just pay the taxes and everything is on its way to your house." The overhead speakers suddenly shouted out Melanie's name. "Customer on line two for you, Mel." But Melanie never even bothered to pick up. This should've told Ian something, but it didn't.

"Alright Ian. And for that, I might as well tell you that Frank approved you for an area rug. Free of charge. Just go pick it from our rug collection. In the meantime, I'll go set you up in our computer." And like that, the deed was done. She was exaggerating, though. Discounts, freebies, and 'buy now/pay later' was how the store got 90% of its business.

That's when Ian read the fine print. "Melanie! This fine print says I get hit with 23% interest if not paying off the ten grand! Are you crazy? I'm not giving away my money!"

"Hey, but we talked about this. You were going to have it paid off before your first payment, remember? You won't have any interest to pay if you do that." But Ian kept holding onto the paperwork. "I don't know, Melanie." But then his mind did a strange thing; it led him to ask Melanie if she had any kids.

"Kids?"

"Yeah, you know . . . mouths to feed."

Ian's heart was at it again.

Melanie was surprised by the question, but quick on the draw.

"Uh, yes, of course. I got three kids, in fact. Why do you think I work 60 hours a week here?" Ian was more shocked to hear about her having 3 kids. "Three kids? But you don't look old enough to have three kids."

"Yeah, well that's kind of you to say that, but yep, I got three kids. So? Are we good?"

"Started young having kids, didn't you?"

"Too young. So am I putting you in the computer?"

"Guess I'm helping to feed your little ones if we do this, huh?"

Melanie *was* quick on the uptake there too. "You better believe it. You know the drill. No sell. No eat."

"I do indeed." Memory of his mother's charity fund and his bank employee fund was working on him again. "What more can you do for me before I say yes?"

"How about a pair of lamps for that bedroom set?"

"Done." A few minutes later and all the furniture was his, well, his and the store's credit department anyway. *But hey! At least I'll be sleeping good tomorrow.*

One thing that irked Ian before leaving the store was *how in hell does Revenue get theirs before I even get to lay my head on my new bed? Something's just not right with that.* Thinking of Melanie having money to put food on the table for her kids made him smile. But though his heart was in the right place, Melanie's wasn't. Melanie hadn't lied about having three little ones, per se, though the three had been taken from her and given to their biological father after she'd been ruled an unfit mother by the courts. As for Ian, his humanity had just shone through, and shown its flaws. But when it rains . . .

Across the street from the Mega furniture store was the town's largest car dealership, called Handel Motors. It too had sales banners flying. 'No Money Down.' 'As little as $99 down.' 'Zero financing (w.a.c.)' 'Overstocked and gotta move 'em!' 'Below factory invoice.' 'Make your own deal.' Ian walked past all sorts of fluttering sales banners when entering the Handel showroom.

Here also, a salesperson was onto him right away. The thought was that Ian was there to use the new 'cash for clunkers II program' for trading in his car. But even with using the latest G program, the best deal Ian could get on a late model used cruiser was 21.9% financing. "What! So where's my 'make my own deal' come in?" Ian was still reading through the paperwork while the Handel finance guy said, "Sorry, Mr. Suarez. Banks are hurting, too. Your credit score didn't come back high enough to qualify for anything less."

"And that's *with* a discount?" Ian was again thinking of leaving, until looking out the window and seeing a Handel Motors service tech already switching his clunker plate to the late model cruiser. The finance guy was antsy for his lunch break.

"So, are we good? Do I run your paperwork through? Of course it will require the $2,200 you mentioned earlier as a down payment."

"I don't know . . ." Ian did like the look of the cruiser. *What's not to like? It's a million times better than what I've been driving, and it's got a/c.*

"I can float you an extra month before making your first payment, but that's it, Mr. Suarez. If you're good with that, then I'll need you to sign here." Ian handed over what was left of the original $3,000 he'd left home with. A free fill-up and he was done.

Ian's conscience tore him to pieces while driving home. But he won over his conscience by convincing himself that the purchases he'd made, albeit all on credit, had been good for the economy. *I think I did my part to grow this local economy.* But the credit thing still annoyed him though.

Back at Handel Motors, the finance guy was sharing a laugh with his co-workers after telling of how he'd fooled Ian into believing the kids in the photo on his desk were his, when in fact the office had been borrowed for loan signing. "But hey, anything to get a sales these days, right guys?" Their laughter ended at the sight of a new victim coming through the door.

Ian by then was in the local supermarket shopping for a turkey to cook the next day, where he would invite his Smith friends over. He had to use his debit card since he'd no pocket money left.

But his feel-good moment would end the moment he got home and checked his mailbox. Among the stack of junk mail was an Association letter telling of his liens, another from Diamond Bank reiterating the liens, and even worse, a new Revenue letter telling of his supplemental income possibly being garnished.

The only way for him to blow off steam was to do a little house painting. After painting his front door a glossy green, he went and dug a hole in the front yard where he put in a new flagpole, which he'd bought days earlier on sale at the Smiths' store. The pole was for flying his new QYB logo flag (given to him as a gift from his print shop buddy). Both the flag and his flashy green door got Ms. Brown calling Weaver again. But Ian had plenty of Jenna emails with more photo attachments waiting for him to care much about how Ms. Brown felt.

Stress from his supplemental income about to be garnished *did* affect his health, though. Staring at a computer screen for hours at a time, while drinking more soda than water, did not help his diabetes. But he did have a miraculous level of energy for writing, hours upon hours until . . . lethargy set in. That's when he succumbed to looking through his Medicare handbook for a local endocrinologist.

"No, Mr. Suarez, the doctor will not see you without you first having your blood drawn. And no, he will not prescribe you anything until seeing you."

"But you said you already had my medical history from the COL, right?"

"Got it right here on my computer screen, Mr. Suarez. But you still gotta get your blood drawn. You can get that done at the local lab. That's no problem. But the doctor still needs to see your results before prescribing you anything."

"And the only appointment you have available is on the 30th?"

He felt queasy and his hand shook a little as he held the phone.

"Sorry, Mr. Suarez; that's the only date open for now. I can call you if someone cancels before then, but I wouldn't hold my breath. We're still getting loads of new patients from the healthcare law. We're still playing catch up with that."

"The healthcare law? But that was years ago."

"Still playing catch up, though."

"Can't you at least give me some sample packs of Glipizide or Metformin until I come in?"

"I wish I could, Mr. Suarez. But the pharmaceutical reps don't ever leave us samples of that stuff anymore. In fact, they barely leave us any samples at all these days. But remember, you live in an area of retirees, and lots of them have health issues. Add in them, and you can see why the long wait." She heard him sigh over the phone. "Look, I promise if someone cancels, I'll call you. Just not that a lot of folks are canceling these days. But listen, you start to feel worse, you get to the hospital. At least there they'll give you enough medication to hold you over until seeing us."

"You mean like go to the emergency room?"

"Only way they'll see you."

"You're kidding, right? I'll need a pillow and a blanket for that. No thanks, I'll pass on that."

"Well, I will be sure to call you if someone cancels."

"I'll keep my fingers crossed for that."

"You do that, Mr. Suarez. Either way, you're down for the 30th."

"Thanks so much for your time."

But an enemy mind that never rests, in a realm of its own reasoning, convinced Ian that if he gave up his snacks, in particular his favorite late night ice cream, that his sugar levels *would* get better. His actually feeling chipper on the 29th got him to blow off his doctor appointment *and* another Association Board meeting.

It started as a glitch in the car's onboard computer, caused by a tiny short circuit that altered the car's electrical system. The short even wound up affecting the car's gear shifting, and fouled the register readings of both the oxygen and fuel sensors. Even the car's timing was altered. Ian had to fight his car onto the service rack, to then deal with Randy, Handel Motor's service manager. Randy got Ian's cruiser up and running right again after some minor adjustments and a reset of the onboard computer. "But that's it, Mr. Suarez. No more freebies."

"What do you mean no more freebies? My car's only got 19,000 miles on it. It must have some sort of warranty for stuff like this, don't it? I mean, you hear about 36,000 mile coverage all the time."

"Not in your case. That's the problem with buying an 'as is' car, Mr. Suarez. What you need is extended warranty, and you'll need to see our finance guy for that."

"Hey, call me Ian."

"Okay, Ian. But the bosses will have my ass if you have any more problems and I fix you without you having warranty. Nothing free with the bosses around here, Ian."

"But Randy, 19,000 miles . . ."

"It's plenty of miles for trouble. But hey, maybe all it needed was a reset. Just see finance while I get you off the rack. They might have some discount going on extended warranties."

"Um, extended warranty . . . Sounds expensive."

"Well, you did buy an 'as is' car, Ian. Says here there was no first owner transfer on your vehicle."

"Whatever that means." But Ian did go see the fellow who'd laughed about the photos on his desk, and where moments later he was raising his voice. "What! $2,200 *more* for warranty? Tell me you're kidding." Handel's finance guru was at the time inundated with paperwork and didn't want to bicker with Ian over something that might net him, at best, a $50 commission. "We've got cheaper rates for lesser service, but it won't cover stuff like your transmission, which Randy seems to think might become the worst of your problems. Buy hey, I'm here until 6."

"Still $2,200 though."

"$2,800 if you want the Platinum plan, which is the one I would recommend. Covers most everything but a rental." Ian had money in his pocket from sticker sales, but nowhere near enough to splurge on a $2,800 warranty package.

"Forget it," Ian started for the door, "I'm sure whatever Randy did will work."

"Hope you're right, Mr. Suarez. But remember, repairs *are* costly."

"You don't have to remind me."

"Suit yourself. Just trying to help."

"Yeah, I've been getting a lot of that lately."

"Huh? I don't follow."

"Never mind."

On the way back to service, Ian noticed his old clunker still parked out near the back fence. *Doesn't look like they have much hope in selling my old heap.* (Fact was, his $2,200 down payment, plus his 21.9% interest on his car loan, *plus* the cash for clunkers credit the dealership did finagle the government out of, gave the Handel brothers the chance of making an additional $250 in scrapping Ian's heap. The junkyard just hadn't gotten around to picking up Ian's clunker.) But at least his new cruiser was running right after leaving service, though he did have to play off the slight hesitation in shifting as mileage related.

*   *   *

Jenna had done all she could to avoid meeting in person with Ian. He was angry about that, and with good reason, since their texting and online chats went on for hours. One night, they got into a spat after chatting for two hours, over her constantly wanting to know more about his father, the Wolfe. Jenna wanted to know all about his days as a kid in Cuba, but he had other postings to attend to, so he said goodnight, and signed off. Jenna wasn't too happy about that.

That night, he wrote about the damages QE4 would cause to the economy if approved. (QE 2 & 3 had seen trillions printed out and eased onto markets that only made the 1% within the 1% richer. The rest of it, the banks hoarded away. TARP hadn't even been included in all this benign printing, which had thus far devalued the dollar to 7 cent buying power from 25 ago.)

IRSuarez: Printing money for money's sake is a definite no-no, my friends. Just look at history. Remember Germany and their inflation crisis right after WWI? Germans needed a wheel barrel full of money just to buy bread. And what about Argentina and its stagflation days; where inflation got so bad that Argentine restaurants were raising prices *while* customers ate. We're doomed if we let the G continue to print more money. Those 12 chairs at the Federal Reserve are the only ones benefiting from these printouts now. Look at the hoarding that went on with QE3. I urge you to contact your representatives by mail, email, phone, or by text; camp out if you have to, whatever it takes to get them to vote 'NO' to QE4.

But QE4 passed anyway, and sure enough, as Ian had posted, the freshly minted greenbacks started right away to weaken the dollar even more.

His ex-banker talk, and the fact he'd lost his wealth to confiscations and fines, proved to the additional 500,000 new QYBers that he had nothing to gain by bad talking the economy. The economy was bad enough in itself without his having to say anything about it. But he had plenty to say about the direction the economy was headed.

He got another 500,000 subscribers in the month of April when posting about the bad blood QE4 had created with OPEC. As he predicted, OPEC's answer to the weakening dollar was to remove it as the standard and replace it with the new Riel. Now America was forced onto the liter system, which thus made a gallon of gas almost $9. It went from 'grin-and-bear-it' to 'grit-your-teeth.' Gun shop owners saw another record year in sales. Ian had predicted that, too. But it wasn't just citizens buying ammo. Homeland bought another 200 million rounds to add to the 200 million it had already bought back in 2012. (The Iraq war had 75 million rounds distributed to troops). Unlike citizens paying for their rounds in earnings, Homeland was still paying for its rounds courtesy of the U.S. taxpayer. Ian wrote about that, too.

He wanted more input from his classmates, Street info mainly, but some of his classmates went suddenly silent with the blogs as QYB was viewed as an anathema by their bosses. The warning to his friends was clear, either cease and desist with Ian and his QYB site, or lose their cushy Street jobs. Yet some of his classmates blogged on the sly anyway.

No sooner had he been getting the rundown on some more QE4 numbers, when Jenna suddenly wanted to chat. She sent a flirtatious email which she knew would entice him to sign off with his friends and chat with her (though she was still refusing his webcam requests). But that night, too, they argued.

IRSuarez: Quit asking me about my father. You're annoying me with that. You already know that I don't remember much about him. I was nine when he died. He's part of my past, much like my mom and brother are part of my past. Today is *my* future. Let's talk about that, and leave the past behind. Plus, what's so important about my Cuba days, anyway? You writing a book? (I meant that facetiously.) And why aren't we webcamming? I want to see you when talking to you. We got that technology, remember? Oh yeah, that's right, you *own* a software company. Come on Jenna, be nice and click on camera.

JennaCal412: We could be talking by phone, but you changed your number again.

IRSuarez: Hey, I got my privacy issues also, just like you. But I don't hide behind a cartoon character. But here's my new number, just for you.

He sent her his number, to which she replied,

JennaCal412: Good. Pick up when I call. *OUT!*

He didn't have to wait long. He picked up on the second ring. But their phone conversation didn't go much better than their chat email had gone, with Jenna's accent being even harder to decipher, and . . . there still being that strange reverberation background noise from their earlier phone conversations. That can sound. But at least he did have her on the phone, which meant something. "But Jenna dear, I'm just saying the sound of your voice is funny. You're in software; you can relate to something not sounding right. And I don't believe it's our connection. Tell you what, you sent me a laptop; I'll send you a new phone. How's that?"

Jenna was regretting having called. "New phone? Why?"

"Because that phone of yours makes you sound echoic and robotic and hard to understand."

"Uh, sorry love, but it's probably my phone's roaming signal. Plus the weather's got me rundown with the sniffles these days. Maybe that's what you hear. I envy you being in Florida."

"So come on over to Florida. You can stay with me until you get over your sniffles, hint-hint. Tell you what; let's just do some webcamming. Come on." Jenna knew to be careful here.

"Not with the way I look right now, we don't, love. I look like shit." (She made it sound like kite.) "Maybe when I'm feeling and looking better, we'll Skype."

"With as beautiful as your pictures are? I don't see the problem."

"Man after my own heart. But there's no way I'm putting on my web cam for you tonight."

"So when *are* we going to meet? You must have some stateside business that can bring you to me, don't you? I mean, I can rent us a car and drive us wherever you need to go."

"Ah, that's nice of you, dear. But why rent a car? Didn't you tell me you bought a car not so long ago?"

"I did. But it's been giving me problems lately. And there goes your voice, cutting in and out again." Her voice was cutting out because of low battery again.

"Listen love, I've got to ring off now. I got a meeting tomorrow and I still feel like shit. I need my beauty sleep. But I will web cam with you next week. In the meantime, keep my, I mean *your* laptop on, so I can send you some updates to your software. I notice your signal's been off these days."

"Now how in the world would you know that?"

Jenna just had herself a *duh* moment. But she regrouped quickly.

"I encrypted your laptop against theft, so I can tell by your signal pattern that it's not being used. Use it. It's a good laptop. My people will keep your software updated with the occasional download. But my, aren't *we* testy tonight." Her indicator light blinking quicker meant her voice was near garbled.

"I can barely make you out now, Jen. And no, I'm not testy; I'm just going gangbusters crazy with my site, plus having lots of problems with my homeowner's Association. And you're right. I have been keeping your laptop off, but I'll keep it on standby from now on. How's that? Jen? Jenna."

Jenna was gone.

It was right as he got up to hurry to the bathroom, that the back of the chair he was sitting in made a weakening sound, right before the arm of the chair broke off in his hand, and sent him falling to the floor!

It took a few minutes to let his anger settle before calling the furniture store. It took several minutes more to get Frank on the phone, during which time Ian started inspecting the other five chairs more closely. He found some that not only had loose arms, but two had loose legs also. That's also when he discovered that the chairs nor the table were of wood at all, but made of some fibrous pressboard plasti-blend material that once loose, was hard to re-bolt together. He gave the table a shake and found it a bit wobbly. *Oh-oh, I better check the rest of my stuff.* But by then, Frank was on the phone.

"I got a serious gripe with you, Frank."

"About what, Mr. Suarez?"

"I just had one of these marvelous chairs you sold me break on me. The dining table also has a leg on backwards. It isn't looking too good, either." Frank didn't make Ian's situation any better when checking his chair's stock number and finding that model had already been discontinued. "So what's that mean, Frank? I can't get a replacement for the one that broke?"

"I can give you a replacement. It just won't be the same chair. Just get in here. I'll fix you up."

"But I want a chair that matches, Frank."

"Just get in here. And I'll give you extra hardware for your other chairs, plus I'll have my boys stop by your house when they're in the area and take care of that table leg. Now listen, I really gotta go. I got the store *full* of people and I got Melanie out sick. But you get in here, alright?"

"This stuff's looking like junk, Frank."

"Oh, come on now, Mr. Suarez; one busted chair doesn't make them *all* bad. Just get in here." Ian sensed Frank was thinking sales.

"I'm not spending any more money, Frank."

"Shouldn't have to, if all we're doing is a swap."

"On a chair you can't exchange with an exact chair? How is that a swap?" But Frank had already hung up. That's when Ian went to checking all his furniture and found . . . his night table drawers were coming loose; the stitching to his sofa was coming undone; a coffee table leg didn't match the staining of the other three legs; even the teaser rug was starting to fray. Ian suddenly felt like the cartoon character that turns to a sucker pop during a *duh* moment, more *duh* when remembering his using credit to purchase the stuff he now considered junk. He felt like a real sucker then.

He did try tightening what he could, which was none, since the plasti-blend stuff got worse the more he tightened the bolts and screws.

That night, instead of continuing with QE4, he posted about the downside to purchasing with 'buy now/pay later' credit. He was amazed at how many other QYBers had been taken in by the same chain store's 'buy now/pay later' mantra. But as bad luck would have it, it also drew in his computer, for when coming from his bedroom after checking his night tables, he found that his PC had crashed again! He was fit to be tied after that. He suddenly felt like somebody was holding an effigy of himself over a fire and sticking pins into him good. Morning could not come quick enough.

He was in such a rush to head to town that he spilled his milk and cereal. Once he got outside and loaded his PC and busted chair in his car, the car wouldn't go into gear. He had to jam the shifter into drive and hold it there until getting to the local auto parts store, where he bought a bottle of Teflon sealer for the car's transmission. It did the trick, but it was still nerve-wracking to drive the car in traffic. He finally got to the electronics store, where he dropped his PC for yet another repair bill, before heading to Handel Motors. All service bays there were full, so he left his keys with Randy while he carried his chair across the street to Frank.

Things didn't go well there, either.

"For crying out loud, Frank, you said an exchange. I'm not dropping another $40 on a chair that doesn't match the others. Come on now; this isn't a swap." Frank was actually looking to pocket Ian's $40 for gas. "But Mr. Suarez, I'm giving you a $279 chair for just $40."

"Yeah, to replace a chair that's been discontinued, *duh*!"

"Look, $40, and forget the tax."

"Ooh, you better not let Revenue hear you say that."

"Oh, that's right. Your initials."

"Forget my initials, Frank. Look, I got a better idea; why don't you just take one chair off my bill, that's $239 for the chair, and we're good."

Frank had caught sight of a few browsing customers looking their way. "Uh, no Mr. Suarez, I can't do that. I don't even have a code for doing something like that."

"The hell, you say. Look, now you're starting to make me feel like I got taken by your 'buy now/pay later' scheme, so please, just do me right with the chair, will ya? If you don't do me right and remove $239 from what I owe, I walk, and if I walk, I don't pay. It's on you, Frank. I'm here for my chair." This got more browsing customers eavesdropping. "Hell Frank, even that freebie rug you gave me is starting to fray." Frank noticed the eavesdroppers.

"Mr. Suarez, first the chair and now the rug, too?"

"Told you Frank, this stuff of yours is junk."

Frank did the parting of the waves thing to show his store's large inventory. He did this more for the benefit of the eavesdropping customers. "You didn't think our furniture was junk when you picked it out."

"It took living with this furniture to find out it was junk, Frank."

"Come on, Mr. Suarez. Our furniture's top-notch, not junk. We've got tons of satisfied customers to prove it."

"Tons of 'buy now/pay later' customers, you mean," shot back Ian. "And your stuff's far from top-notch, my friend. And by the way, why is it you don't sell anything American here?"

"We've got American pieces. They're more expensive, but we got 'em."

"Yeah? Well I looked for American stuff in here, but didn't see any."

"Blah! I've got no time for this."

"That's because you got nothing that's made in America here. You know it. I know it. Not one tag in here says made in America."

"Look, Mr. Suarez; seems to me like maybe you need to deal with our customer service and settle things with them."

"You would go there, wouldn't you Frank. Well, that's a bad answer on your part. You're the store manager, for crying out loud. You can make things right *and* keep me as one of those satisfied customers you mentioned. So why are you annoying me with your lack of customer service skills? You think my spending $10,000 here was chump change? You should really try making me happy, not mad, Frank." Both men noticed the browsing customers now checking labels. Frank didn't like this at all. "Mr. Suarez, just call customer service and see what they can do for you. All I got is a chair, and I'm sorry it doesn't match."

"I really can't believe you just said that. Well, you know what Frank? Now I want you take back *all* the furniture I bought. In fact, I want you to send your truck to my house today; get all *your* stuff out of *my* house."

"Are you crazy?"

"Hell no, I'm not crazy. I'm just sick and tired of junk furniture. I can't trust sitting in one of your *glamorous* chairs for fear of them breaking; even the dining table's shaky, so hell yes, I want it all gone. I'll admit I should've done a better job of checking your stuff more closely before I signed on the dotted line. But the way you and Melanie worked me over, and what with your freebies and all, so long as I signed, yadayadayada . . ." it was Ian's turn to do the parting of the waves thing, ". . . just send your truck, Frank, so you can have more junk to sell." Frank was now regretting having gone after Ian's $40.

"Look, just take the chair and forget the $40. And bring in your rug. I'll swap that, too. But that's it, okay?"

"You really haven't been listening, Frank. Look, I hate to sound discourteous, but is there someone else here besides you that I can talk to over this? Someone with authority to send a truck?"

More heads turned at that.

"I'm the only manager here, Mr. Suarez, and I'm not sending any truck. You'll need corporate to send a truck, and they're not going to send one, either."

"You don't know me very well then, Frank."

"Mr. Suarez, I'm willing to give you the chair and swap the rug. What more do you want?"

"I don't want to pay for junk, and certainly not $10,000 for junk. Hell, at the rate my stuff is breaking, it will all be broken by the time the first payment's due! Just send the truck, Frank. That's what I want."

"I can't do that, Mr. Suarez. And as for crediting your account, I can't do that either. If I did, I'd have to do it for a whole lot of other folks."

"So then you *are* admitting your stuff's junk."

"I'm not admitting anything, and our stuff's not junk, so quit calling it that. Plus, how do I know that you didn't just break your chair to get out of paying for it?"

"And what . . . waste my time being here with you? Be real, Frank. My time's worth more than a chair. Your time is, too. That's why I don't understand why the hard time. You know, if it wasn't for the fact that I liked the pickling stain on my chairs and table, I'd just be buying me six *American* chairs, which I'll probably do anyway, and be done with it. But nope; I want *your* stuff out of *my* house."

"Ain't gonna happen."

"Oh, it's gonna happen, alright." Ian exaggerated his moving closer to Frank as if sharing a secret. "But you know what, Frank . . ." he said in loud enough voice for others to hear, ". . . if you're worried about me not letting on about you crediting my account, I'll be as quiet as a church mouse, so long as you do me right."

"But you signed a contract for your furniture. We didn't force you to buy."

"I see I'm getting nowhere with you."

An employee of Frank's tried saving the day by waving to him for help with a customer. "Sorry, Mr. Suarez, but I'm being called away."

Frank was already walking away while speaking. "I'll do the chair and rug and that's it. And remember, we didn't force you to buy here. You bought here of your own free will."

Ian responded in raised voice. "And I could kick myself for that, Frank. Hell, I would've kept using my patio furniture for home furniture, if I would've known your stuff was such junk."

Frank was hurrying to keep browsing customers from leaving.

"Chair and rug, and that's it."

"Forget the freebies, Frank. That's how you hooked me the first time." Ian, too, began heading for the exit. "If you're thinking you're washing your hands of me, Frank, you're wrong. I'm not paying anything for this junk. Best send the truck."

Frank was now wishing he'd taken a sick day. "You'll ruin your credit score if you don't pay."

"Credit score? Hell Frank, it's *credit* itself that's got us in the mess we're in."

"Enough already. I tried helping you."

"Yeah, helping me by jamming me up with $10,000 worth of junk. Best send the truck, Frank."

But Frank wasn't sending any truck.

Ian left and crossed the street to get to Handel Motors to continue the adventure . . .

"$300! Come on, Randy. Where does this end?"

"I'm sorry, Mr. Suarez . . ."

"Ian, remember?"

"Right. Well, Ian, I did try to keep your bill as low as possible."

"But it's still $300." Ian had to grudgingly pay his bill if he intended to drive away.

Minutes after that, it was another repair bill that needed his okay before his PC could be worked on. "Best you start thinking about an extended warranty program for your computer, Mr. Suarez."

"Oh geez, not you, too."

"Huh?"

"Never mind. Just . . . when will it be ready?"

"About a week, give or take a day." Ian left the store and headed straight for the library. He had *plenty* to rant about that day. Adding salt to the wound . . . that same night, after finishing up with a favorite read of his, a non-fiction by Dr. Warrick, upon placing her book on the headboard shelf, the entire headboard collapsed! That was when his enemy mind started putting together in his mind: Road Trip.

Chapter 28

"So let me get this straight . . ."

Weaver had been excessively longwinded after hitting the record button to his voice recorder. Ian had not been able to blow off the next mandatory Board meeting at the rec center. Weaver had threatened to bring every one of the Board members to Ian's house, if he blew them off again. ". . . You're going on record as saying that your conscience is the reason why you won't pay your fines? Is that correct?"

"That's about the size of it," answered Ian, while purposely staring at the self-invited Ms. Brown, who was sitting at the end of the table, staring back at him, while the rest of the Board looked to Weaver for direction.

Weaver, too, regretted seeing Emily Brown at the meeting. Others of the Board were just as leery at seeing her there. But there wasn't much anyone could do about that now that the meeting had started.

"Well then, Mr. Suarez . . ." started Weaver.

"Ian, remember?"

"Not for tonight's meeting you're not."

"Suit yourself."

"So I think I speak for all of us when saying that your excuse for not paying your fines is patently absurd."

"More like crazy talk," interject Brown.

Weaver not only waved off Ms. Brown's interjection, but another member who wanted at Ian. "I've got this, Fred. And Emily, please." Emily Brown's *humph* was clearly heard by everyone.

The spiel had been going on for over 30 minutes. Every member of the Board had gone at Ian, except for the two lone women members who continued to sit quietly at the table, taking it all in. Emily Brown was not of those women staying quiet. She constantly made noise even when not talking. Her fidgety cigarette habit was the cause of that.

Ian had already come to the conclusion that instead of working anything out, the meeting was just a charade. He went back to focusing on Weaver's ring and blocking the arguing out.

That's when he noticed the matching lapel pin.

Well I'll be damned. This Weaver was a high up in PSG's shenanigans. I can't believe he dares to keep wearing that stuff. Ian remembered the Prince Sanford Group trying to run an investment gambit on him during his RMF days. He'd read through their math and decided their math wasn't for him. *But why Weaver? Unless of course his bank, being in Florida and all . . .* but Ms. Brown's gravelly smoker's voice broke him from staring at Weaver's ring.

"I haven't heard anyone mention anything about his fence still being up." Ms. Brown made quick work of giving everyone the evil eye before setting her sights back on Ian and pointing her finger at him. "How many more damn rules do you intend to break?" To the room, she said, "How much longer are we going to keep letting him continue to break the rules before voting him out of DHE?"

Weaver feigned impatience by looking at his watch. "Emily, please, will you can it? You're no longer a member of the Board. We'll handle this."

"You sure haven't been doing a good job of that lately, I can tell you that." Emily ended her rant with another loud humph.

Weaver wasn't looking to fight or to confront. He just needed stuff on the record so he could put his plan into motion. He had a sit down with his mother-in-law right after the meeting and he didn't want to be late for that. Ian's house would be the main topic of discussion between he and his mother-in-law.

"Say Emily," Weaver sidetracked Emily Brown from interrupting, "How *did* you find out about tonight's meeting anyway?"

"It's *still* Ms. Brown to you, Dick."

Oh, brother, here we go!

"And you forget that Dolores Green and I are friends." That was a stretch, Ms. Brown calling Dolores Green a friend, but since Dolores wasn't there to refute it, and since Mr. Green *did* have a thing for Emily Brown, her claim stood. "But forget all that, Dick. Just get to what needs doing and be done with it. You said you're handling it, right?" Emily Brown was so wound up she couldn't sit. "And who gave him permission to put up such a huge birdbath?"

Another Board member interjected with, "Emily Brown's right about him having broken quite a few rules." Instead of feeling placated, Emily Brown turned on the man. "You're a fool to think just a *few* rules? You don't live next door to him. I do. I mean, just start with my car and what it looks like each morning with all that bird crap all over it! Few rules, my ass." Emily Brown was not to be placated. "And those lights around his birdbath keep me up pretty much all night now." That was a stretch too, since Emily Brown was a big fan of Ambien sleep aid.

Ian was now wishing he had taken up Nancy Smith's offer to accompany him to the meeting for support. But he'd needed her to upload his latest postings from her computer, as his PC was still being repaired. The Jenna laptop hadn't sufficient enough RAM to handle QYB business (an error on Jenna's part), so it had been slow in uploading stuff, so he'd just shut it off.

Nancy was at that very moment logging onto QYB to post his stuff when catching some of the chatter on Ian's 'Posted for Discussion' page. She was surprised to learn not only how many QYBers were in tune to Ian's Association nightmare, but how many had their own Association nightmares stories. There was even a couple asking for Ian's help in resolving a co-op issue that was forcing them out of their apartment that very night. It was Nancy who was now wishing she'd gone with Ian, but by then his postings were coming online. And so while NancSmit147 sat and read . . .

Back at the DHE rec room . . .

"I thought retirees were supposed to be good managers of their time?" Ian had nothing else to say while catching a sideways glance of Weaver's ring. His reference to time just irked Ms. Brown more.

"You jerk! You're the one wasting *our* time with your driveway, fence, and birdbath, jackass!"

Ian was about to go at Ms. Brown again, but his voices stopped him. *"Easy, Ian. Just forgive Ms. Brown her ways. Forgive the Board their ways, too. Forgiveness works, Ian."*

"And let's not forget the mess you made of our cul-de-sac with your pile of garbage," said another from the cul-de-sac.

Forgiveness hell!

"To all of you here, what am I, your only source of entertainment?"

Ian's anger got Mr. Green saying, "It's not our fault that we're here. And Emily Brown has every right to be mad at you." Ian didn't want to be combative with the 70-year-old Mr. Green. "We all wouldn't be here tonight, if not for you."

"You make it sound like I *want* to be here," replied Ian before looking at Weaver. "And all this because of my wanting to make my house look better."

"Your house was fine prior to you moving into it," said Weaver.

"Forget his house," yelled Emily Brown, "the rules, damn it! Remember the rules."

Ian turned to her at that. "Here we go again. You and your rules."

Ms. Brown didn't like being interrupted. "Listen here, fool; it's not *my* rules. It's rules we *all* have to live by."

"You call me fool, but you're the one sounding as long-winded as my banker here." Ian pointed at Weaver.

"Well, I never!" shouted Brown.

"You can never all you want," said Ian, while catching sight of the other two women members smiling at his going at Ms. Brown.

"Mr. Green is right, though," interjected another of the members. "We wouldn't be here if it weren't for you. Fences and red driveways aren't allowed."

"You all really should relax yourselves," said Ian, "before one of you has a heart attack. I don't want to be fined for that too."

"Oh funny that," said one of the members.

"Well, I never!" reiterated Ms. Brown.

"There you go again with the 'I nevers,'" mocked Ian. He was starting to lose his voice, and it sounded it, when saying, "Folks, please; look, I'm sorry. No. Check that. I hate the word, sorry. Instead, forgive me if I've caused you all grief. If badgering me makes you all feel good, then fine, badger me all you like. But know this; I'm not paying any fines."

"We'll see about that," interjected another of the members.

"You can *see* all you want . . . ." Ian turned to Weaver, "you know, as Board President *and* my banker, you can make this all go away. I don't understand why you don't just end this taunting tonight."

But wearing that ring and pin does tell me why you won't.

"Make all this stop?" Weaver feigned a perplexed look. "You're kidding, right? It's your insolence that has us here, so stop."

"It's *you* wasting *my* time that has *me* here." Ian tried up and leaving then. "What part of my *not* paying any fines are you having a problem with?" Ian's throat was now hurting terribly. But he still had enough in him to say to Ms. Brown, "and you, as my neighbor, causing me such grief. Shame on you." Ian turned back to Weaver. "You want my driveway gray? Fine. I'll paint it gray. I'll paint it whatever color you like. You want my fence gone? No problem. Soon as I have it sold, it's gone. Don't want me having bricks on my columns? No sweat. I'll use them around my birdbath, which, for the record, I got a birdbath because this *is* a *bird sanctuary.*" Ian had to massage his throat to continue. "Don't like my window shutters being red? I'll paint them hot pink, whatever, so long as this façade stops right now. And while on the subject of fines, is there a fine for putting a For Sale sign in my yard?" He looked to Weaver for the answer, and caught Weaver smiling an odd smile.

Bingo! It was *exactly* what Weaver was wanting to hear. But Weaver kept his demeanor neutral, so as to not give away his joy at hearing Ian surrender.

"Mr. Suarez," Weaver began straightening his tie in preparation for a vote, "there is *no* fine for putting up a For Sale sign. But I can tell you now that if you don't pay your fines, we'll be forced to put a lien on your property, and that *does* make selling your place a wee bit more difficult."

"We'll see about that."

"I'm your banker, remember? I would know."

Emily Brown couldn't stay quiet. "This is what happens when you move *his* kind here." Ian did a double take at that.

"What do you mean *my* kind?"

"Emily, please!" Weaver wanted the Board to vote, not to hear more bickering. He needed the vote so he could leave. "Emily, please hold your tongue." But it was too late. Emily Brown had let the cat out of the bag when staring at Ian and mockingly saying, "I guess it's probably best to just call you señor Suarez, no?" Emily Spanglish was horrible.

"Emily, enough already!" shouted Weaver while wanting no more distractions. Emily Brown was all that and more. He wanted to wrap up. He still had his mother-in-law to deal with. "We need to vote, Emily, so stop. Just stay quiet, okay?"

"Then vote already!" she huffed back.

Ian wasn't letting her off the hook that easily. "Boy, did I draw the short straw with you as my neighbor, eh señora Brown?" Ian shook his head and tut-tutted her. "And a racist to boot. What a shame."

"You're in *my* country, you Mexican spic bastard; I'm not in yours."

"Well, news flash for ya, señora; but I'm *not* Mexican, which by the way, Mexicans are far better people than you. I'm Cuban American and as much American as you."

This absolutely infuriated Emily Brown. The entire room could hear it in her voice when she said, "You? As American as me? Why you wetback piece of shit, my kin have been here going on six generations." She was beyond infuriated by Ian actually laughing at her saying that.

"So what? Where did your first generation come from, eh chica? Certainly not from here, unless you're Indian, and you're too white to be mestizo. So which is it? Maybe it's *you* who has a little Mexican running through you."

"Cuban. Mexican. You're all slices from the same turd."

Ian looked to Weaver. "So on top of everything else, I come to get insulted by her, too?"

"You brought this upon yourself, mister," said Mr. Green.

Ian turned to Green. "You, my man, are starting to sound like a broken record." Ian turned back to Ms. Brown. "So six generations, eh? Well I think you should go stand by the door and collect your trophy. I hear the trophy truck coming."

"Fuck you!" shouted Emily.

Ian noticed the other women could barely contain their laughter while prepping to go. He turned to Weaver and said, "You should have warned me that I was moving next door to Irma Grese."

This got Green jumping to his feet. "How dare you!" Green's voice shook a little when saying, "Emily's Jewish, you asshole."

But Emily Brown didn't need anyone defending her.

"You spic bastards are all the same. You come, and you take, and then you take some more, and then you fuck everything up." Ms. Brown, too, prepped to leave. "I'm glad you're getting your ass voted out of here." Ian made for the door, but was held up by Weaver waving his voice recorder at him. "Uh, Mr. Suarez, it would behoove you to stay. At least until the voting is done. That includes everyone. But not you, Emily. You can leave." Weaver looked to everyone else.

"We have a vote to finish."

"I'm leaving," said Ian.

"I really think you should stay and see how the vote goes, Mr. Suarez. After all, it does pertain to two liens against you."

"You *would* lien me, wouldn't you?"

"Not me, Mr. Suarez. The Board, and for breaking the rules." Weaver looked at the quickly retreating Emily. "And *you*; you really need to reel in all those racist remarks. He's still your neighbor, you know." Emily had already reached the door and could've cared less what Weaver said. "That spic won't be my neighbor for much longer, if you do what's right. Oh, and fuck you, Dick." She gave him the finger and left.

Weaver had accidentally recorded Ms. Brown. He would have to delete her later. "Okay folks. Didn't mean to get sidetracked. Now let's focus on what needs doing." Weaver waited till absolutely certain that Emily Brown wasn't about to storm back while eyeing Ian. "You had all the time in the world to make things right with us. But instead, you chose to go left when you should've gone right, and so now here we are at right, Mr. Suarez."

Ian simply went back to staring at Weaver's ring again. "Sure, Weaver. Whatever you say." Weaver caught Ian staring at his ring.

"This meeting's a no-brainer, Mr. Suarez."

A no-brainer is you wearing that ring thought Ian.

Weaver caught Ian eyeing his ring again, but made as if it were just a coincidence *though I don't think that's coincidental staring* thought Weaver. "Uh, Mr. Suarez, do you want to add anything before we vote?"

Ian was caught by surprise by that. He breathed deeply before speaking. "You mean like in defense of myself?"

"You have a minute."

"Then let me begin by saying the grief you've caused me has been ridiculously unbelievable. And while on the subject of making my life miserable, why haven't you gotten on my neighbor's case about her house being a wreck? Why hasn't *she* been fined for her rotting shutters and torn screens? I'll end by saying that I never thought a place called Dream Harvest Estate would have so many asinine people living in it. And as for my fines, to which I also just paid the new Homeowner's Association fee, that means I'm due some money against my fines. But if you're planning on voting me out, than I expect my money back. That's all I have to say." Mr. Green was left staring at Weaver, because he had nothing in the books about Ian having paid that year's increased fee of $2,400. (Having paid his fee in cash to Weaver, had given Weaver the opportunity to just deposit Ian's fee in his pocket.) Green was in fact getting ready to send Ian a non-payment letter right after the meeting. Green was still looking to Weaver to confirm or deny what Ian had said about his having paid his fee when Weaver waved him off also. "Don't worry about any of that, Stan. We'll catch up on that later." To the others, Weaver said, "Let's get the voting done and over with." Weaver raised his voice for his recorder's sake. "Okay then, let's see a show of hands of those rescinding Mr. Suarez's privileges for living here."

Ten hands shot up.

The two abstentions were the two women members.

"Okay, vote is 10 for and 2 abstentions. Joyce and Kim, I'm putting you down as no votes." Weaver turned to Ian. "There it is, Mr. Suarez."

"It is what it is, Weaver."

"I warned you something like this might happen. And by the way," Weaver began putting on his suit, which gave Ian another chance to stare at Weaver's diamond crusted lapel pin, "it's come to my attention that there's also a tax lien placed on your house."

"Tax lien? Won't surprises ever cease? When do you stop piling on?"

"Not me piling on, Mr. Suarez. That's Revenue piling on, which along with the two liens we're proposing here tonight, does change your loan terms with my bank."

"And now you blow my anonymity, too?"

"Your anonymity?"

"You don't think I really wanted anyone here to know about any tax lien, did you? Or any liens, for that matter."

"Come on, Mr. Suarez, we're all adults here."

"Adults, my ass. No one here's acted like an adult since I put up my fence. Well, except maybe for them." Ian pointed to Joyce and Kim. "And my friends the Smiths." Ian right then started for the door, but then suddenly turned, as if remembering something. "Say Weaver; whatever happened to you telling me that so long as I paid my mortgage, I would be building up equity, and that would cancel out my fines? Tonight sure was a helluva way of canceling out my fines."

Ian did some quick math in his head and concluded that his salvation would have to be in sticker sales. But he would need $5,000 just to pay off his fines, and with his monthly disability on the verge of being garnished by Revenue, $5,000 a month seemed like a fortune. He realized then that 34 Starling Circle had just become his own Alamo. "Weaver, why are you continuing to hammer away at me like this? Are you trying to get blood from a rock? Where does this all end?"

"Voting's done, Mr. Suarez. I can't change the vote."

Ian let Weaver catch him staring at his ring while saying, "But ah—contraire, Weaver. You might not be able to change the vote, but you sure can change the outcome. Instead, you throw out liens and fines and loan contracts that now change. What's with you? You're acting more like a bloodsucker, just like Revenue."

"I don't know about your issues with Revenue, Mr. Suarez, but I can assure you, if you don't square with them, bloodsucker or not, *they'll* run ya outta Dodge quicker than any of us here can. Just don't go throwing away tonight's transcript when it comes in the mail. Maybe then you'll see what you've done to yourself."

"I don't need a transcript to know what's happened here tonight, Weaver. You can still make all this right, and you know you can."

"If only that were true, Mr. Suarez."

"Yep. Been getting a lot of that lately."

"Been getting a lot of what lately?"

"Never mind. Well, if you're still kicking me to the curb, then know that I'm not going without a fight."

"I didn't expect you would. Are we done now? Can we all go home?"

"You could've all *stayed* home, as far as I'm concerned," said Ian to the room of Board members. Weaver was already heading to the door. His haste was so he wouldn't have to hear his mother-in-law bitch at him for being late again. She was already busting his balls over his delayed payment to her $100,000 secreted loan to him, which she wanted paid back with interest. *This vote tonight assures me of the home coming back to me, and she already said she'd take it in trade.* Weaver would have loved to have raided his bank's coffers and taken money to pay her, but he'd already hit the coffers one too many times, and because of it, had gotten onto regulators' radar. *Her money, along with what I've hidden away from my pocket mortgages, oughta get me outta Dodge real soon.* But for Weaver, soon wasn't soon enough.

Though nowhere near as invested as Ian had been when running RMF, Weaver still had played the markets enough during the glory days of securitization to lose his shirt through bad investments and splurging. Having a trophy wife *and* a trophy mistress were the reasons for his splurges. Being part of a financial group of thieves had been the bad investment side to things. Weaver, too, had become paper-heavy, but cash-strapped like many during the heydays, and though he like to think Ian was just like him, Ian's fall from grace had been more due to his $20 million fine and the confiscations that took everything from him. Weaver wasn't like Ian at all in that regard. Weaver had also broken the law many times through deceit and treachery to sustain his lifestyle. Joining with fund managing groups like Prince and Galsworthy had been a bad decision, too. Now, if *not* going through with becoming the Fed's star witness, he, too, would be headed to jail. His financial misdeeds could only be rectified by turning state's evidence and throwing certain people under the bus. Federal prosecutors had convinced Weaver that redemption was the only way of staying out of prison. (Prosecutors were promising anything to get convictions.) Weaver's last cash resources were his pocket mortgages. That's what he called them, his pocket mortgages. Trophy wife #3 didn't much care about his pocket mortgages, so long as there was always money in her account. His trophy mistress was another who needed spending money, a woman who could outspend wife #3 *and* compete with government spending!

Because his cash reserves were dwindling, Weaver was looking to bolt. He'd also gotten word that those he was looking to toss under the bus weren't going to let themselves get tossed so easily. Certain jailed associates already had people looking to silence Weaver before he went to turn state's evidence. And now here was Ian, eyeing his ring, and making him nervous. *Stupid ring! I should've sold the damn thing years ago.* Ego and vanity had kept Weaver wearing it. In addition, his mother-in-law was making his life miserable because she knew about his trophy mistress, which she held as a weapon against him. That's why 34 Starling Circle was so essential to his biding his time.

"**M**r. Suarez." They were now outside, Weaver and Ian, while waiting for Mr. Green to lock up the rec area clubhouse. "I should remind you that I went to a lot of trouble getting you voted in here. I never imagined it would come to this."

"You don't fool me, Weaver. You did all that because you wanted my money. And in case *you've* forgotten, I paid you top dollar for my house, so don't go thinking I owe you any favors. And so what of my disability? Doesn't that count for something? And what of my opening my account in your bank with my offshore funds? Those were big deals when you approved my house loan. So now what? I'm still disabled, you know."

"Your disability hasn't stopped you from spewing all that nonsense you write about on your site."

"What's my website got to do with anything?"

"It doesn't. But your name's been coming up a lot around the bank lately, if you catch my drift."

"Still piling on, I see."

"Stop with the melodrama. You brought this on yourself. Me, I thought you were a good fit here. Guess I was wrong. End of story."

"End of story, my ass. And what of the $2,400 I paid you for this year's Association fee? I mean, if you're looking to boot me, then I want my money back." Weaver had plans for 34 Starling Circle, and with the exception of Mr. Green's treasury book, nothing was getting in the way of that. "Look Mr. Suarez; whatever money you're due, we'll apply it towards your fines. End of story."

"Bullshit to that."

Green was overhearing what was being said, and his conscience was starting to make him think he might have been a little too hasty in judging Ian, no less voting him out, especially with it looking like Ian had paid his fee after all. But then Green remembered Weaver held the paper on *his* house, so conscience be damned. Green would learn to live with his vote.

"So now what, Weaver?" Ian asked. "Burning me at the stake next?"

"Still with more melodrama, huh? It was you not taking this Board seriously; you choosing to break the rules; you choosing to not pay your fines, that got you booted. Now you have 30 days to pay up, and that does include your liens, or it's court for you. Your choice."

"Just like that?"

"Just like that."

"Even though I'm current on my mortgage?"

"Current hell. Seems like I've been seeing you as a regular on our hot list."

"You really are after blowing my anonymity."

"Will you stop that? The IRS doesn't much care about your anonymity, so why should I? And they're your biggest worry now, not me."

"But . . ."

"Look Mr. Suarez, don't confuse me with someone who cares. You've got 30 days. End of story. And turn that damn driveway of yours seagull gray, will ya? I don't want to hear any more of Emily Brown's bitching."

"My driveway looks fine in red."

"No, it does not. Nor do your shutters. The Board don't much like your birdbath either, and your fence, well, we've already gone through that enough. You either start making right, or start packing." Weaver was 6'4" and outweighed Ian by a hundred pounds, so there wasn't the worry of their talk becoming physical. Ian was all about diplomacy anyway, and the thought of going at Weaver hadn't entered his mind . . . yet.

Ian waited until Weaver was in his car and strapping himself in, before saying, "You remember my being in banking once?"

Weaver lowered his window to answer. "Yeah, sure, I remember reading about your banking days. I also remember you almost took down your bank with some lousy investments, or some such, so yeah, I know of you being in banking once. Correct me if I'm wrong, but didn't some South American bank have to bail you out?"

"It was a merger, and in fact, Family Bank wasn't anywhere near going down at all. We merged with Sinn because it was a sweet deal for their Board, too. But that's not why I bring up my banking history." Weaver gunned his car to show his impatience. Instead, Ian gave his ring another hard look before locking eyes with Weaver.

"Lousy investing isn't what got me; it was me holding over 80,000 bad mortgages that got me. I don't think you've ever seen numbers like that,

Weaver. Or have you? I don't think there's 80,000 homes in this entire county, is there?"

"Your point?" Weaver gunned the car again.

"In all those bad mortgages, I never once got involved in kicking people to the curb; not like you're doing me. Hell Weaver, I even gave folks extra time to move, even after the courts said . . ."

"Whoa now, wait a minute; don't go confusing me for someone who's going to give you extra time to move, cause I'm not." Weaver gunned his car for emphasis.

"You aren't fooling me, Weaver. I know this isn't about any driveway or fence. There's something more going on here." Ian stared at Weaver's ring again. "And I bet it's got something to do with that there." Ian knew he'd struck a nerve when hearing Weaver switch to a mite friendlier tone. "Look, Mr. Suarez . . ."

"Ian, remember?"

"Right. Well, Ian, how about we just stop trading barbs? How about you just accept what's happened and move on."

"I'm not going to be bullied over this, Weaver."

The mite friendlier tone vanished. "Well good. Save it for when the sheriff comes to put your ass out." With that, Weaver hit the gas and roared off.

(Even though the county courthouse was bogged down in foreclosures and bankruptcies, Weaver's knowing people at the courthouse is what would get Ian's eviction paperwork expedited. His liens and foreclosure proceeding, leading to eviction, was on the clock.)

Ian had plenty to write about that night, and could've written till sunup, if not for the Jenna laptop crashing also! He was in the middle of posting a scathing blog about the bullying that went on with some Associations and co-ops when the Jenna laptop blew up and wouldn't reboot. Adding to his annoyance was his inability to save to his flash drive what he'd just spent hours writing. He had no choice but to wait until morning to post from the library. By then, the agency van parked out past the circle had done its deed and been long gone. From the van, the new Subnet/Zero virus, a virus developed on taxpayer-funded dollars, had been unleashed. Subnet/Zero was a virus created for disrupting sites like QYB. But unbeknownst to agents, Subnet did more than just take out Ian's laptop. Once Subnet was unleashed, it went viral and pinged into many home computers in the area. But it didn't stop there. Subnet would even find its way into Diamond Bank's servers.

Released from a simple thumb drive (much like the Olympic Games virus had been unleashed years back to disrupt the Iranian nuclear program), the results to Subnet/Zero was to crash several hundred thousand computers before spyware could stop it in its tracks. This was just another example of the government's left hand not knowing what the right hand was doing. Agents in their 'oops' moment failed to see the result to Subnet, another intrusive virus protected under the PATRIOT and SOPA acts.

But Ian's problem was more than a busted laptop. At that very moment, Miami's Homeland Special Agent-in-Charge, Carmen Rubio (Miami was where QYB had officially begun online) was just then getting the goods on Ian. SAC Rubio was already plenty busy without the added file on Ian. But a red flag (like those tagged to WikiLeaks and Snowden) had come with Ian's file. Rubio couldn't downplay that. "Quit your bitching and start the revolution, huh?" Rubio said aloud while reading more about Ian, before checking his site. "So, let's see who you've been chatting with today, Mr. Ian Red Suarez; . . . oh, and lookie there, the IRS initials too."

Once bringing up QYB, Rubio discovered Ian had some pretty strange bedfellows for chat mates. A dozen were already on Homeland's watch list. This included his favorite author, Dr. Dana Warrick, and the far more dangerous militia-type, Michael St. Donovan, owner of Liberty site and press, better known as Missouri Mike. Missouri Mike had multiple flags on him.

It was Ian's association with Missouri Mike that got Rubio gathering her troops. She even brought in her best tech agent, a girl named Lloyd, to handle snooping through Ian's webpages. But Subnet/Zero was making that difficult, even for the likes of tech Lloyd. "Then redirect to the Liberty site, Lloyd. Check what that scoundrel Missouri Mike's site got going with this Ian fellow. I'm sure you'll find plenty to record." The Liberty site, along with Rage and Strike.com, were sites high on Homeland's watch list. Adding QYB wasn't a problem.

Lloyd would try getting a bead on Ian while he posted from his local library the next day, but Central Florida libraries had recently installed some pretty darn good privacy filters to combat against a rash of identity thefts that had been happening around the area. It would be weeks before SAC Rubio and her team could get a bead on Ian. Surprises kept coming though for SAC Rubio, as SA agent Landers Ferguson made his acquaintance known. But Ferguson was more annoyance than help, and his having been in South Florida for years running surveillance on Ian was again another instance of the right hand not knowing what the left hand was doing nonsense.

"So, why didn't I know of you?" asked Rubio.

"Because you were working for DEA, while I was working with Homeland in Homestead." Ferguson almost ended with *mate,* but didn't think one so pretty as Rubio (though she was nearing 50), plus the photos in her office of her previously being a champion kick boxer, wouldn't have liked being called *mate.* Ferguson's impeccable credentials, though would keep him on her team, plus . . . there was still the Eye-for-an-Eye mission.

Rubio's phone rang while she was still reading through Ferguson's smudge smile. The call was from the OJI in Atlanta wanting to know more about Ian, the possible fraud and avoidance charges coming his way, and requesting to be brought into the loop. This just annoyed SAC Rubio more. "I'll have to get back to you on that, agent Terrence." She hung up to his asking for her email address. Rubio had had all she could take for one day. Having the new 'Ian target' on her radar had done that. *And having nearly a million subscribers and friends like Missouri Mike and a microbiologist who is an expert on terrorism makes our boy out to possibly be a serious problem.* She ended her day by kicking Ferguson out of her office.

Chapter 29

"Wow! It's going to cost me that

much, huh?" Ian was back checking on when his PC would be ready and to get a repair quote on his crashed Jenna laptop. "I mean, wow, another $600 in repairs? Don't you think that's a bit much . . ." he eyed the tech's nametag, ". . . Cheryl?" He had earlier emailed Jenna about the crashed laptop, asking if maybe the laptop still might be under warranty and save him some money. But Jenna hadn't responded to his email yet.

"Well sir, I'm really sorry . . ."

"Call me Ian."

"Alright then, Ian. But you did ask for the 'best money could buy' replacement parts for your PC. You wrote that on the repair slip yourself. I'm assuming you want the same for your laptop, which by the way, my diagnostic shows your motherboard's fried."

"Fried motherboard?"

"Crispy fried, Ian. I imagine you want 'best money could buy' parts for that too, right?"

"So no discount or anything?"

"Sorry Ian, but I just work here. The prices are what they are. And by the way, I could've saved you a trip on the PC, but your phone's not accepting any calls."

"What? Not accepting calls?" While Ian checked his phone, Cheryl checked his laptop more. "Oh-no."

"What's up? Something wrong with your phone too?"

"I forgot to top-up. It's been one of those days."

"I hear ya. Well, as for your computer, you know you could save yourself some money if you had one of our extended warranties. And if your laptop's going to give you trouble, well . . ."

"Oh please, Cheryl; you're starting to sound like my car mechanic over at Handel Motors."

"Huh?"

"Never mind. Look, just go ahead and fix my laptop instead. I've already put enough good money into the PC. Leave it broken. And you did say you could speed up my laptop, right?'

"I can."

"Good. Do it."

"I can also install some more virus protection."

"Will it help?"

"Sure it will."

"Then do that, too. But no more, okay?"

"You got it. I can add another 8 gigs to your RAM and load you up with some pretty sweet software protection. So what about the motherboard? You want the best money could buy, right?"

"I thought I just told you, no more; oh, but wait, that was the original problem, wasn't it?"

"It was. And you can't use your laptop without a motherboard."

"Right, well okay then, just hand over that crap PC of mine and start on my laptop."

"Sorry about your PC, Ian. But you know *I* didn't build it."

"Oh hey, I'm not mad at you, Cheryl. I'm just tired of all these costly repairs. It's not like I have a money tree growing in my backyard, you know. Bad enough I'm running a website that's draining me; now all these crashes have got me stuck using a library computer."

"Sorry to hear that, Ian." Cheryl went to get his PC, which was among a number of PCs lined up on her work bench. When she came back, Ian asked her, "So what do you think fried the motherboard in my laptop, Cheryl? I mean, spending this kind of money makes me think I'm better off buying a new PC."

"Your laptop's well worth spending the money to repair it. As for a new PC to run a website? You should've started with something more geared to heavy workloads, not a gaming computer."

"Gaming computer?"

"The 'best money could buy' gaming PC is what you got."

"Well hell, that teaches me never to ask a young geek gamer to show me to the 'best money could buy' computers."

"I bet you bought all the bells and whistles that came with it, didn't you?"

"Sure did, including upgrading to the 7.1 surround sound speakers plus the touch screen monitor. But about the motherboard, remember?"

"Oh yes, well, I venture to say you caught one bad bug."

"Bad bug, huh?" Cheryl pointed to the other PCs on her work bench. "You see those? *All* came in this morning, so yeah; one *bad* bug fried your motherboard. Probably the same thing that fried your PC. Who knows? But whatever it is, it's one mean bug. You're doing right by buying more software protection, and no, I'm no gaming geek, so I'm not just trying to sell you."

"I just thought, since the laptop's so new, that maybe the manufacturer's warranty might cover some of the cost. I have already spent nearly $4,000 on that stupid computer, and another grand to repair it, so maybe . . ."

"Well, if you had one of our extended warranties . . ."

"There you go sounding like my mechanic again."

"Huh?"

"Oh, never mind. Just me rambling again."

"So Ian, why don't you have me *build* you a new computer?"

"Please, Cheryl, no money tree, remember? And say, while we're on the subject of money, is there a charge for your diagnostic check? I don't see it here on the bill."

"Nope. Diagnostic's free."

"And all this over some bug."

"One badass Trojan or worm. Maybe both. I will most definitely put in the 'best money can buy' virus software in your laptop."

"Say Cheryl, what about the Lemon Law on my PC?" Cheryl was the store's best repair tech, though her tats and piercings are what probably kept her from climbing any further up the corporate ladder. But Cheryl knew store policy, and knew Ian hadn't a leg to stand on when it came to the Lemon Law. "Sorry, Ian, I already tried that one on the manager. We can't lemon law you if diagnostic shows it's not a defect, which in your case, diagnostic showed your PC crashed due to a virus, not a defect. Can't lemon law you if we can fix ya." Cheryl had already made quick work of tearing out the motherboard from the laptop and set it on her bench. "Give me a few days to work on it. I'll call you when it's ready, so go get your phone topped-up." Cheryl pointed to the courtesy phone near the restrooms. "And if you want, you can always try getting someone at your computer manufacturer's customer service. But good luck getting a human to speak to you."

But Ian had already been sidetracked by something hanging on the display rack near aisle #4. *Damn, if that wouldn't make the perfect consolation for me spending so much money here. And with my road trip coming up . . .*

"Ian?" Cheryl broke him of looking at the rack near aisle #4.

"We got cell phone top-up cards here too, you know."

"Oh, yeah, right. Well thanks, Cheryl."

"You really should be thinking of buying a service plan for future possible repairs on your laptop. And that stuff you're looking at over there . . . that's all generic off-brand component stuff, in case you're thinking of building one yourself. The stuff you want, especially for running a website, is right here behind my counter. And by the way, what's the name of your website, anyway?"

"Oh, I never did tell you, did I? It's called Quit Your Bitching and . . ."

". . . Start the revolution! Dude, I know your site! My roommate and I check your site daily. Wow! What a small world." Cheryl was now even more glad to know him, and it sounded it. "Well it's no wonder you're having so many crashes!"

"What do mean?"

"The stuff you've been writing about; the government and the Associations and all. Plus banks and Corporate America. Dude, you gotta know the powers that be must be wanting at ya. I'm surprised the government hasn't shut you down already."

"Yeah, well they don't run the Net."

"They will one day."

"That'll shoot my numbers up even more, they ever try controlling the net."

"Well I'm just glad to know you. My roommate and I, we go on your PFD page all the time to chat. We've been having our own Association mess, ourselves."

"Yeah?"

"I live over at Blyleven Estates. You've probably passed it on the way into town."

"Yeah, I know Blyleven."

"Well, it looks like *our* Association Board is taking a page from *yours*."

"How you mean? What's your Association doing to you?"

"Screwing us around is how I mean. They got a new dog clause that went into effect this year. They want me to get rid of my old mutt, which I won't do. Hell, I've had my dog since he was a pup. Now, because of some new insurance clauses, they want me to get rid of my dog. Well, screw that. What the hell's wrong with people nowadays, anyway?"

"Your guess is as good as mine, Cheryl. But you've heard it said, the more we get to know people . . ."

". . . the more I love my dog. I hear ya, Ian."

Cheryl suddenly spotted her manager eyeing them from afar. She made as if needing to look inside his PC again. Her loosening the screws on his PC gave him an idea.

"Just leave the screws loose," said Ian.

"Why?"

"I may want to pour gasoline in it when I get home."

"Get out! You're kidding, right?"

"Yes, I'm kidding. So anyway, your Association at Blyleven?"

Ian loosened the panel screws some more while she talked.

"Our Association has already fined me for my dog. I had my dog grandfathered into my homeowner's contract, which they upped and changed. A vote or something nixed the grandfathered clause. It don't count for shit anymore."

"So they basically made a new rule and out goes your dog."

"Screw that, but right you are. But hey, look at who I'm talking to. What with your own issues over there at Dream Harvest. Man, it's like people vs. people out there."

"Sort of reminds me of the crap I went through in Cuba. My mother and brother both lost their lives over crap like this."

"Yeah, I read your bio. Pretty wild stuff you being rescued at sea."

"Yeah, well, don't forget my getting struck by lightning, too. Now *that* really hurt."

"Yeah, I bet."

"Hate to say it, Cheryl, but all this bullying legalese, and all these regulations, by-laws, codes, and fines, if we don't do something, it'll only get worse. Just look at government, for example. Their antics continue to set communities on edge. I guess that's what we get when we vote so many lawyers into office."

"Funny you should mention lawyers, cause our dickweed Board President, he's a lawyer. Bastard even sent his son over to my house, while my roommate and I were at work, to pressure wash my house because of mildew on my awnings. Bastard then charged me $250 for the washing, and when I refused to pay, I got slapped with a fine. You believe that? What kind of shit is that?"

"I feel ya, Cheryl. But you know you just gave me a great idea for a new topic of discussion on PFD."

"Oh? What's that?"

"You mentioned it being like 'people vs. people' out there. Well, I'm going to run with that as a new polling segment."

"Polling segment? I don't get it."

"You will. Just keep watching the site. And chime in when you can, cause I got a funny feeling 'people vs. people' is going to take off. Hey, with this economy, and what it's doing to people, making them behave the way they are . . . why should it not?"

"Well, then look for me, Ian. I'm Cherylheart03."

"Okay, Cherylheart03. But don't get mad if I don't get right back to you. I've got over 200 emails to clear from my inbox each day before I can even get to chat. But do continue to email me, okay?"

"I will. Oh, and Ian, your initials. Did your mom do that on purpose?"

"Crazy that, huh? Nah, the IRS thing is strictly coincidental."

"And *you* having all them IRS troubles."

"Don't remind me. Still got troubles with them. Bastards even want my disability income." The thought made him suddenly scratch at the bald spot on his head, hidden by a ball cap. He'd gotten into liking wearing caps.

"Well, Ian, I do remember hearing about some guy flying his plane into the IRS building in Texas somewhere."

"People vs. people, Cheryl, remember? IRS are people also."

"Yeah, but *government* people."

"We're all from dirt, Cheryl."

"Yeah, but some are . . .

". . . dirtier than others. I hear ya, Cheryl."

Ian didn't mean to look again at the display rack near aisle #4, but did anyway. "Dude, forget all that DYI stuff. I told you, if you're thinking of building, the stuff you want's right here behind my counter."

"Nah, Cheryl; if I wanted to build a computer, I'd have you build it."

"Well, if you decide to build . . ."

"Let me go top-up, Cheryl. See you later."

"Oh, and Ian, you know that furniture store you've been ragging about on your site? I had trouble with them, too. I bought a sleeper sofa from them once. Damn thing got to where I had to fight with it just to get it open. They couldn't do anything for me either. Said my sofa had been discontinued. I had to eat it. It was a cheap piece of junk, too. I was so glad to start my burn pile with it! You're right about that store selling junk. I've never shopped there again."

Ian had liked interacting with the heavily metaled and tattooed Cheryl. She thought his smile was for her, which made her smile, too.

"Well Ian, it was nice chatting with you. I'll call you soon as I have your laptop ready." They actually high-fived before Ian headed for aisle #4 with his PC in hand.

Cheryl right away got busy with a new customer, which gave Ian the chance to run his ploy and get down on a knee and make like he was tying his shoelaces. He quickly unscrewed and opened the side panel to his PC then grabbed the vacuum-sealed package off the display rack, shoved it quickly inside his tower, and then retightened the screws. Next was getting past the door scanner. He had anticipated the scanner alarm to go off. No sooner did the scanner beep then Ian yelled to Cheryl while smiling at the store's part-time helper who was lazily checking packages. Ian pointed at the numerous repair stickers already on his PC while pointing over at Cheryl. "She's done so many repairs to this thing, that I'm not surprised your scanner went off." Seeing Cheryl waving okay from the repair department got Ian waved through. "You're good to go, sir," said the store employee with barely a cursory nod.

Ian next hurried to his car, where moments later he was fighting to open the tightly sealed vacuum-packed new 8GB video pen, which he immediately clipped to his shirt pocket once he got the package opened. He struggled with his conscience afterwards. But first there was the issue of his car acting up again . . . while at that moment 11 miles east, his expedited paperwork was being reviewed by a judge, prior to signing his eviction papers.

Fees, fees, and more fees. Furniture that was barely making the grade. A computer far from being 'best money could buy'. A gifted laptop that wasn't much better. A low mileage car testing his patience with high mileage repair bills. Car payments with late fees. Home payments with late fees. Fines, violations, and taxes due upon receipt. An increase in home insurance. An overdue printing bill. And as if his money woes couldn't get any worse, gas prices were on the rise again. Even his favorite breakfast cereal had gotten too expensive, which had led him to buy the generic, which tasted like generic. But at least his QYB stickers were selling, though not at the rate to help him much past sticker expenses. The attorney he had hired to fight his foreclosure had wanted a $5,000 retainer (and never even got Ian's foreclosure proceedings to slow down). Cap and Trade made buying electricity so expensive, that as summer heated up, so too did everyone's electric bill. Ian's May bill alone was over $400. Robbing Peter to pay Paul (Peter being Ian and Paul the economy) was turning Peter into a pauper, if not catching a break. But at least Paul was happy.

Extreme frugality is what got Ian squeaking through May and into June, where at least in June, his luck turned a little with 16,000 stickers sold, and most paid for. But his mailing list had already made it onto Revenue's radar (their reach now included the Net), and his disability income garnishment was no longer a threat. The Revenue letter mentioned that in most cases, the maximum allowable garnishment was 22% as set by SSI. But Ian was not most cases, and at the OJI's signing, Revenue garnished his entire monthly supplement. Agent Terrence wasn't playing games with Ian, which forced Ian to put his Road Trip on hold. To make his Road Trip happen, he would need to catch a financial break. That break came in July.

A Cincinnati Homeland agent, driving home from her office, noticed the QYB sticker on the car ahead. *Been seeing a lot of those lately.* While stuck in traffic, the agent fired up her laptop to catch some of Ian's website. What she saw of QYB annoyed her. What she read of Ian's candid portrayal of most government agencies annoyed her even more. (Ian was starting to rattle cages with his new 'We the People Movement.') Just as troubling to the Cincinnati agent was the three million subscribed viewers calling themselves QYBers. The agent made a note to check Ian's background when getting home before jotting down the license plate number of the car ahead.

Once home, the agent found she was behind the curve when it came to Ian and QYB. SAC Rubio in Miami not only had the lowdown on QYB, but she was already planning the takedown of sites like QYB, Liberty, Rage, MilitiaDawn, Strike, and others that had made it onto Homeland's radar. Agency eavesdropping was covered under the **U**nited and **S**trengthening **A**merica by **P**roviding **A**ppropriate **T**ools **R**equired to **I**ntercept and **O**bstruct **T**errorism Act.

An increase in anti-government rants and writings, a majority of which came from the net, made PATRIOT a must, and gave reason for more SOPA intervention. Tons of 240-filings had given agents the right to snoop into people's lives, which had begun years back during the NSA snooping days. But the government was going beyond the usual phone tap and intercepted texts; emails and even library checks-outs were considered when gauging a person's stance towards government and the future. Fishing the Net under the pretense of 'terrorist watching' made Ian's friends, like Missouri Mike, and others like him, prime fish of the day. The fact that Missouri Mike headed the Liberty website pushed him to the top of the list. But Missouri Mike was pushing buttons much harder than Ian.

His real name was Michael St. Donovan. He was called Missouri Mike because he'd been born and raised in the hills of northern Missouri. It was in northern Missouri where he also had his Liberty print shop (publisher of the Liberty Press) and from his print shop also ran his Liberty site.

Mike had known plenty about Ian's father 'the Wolfe.' It's what had made them friends from the get go, especially when learning that Mike's parents, the St. Donovan's, had known Ian's father personally. They had met the Wolfe during 'Bloody Sunday,' (where in January 30, 1972 British paratroopers killed 13 Irish citizens at a civil rights protest in Derry, Northern Ireland). The Wolfe's time-delayed fuses had added to the conflict in the streets. From then on, the Wolfe had become like a sort of hero to the St. Donovan's, and thus also to Michael.

But to SAC Rubio, she did not view Ian and Mike's online relationship as just friends sharing a common bond in websites. Rubio, who was already bogged down with enough work to last her through the year, saw Mike and Ian's chat relationship as just another hassle for her and her team, beginning with Mike's Liberty Press.

Mike's Liberty site and press had for years been spewing lots of anarchic comments, angling towards revolt, which was the feeder paper to the northern militias. But birds of a feather *were not* Liberty and QYB.

Ian's approach to change was different than Mike's. Ian was more into wanting downsized government. Mike was more into State's rights. "All states do have Capitols for a reason." This was one of many of Mike's comments.

Mike's staff of volunteers were also a problem. Most of those manning his presses were believers in anarchy and state's rights. Several were troublesome anarchistic believers, with some having serious criminal records to prove it. Liberty was a site that spoke loudly to those no longer believing in federal democracy, and hence the reason why Liberty was on radar. Mike was the center stone to a website gearing towards trouble. To agents, having Ian chatting with Mike meant Ian was trouble, also.

Mike was 20 years older than Ian. But Ian was far better with words than Mike. Mike was a more radical writer. Ian was more to-the-point with details. Mike liked pushing buttons. Ian liked feeding facts and figures to people and wanting them to make the choice of whether happy with the status quo, or wanting change. Thus began the 'We the People' movement.

Another of Missouri Mike's maxims was 'Out with the Old and In with the New." But his New meant pointing people towards Liberty, Rage, and Strike.com as their choices.

But ironically enough, it was QYB getting most of Homeland's attention, and that was because of its use of the word 'Revolution' in its title. It's growing numbers, surpassing even Liberty, meant more eavesdropping by agents and more overtime approval for SAC Rubio and her team, at a time when it was hard to get approval for anything pertaining to money from her superiors.

Ian's timing had been as near perfect as Periclean Athens, Medicean Florence, Persia's rise, Elizabethan England, and Jefferson's Williamsburg. But in Ian's case, to make his timing *more* perfect, he would need his Road Trip, and a car that ran correctly. While he struggled getting his car to Handel Motors for service, and while it was on the rack, onto his door was taped a 30-day eviction notice.

Chapter 30

Ian first switched on his pen
camera before dealing with Randy's new assessment of his car troubles. "You need a new transmission, Ian. And you already know what the bosses are going to say to that."

"And *you* know I can't afford a new transmission, so don't even go there. Can't the bosses do something?"

"I already ran your problem by Brian Handel. He was real quick to remind me of your 'as is' situation."

"I'm going to go crazy if I hear one more time how my car's an 'as is' car. It's not like I'm not making payments on the damn thing."

"Sorry, Ian, but having warranty would help."

"Oh, don't start that again. So pray tell, Randy, what's a new transmission cost these days?"

"I got you an estimate written up right here." Randy handed over his estimate, to which Ian whistled when seeing the bottom number.

"$3,400! Are you kidding? What the hell's it made of . . . gold?"

"Sorry, Ian, but remember, I just work here. And I gotta get you off the lift, if you're not paying. Either of the bosses sees your car on the rack without a work order, and it'll be my ass."

Ian remembered his camera and played to it a little. "But Randy, my car doesn't drive right. You would think, after paying what I did for my car, that I could at least get better service."

"I'm trying, Ian. I mean, I can give you all the service you need, but I can't do it for free. You need warranty, my man. Go try finance again. I think they have a sale on their warranty packages this week. Maybe they can do you a deal."

"Yeah, I can only imagine their deal. Look, how about the Lemon Law? Doesn't my car qualify for the Lemon Law? It's only got 19,000 miles on it, which would be early for a transmission problem, don't you think?"

"There's never been a recall on your car's transmission, so it's not defective. That's the only way I could run the Lemon Law past the bosses. Plus you buying an . . ."

"Don't say it."

"Right. Well listen, Ian, if it's any consolation, I'd be pissed too, if having your car. I'll put in some Stop Leak for ya, get you back running again, and even toss ya a couple of cans onto your backseat. But that's all I can do, and I gotta do it on the sly."

"But Randy, really? Just 19,000 miles."

"That's actually plenty of miles for having trouble. Granted, not *new* transmission troubles, but I get cars in here all the time with less miles and having plenty of trouble, so no, it's not the miles. I mean, if you only had, say 90 miles on the odometer, than sure, you would probably qualify for a new car. But I don't make the rules, Ian. The first buyer of your car was probably hard on the shifter. I'll do the Stop leak. You go try finance."

But Ian was stopped from going anywhere when the more profit-minded of the two Handel brothers, Brian, walked into the service area. Brian was there to check on another customer's car when seeing Ian's car on the rack. Brian hurried right over.

"So, I see you got your car back on the rack, eh Mr. Suarez? Getting it fixed proper this time, I hope."

"He still can't afford a new transmission, boss, which is what he needs," answered Randy.

Brian Handel immediately looked at Ian and asked, "Can you afford our warranty service?"

"Too expensive."

"Well, then there are other shops in town you can see." Brian turned to Randy. "I got Miss Jean's car coming in for service. Put her on this rack here."

Brian Handel's body language while swaggering off was recorded perfectly onto Ian's camera and would show he was done with Ian.

Randy waited until his boss was out of earshot before saying, "Ian, go see finance. I'll get the Stop Leak."

"Thanks Randy. At least *you're* trying to help." Ian slipped $20 into Randy's shirt pocket before going to see the finance guru. The camera did not catch that, though.

"Your car will be waiting outside for ya, Ian."

"Thanks again, Randy."

Ian's camera would also do a good job of recording the finance guy's disinterest in him. "Sorry Mr. Suarez, but that's the best I can; $700 down and payments of $164 a month for two years."

"Come on now . . . best you can do? And where's the discount, like your sales poster says? $700 and $164 a month? Where does this end?"

"I don't follow, Mr. Suarez."

"Ah, forget it. Just talking to myself." Ian took a deep breath before continuing. "Look, can I give you what cash I have until I check my P.O. Box? I know I have some money in my Box, but I won't know how much until I go check. Will that at least get my paperwork started, so that Randy can start working on my car?"

"Oh no, Mr. Suarez; we're just underwriters here. I still have to shop your contract. Once I got you a provider number, then we can start working on your car."

"So how long will that take?"

"About a week."

"A week! And until then what? I ride the bus while making payments on a car that don't drive right?"

"Sorry, Mr. Suarez, but we don't build 'em here, we just sell 'em."

"I've been getting that a lot lately."

"I don't follow you there either, and remember your problem was buying an 'as is' . . ."

"Stop right there. I don't want to hear about that 'as it' nonsense anymore." Ian reached for his wallet, which got the finance guru's attention *ooh, I make commission after all* until seeing Ian hand over just two-$100 bills.

"Can you at least start my paperwork with these two Benjamins here? At least until I go check my Box?"

"Sorry, Mr. Suarez, but I need the full $700 before I can start your paperwork."

Ian flipped his wallet upside down to show it was all he had.

"Look, let me check my P.O. Box, though I can't guarantee I can give you the full $500 today, but I'll bring you what I can. If not, in a day or two I'll have the rest. But I really need you to start my paperwork."

"Don't you have a major credit card? We do take those, you know."

"I know that. But I'm not much into plastic these days. I'd much rather pay you in cash."

"As you wish. Cash does always work."

"So? Will you start my paperwork with my $200?"

"No can do, Mr. Suarez. I can keep your $200 as a deposit, but I can't run your paperwork without it being paid in full. Those are the rules."

"Yeah, right, the rules. And so what about a loaner? Do I get a loaner while my car's being repaired?"

"Well, we don't do loaners, per se; but we can get you home and pick you up when your car's ready. If you need a rental car, you'll have to work it out with your provider. But they usually reimburse people for car rental expenses." (That wasn't necessarily true. Not all providers cover rental expenses.) "Best go check your P.O. Box. I'm only here till 4 today."

Ian instead put his $200 back in his wallet and walked. He went back to the service area where he had to wait on Randy to give him his keys.

"Sorry. I meant to leave them in your car. It's a habit, tossing them in my pocket. Sorry things didn't work out for you, Ian."

"I've been getting that a lot lately."

Fifteen minutes later, Ian was at his P.O. Box, but only to find a $1,000 in sticker sales, with most paid for by check or money order. Less than $200 came in cash. Among the mail was also another Revenue letter to anger him. *How in the hell did Revenue find my P.O. Box? I used the Wolfe name to open this damn Box. I sure hope they're not onto my sticker sales.* Ian's worry should've been more on his Wolfe name.

The new Revenue letter threatened criminal charges because of his having an offshore account during a time of confiscations.

Ian's voices started right then. *"Big trouble for you now, Ian."*

"They're gonna stick you in the slammer over this."

"Best get you a better getaway car."

It was all he could do to keep from tearing his hair out (and from then on, he was always watching his rearview mirror). From the post office he went to see his print shop buddy, where he handed over the $1,000 in sticker orders and then drove home. His transmission began slipping the moment he pulled into DHE. But his transmission was the least of his worries when compared to the eviction notice on his door.

Having his supplemental income garnished, and being threatened with criminal charges, is what forced Ian to visit the Revenue office in town. But simple diplomacy didn't work there either.

Ian's troubles were centered around lines 15a & b of his 2009 to 2013 long form. (Line 15a is where taxpayers must declare any extra income from things like pension plans, Roth IRAs, 401ks, and the like.) While sitting in the Revenue agent's office, there was mention made of his stickers being undeclared income. *Oh-no! So she does know about the stickers.* There was also underreported income from cashing out on stocks totaling $270,000 in 2010. That income had put him over the middle-income percentile, thus placing him in a higher tax bracket (2010 had seen Revenue's $2.2 trillion yearly take-in as not being nearly enough to cover governmental expenses. It had since gotten worse). "But ma'am, 2010 was years ago. All I've got left now is my disability, which you people are garnishing. And what of all my charity giving? Doesn't that count for anything?"

Agent Philips had gotten too busy reading off her screen the OJI's transcript from Atlanta to give Ian her full attention. "Yes, well Mr. Suarez, it says here that Atlanta has you down for using money from an offshore account to buy a house here in this county."

"So? What's wrong with that?"

Agent Philips continued to read her screen while answering.

"What's wrong with *that* is having money *after* telling adjudicators you were broke; that doesn't sit well with the CID investigators." Agent Philips lowered her glasses to look at Ian. "See where I'm going with this?"

"But you IRS people already clobbered me once. What more do you want?"

"The taxes on that $270,000 cash-from-stock buyout, for starters."

"But that was years ago, and the money's already been spent."

"On what?"

"Living and medical expenses! I know you *must* know about living expenses, right? You *are* feeling the pinch like the rest of us, right? Besides, all that stock, I sold short, just to survive. You people got part of that, too, when you took the house. So why do you continue to hound me?"

Agent Philips scooted her glasses back up on her nose and sat back in her chair to deliver her spiel. "Atlanta is your biggest problem right now, Mr. Suarez. They seem to think you've done something illegal and that's what matters. You were CEO of a troubled bank. You, of all people, should've known what trouble an offshore account would bring you. Especially during a time of confiscation and forfeitures."

Ian sighed loudly before answering. "So I have a friend at a Montserrat bank. I put what money I had left in her bank. I did nothing illegal there."

"You had money parked in an offshore bank *during* a time of confiscation. Don't you get it? This isn't going away."

"But I'm flat broke now! Don't *you* get it? And what of my almost being killed by lightning?"

"You get disability for that."

"Not anymore, I don't. You people are taking that, remember?"

"Well, we in this office had nothing to do with that, Mr. Suarez. I'm just reading what Atlanta sent me on you."

"Well, the black and white of this is that I'm broke, flat busted broke, and you can't get anything at all from flat busted broke."

"The OJI will try." Agent Philips stood to put on her jacket. It was time for lunch. "Mr. Suarez, your black and white is different than the CID's. It's not the black and white the OJI is after; it's the green that CID wants." She tapped her monitor screen. "Before I leave for lunch, I need for you to confirm this amount that our auditors say you owe. Making arrangements to pay this might get your garnishment lifted."

"It should be illegal for Revenue to garnish mine, or anyone else's disability. Heck, the way I see it, it should be Revenue giving *me* money."

Agent Philips actually laughed at that. "Ha! Not in this lifetime."

Ian also stood and made to leave. "Look, the IRS has already taken me to the cleaners once. That's not going to happen again. If Revenue feels like it has to garnish my disability, then so be it. Either way, I'm out of here."

"Ah, Mr. Suarez, your confirmation? On this bill amount, please?" She tilted her screen so Ian could see what CID/Atlanta had sent.

Ian's eyes widened. "But that says $51,000! Revenue wants me to pay $51,000?" His voice sounded incredulous.

"I believe that's an approximate. There could be more. You'll know if you receive another balance due bill."

"Uh-uh. No way. I didn't survive the ocean and lightning so you people can railroad me again. Uh-uh. You get on the horn with whoever in Atlanta and tell them they're crazy to think I'm going to continue playing this game. I'm leaving." Ian made for the door.

"What about your stickers?"

"My stickers?"

"You know, Mr. Suarez, I already had enough on my plate before your file got to me. You're just more that I need to contend with now, so please don't play coy with me. Yes, *your* stickers, those damn QYB stickers I keep seeing around. I know you're making a few bucks off them. You're in enough hot water already, so why not pay down your bill with your sticker money? This isn't going away anytime soon, and I hate to see you end up in prison over this."

"In prison? Why? Because of stickers? Say, when in the hell does this all end, anyway?"

"When it ends depends on you. But I would highly recommend you use your sticker money to pay your bill."

"You sound like my Homeowner's Association, and they're a bunch of crooks, too."

"Atlanta wants closure, Mr. Suarez. Or is it Wolfe? Cause that's on your file also. Something about hiding golf earnings under Wolfe, whatever that means?"

"I haven't seen golf earnings in years, since being struck by lightning *on* a golf course! Look, IRS already took my house. I think that's enough. Now I'm about to lose another one. You think I'd lose my house if I had any money?"

Agent Philips reached over and clicked her PC into sleep mode.

"Whatever, Mr. Suarez. Have it your way. How you handle your evasion problem is your own business." Philips handed Ian her card from her card holder. "I need you to come see me next Thursday. That should give you plenty of time to figure out where you want to go with this. I'm willing to work with you, but you're going to have to work with me. Don't blow me off. This isn't going away. Believe that. And remember, if you don't pay, you could end up in prison."

"So what? Are you intending to arrest me next Thursday? If you are, then I'm not coming."

"CID still wants to work with you, so no, no jail time yet. But you're on their short list, and even I wouldn't want to be there. I've seen them send people up the river for a lot less than what you owe."

Philips looked like she meant what she said.

"You make me out to be as bad as Capone," said Ian.

"Nah. Revenue keeps much better records now."

"Not in my case they don't."

"Double or triple your sticker sales, Mr. Suarez. That's my advice to you. Do whatever it takes to pay down your account."

"Yeah, right."

"Oh, and I got one more bit of bad news for ya."

"Oh? So tell me, when does this end?"

"Atlanta just froze your bank account here in town"

"What!" Ian was now more incredulously angry. "Tell me you're kidding." He could tell she wasn't. "But that's the last of my money!"

"Sorry, Mr. Suarez, but that's CID's power, not mine. And before you ask, cause I see the look, no I *cannot* overturn Atlanta's decision."

Ian was beyond angry when told that, and fuming by the time he got to his car, which naturally gave him trouble staying in gear. He had to stop and buy more Stop Leak to get home. Even a passing RV with a QYB sticker on its bumper couldn't lift his spirits.

He had been running film the whole time with his pen camera, which once home, he took his tax clip and edited it into a seven minute segment (after learning the ins and outs of editing by watching YouTube). 'Bullied by Revenue' was his first clip loaded to QYB. There would be others.

The next 27 days went by like a flash. In that time, more of his furniture broke. His car sucked up Stop Leak like crazy. His PC he set to the side. Even the laptop was making an annoying hum after booting up, and this after Jenna *finally* got back to him, and sent him an update to his operating system, which left him wondering why the Union Jack icon in the taskbar was suddenly blinking faster. She never did answer him about that. Regardless, it was easier to write on the library's computer, so he once again shut down the Jenna laptop and went to posting from the library. He became such a regular at the library, that for the librarian's grateful coffee offer, he always brought donuts.

He had by now planned the phases to his Road Trip. All he needed was trip money. But though hindsight told him to raise his sticker prices, he still kept them at $5. (Even political hacks were getting $25 or more for their stickers to be on people's cars till election time.) But Ian wasn't about the money or contributing to any candidates as much as he was for the people. He knew he could always find a way to keep his QYB mission statement alive, just didn't know how with an eviction, garnishment, and more tax problems coming.

Many college students became fans of QYB. Stickers were seen on many college laptops, cars, motorcycles, and bikes, with a few skateboards touting QYB stickers also. (A dean at a major university had a QYB sticker on her car). But though desperately needing money, Ian still refused to raise his prices past $5. He continued in the hope of the honor system, which had its ups and downs.

But a big pay off came just 71 hours before his eviction was to take place. In his P.O. Box he found close to $7,000 in sticker orders, his largest single day order yet, and with most of them paid for in money orders, checks, and some folded cash. Another just as large an order would arrive the following day, and from then on, sticker sales grew exponentially. His $7,000 day led him to post a heartfelt thank you to all those buying stickers and becoming QYBers. An error in judgment was his using the Jenna laptop to post his thanks.

IRSuarez@QYB.com: Even though I sit waiting on the hour when the sheriff will come to toss me from my home, I still want to say thank you to all who are buying my stickers. The proceeds, after paying for the stickers and the mailing of course, will help to fund my QYB Road Trip, which I will post about later. I am about to add 'Payback' as a new segment to Quit Your Bitching, so do stay posted.

Missouri Mike chimed in through facebook.

IRSuarez: Hey Mike. What's up?

Turbold183@Liberty: What's this about a road trip? And why is it capitalized?

IRSuarez: Nothing gets by you, eh Mike? Road Trip is capitalized because it's going to be a BIG THING! How's that for capitalized?

Turbold183: You're off the chain, Ian.

IRSuarez: I'll take that as a compliment.

Turbold183: And why haven't you just gone vender status with them stickers of yours? Make more money that way.

IRSuarez: I'd rather give away my stickers before seeing people using a credit card to pay for them. I feel stupid enough already having used credit for buying my crap furniture

Turbold183: Your trip bringing you up this way?

IRSuarez: Sorry Mike, but my trip starts with payback right here in town, and then works its way to California.

Turbold187: I had a feeling you had something up your sleeve with this road trip business of yours. Look, I know this is *your* world and *I'm* just living in it, but you be careful what you do. And be careful with posting stuff like 'payback.' Lots of eyes and ears, buddy.

It was Jenna, or rather the Betty Boop caricature, that chimed in through facebook then.

IRSuarez: Gotta run, bud. Jenna's wanting to chat.

Turbold183: You be careful with her, too. Something strange about a woman who won't show her face. Chat at ya later, bud.

Ian clicked off and accepted Jenna's chat request. But she didn't want to chat at all; she just sent a 'check your email' memo. Ian noticed the Union Jack had suddenly started blinking even faster. *Hmm, I wonder why that is?* Ian checked his inbox and did a double take at seeing Jenna's new yum-yum attachments. *Man, this woman looks good. But she sends pics, and no chat? Mike's right . . . Jenna is strange.* He broke from facebook and went to his website, where he found an additional 6,000 new added subscribers to QYB. *Calls for some good writing tonight.* He next checked his total count. *Whoa . . . 4 million! Yep, people are due some seriously good writing tonight.* He no longer cared about the flashing icon.

Weaver was sitting at his desk and staring at his calendar while pondering the inevitable. His mother-in-law had agreed to take 34 Starling Circle in trade for the money he owed her. He now needed Ian gone more than ever.

Ian had made things easier for Weaver when avoiding to defend himself in court against his eviction proceedings. That pretty much sealed his fate. Ian's attorney did file an appeal, but it was denied for lack of evidence. Ian was on his way out. All Weaver had to do was wait his time and 34 Starling Circle would be his again.

But one thing kept gnawing at Weaver. It was the way Ian had kept staring at his ring.

Weaver hadn't run Ian's mortgage in the conventional sense. Ian was another of his pocket mortgages. But banking regulators inspecting Diamond Bank's books got onto Weaver's 160 some odd pocket mortgages. His excuse had been that he was holding these mortgages on his own dime until these customers could better their credit scores. "But they're already in the homes," had said one regulator.

Weaver's pocket mortgages were netting him $200,000 a month, which was another reason why regulators wanted those mortgages in the books. His claiming they were all troubled mortgages was false. Other than for Ian, and a few others, who were late a time or two, his pocket mortgages were as stable as all the others in the books. Regulators had gotten onto that, too.

But Weaver wasn't about to just turn over his main source of income, especially when thinking to bolt on trophy wife #3 and his mistress. A memory of his last conversation with his wife reminded him of her talking about her favorite subject, how much she'd spent the day before in Orlando. *That there's reason enough for me to bolt!*

Weaver's trophy wife had never much cared how her husband made his money, so long as there was money to spend. Even their abrupt move from their lower Manhattan digs back to Florida hadn't bothered her much. Yes, she'd been a little miffed at losing all that New York City shopping, but she got over it.

Weaver thought to pick up the phone and call his 23-year-old mistress. But talking to her was even worse. *She out-spends my wife 4-to-1! I gotta leave these two bimbos behind, before they break me.*

Weaver had dug a hole so deep he forgot to stop digging. Turning state's evidence only helped so much, and it didn't assure him that he'd be safe after ratting out his Sanford, Singe, and Chandler associates. He knew time would reveal his own ill-laundered past, which included hiding his illegally gotten gains in his bank. His ring and pin were a sign of how much gains. *And this Ian's onto my ring and pin. It was stupid of me to take him for granted, his being in the banking game himself once.*

Ego and status had gotten the best of Weaver. His last hoorah would have him living in some hidden village in the Amazon. *Might even be better hiding in the Arctic!* Weaver had also ruined his own bank's credit worthiness. When thinking a new homebuyer program might bail him out . . . no program came. When thinking Fannie and Freddie might rebound and serve him up more mortgages . . . no mortgages came (once the MAEs flamed out). When needing a boost in housing credits . . . Countrywide and Amerifirst went belly-up. Bear Sterns had been his big money lender with low points . . . but now Bear was finished. All that was left was to become a whistleblower. But there was still Ian to contend with.

Weaver absentmindedly fiddled with his prized ring while thinking of Ian. He kept taking the ring on and off while trying to convince himself that Ian was just a momentary bump in his way. He glanced out at his V12 Mercedes in the parking lot. The shine of the car in the noonday sun made him regret having bought it with his ill-gotten gains. *Damn shame to lose that ride.* He looked at the pale spot on his ring finger without the ring on. *Ah, what's the point of hiding it? Any idiot can see I'm missing a ring.* Weaver continued in his gloominess until his stomach reminded him it was nearing lunch.

Ian had by now resigned himself to losing his home. While *he* was waiting on the inevitable, he began loading his car. The first thing he put in it was his busted PC, then his clothes, his backpack full of journals, his laptop, 2 cases of bottled water, a full case of Stop Leak, all in preparation for his road trip. He still had his furniture to load, but he had plans for that. His plans did, however, require borrowing the Smiths' truck. While waiting for the Smiths to arrive home to ask to borrow their truck, he Skyped.

Among those he most like to Skype with was his favorite author, Dr. Dana Warrick. No sooner had he started chatting about Dr. Warrick's new book, 'Terrorism in a World of Terrorists,' when agents in Miami started recording.

Ian's author friend, Dr. Dana Warrick, was not only a writer of seven books, but she was also a teaching professor at the War College in Maryland. The fact that she and Ian were kindred spirits did not sit well with SAC Rubio in Miami. In fact, she was most worried about Ian and his relationship with a microbiologist. Dr. Warrick being a fan of QYB troubled Rubio that much more.

Ian had never been much into educational writers. He hated books written by grant-sponsored professors. He considered their books boring and lacking in people-speak. Ian was all about people-speak. It's what made QYB so popular. But in Dr. Warrick, he was positively thrilled with her people-speak, and the fact she wrote and published on her own dime. Ian thought the world of Dr. Warrick, and she of him. Besides being a writer and a biochemist, Dr. Warrick was also an epidemiologist. She had recently taken part in vaccinating thousands of people who were in the Nile region, where many were infected with the deadly Steiner virus. Never once did she fear contracting the Steiner virus while there, and for her assistance, she received a World Health Organization award. It was the fact she was interacting with Ian that had Rubio's agents working overtime listening in to each of their Skyping sessions.

DocDanaWar: You can use my guest bedroom, if your road trip brings you this way.

IRSuarez: Thanks, doc. But I'm headed west, not north.

DocDanaWar: I also wanted to thank you for posting about my book on your website. My publisher thanks you, too. He says he can't keep up with all the new orders.

IRSuarez: Least I could do for someone who donates their profits to charity.

DocDanaWar: You've given plenty to charity also.

IRSuarez: Neither Revenue nor my banker care anything about that right now.

DocDanaWar: Well, I and my charity thank you.

474747

47474

IRSuarez: So, did you get around to writing me that article I needed? This little gem got bored agents at full attention.

DocDanaWar: I did. Check your email.

IRSuarez: You're the best, doc.

Rubio wanted whatever had been sent to Ian on her desk immediately. But there was a problem breaking through his IP address. She was just getting the low down from her tech agent Lloyd when her boss in Langley called. The topic of possible 'code-speak' regarding Ian was discussed. But Rubio knew code-speak. She had been dealing with the cartels during her stint with the DEA to know lots about code-speak. "I don't think so, boss. But I have to wonder why a woman her age would even be spending time talking to our man."

"This woman's a terror onto herself," said her boss. "She leads a science department, does bio work, and writes bio-terror books that sell like hot cakes. I *do* think there's code-speak in their chats. Just keep your people listening in."

"We got a problem getting into his email account."

"You'll figure it out."

"Well, I wouldn't worry too much about that code-speak stuff, sir. Their chats are sounding legit. Nothing but talk."

"You need to get focused on this Ian fellow, agent Rubio. Work him 24/7 if you have to, but get the goods on him before your vacation time comes around. I know you got plans later this year."

"But sir, that's in December."

"December will be here before you know it. Just site in on him exclusively, 'cause up here, his site means trouble."

"I will, sir. But remember, I already put in my request for December. My family and I are already booked aboard a cruise ship for three weeks."

"Sorry, agent Rubio, but this is priority #1. And you best get the goods on this Missouri Mike fellow that Ian is always talking to. We're seeing lots of chatter between their sites these days."

"Roger that, sir." This was one of those rare times when Rubio hated being a 'can do' agent. But as she worried about her vacation with her family, on her computer screen, she saw where Missouri Mike was trying to interrupt Dr. Warrick and Ian's conversation through facebook. *Oh? So what's this? First a microbiologist and now a militant wanting at the microbiologist?* Rubio keyed up her speakers to listen in.

DocDanaWar: Hey there, Liberty man.

Turbold183: Hello, doc. I noticed you were talking with Ian.

DocDanaWar: He just rang off.

Turbold183: I'm having trouble logging onto his facebook *and* his Skype page. I tried tweeting him, but apparently he's not checking his tweets. Might be trouble on my end.

DocDanaWar: I'm not surprised, all the trouble you bring yourself with that Liberty Press of yours. You know you must be persona non-grata to the authorities.

Turbold183: I'm not the only one causing trouble. Ian's another who's begging for trouble with this road trip talk of his.

DocDanaWar: We'll see. I don't think Ian's that crazy.

Turbold183: He wanted me to write an article about the militia activity up this way. Said it was supposed to tie in with something he was having you write. Can I send you that post, and you send it to his account page? I can't seem to get onto QYB either.

DocDanaWar: Now that *is* strange, and sure, I'll get your stuff to him.

Turbold183: Thanks, docs. I'll attach it to your email right now.

DocDanaWar: Have you ever gotten a chat request from this Jenna woman Ian's so hot about?

Turbold 183: I have. In fact, she sent me some anti-virus upgrades to help with my site, but it fouled me up more than helped. I eventually uninstalled it. Why do you ask?

DocDanaWar: Cause I got a chat request from her last night wanting to send me the same stuff. Hasn't given me any trouble, and Ian vouches for her, although he's upset he can't ever meet with her.

Turbold183: Ian should be upset. I don't trust a person who won't do live chats. And be careful what she sends you. Ian's such an innocent, he won't see trouble coming until it's right in his face. And if I were you, I'd uninstall whatever it is she sent you until we know more about this woman.

DocDanaWar: Funny you should say that, because I *was* going to accept her chat request for later this evening. But if you say beware . . .

Turbold183: I do say beware. And next time you chat with Ian, tell him he's stirring up a hornet's nest with this Revenue video he posted. And his commentary on the Federal Reserve and Homeland isn't going to get him any awards with the government, either.

DocDanaWar: Let Ian be. He's got enough going on without you mentioning hornet's nests.

Turbold183: True that.

DocDanaWar IRSuarez: I'd love to chat more, but I got a class to teach.

Turbold183: I'm sending my attachment now.

DocDanaWar: I'll be sure to forward it to Ian. Bye for now.

An abrupt entry by federal agents into Missouri Mike's shop delayed his sending his post to Doc Warrick. At the exact time of the entry, Ian was getting a knock at *his* door from the pizza delivery guy. And at the exact moment that Ian bit into his first slice, Mike got away from agents and took off running.

Chapter 31

And Jenna *continued* to send Ian

stuff; stuff like downloads, attached pictures of herself, *always* sending stuff. But other than for a few text messages to say in which part of the world she was doing business in, she never again made any attempt to make an actual phone contact with him, and her excuse for not meeting in person continued to be business. But she did keep the carrot on the stick with a possible Florida rendezvous in the near future. This kept Ian hopeful, and her more enticing attachments even more hopeful. But his road trip took precedent over JennaCal412.

Ian continued to post from the town library. He went from bringing donuts, to buying all the library staff gifts, like flea market sunglasses and watches. As for Jenna, Ian had come to the conclusion that she was either married, engaged, or had a boyfriend *or maybe all three.* Her pics and emails just made her out to be even more mysterious in Ian's eyes. Jenna had her reasons for being mysterious.

He finally got Nancy on the phone. "Ian? Coffee? Really? But you should be trying to work things out with Mr. Weaver, shouldn't you? How can you have time to invite me for coffee?"

"Cause I need a favor, and that's why I'm calling."

"Does your favor include us helping you with your fines? Cause if it does, you know we will."

"No, it does not."

"No? You sure?"

"Yes, I'm sure."

"And you say the coffee's already brewing?"

"It is."

"Well, then I'll be right over. I got to hear this favor you need."

"The start of the favor is you making those nice lemon muffins of yours. Oh, and it's not money that I need, by the way."

"Muffins will be ready in 20. I'll be over in 30."

True to her word, Nancy walked through the door exactly a half hour later. But she first had to work around the piled-up furniture that Ian had stacked on his patio. "What's with your furniture all piled up outside?" she asked once coming through the door.

"That's the favor I need. I need your truck so I can take all that stuff to storage."

"To what storage?" Nancy smelled the coffee. "Umm, smells like the good stuff."

"Only the best for you, Nance."

Nancy worked her way to the kitchen where she set down her muffin basket. Ian was reaching for the cream pitcher when she asked again, "so what storage?"

"The storage place down the street from your shop. I was hoping you would lend me your delivery truck for a couple of hours, so I could load and unload my stuff." Ian got a text message right then. *Hmm, only my closest friends know my number. I wonder if it's Jenna?*

"Sorry, Nance. I gotta check this text message. I'll be quick."

But it wasn't Jenna. It was an SOS message from Mike, who was wanting to Skype ASAP.

"Take your time, Ian. I'll bring the coffee and muffins to the table."

Ian gave her a smile while booting up the laptop. "Thanks, Nance. I swear I'll be quick." But he wouldn't be quick at all.

Ian's first impression of seeing Mike on camera was that he was flustered.

IRSuarez: What the heck's up? Something wrong?

Turbold183: I got trouble.

Ian could tell from all their earlier Skyping that Mike wasn't in his office. Nancy was too busy getting things ready to notice Ian take the laptop from the table to the sofa.

IRSuarez: So where are you at? It doesn't look like you're at your workshop.

Turbold183: I'm in one of my cabins.

Mike swept his web camera around so Ian could see the cabin.

Turbold183: For obvious reasons I can't tell you my exact location, but this cabin's yours whenever you need it.

IRSuarez: Thanks for that. So . . . what's the trouble?

Turbold183: Feds came storming into my shop yesterday morning. They were looking for some of my workers. Something to do with some Armory heist.

IRSuarez: Did you have something to do with this Armory heist?

Turbold183: No. But they still had a warrant to search my place. Anyhoo . . . they confiscated my computer before starting to tear apart my shop. The lead agent said they were looking for weapons. I waited my turn before skedaddling. By then, the bastards had found my emergency money stash, so I'm flat broke with no way of getting into town to withdraw from my bank without getting popped. They probably think my stash is from this heist I know nothing about. I don't need much, since I am heading north for a while and I have some money waiting for me where I'm going. But in the meantime, I gotta eat and I need fuel. Can you help?

IRSuarez123: Sure thing, Mike.

Turbold183: I've also got Doc pitching in, but that could be a problem if the Feds are checking her, too.

IRSuarez: Why would they be checking her?

Turbold183: Eyes and ears, remember?

IRSuarez: I can send you cash, but I've also got to avoid a money trail. I'll text you a drop method I learned from one of Doc's books. Use it. (Ian was referring to a drop tactic that the early al-Qaida members used for sharing information. It began with a common password protected e-mail account. A draft would be started, but not finished. This gave others the ability to add or remove from said email just by knowing the password. This was how a constant flow of information was transferred among cells worldwide without needing a drop site. It worked for al-Qaida. It would work for Mike and Ian as well.) While they were Skyping . . .

In Miami . . .

Agent Rubio was just then getting the low down on the Northern Amory break-in. She hadn't a clue as to Ian's new phone number, as he was changing numbers periodically and using different SIM cards that did a fine job of keeping him off radar. Mike, she had dead to rights. Having transcripts in front of her of Ian and Mike's earlier chats (before Subnet had taken out Ian's computer) gave her reason to think code-speak. *Could Ian have known of this heist? After all, he is planning a road trip, and it was a big heist; many weapons and much ammo stolen. Could he be wanting weapons through code-speak?* Rubio rushed from her office to check in with SAT and see if SAT had anything on either Ian's or Mike's whereabouts.

Landers Ferguson was just then coming from the elevator, his laptop under his arm, and when seeing Rubio trying to avoid him, he hurried towards her. "Agent Rubio."

"Not now, Ferguson. I got no time to talk now."

Rubio noticed that on Ferguson's laptop, he had Ian and Mike's Skype chat going. But then the chatting stopped. Mike and Ian had ended their Skype session. It was Ferguson who was angry then, especially when Ian's entire web signal went off-air from his shutting down the laptop before packing it in his car.

As soon as Ian finished chatting with Mike and shut off the laptop, he heard the all too familiar sound of another chair about to break.

"No, Nancy! Don't sit there!" But it was too late. Nancy was already headed for the floor.

Ian cared nothing about the chair. All the chairs could break to pieces as far as he was concerned. But seeing his friend hit the floor *did* concern him, especially Nancy with her bad hip. Ian hurried to help her off the floor. "Oh, Nance, tell me you're alright."

Nancy had coffee, muffin, and pieces of shattered mug all over her new dress. Nancy, the humble soul that she was, instead of being angry, just let Ian help her to her feet, while trying to laugh it off. She was a small woman, so it was easy for Ian to get her to her feet, but he did it way too fast. "Easy there, Ian. I've got plenty of breakable parts, you know." Nancy's smile eased his worry of her being hurt, but then became angry when looking at the chair, so angry when seeing her nursing her hip that he kicked at what was left of the chair and sent it crashing into the wall. Nancy was startled by that. "Oh Ian, please control yourself. You won't have any chairs left, you keep doing that. I'm okay, really."

"To hell with these chairs, Nancy. I just had to watch you bust your ass because of this junk, junk I wanted out of my house months ago."

"Junk or not, it's what you've got. I've had harder falls. Don't worry. Why do you think I had to have a hip replacement?" She emphasized this by giving her hip a gentle tap. "See? I'm alright."

Ian by then had Frank on the phone.

"No, Frank, she's not a heavy woman. In fact, she's small and frail," Ian waved off Nancy's 'don't worry about it' look, "who, thank God, did not get hurt when the chair broke. But I told you this would happen. One chair has already shown it was junk, now they're all falling apart. No, Frank, you can chant me your store's policy all you want. But you gotta send your truck, you hear me?" Ian's anger boiled when seeing Nancy going for the dustpan and broom. "Nancy, please sit down. I'll clean up that mess soon as I'm done with Frank. Go sit on the sofa. I don't anticipate *it* collapsing on you."

"Mr. Suarez; we've been through this already," said Frank. "I cannot take back any of your furniture."

"I'm sick of your 'I can'ts' Frank. *Sick* of hearing it! Repo this junk, or whatever you people call it. Do whatever it takes; just come get this stuff out of my house." Ian remembered his eviction. "And do it *today*."

But all Frank wanted to talk about was beacon scores.

"Forget beacon scores, Frank. I want this stuff gone. You hear me Frank? FRANK?" But Frank had hung up.

"Why that mother . . ."

"Lord Ian, listen to yourself. Forget all that arguing with that man and come finish your coffee and muffins. Or why did I bring them? Come on, you got no time for this, with your eviction just days away."

"Tomorrow to be exact, Nancy. And that's why I need your truck. And forgive me for getting so riled up. It's just tough watching you fall like that, on crap furniture that brings out the worst in me."

"Seems like you got your priorities all mixed up, Ian. It's not your furniture that should be bringing out the worst in you; it should be your eviction."

"Well, that too. But what's done is done, and I'm not paying any money to some heathen Board of crooks, either." He pointed at the stuff piled outside. "But *that* I have to get to storage."

Something about Ian's behavior troubled Nancy. "You sure you're just going to storage?"

"Sure. Where else would I go? And to think I come from a long line of excellent furniture builders."

"I caught that in your bio."

"So, the truck?"

"You got that look about you, Ian. You sure it's just storage? What you got going on in that head of yours?" Nancy came close enough to pinch his cheek . . . hard.

"Ouch!" yelled Ian.

"Forget whatever craziness you got going on in that head of yours." Right then, one of his inner voices started shouting *Road Trip! Road Trip! Road Trip! Road Trip! Road trip! Road Trip! Road Trip!"*

"I just need your truck before the sheriff comes a-knocking."

Nancy read something in Ian that made her feel like he wasn't being truthful. She sipped her coffee slowly before saying, "So nothing more than storage, eh?"

"Geez, Nance. You make it sound as if I were planning a heist or something."

"Are you?"

"Come on, Nance. I don't want to have to spend $300 on a rental. Plus your truck has that great lift gate, which will help get my stuff inside. Storage and back. Promise. I'll fill the tank before returning it."

"Don't make promises you can't keep." Nancy already had her phone out to call her husband, Willard.

Road Trip, once started, would mean no turning back.

The Smiths had been Ian's one positive to a whole lot of negatives occurring at DHE. The Smiths had been good friends to Ian, wonderful people, really. But Nancy was the more savvy of the two when reading people. In Ian, she read a genuine fellow. She also liked his Quit Your Bitching concept, enough to become a subscriber herself. But she sensed trouble in Ian even while talking to Willard.

"Ian, Willard says he can't loan you anyone from the store to help you. He's got two that are out sick for tomorrow, so you're on your own. Can you handle loading your stuff yourself?"

"I can go to town in the morning and find someone to help me, don't worry."

"Willard says you're cutting close with the sheriff, and I agree."

"If it's still about the furniture, then I have most of the heavy stuff already out on the patio. I just need to drag the sofa and the bed out tomorrow." Ian was still suffering through the voices while Nancy spoke to Willard. She then hung up and gathered her things to leave.

"Well, the truck is yours, but . . ." Nancy came closer, ". . . I'm going to be brutally honest with you, Ian . . . if borrowing our truck brings us trouble, then here's the brutal part . . . our friendship, as you know it, will be over. Capish?"

Nancy's candid honesty shocked Ian a little. It even sounded in his voice when he replied, "No way, Nancy. Just storage and back."

"You've got something up your sleeve, I can tell. But hey, you got *our* truck and *your* conscience to deal with, so let that guide you." She was at the door when she turned to say, "I'm going home to soak in a warm bath. But do remember our friendship, Ian. I'm giving you the benefit of the doubt. But please, do hurry tomorrow, cause I'll be worrying about you the whole time you're gone."

"Put salts in your bath and quit thinking such crazy thoughts about me. I'll have your truck back before you know it. Promise."

"There you go with the promises again."

Ian gave Nancy time enough to reach her house before clicking on his pen camera. He had already recorded his dragging furniture out to the patio. It was time to finish the job, which meant dragging the sofa, dining table, and chairs out to the patio, also. Last thing he tossed out was the frayed rug. He left his mattress on the floor for another night's sleep before dragging that out, too. The following day was going to be a busy day.

Part V

Road Trip

"Economic activity has a huge impact on the budget. As the economy grows, so too does tax revenues as more people work to pay more taxes."

Mentioned on QYB

"Blind respect for authority is the greatest enemy of truth."

Albert Einstein

Chapter 32

In the truck beside him was one

of his Mind journals with the words 'Road Trip' written in black marker on the front cover. The first page of his Road Trip journal was titled: 'Payback'. At the top of his list of payback was 'Furniture Toss.'

It was no easy feat loading all his furniture by himself into the Smith's truck. His sofa had been one of the toughest to load.

The dining room table hadn't been that easy, either.

He damaged one of the legs of the dining room table when dragging it to the truck, and this after ripping a hole in his newly screened door when dragging it. Adding to the ripped screen was a dent to the door made when he carried out the headboard.

The desk hadn't been that easy to load, either.

The mattress fell off the truck ramp while he tried to push it into the truck.

Not only did his camera film him loading all his furniture, but it also captured the amount of energy his manic mode was instilling in him that morning. But what his pen camera could not capture was what his enemy mind was doing to him, screaming in his head . . .

"GET TO THE STORE! NOW!"

He put the truck in first gear, and since this would be the last time he would be at his house, he absentmindedly waved goodbye to it. (He'd driven his car to Nancy's house already and left it there parked, packed, and ready to go.) He missed seeing Ms. Brown at her window when he waved goodbye to 34 Starling Circle.

Ms. Brown had been watching him the whole time he'd been loading, smiling each time he hurt himself, thinking it was fine retribution for all the trouble he had caused while living on the cul-de-sac.

But to Ian, none of that mattered now that his Road Trip had begun.

He drove the Smith's truck with great care after clicking off the camera for the 14-mile trip to town.

Ian next clicked on the camera to capture the beeping of the truck while it was backing up to the furniture store's customer entrance. The pen camera recorded him jumping from the cab of the truck and hurrying to open the rear doors of the 20-foot panel truck. Ian then made sure his camera was firmly clipped to his shirt pocket before jumping in back and . . . pushing everything out!

The chairs, the dining room table, desk, headboard, sofa, recliner, mattress, box springs, coffee table, loveseat, two night tables and their lamps (their bulbs shattering when the lamps struck the concrete walk) all got tossed from the truck. His recliner was the last of his furniture that he pushed from the truck, with his frayed rug topping off his furniture pile. He missed seeing one of the dining table legs break through the bottom half of the store's glass door.

Ian next aimed his pen camera up at the store's large 'Buy Now/Pay Later' banner. "That's how they get their junk into people's homes." He aimed the pen camera at his piled up furniture. "And this is how you bring it back."

Ian hadn't noticed the broken glass door, but Frank's employees did. A call up to his office had Frank coming on the run.

Seeing Frank hurrying towards the front of the store got Ian rushing to shut the truck's rear doors before jumping back into the cab and getting the truck started.

Frank had to step around broken glass before getting to yell at Ian to stop. "Whoa! Stop right there, mister. I don't know what the hell you think you're doing, but you can't leave that furniture here. You need to put all that stuff back in your truck."

Ian let off the clutch and got the truck rolling forward. "Your stuff now, Frank. Do with it what you want." The camera captured Frank's bewildered look as he jumped aboard the truck's running board. "You need to stop this truck now."

Ian didn't want to see Frank get hurt while hanging onto the side mirror, so he stopped.

"Back this truck up and load up all your stuff," said Frank angrily almost in Ian's ear, "load it now, or I call the cops."

Instead, Ian gunned the truck. "Save your threats, Frank. And I suggest you jump before you get road rash. Your choice. But I'm leaving."

"Look, man," Frank tried a friendlier tone, "if you've got a beef, take it up with corporate. Not me."

"How can you say that? I bought all that crap furniture from *you*. And remember my neighbor and the chair?"

"Look, tell you what, uh, Mr. Suarez, right?"

"Ian will do."

"Okay, Ian. Look, you load up your stuff and park, you come inside, and we'll deal with this. But you gotta load your stuff."

Ian gunned the truck again. "Best jump, Frank."

"But you can't leave your stuff here, Ian! Look, tell ya what; I'll get someone from corporate on the phone to talk to ya. We'll deal with this. Promise. But you gotta load your stuff. I can't have your stuff piled up in front of the store like this. And you also got a busted glass door to pay for."

"I didn't come to discuss terms, Frank." Ian let the truck roll a little before braking hard. "You gotta get off Frank, cause I'm definitely headed home."

"You're insane if you think you can just leave your stuff here!"

"Stuff's already here, Frank."

"Look, okay, forget the glass door. And I'll even get some of my people to help you load up. But ya gotta load." Ian again popped the clutch and made the truck lurch forward before hitting the brakes. This did get Frank to finally jump from the running board, but only to be replaced by his new part time hire, a teen!

Ian was surprised to see the teen at his window.

"Boss told you to load your shit, mister. You best load up your shit, or I pull you from this truck."

Ian wasn't at all worried about the teen's threat. What he was more worried about was the big kid getting hurt. Thus far, he knew he had recorded a pretty good video. But if the kid got hurt, the video would be useless. He was thinking this right as the teen grabbed his shirt, and in the process came close enough to touch the pen camera.

Ian looked to Frank and yelled, "Call your dog off, or he rides, Frank." Hearing that, the teen twisted Ian's shirt some more.

"Call him off, Frank!" Ian gunned the truck for emphasis.

But the teen wouldn't budge.

"His getting hurt's going to be on you, Frank, so call him off."

Ian wasn't about to go anywhere while the teen was still hanging onto his shirt, but he wanted the teen to believe he was.

"Daniel! Get your ass down off of that man's truck!" Ian was relieved to hear that.

"But I got a good hold of him, boss." The teen still hadn't let go.

"Kid, you're going to get yourself hurt, if you don't let go of me."

Seeing the truck moving forward got the teen jumping off.

But not before ripping Ian's shirt pocket.

Had it not been for Ian's quick reflexes, he would've lost the camera.

The camera next recorded sirens coming from in the distance as Ian merged with Main Street traffic.

Ian's next stop was the Post Office, which was a few miles down the road from the store. He pulled to the back of the Post office where he took time to settle his nerves before going inside to find more relief in the form of $3,500 in cash and money orders for sticker orders in his Box. While still opening envelopes . . .

Two police cruisers had parked right near Ian's piled up furniture. Deputies had begun taking pictures of some of his busted furniture and of the broken glass door, and they took down information from Frank and his help, including info on the well-advertised Smith truck.

Ian was on his way back through town and was about to pass Frank's store, when a passing tractor trailer rig gave him the opportunity to hide from Frank and police. He used the cover of the big rig all the way to the stoplight.

He was pulling up to Nancy's house right as deputies were dispatched to 34 Starling Circle, where they would find Ian's eviction notice replaced with 'No Trespassing' signs recently taped to the door.

He had to use his breathing exercises to calm himself once parked at Nancy's. He then used his best diplomatic skills to explain to Nancy what he'd done.

It was Nancy's turn to use breathing exercises before erupting with, "Ian! How could you?"

But it hadn't surprised Nancy that much that Ian had done something so shocking. She'd read it in his demeanor days before. But she was still disappointed in him and showed it. "And you used *our* truck for *your* craziness. You know Willard is going to be *awfully* mad at you." Ian had nothing to say to that. He stayed silent and let Nancy rant. "And I sure hope your craziness doesn't bring us any repercussions because of you using our truck. Oh, Ian, how could you? Why didn't you tell me what you were planning?"

"You would've tried to stop me."

"You're right there."

"And I didn't want to be stopped."

"That's pretty obvious."

"Now, can I use your computer, so I can show you my video?"

"And a video, too? Well, I might as well witness your craziness in action." Nancy had by then calmed down enough to watch the video, which she thought, was pretty crazy. She did allow Ian time to edit what needed editing before posting to QYB though. "I'll allow you time at my computer because you're a friend. But you really need to be thinking of where you're going to live now."

"I'm on the road next, Nancy, so a place to live, I'll worry about when I come back."

"That darn site of yours is making you crazy, you know that? And now a road trip, instead of looking for a place to live? Crazy, I tell you."

"Don't tell Willard about any of this until he gets home, alright Nance? I don't want to ruin his workday."

"I just hope that store manager didn't catch the name on our truck." But it was too late for that. The police were just then visiting Willard at the store.

It was right after editing and posting 'Furniture Toss' from Nancy Smith's computer that the knock came at her door.

Handcuffs came next.

It was while riding in the back of the transport car that Ian got to wondering what Willard would think of him when finding the filled gallon gas can still strapped to the inside ribbing of the truck.

Ian had a difficult time staying quiet in court when hearing the charges of: "Disturbing the peace. How do you plead?"

"Disturbing the peace? Get out."

"Mr. Suarez. You will respect this court. Now how do you plead?"

"Absolutely *not* guilty, is how I plead."

"As to destruction of private property; how do you plead?"

"Destruction of *what* property?"

"How do you plead, Mr. Suarez?"

"Not guilty again, your honor. It's that store that's guilty of . . ."

"There is here an attempt to harm someone with your truck. Is that right?"

"They jumped on my truck. I didn't attempt to harm . . ."

"So what is your plea to that then?"

"Not guilty again, your honor. Not guilty to any of it."

"What about this illegal dumping charge?"

"You *must* be kidding. Illegal dumping?"

"You *are* trying my patience, Mr. Suarez. I'll charge you with contempt of court in a minute if you don't start taking this more seriously. Now, as to illegal dumping, how do you plead?"

"Not guilty. Not guilty to *any* of *your* charges."

"That's it. Bailiff."

(Ian's more serious charge of 'intent to incite' would come once 'Furniture Toss' went viral.)

"Where are you sending me, your honor? You should just let me go. You've got no right to jail me. If anything, you should be jailing those on the Board of such a crappy furniture company!"

His outburst actually got him Baker-acted.

Ian was remanded to the psyche wing of the county jail for a 72-hour observation period. He was kept separated from the general population at the jail, which was a good thing, though held naked while under suicide watch. He was given a furniture pad to ward off the intentionally cold a/c and left alone for 3 days. He suffered through his 3 days in his quiet place.

Three days later, he was in front of the same judge, who in seeing a much calmer Ian, and after checking his background for priors, decided to let Ian go free (the county jail was severely overcrowded at the time), but not before Ian signed court documents assuring the judge he would appear on his trial date.

But much like he'd done with his mandatory meetings with the DHE Board and Weaver, and his doctor appointment, Ian would also blow off court.

Nancy was who picked him up and drove him home once he was released from jail. She even allowed him a shower, fed him, allowed him some time at her computer (where Furniture Toss already had 40,000 views with 95% likes) before getting on his case again about his living situation. "You lose your house over your nonsense; get yourself jailed over your craziness over some furniture, and now a road trip?"

"I gotta do what I gotta do, Nance."

"I'm sorry to hear that. And so I'm assuming there's more in the line of payback videos?"

"Nothing gets by you, Nance."

"A few days in jail and you become a smart ass."

"I'm sorry, Nance. I didn't want us parting like this."

But Nancy wasn't about holding any grudges, especially against Ian, whom she really liked, and thought the world of because of his moxie. Instead, she offered him a hug at the door. "You're a fool, Ian, you know that? But you be careful in whatever you do. And do see Willard before you leave town. He's mad, but not mad enough to not forgive you. Quite a fiasco you caused with our truck, though."

"Yeah, I'm sorry about that, Nance. I hadn't planned for it to go that way. And as for Willard, I would've seen him anyway without you reminding me. I don't want Willard mad at me forever."

"That's good then," said Nancy.

Ian took that as his clue to leave.

He had to first pour in a whole bottle of Stop Leak before starting the car. (The bottle would take him to the state line before needing another one.)

While passing by his old house, he noticed a late model Jaguar parked underneath the carport. *Wow! Got people living in it already?* He got to smile though when seeing his QYB sticker still on Ms. Brown's Cadillac. (Ms. Brown still hadn't figured out why she got the occasional honk, thumbs up, or "you go, mama!" from motorists.) His smile grew bigger when in his rear view mirror he saw an older woman standing on his old front porch yelling profanities at Ms. Brown, who was yelling back from her front porch. *Wow! That woman never quits.*

He next stopped to see Willard, where sure enough they were back to being friends in no time, and even sharing a laugh over Furniture Toss. (Other than for a call to them days later, Ian would lose contact with the Smiths.)

After visiting Willard's store, Ian went to see his friend Cheryl at the electronic box store. He was there not only to pick up his laptop, but to also buy the latest Lockout software for his laptop. He'd read about how Lockout was used by pharmaceutical giants to guard their most intimate R&D secrets. (Lockout is a security program that changes pass code numbers 250 times a minute.) Ian's need for Lockout was because he knew the courts and the attorneys for the furniture company would probably want to trace him using his laptop while on his road trip, and then use that as evidence against him. So Lockout it was . . . which also inadvertently canceled out the Union Jack tracking software.

"Geez, my roommate and I laughed watching you toss out your furniture like that." Cheryl was still waiting for Lockout to finish installing.

"I wound up in jail over that."

"I'm not surprised." Cheryl handed over the laptop once the download was done. "That's a hell of a good program you got for yourself, Ian. Use it wisely." Ian handed over his new pre-paid money card, loaded with trip money from his P.O. Box offerings.

"You know I will, Cheryl."

"We'll be watching for you, Ian."

"You do that. And enjoy my next video, cause 'Quit your bitching' is on the road now."

"I like the sound of that."

Last friend to see was his print shop buddy, who had another 2,000 stickers to mail out.

In Mapquesting his Irvine, California trip a week before at Nancy's, Ian had also gotten info on the computer company he was about to visit. He knew the company had a quarterly share profit meeting coming up in a few days, and he wanted to be there for that. His car did not have a GPS screen, so he taped his MapQuest to his dash, jotted down a few things in his Mind journal, and hit the gas to start his 2,300-mile journey west.

Last stop in town was for buying a whole case of fluid for the car.

He kept his laptop off during his drive, not so much because of the distraction, but because the car needed his attention.

He was at the halfway point to his trip and had already gone through half the case of fluid.

But had he been online, he would've noticed Furniture Toss had gone past 80,000 views with very few dislikes. Also, more people were wanting stickers than ever before. But Ian's mind was on revolution, and his next Battle of Lexington was in California.

Chapter 33

'Furniture Toss' made lots of

trouble for the furniture store giant. Within days, 30,000 stickers were sold due to Ian's Furniture Toss, with many of those who bought stickers asking themselves *why* Frank just didn't do right by Ian and avoid the whole furniture toss mess. It not only affected sales in his store, but as the video went viral, it hurt sales throughout the conglomerate's entire chain of stores. Ian's toss video also got QYBers sharing in their own sales horror stories with this particular conglomerate, which drove the store's sales down even more. Some stores reported sales being off by as much as 50%. Ian's toss video even affected the conglomerate's stock prices. That's when the furniture conglomerate hired lawyers to file additional charges against Ian and his QYB site. Ian had no way of knowing any of this because he still had the Jenna laptop turned off. He also didn't know about his buddy Missouri Mike's troubles up north. Among his many emails waiting to be read were several from Mike, but Ian's car still needed all his attention. He just wasn't in the frame of mind to chat while the car continued to act up on the way to Irvine. The only thing he had in his mind was making it on time to the computer company's share meeting. But had he checked his inbox, he also would have found several emails from SAC Rubio in Miami wanting to chat also. But hers was more an ASAP chat. His pay-as-you-go phone, sold to him by Cheryl, came with the added privacy filter provided by his SIM card which also helped keep him off radar. It was all road trip now. Mike's troubles, along with Rubio's demands, would just have to wait until the next phase of Ian's road trip was complete.

Ian's actions were being compared to actions that the Occupy Wall Streeters from years back would've loved. Some on the Left even considered Ian as being one of theirs, while some on the Right thought him an enough-is-enough type and one of theirs, also. Both sides accepted his actions as a sign of the times. But Ian was more a centrist type; a man who knew hard work always paid off, which was what he was hoping for in Irvine.

His thought processes had led him to think outside the box, more so since waking from his coma. But his thinking never led him to believe he was being looked at in connection with the growing militia activity going on, particularly in northern Missouri and Wisconsin, with some militia activity even reported in the forest of Manistee, Michigan.

Ian knew nothing of what Mike's buddies were up to in the north while he was making his last fill-up before Irvine. He thought of checking his inbox, but the rock group, 'The Hell with Government' was playing on his radio, and he preferred listening to them to turning on the laptop. But his radio was suddenly drowned out by a microbus blaring Pink Floyd's 'Comfortably Numb.' The bus pulled up to the opposite side pump.

What happened next really threw Ian for a loop, as the young couple in the bus came hurrying over to him. The QYB sticker on their bus was the reason why.

Ian didn't want to be rude, but he really needed to go. The following morning was the computer company's share meeting and he didn't want to miss it. It was also while chatting with his new friends that all hell was breaking loose in the northern woods of Missouri.

Three of Missouri Mike's friends, who were employees of his shop, were part of a group of six men and two women who raided, in similar fashion as Harper Ferry, the Grand Northern Armory of Northern Missouri. The group succeeded in stealing weapons and ammo, while at the same time getting into a shootout with police. The running shootout led police right to Mike's shop. One of his employees had keys to Mike's shop, which gave them access to a fortress-like office building, which they then turned into their own Alamo until the shooting got too hot. The group of eight, with two injured, split out the back in pairs and ran deep into the surrounding woods. Most of the stolen weapons were found inside the three vans driven by the group which were left shot up and undrivable in front of Mike's shop. Some left their weapons inside Mike's shop, which made Mike seem to be an accessory to the heist. Having info about this particular Armory on his computer sealed his fate. This was all going down while Ian was pumping gas and chatting with his new fans.

"So what are the odds of meeting you here after your furniture toss, eh Ian? And great job of that, by the way."

He could tell the young lady was stoned by how red her eyes were. Her boyfriend's eyes were even redder. He could also smell the marijuana coming from their bus, which had a Colorado tag on it.

"Well, if you liked my furniture toss, wait till you see what I have planned next."

"We watch your site all the time, man. But that furniture thing is the bomb!" The girl slipped her John Lennon shades back on and went to buy some munchies.

It was right as Ian was pouring in the last of his fluid . . . that Missouri Mike's friends were continuing to return fire from within the woods near Mike's shop. But the authorities held superior firepower, and hours later, six of the eight from the group were dead, with the two still alive seriously wounded, along with four police officers and two federal agents dead.

As Ian got in his car to drive . . . a judge in Florida was signing additional charges against him, brought by the furniture conglomerate's lawyers. The judge was also angry at Ian for having four million plus viewers agreeing with his actions. A warrant was also signed for Ian failing to appear in court on his charges.

"So California is where you're planning your next video, eh Ian?" She was back just as 'Comfortably Numb' was finishing. "Or are you on vacation?"

Ian smiled at that. "No time for vacation when I'm looking for payback. You just keep watching the site."

"Cool, man, I will." She went back to the van and moments later she, her boyfriend, their QYB sticker, Pink Floyd's 'The Wall' and their marijuana smoke were gone. Ian made tracks too, though his was more a continuing struggle with his gear shifter while heading back west on CA91. He started to feel pretty comfortably numb himself when seeing the lights of Irvine ahead, just as the sun was setting over the ocean. Instead of a motel, he decided to save money, found a spot to park at, and slept overnight in his car.

Phase two of Ian's road trip almost ended when he turned down a one way street and nearly got hit by head-on traffic. It was with incredible luck and driving skills that he managed to get around cars, including some parked, to avoid an accident and injuries in a car that wouldn't shift correctly. Ian wound up jumping the curb to avoid traffic, to then work his way *back* into traffic during his quest to find the computer company. Having woken late for the company meeting had him rushing to look for it. Not finding the company using his MapQuest printout just added fuel to his anger. It was minutes after his one-way traffic debacle that he finally saw the company headquarters . . . but it was on the other side of the freeway!

It took another fifteen agonizing minutes of driving before finally getting to pull into the computer company's parking lot. He then had to search for a spot where he would feel less conspicuous. He found the perfect spot under the shade of a large sycamore tree. But his car wouldn't take reverse, so he had to open his door and push with his feet to get it parked. Once parked, he shut the car off and started his breathing exercises.

It was crunch time. He spent a minute gathering himself, and when feeling ready, went to the back, opened the hatch, and got his PC prepped and ready for delivery. Done with that, he used his dirty clothes to pile on top of his laptop, backpack, what remained of a case of bottled water, and the last few cans of Stop Leak. He shut the hatch, but left the car unlocked in case of a quick getaway. He clicked on his camera, picked up his PC, and started for the main entrance of the company.

But something kept gnawing at him while walking. It was as if he were forgetting something. *But what? I left the car unlocked. Everything's pretty well hidden. So what is it?* Seeing the roving patrol coming on his cart, got Ian focused back on his mission.

His camera next records him passing by the company's three large flags, the American, State, and company logo flags flapping loudly in the breeze. Ian spoke softly into the camera while walking.

"I believe that logo flag pretty much tells where I'm at."

He kept his breathing exercises up while the rover approached in his cart. But seeing the familiar brand PC that Ian was carrying just got him a cursory nod from the rover, who thought Ian either a new employee or someone headed to the company's R&D department.

The camera here records Ian's deep sigh of relief.

Moments later, Ian is recorded climbing up some highly polished granite stairs that led to a carousel of doors before entering the company lobby. Just before entering, Ian stepped to the side and recorded this message. "This company merged with the Chinese a few years back, so they're American in name only. They are another of these conglomerates who have sold out for quantity over quality, and that's why I'm here."

Ian entered a monolithic lobby with a large glass atrium that housed the security counter. The custom porcelain clock near the bank of elevators showed it being almost 10 o'clock, which meant he was an hour late. *Damn it! I gotta hurry!* His sneakers squeaked loudly on the highly polished floor as he approached the security counter.

Ian sighted in on the array of monitors behind the security counter while asking if it was okay to put his PC on the counter. *Looks to me like the meeting's wrapping up. Either that, or they're about to take a break.* "Yes sir; go right ahead and place your PC there, and if you would, just sign in and tell me where you're headed."

Ian spotted the man's nametag. "Thanks, Jerry."

The ex-cop handed Ian the sign-in board while saying, "beautiful day outside, isn't it?"

"It sure is." Ian put his name on the sheet and handed the clipboard back to Jerry.

"Okay, so Mr. Wolfe; how can I help you?"

Ian pointed at his PC and said, "I know I'm late, but I'm here to demonstrate some new software your company wanted shown at today's meeting. I'm from Florida and got lost getting here, so if you'll point me in the direction of the meeting room . . ."

Jerry's look turned a bit incredulous. "But Mr. Wolfe, didn't you get the memo?" Ian was too busy running through his mind what he was to say next to get the gist of what Jerry was leading to.

"Memo?"

"Mr. Wolfe, today's meeting started at 8:30 a.m. sharp." Jerry turned to his monitors and said, "And it looks like that meeting is just wrapping up."

"Oh, no!" Ian sounded genuinely distraught. "Shit, I can't believe I drove all the way from Florida . . ."

"Well, now hang on a sec, Mr. Wolfe. All may not be lost. Just give me your contact name and I'll call you in."

"Call me in?"

"Sure. I'll let them know you arrived late, but that you are here."

But the only name Ian could remember was the company CEO's name. "Contact name. Uh, right, well, umm, I sure won't be needing any contact name if I go back to Florida and tell my boss I missed making my presentation. Mr. Scanlon's my contact."

Mentioning Mr. Scanlon, the CEO, definitely got Jerry's attention. "Well now, Mr. Wolfe; Mr. Scanlon *is* quite the contact, except that Mr. Scanlon hasn't left me any message about a Mr. Wolfe from Florida coming to visit today." Jerry checked his message board again. "Nope. Nothing about a Wolfe from Florida, pardon the pun, coming to today's meeting. You sure you're not supposed to see someone in Research and Development? Cause I can get someone from R&D to come see you right away."

Jerry was suddenly bothered by Ian's blank stare. The ex-cop in him said something was fishy. He'd seen the look before in people with agendas. "Uh, Mr. Wolfe? R&D? Do I call them for you?"

Ian knew he was in a pinch when seeing Jerry waiting to punch in an extension number.

"Yes, right, R&D. Well, Jerry, I would uh, I would need to go back to my car to get a name for someone in R&D."

Jerry, the ex-cop, wondered more after that remark. "Mr. Wolfe, you can't remember the person who set up your appointment?"

Ian's continued blank stare concerned Jerry.

That was when the elevator opened and out popped the CEO.

Along with Mr. Scanlon were his Asian counterparts, and some others from the Board. It was all Ian needed to see. He grabbed his PC and headed straight for the group.

Ian's body language set off Jerry's internal alarms, especially after grabbing his PC the way he did. Jerry started from around the counter while raising his voice to Ian. "Uh, Mr. Wolfe, please return to the counter." But Ian was not going to miss his one opportunity now. "Mr. Wolfe, I'm ordering you to return to the counter. Do not approach Mr. Scanlon or any of those people."

Ian looked back and asked, "why not?" though he never stopped moving.

"Because that's not how we do things here."

But it was too late. Ian had already reached the perfect spot for tossing his PC at Mr. Scanlon!

His 'Computer Toss' was as perfect as 'Furniture Toss.' He slammed his PC so hard on the floor that it scared pretty much everyone in the vicinity of hearing it . . . except for one. Scanlon seemed unfazed by what Ian had just done.

Prepping his PC before throwing it had been a great idea. His motherboard, two RAM cards, his video card, power supply, fans, and even his burner went flying when the PC struck the floor. Pieces went everywhere, with the PC tower itself ending up at the CEO's feet. But still Mr. Scanlon seemed unfazed.

Scanlon's company members looked to him to see how he was going to play this. It was obvious to all that what Ian had just done had not been an accident. Jerry by then had grabbed Ian and wasn't letting go.

The CEO kicked away Ian's PC, and then took in the new scratches to his favorite shoes. Mr. Scanlon next took in Ian's busted motherboard lying near his CFO's feet. The hard drive had also ended up right near his advertising director's feet.

The camera couldn't show Ian smiling, but his was a big smile, elated over his 2,300-mile trip ending with such success. A second guard approached Ian's other side, while a third guard came from the stairwell. The rover was on his way and would be in the lobby shortly.

Mr. Scanlon approached Ian and asked, "Are you mental? Insane? What? Why would you intentionally throw your computer at me? You on drugs or something?"

Ian took a deep breath before answering. He wanted his response to sound good for the camera. "I'm no druggie, so you can forget that. As for my being insane, well, I might be a little, though made that way by your crappy product, which I came all the way from Florida to deliver back to you."

"You came all the way from Florida to deliver me your computer, and you say you're not on drugs?"

Ian suddenly pulled away from Jerry. "Let go of me."

The CEO waved Jerry away from Ian and said, "So why throw your computer at me? I didn't sell it to you."

Ian knew to tread lightly. He did not want to get into a war of words with this man. "You are the head of this company. Who else could I blame for stealing my money? I spent $4,000 on your crappy product, $4,000 *hard*-earned dollars, by the way, for something that crashed more than worked; so yeah, as CEO, you get back your crappy product. I also came to tell you that I wasn't going to stand for you stealing from me."

"And you say you're not on drugs?" This got a few of Scanlon's Board members to snicker, which included Jerry.

"I've never done a drug in my life, Mr. Scanlon."

"So you know my name."

"I know a lot about your company. You made a good product once. Not anymore. I came all this way so you can see how angry your crap product made me."

"So why didn't you deal with this through our customer service?"

"They're worse even than your product! You don't even have a human to answer a phone at your customer service. And when the store in town where I bought my PC tried getting approval for warranty service, it was refused, even though the damn thing was still a brand new computer! I wound up spending an additional $2,000 on repairs on this crap."

"Stuff happens."

"Stuff happens to *your* computer. *My* money, remember?"

"What's your name, anyway?"

"My name's Ian. Ian Suarez."

"But you signed in as Wolfe," interjected Jerry while holding out the clipboard so that Mr. Scanlon could see it. But the CEO didn't care to see Ian's name.

"So Mr. Ian, what did you intend to accomplish by throwing your PC at me?" The camera captured Mr. Scanlon purposely stepping on and crushing the motherboard while signaling his other guards to start shooing milling onlookers away.

"My intent is the look on your face, Mr. Scanlon. I am now satisfied that you have received my message. You can keep my money now. I am love offering it to you. You will not steal it from me."

"You came all the way from Florida to tell me that? And you think this is a sane thing you've done . . . throwing a computer at me?"

The CEO looked to the others before studying his watch while Ian spoke next . . .

"It's *your* customer service, *your* computer, *your* crappy line of products that brought me here. I didn't want to be here. I would have preferred my money buy me 'the best money could buy' product, which *yours* is not! For $4,000 plus my $2,000 in repairs, I'm due a little vindication, I think. Now, maybe if you'd like to do the right thing and refund me my money . . ."

"Yep, yours is a definite mental issue, Mr. Ian, Wolfe, Suarez, or whoever you are."

"Just Ian is fine."

"Well Ian, you're definitely *not* getting a refund from me. Not after throwing your computer at me. And now, if there's nothing else, I want you to pick up every piece of your computer and get the hell out of *my* building."

Ian was suddenly distracted by Jerry lifting his shirt roughly from in back. "What the hell are you doing?"

"Checking for a weapon, bub," said Jerry. "Can't be too sure with you kooks these days."

"I came to make a point, not to shoot anybody."

"Mr. Ian, or whoever you are," continued Scanlon, "just gather your stuff and leave, because as of now, you're trespassing. Buy your next computer from the competition. I don't care. Just get out of here."

Ian first straightened his shirt before saying, "You're sadly mistaken if you think I drove 2,300 miles just to take back *your* crap."

"You either pick up your stuff now, or I'll have Jerry here call some of his buddies at the precinct. Your choice. How this ends is on you."

And that's when things got stupid.

That morning's hired temp, brought in from the secretarial pool to record the meeting, too strung out on coffee, from out of the blue, shouted, "I think you should check his computer. That's how these bastards do it nowadays. They stuff toxic shit inside them things, then leave, and we're stuck getting sick. Check inside his computer."

Stupid woman thought Ian. "Hey, can that talk, will ya lady? I'm a pissed off customer, not some terrorist. What was inside that tower is spread out on the floor before you."

"Yeah, well I bet you got ricin, anthrax, or some other shit just waiting to go off once you leave."

Ian looked at the CEO. "I think you're the one with a drug problem here, Mr. Scanlon."

Another from the group took the side of the woman temp. "No harm in checking inside his PC. What if she's right? Plenty big to put most anything inside it." The murmuring started then. It was all the CEO needed to hear. He turned to Ian and said, "See what you started?"

"Give me a break. Had your company made a better computer, I wouldn't even be here. All I wanted was service. Instead, I get more grief from coming here." Ian turned to the woman temp. "And stop with your fear nonsense. I wouldn't know the first thing about any ricin or anthrax." But it was too late. Fear had taken over; fear that led Jerry to call in a hazmat team. Knowing that this would probably get him jailed, Ian had no choice but . . . to run.

He had never run so fast in his life. He ran through the doors at top speed and hit the stairs two at a time. Behind him came Jerry and the other guards, their two-way radios blaring.

The ex-cop Jerry yelled at him to stop. But Ian wasn't stopping for anyone. He juked past the rover's cart then started looking for his car while running. Once seeing his car, he ran faster.

Coming from the building to take in the chase and direct his troops was the CEO.

"Cops are on their way, asshole!" yelled Jerry some 40-yards behind Ian. "Might as well stop. You're making it worse by running." Ian's camera couldn't record his flipping off Jerry.

Ian made it to his car with just seconds to spare. He just did get the car locked before Jerry started manhandling his door handle.

"Come out of there, Mr. Wolfe!"

Once Ian got the car started, Jerry straightened. But it was what Ian did next that got Jerry backing away. Ian took from his pocket the pen camera and placed it in the plastic bin underneath the passenger seat. This got Jerry thinking gun, and stopped his fellow guards from coming closer.

The camera had already recorded the sound of sirens coming closer before Ian shut the camera off.

"You sure you saw a gun, Jerry?" asked the rover.

"Sure as shit did."

Ian heard Jerry from inside his car. "I told you already I have no gun!" *And why isn't this car moving?*

And that's when the gnawing from earlier caught up to him. He wasn't moving because he'd forgotten to put in fluid in the leaky transmission. All he got was an engine at high rev with no going forward.

Moments later he was being taken from his car by police.

Dejection was written all over Ian's face when he was taken back to face Mr. Scanlon. One of the deputies was holding Ian's license when Mr. Scanlon asked, "So is he really from Florida?"

"Yes sir, he sure is. We ran his ID and found he's got some trouble back in Florida also. He's got no record, but I think that's about to change."

"Good. I'll file whatever charges you fellows need for taking him in, and I'll have my lawyers draw up more charges later."

"Yes sir. He won't be bothering you anymore."

A flatbed tow truck came roaring into the parking lot for Ian's car just as Ian was being placed inside the transport car. By the time they'd chained his car to the flatbed, Ian was in his quiet place. The city of Irvine went by in a blur after that. But at least this time he remembered to keep calm before the judge.

Chapter 34

The Irvine jail was even more

crowded than the central Florida jail Ian got put into after his furniture toss. But Irvine wasn't the only place with overcrowded jail cells. All over America, inmate population had risen four fold and was getting worse due mostly to the economic downturn. America, already leading in inmate population around the world, was jailing even more per capita inmates. The right to a speedy trial had become a misnomer, with some prisoners, especially during Southern California's backlog, had to wait upwards of a month before seeing an arraigning judge. Overcrowding was a national widespread problem, with some local and county governments giving in to using imminent domain for confiscating properties to use as temporary shelters for housing those arrested. Abandoned buildings and some parks were also turned into stockades for easing prisoner overpopulation. Judicial had gotten the word from Legislative that Executive wasn't going to deal with the overcrowded jail mess. Executive was only going to deal with the country's economic woes, also a nationally widespread problem.

Waiting 11 days to see the judge zapped Ian's calm, so instead of being calm, when it came time to plea, Ian shouted that he wanted "OUT!" The judge, already reading about Ian's earlier Baker-act, Baker-acted him again.

As when in the Florida jail, Ian was again stripped naked of his clothes and given an even thinner pad for warding off Irvine's colder a/c. But unlike in Florida, Irvine's psychiatric wing of the jailhouse was severely overcrowded with those more mentally unstable than even Ian. His three-day Baker-act was a living hell.

When back in court, instead of being calm, Ian went ballistic again, this time because no judge came to the bench that day. (The judge had at the last minute gotten sick and decided to stay home. No other judges had been available to rule over the dozen prisoners who sat chain-gang style for hours before guards took everyone back to their respective cells.) Back to the psyche wing went Ian, only this time he was placed inside a cell with a Plexiglas front panel through which a rover could watch him. It was then that Ian decided to conform to the jailhouse psychiatrist's wishes, and he was put back on his old Lithium/Ativan mix. The mix of drugs did help to quiet his anger some, though he felt so out of it that he went and sat Indian style underneath his tented blanket while waiting for his new day in court.

Exactly 72-hours later, he was in front of a new judge.

He was fifteen pounds lighter since Road Trip started. He had a terrible ringing in his ears caused by the interaction of his meds when standing before the judge, who then angered him plenty when setting his bond at $50,000. Ian was about to go ballistic again, when a well-suited man with a heavy Welch accent approached the bench to say he would pay Ian's bail. Ian didn't know the man, nor did he get a chance to thank him, for the Welshman immediately left the courtroom. It was the bailiff who told Ian that the Welshman would be waiting outside for him.

Marshall Evans hadn't been all that keen about flying all the way to California to bail Ian out of jail. But he couldn't overrule Chief's ordering him to do so. Worse was having to spend an additional 17 days because of the overcrowding and Ian's Baker-acts. Evans' resolve was again being tested when having to wait an additional two hours before Ian was processed out of jail.

Marshall Evans wasn't there on just London's behalf. There were other agencies wanting Ian free, like Homeland and the FBI. Even SAC Rubio had tried getting approval for Ian's $50,000 bail amount. But S/A London had precedent over Ian, and so Evans had drawn the shortest straw in a pool of short straws.

Evans shoved in his glove box the money he'd stolen from Ian's car when seeing him come from processing. He wondered about Ian's slight trembling when shielding his eyes to the sun to find Evans, who waved Ian to the rental car. (The trembling was due to Ian missing his a.m. and p.m. doses of meds because of court.)

Instead of taking Ian's proffered handshake, Marshall Evans went ahead and placed in his shaky hand a manila envelope.

"No name and no handshake? This is too weird," said Ian while studying the envelope. "So I'm supposed to feel comfortable with this? You paying 50K for getting me out?"

"My name's not important. And who sent me to bail you out was Jenna Davis. I'm just her messenger." To Ian, the man's Welsh accent seemed to get thicker as he spoke.

"Okay, so Jenna." Ian held out the envelope. "And what's this?"

"Mr. Wolfe, I'm short on time. Or should I call you Mr. Suarez?"

"Just call me Ian. It was my father who was Wolfe."

"Oh, he most certainly was, mate."

"Huh?" Ian got to opening the envelope when asking Evans, "So you knew my father?"

"Not exactly. But I got no time for that, either. I've a plane to catch in an hour and really need to get going. Your shenanigans and your lousy court system here has already cost me almost a three week stay. But all water under the bridge now, right mate?"

"Whatever that means. But I do have one question, if you don't mind."

"Sure mate. Just one though."

"How did Jenna know of my arrest? I haven't posted my video yet."

"Video? What video you talking about? And as for knowing of your arrest, you gotta remember, Jenna's always searching the Net for you. But look, never mind all that. Just take your money and start getting back home."

"So you bail me out, just to bail on me. I don't get it."

Ian got to counting what was in the envelope. "So what's this thousand dollars for?"

"To get you back to Florida."

Last thing out of the envelope was his impound slip stamped: Paid. "This come from Jenna too?"

"Yep. Thousand and the impound slip. Should be enough to get you home, eh?"

Ian started handing over the $1,000. "I don't need this. I got money stashed in my car."

"Sorry mate, but there you're wrong. Seems the coppers, uh, in searching your car, found your money, and confiscated it. They think it might be evidence of you being paid to harass that company exec. I would say take the $1,000 and be happy."

"Be happy? But that would mean me giving away close to $7,000! Plus, no one gave me any money to harass anyone. That money's from my sticker sales. Shit! I can't believe this."

"Well, you can always go back inside and argue it with someone in there." Marshal pointed back at the jailhouse. "But I got to go, mate."

"Listen friend, since you won't tell me your name, can you at least take me to my car?"

"You already know the answer to that, mate. But the copper inside told me that if you go sit on that bench over there," Evans pointed to a bus bench across the street, "the number #14 bus will take you right to the impound yard."

"So I'm supposed to catch a bus in a city I don't know? And so why didn't Jenna just come herself? I'd be lying if I said this whole thing seems normal, which it absolutely does not . . . a woman I've yet to meet in person, sending someone to pay fifty large to spring me from jail. This is one strange day and getting stranger."

"Well, if it helps to calm you, my name's Marshall Evans. But enough of this chatting stuff. You've got some driving to do, and I, some flying, so let's get cracking. Oh, and do send Ms. Davis an email while on the road. She will be most happy to hear from you." Evans put his rental car in drive. "Ms. Davis is very much wanting to get together with you, Ian. I do believe you two will be meeting in person real soon."

Ian's heart skipped a beat when hearing that. "Really?" But his withdrawal shakes started in then, and he had to deal with that. "You sure you couldn't just drop me off at my car?"

"Sorry mate." (Evans wasn't hurrying to any airport. He was driving to Vegas with Ian's money, where he would spend it on booze and hookers for a few days before heading back to London.) Ian had no recourse but to cross the street and wait on the #14 bus, which came shortly thereafter. By the time he got to his car, his hands were shaking terribly.

The car reeked of stale, sweaty clothes that had been left in the sun too long. But his car, his clothes, his laptop, all took second place to his pen camera, which was still where he'd left it. Relief washed over him when pulling out the bin under the seat and seeing it there. He clipped the pen camera to his pocket, opened the windows, and then poured in the last of his fluid before pointing the car east. He stopped at a parts store to buy more fluid right before hitting the highway.

Ian next needed a place where he could edit and post his 'Computer Toss' video. He stopped at the same rest area where he'd slept in his car. It was a perfect spot for spending some quiet time without anyone bothering him. Except, that once parked, he found the laptop was completely dead. He had to wait on a trickle charge, catching a nap while doing so, but sleeping only minutes because his withdrawals refused him sleep. Instead, he went to walking, loosening his legs a little while waiting for the laptop to charge up. Once charged up, he spent an hour editing his 'Computer Toss' video before posting it and driving off. (The first five to see Computer Toss were the stoned-out couple in the Microbus, Nancy, his print shop buddy, and Steve in Doral. Those five would soon become thousands; hundreds of thousands by month's end. It was also Steve who posted Computer Toss onto YouTube.)

Ian thought to answer some emails, but decided it would take too long, and he really wanted to get back to Florida for phase three of his road trip. As it was, his shifting was awful when getting into New Mexico. He thought of an idea that worked. He bought duct tape to wrap around the gear shifter and the seat buckle. With pressure, he was able to keep the shifter from sliding. With the occasional bottle of fluid, he was able to get back to Florida.

He was ecstatic when finally pulling into town. But though weary from his road trip, he still needed some financial aid from his P.O. Box, where he was shocked to find nearly $17,000 waiting for him! (The post office worker needed to bring the rest of his mail from in back.) With his monetary blessing, he was able to afford a stay in the town's best motel, where a shave and shower, plus a late lunch, invigorated him enough to visit his print shop buddy who was also happy to get paid.

Paying cash for his purchases and using an alias to hide his whereabouts did help to keep Ian off radar. But that didn't go the same for his print shop buddy. Ian was taking a nap as the first federal cars pulled up to his print shop buddy's shop.

Chapter 35

Ian's 'Computer Toss' did to

the computer giant what his Furniture Toss did to the furniture conglomerate; it hurt sales tremendously. Customer service at the computer company got so bogged-down with call-ins that they needed to answer phones with a prerecorded message telling of how long the wait time and repair times would be. Service techs at the company got inundated with repairs. DIY computer kits were suddenly outselling manufactured computers four-to-one. Both the furniture company and the computer company were looking for Black Friday to save their products and their stock prices. At both corporations, their Asian counterparts had already begun to unload themselves of their investment stock.

Ian was too busy posting for his 7 million plus QYB subscribers to concern himself with his growing legal issues. His People vs. People poll had taken off and was taking a lot of his time, so he treated his legal issues like his homeowner fines; he put them on the back burner. The only thing he cared about was his site and phase three of his road trip.

Handel Motors was phase three.

Ian had his camera rolling when entering the Handel Motors service bay. He went searching for Randy, who he found under the hood of a late model car. "Hey there, Randy."

"Oh hey, Mr. Suarez."

"Ian, remember?"

"Right, Ian. So don't tell me . . . you need more service."

"You got it."

Randy turned the rest of the repair over to his tech while wiping clean his hands. "Ian, now you know the bosses will have my ass if seeing your car back on the rack without you paying for service."

"Damn it, Randy. I had to nearly push my car to get it here. Isn't there something you can do without charging me for it? I just don't have $4,000 for a new transmission."

"Come on, Ian. You know the drill. I can't touch your car if you're not paying. And remember, I just work here. You can get me in a lot of trouble if I put you back on the lift without . . ."

"You're repeating yourself, Randy."

Ian suddenly had someone new to deal with.

Brian Handel had seen Ian pull into service from the showroom floor. Moments later Ian was bickering with Brian Handel again. The camera captured all of it.

"Save the good mornings. What I want is service. I don't want to hear any more about how I need to buy warranty, so you can then service my low mileage car. You're one of the owners here. You can make things right with just a signature and you know it. So think less profit and more customer service and we'll be good."

"Sorry, Mr. Suarez, but that's what comes with buying an 'as is' car." Ian moved from Brian Handel's side so he wouldn't see the camera's tiny recording light while speaking.

"I'm also sick and tired of hearing all this 'as is' car nonsense. I bought a car from here with under 19,000 miles on the odometer. I *demand* you get my car running right. If it needs a transmission, then *you* should pay for it."

Here the camera recorded Brian Handel starting to smile.

"You demand, huh? Oh, I needed a good laugh right about now. But you're shit out of luck if you think I'm paying for *your* transmission. You'll need a lawyer for that, and I'll paperwork the two of you to death before I give you a free transmission. I would suggest you just get in your car and go check out some of those rinky-dink repair shops in town."

Ian had actually been hoping for an exchange like that. He felt his camera had just captured a David and Goliath moment.

The car he was actually sick of, and for good reason. Had Brian Handel come across with a free transmission, phase three might have been eliminated. But Brian Handel belittling Ian his repair was all Ian needed for continuing with phase three.

Randy was left wondering why the strange look on Ian's face when getting back in his car and pulling away from service. Randy could hear Ian's transmission slipping as Ian struggled to drive away.

Randy felt Ian had a right to his repair, but with Brian Handel wanting assurances, Randy had no choice but to say, "Sure boss, I'll watch for him." Brian Handel went back to the showroom to await his next victim.

In order to set up for his next clip, Ian needed to park. Once settled and ready, he took from his pocket the camera and pointed it at himself.

"Well folks, I'm about to do something that some of you will think is crazy. No, let me take that back, *most* of you will think it is crazy. But like my furniture and my computer, my car leaves me no choice, either. All I wanted was service for this piece of junk ride. As for this extended warranty nonsense, I don't get it. Heck, I bought this car because of its low miles. I mean, maybe if it'd had sixty or seventy thousand miles, I could see needing a new transmission, but not with just 19,000 miles on it. So no. Now I'm looking to maybe even get myself hurt on this video." Ian got the car started back to Handel Motors. "And you all ever wonder why we need to spend so much time at a car dealership, anyway? I mean, we're in the computer age; why do we need to waste so many hours waiting to get approved? I mean, we can just as easily choose our own make, model, color, leather seats, pick even our own engine, and heck, even pick extended warranty if you like." Ian had the car pointed right for service. "We could even use a dealer's own computer, and if approved, bam! Out pops your new keys, and away you go. Simple as that. No need for any gimmicks or haggling over price. Anyhow . . ." Ian re-clipped the camera to his pocket and focused on aiming for bay #5. "Well, here goes nothing, folks. Enough's enough. And to those who won't agree with what I'm about to do, then let me apologize ahead of time. But I'm doing it." He was almost at bay #5.

"I did think of just using my car to block the doors to their showroom; break the key in the ignition; maybe pop out the tire stems. But I'm pretty sure a tow truck would get my car out of there in no time. No my friends, this is better."

His front tires hit the rack hard!

"Here goes nothing."

The camera next records the sound of screeching tires as his cruiser hit the lift too fast. "PAYBACK TIME!"

The first thing damaged was his oil pan rupturing when hitting the safety lip on the ramp. A loud whining noise, as if in protest, came from the engine compartment, just as his front bumper struck the large rollaway toolbox in bay #4. The toolbox wound up smashing into the repair car in bay #4.

Milliseconds later and Ian went crashing into the block wall ahead!

The loud crash got everyone's attention in service. Even some in the showroom heard Ian's crash.

The sound of hissing air hoses was what Ian heard next when accidently hitting his horn while attempting to open his door. His hitting the wall so hard had folded up the front end of the car like an accordion. Both doors were jammed and he couldn't get out that way. He next struggled with his belt, while at the same time hitting the hatch release button. Both belt and hatch released at the same time.

A service tech came running over to Ian, asking if he was alright.

"You need me to call an ambulance?" It hadn't dawned on the kid that Ian had intentionally just crashed his car.

Instead of answering, Ian tossed out his backpack before he crawled out of the back of the car.

Here his camera recorded blood dripping from his mouth to his hands while he stood up. He had busted his lip and had a nosebleed.

Ian staggered a little while walking, using mind over matter to calm the pain he felt in his back and sides. But that didn't slow him down a bit, as he removed the pen camera from his pocket, aimed it first at his totally wrecked car, pinned between wall and lift, and then at himself. "There you have it, folks. Payback."

Ian had to pick up his pace when seeing Brian Handel hurrying from the showroom. Once outside, Brian yelled for him to stop. But professional linebackers wouldn't have been able to stop Ian on that day. (Ian's flip-off of Brian was again missed by the camera.) Ian ran past the tree line and moments later was deep in the woods.

Brian had several of his salespeople beside him when stopping short of the tree line. "Hey, you guys go in after him. I'm calling the cops."

"Uh, you're crazy, boss. That guy had a backpack. No telling what he's got in his backpack."

In the distance was heard sirens. Someone had already called the sheriff's department.

Seeing as how no one was following him, Ian had the impetus to slow down his walk in the woods and talk to the camera. "I hope you who watch this don't do what I just did. I just couldn't think of any better payback. I'm Ian and I'm out!"

The remainder of his clip shows him cutting through the municipal golf course before reaching the movie theater parking lot. From there, he chugs a bottle of water while making for the bus bench, where the Bluebound bus came just a few minutes later. The Bluebound took him right to his motel, where after a shower and shave, he spent a half hour editing his 'Car Crash Payback' video. He was so happy with the results of 'Car Crash Payback' that he treated himself to an early dinner and a movie. It was while posting his video . . . that chaos reigned at Handel Motors. Especially in bay #5.

Randy did his best to explain to deputies what had occurred, this as Brian Handel and his brother Fred screamed for Ian's blood.

"So let me get this straight," asked the deputy of Randy. The deputy had already run Ian's tag and a police cruiser was in route to 34 Starling Circle. "You say this man crashed his car over not getting service?"

Randy looked down at the $20 Ian had put in his pocket after Randy had snuck him another bottle of Stop leak. "You see the bosses over there? The ones screaming for this guy's blood? They're the ones who refused him service. Not me." Randy waited until Brian Handel wasn't watching, to continue to say, "They've been riding this fellow pretty hard about his needing to buy warranty so we could fix his transmission. This guy just snapped, I guess. I was working on that car over there, or I could've probably stopped the guy from doing what he did." Randy peeked at the $20 again. "Right fine fellow though, for being crazy."

The deputy continued taking in the wreckage of not only Ian's car, but the damaged car in bay #4. From Ian's car, fluids leaked from every hose and seam. The car in bay #4 had a $2,000 dent in the right front quarter panel.

"Well, you've certainly got quite a mess to clean up here," said the deputy while putting away his notepad. "Seems to me it might've been more cost effective to just give him service."

"What? With them bosses there? You got a better chance of winning the lotto before getting free anything here." The deputy took in the 'Manager' emblem on Randy's shirt and wondered if maybe Randy might've had something to do with pissing Ian off. The deputy took in Ian's wrecked cruiser and said, "kind of new for needing a transmission, don't you think?"

"Ah, we get them in here like that all the time. But hey, I just work here."

"You think this guy might come back and go postal on you guys?"

"Nah. This fellow Suarez was actually a nice fellow. Sounded smart. Dressed nice, too. Nah, I think he just got tired of the runaround, and this was his way of saying 'enough is enough', is my guess."

"Well, if he does come back . . ."

"Call 911. I got it."

"Good. Then we're done here, though I don't envy you your cleanup."

"Me either, deputy."

On the deputy's radio came the call that Ian no longer lived at 34 Starling Circle. An APB was put out on Ian then. Lodging under the Wolfe name would keep him clear for now.

By the time Randy and his crew got Ian's car removed from the rack, Ian was on his second tub of popcorn and watching the number 1 hit movie of the year. But though engrossed in the movie, his mind was already going through the intricate plans that would involve completing phase four of his payback road trip.

Chapter 36

Ian began his next video with a commentary on Mr. Weaver. "My ex-banker, the man who stole my house, is a scoundrel, and not because of his just taking my house. Let me explain." Ian spoke while putting on a new suit jacket. This time he was speaking into a new video camera, one he bought special for his next video. The camera was a spy watch camera, with the lens of the camera at the 12 o'clock position on the watch. The microphone was the actual stem of the watch. The watch came with 8 gigabytes of memory. The 8GB was plenty for what he had planned.

"Through various Google searches, I discovered Weaver has been toying with some very shady characters, starting with self-knighted Sir Hunter Clarke Davit. It is this Sir Hunter Clark who gave Weaver his ring and pin. You, who watch this video, will have your own chance to eye Weaver's ring and pin. Google the now defunct hedge fund group HCD and you will see how Sir Hunter Clarke Davit awarded his best conmen with these self-designed rings and pins. You will also see that Sir Davit is in prison now. His HCD group stole an estimated $65 billion from Wall Street, so yeah, prison it was." He aimed the watch camera at his face before putting it on his wrist. "You heard right folks; $65 billion of *your* tax dollars was needed for covering what *this* man and his associates stole."

Ian held up a printed copy of the Regulatory Commission's proof statement dating back to 2008. "But now, back to Weaver."

Ian began straightening his tie. He wanted to look good when visiting with Weaver. "I do have a more personal grudge with Mr. Weaver though, and it has nothing to do with his essentially stealing my house from me." Ian held up a new picture of an older gentleman with a smiling family surrounding him. "This was a friend of mine named Albert Morella." Ian finished his tie then bent his wrist so he could aim the watch camera back on his face. "I say *was* because Albert Morella is dead now. Weaver and his goons at Sir Davit's HCD fund group were the cause of that. It was their swindling him of his money during our heyday in construction in South Florida that made him put a noose around his neck. The young kids in the picture are his sons. I have already discovered through certain sources whom I still have working on Wall Street that Albert's money was hidden in Weaver's bank here in town and is what probably earned him the ring and pin." Ian smiled for the camera. "I intend to get Weaver to admit to that today." Ian clicked off the spy watch and went to wait on the Bluebound to take him to town. This time he left his backpack behind.

It was while riding the Bluebound that he got to mulling over whether Weaver would see him or not. There was always the possibility that he wouldn't. It worried Ian enough to absentmindedly start fidgeting in his seat while riding the bus. Since the house was a done deal, he worried that Weaver might suspect him of being up to no good. Weaver had already let on that he knew about QYB. Ian was counting on Weaver not knowing of his friendship with Albert Morella of Morella Investments, or of Albert's $18 million swindle. An additional worry was if Weaver knew about his car crash video at Handel Motors. That could also bring the police if he did. But the Bluebound was by then opening its doors directly in front of Diamond Bank. Ian set all his worrying aside and headed for the lobby.

He was thinking to use his best diplomatic skills, not only for getting past Weaver's head teller, Helen, but for keeping himself seated if seeing Weaver. But there was no guarantee that Weaver would even talk to him, let alone let him in his office. It was a chance he took when opening the bank doors.

But life was about to serve Ian another surprise.

The first thing he noticed when entering the bank was that the Bank's new teller seemed very familiar to him. She was working the drive-up window, so her back was turned to him as he approached Helen and asked to see Weaver. But there was still something oddly familiar about the new teller . . . *something about her stance and hair.* But he had Helen's angry stare to deal with, so he had to put on hold his interest in seeing the woman turn around.

"Mr. Weaver's too busy to see you today, Mr. Suarez. I'm sorry. But you really should call ahead next time."

"Yeah, well Helen . . ." but the new teller got his attention again, and not only in how she counted money, but her voice sounded oh-so familiar when talking to her drive-up customer. Ian was positive he knew her, just didn't know from where until seeing her. Something about her though, did get his heart racing a little, enough to get Helen to tap her glass to get his attention again. "Mr. Suarez? Next time? Call?" And that's when the new teller finally turned around. He knew her alright. It surprised him enough to forget Weaver a moment, because there standing before him was the woman who disappeared on him in high school, now reappearing in his life again, his old high school sweetheart, Cathy Hancock.

Cathy, too, recognized him right away. She was as stunned as he was when seeing him. Her eyes widened and her heart also skipped a beat when seeing her old boyfriend standing across from her glass counter. "Oh my god! Ian!" Helen was a little shocked when seeing her co-worker make for the lobby.

The voices in Ian's head started again. *"Focus."* He so hated his voices right then. *"You've got work to do." "Get to Weaver's office, now!"*

But he couldn't just avoid Cathy, especially when she was hurrying to greet him. "Oh my god, Ian! What a small world!"

He agreed it was a small world . . . *but of all days?*

"Just get her number and be done with it."

Cathy went right to hugging him, which he had to admit felt pretty good, coming from her.

"Weaver, Ian, now!" He *really* hated it when they called him by name. *"Get going!"* He had so many *new* voices he couldn't make them all out. It was Helen who finally got Ian's voices to settle when interrupting him with, "So you two *know* each other?"

"The mission, fool." He also hated it when his voices taunted him.

A hug overdue by twenty plus years was a little hard to avoid, though. *"Weaver! Payback! Now!"*

"Helen . . . not only do I know Ian here, but he was my boyfriend in high school."

"Well then you're right about it being a small world," said Helen, while still eyeing Ian, who though giving as much of an affectionate hug back, still eyed Weaver's office.

"Ian, it's payback time, remember?" It was a chorus of voices that were ringing in his head now.

Cathy broke him of his staring at Weaver's office by saying softly in his ear, "it's really nice to see you again, Ian." Her saying that made him feel great, and . . . made his day more difficult.

His voices went to a low muttering then.

Cathy had always been an opportunist at heart. In Ian, she saw a chanced opportunity, destined if you will, as he could so easily fill the void left in her life after her breakup with her boyfriend when finding him in bed with her ex-best friend, Rachel. Ian, showing up at the bank when he did, convinced Cathy that theirs wasn't just a coincidental meeting. This was a reunion that was meant to be, or at least that's what she thought. She also found him to be still quite handsome, which helped. It made her smile, while Ian was still eyeing her boss's office. Cathy was also intuitive enough to sense a bad vibe growing between Ian and Helen.

"Yep, Helen, small world," said Cathy to her co-worker while holding Ian's hand.

"So, Cathy," started Ian, while looking at Helen, "you think we could maybe get together later, say, over dinner? Unless off course, you're married or something."

"I would love to have dinner with you. And no, I'm not married or something." Cathy added a sweet laugh to that.

"So, then let me get your number and I'll call you later."

"You got it. I'll go write it down." While Cathy went back to her cubicle to write down her number, Ian went back to dealing with Helen. "Look Helen, I really need to see Mr. Weaver before I leave town. I promise it will only take a few minutes. I need his take on something I'm buying. I didn't call ahead because I didn't think it would be a problem."

"Well, you shouldn't be so sure he'll see you, cause I don't think he will. At least, not without an appointment. He's pretty busy these days, you know."

"No, I don't know, and I don't see why the big deal. Helen, just two minutes. That's it. You can tell him that. I'm leaving town and . . ."

Cathy suddenly cut in with, "So if you're leaving town, how is it we're going to get together?"

"Oh no, Cath, I'm not leaving town permanently. I'll be back later this evening, in fact, rushing back to see you." He gave her a wink just as the voices started up again.

A new drive-up customer needed Cathy's attention, leaving Ian with Helen again. "So? You going to tell Weaver I'm here, or am I?"

"The man's pretty busy right now, Mr. Suarez. I think you should just call ahead."

"First, call me Ian, and second, I'm already here. Should I maybe just go knock on his door myself and leave you out of this?" The arrival of a new drive-up customer put their confrontation on hold as Helen was needed to attend to the new customer. Cathy hurried over with her phone number soon as she was done with her customer.

"Cath, I gotta see Weaver," whispered Ian in her ear.

Cathy winked and smiled. "Say no more." Cathy turned to Helen, who was still busy at the window with her customer, and said, "Helen, I'm going to walk Ian back to Mr. Weaver's office."

Cathy was stopped cold by Helen's 'absolutely not!' stare.

"Uh, don't do that Cathy," said Helen. "Your Ian needs an appointment to see Mr. Weaver, like everyone else."

"But he's leaving town, Helen."

"Doesn't matter." To Ian, Helen said, "And if this is about the government freeze on your account, it's still on hold."

A new drive-up customer forced Cathy away.

Ian returned his attention to Helen. "I didn't come here to cause the man any trouble, if that's what you're worried about. I just need a few minutes of his time. That's all."

Helen's look was one of impatience. "Okay, since you won't leave, then let me try ringing him and see what he says."

"Fair enough." But Ian saw her ploy right off when catching Helen holding down the receiver button on the bank phone.

"Looks like Mr. Weaver's busy talking to someone else on the other line, Mr. Suarez, uh, I mean Ian. Best you call back later."

"I'll just wait till he's off the phone then."

"I would advise against that, Ian. Plus, we'll be getting our lunchtime crowd here pretty soon, and Cathy and I will be pretty busy, so best you try back tomorrow. I'll let Mr. Weaver know you were here. Be here around ten tomorrow, okay?"

As soon as Cathy finished with her customer, she turned to Ian, and with a wink and a nod towards Helen, said to Ian, "Want to see a movie tonight?"

"I'd love to, Cath." It was becoming like old times with them. "But I got this thing I gotta do and I really need Mr. Weaver's advice on what I'm doing. But you bet I want to see a movie with the prettiest girl in town. You can most definitely expect my call sometime this evening." Cathy's skin was alabaster white to Ian's Mediterranean tan, so her blushing was hard to hide. But Ian missed her blushing because of more customers coming into the lobby.

Helen went from staring at him to smiling sweetly for the early rush of their lunchtime customers. "Okay then, Mr. Suarez; see you tomorrow then."

"Back to Mister again, I see. Well, I'm using the restroom and then I'm gone, Helen." He didn't give Helen a chance to stop him.

"Uh, well you do that and then leave. I'll let Mr. Weaver know you'll be back tomorrow." Cathy again came to the rescue by asking Helen about a particular deposit and giving Ian a chance to get to what she knew would be Weaver's door.

More customers entered the lobby as Ian reached the bathroom. He stayed in the bathroom until hearing the noise level rise in the lobby before exiting the bathroom, and when seeing Helen busy, with a wink to Cathy who was looking right at him, he made for Weaver's door.

"Forget the girl and concentrate, you fool!" The voices were back at it again. *But this is Cathy we're talking about. She's not so easy to forget.* He caught himself right as he was about to twist Weaver's door handle while knocking. *Oh, what am I doing? Now I'm talking to myself within my own head!*

"She let you down before. She'll do it again."

That was then. Plus, I bet her father had a lot to do with taking her away from me.

"Shut up and open that door already."

He was through arguing with his voices.

Soon as Cathy saw Ian make for Weaver's door, she distracted Helen from turning around by asking for advice on a new customer.

With a twist of the handle, Ian and his spy watch were back at work and past the point of no return.

Helen gave Cathy her advice then asked about Ian. "Did you see him leave? I was too busy to see if he left or not." Cathy went back to filling in a second deposit slip when answering, "Yes, Helen. He used the bathroom and left."

As soon as Cathy got done with her three customers, she turned to Helen and asked, "So, what's the big deal between you and Ian anyway?"

Helen was taken a bit by Cathy's question, and it took her a moment to answer. "Well, uh, really not so much a deal with me as with Mr. Weaver. I like your boyfriend."

"He's not my boyfriend . . . yet."

"Whatever. But I can tell ya, he isn't so high on Mr. Weaver's list of favorites. In fact, Mr. Weaver's trying to avoid your Ian because of his website."

"Website? Ian has a website?"

Helen used the lull in customers to bring up QYB on her computer and then sent it to Cathy's computer. "Look for yourself." Cathy was now introduced to 'Quit Your Bitching and Start the Revolution!'

Helen thought showing Cathy Ian's radical website would turn her off to Ian's site. The site had the opposite effect on Cathy. She, like the millions of other QYBers became an instant fan of Ian's site. To her, it spoke of Ian all the way, plus the 9,000,000+ subscribers were impressive also.

Cathy was 34 and looking to settle down. She saw that possibly happening with Ian, if playing her cards right. She suddenly felt like a teen again, and this while watching more of QYB. She thought it was all good while scrolling through the turn pages to QYB until . . . getting to the video page. That's when she started to worry. *Looks like Ian's lost his mind.* Seeing the car crash video really worried her. *Now that looks criminal and he's in there with Weaver.*

"So, Helen," Cathy used Helen's distraction at writing out a check order and avoiding her monitor, to ask, "so you don't keep up on Ian's site?" She clicked off the car crash video when seeing Helen coming towards her. *If Helen sees that video, she'll probably call the cops on Ian herself.*

"No, dear. I don't stay up on that nonsense. Nor does Mr. Weaver." *Thank goodness* thought Cathy, as more customers started coming into the bank.

"I'm not much interested in all that radical nonsense," continued Helen, putting on her customary smile, "I mean, really, 'quit your bitching, and start the revolution?' Come on; seems like your boyfriend's got some growing up to do. In fact, you ask me, I think your boyfriend's got a screw loose. I'm surprised they haven't arrested him for all that stuff he writes on his site. And he's already in trouble with the IRS."

"Sounds like Ian."

"What? And you like that about him?"

"I do. And I like his site."

"Blah! You young folks."

"Hey!"

"Just saying."

"Then you don't know his background."

"His background?"

"His history? You do know he was the CEO of a major bank once, right?"

"I believe Mr. Weaver might have mentioned it to me once."

"He was CEO of Family Bank in Miami. That's no little bank." Cathy's customer thought her smile was for him.

"So what's so special about your boyfriend's history?"

Helen was starting to get on Cathy's nerves. "You obviously don't know about how he arrived in the United States."

"How he arrived in the United States? What's so special about that?" To her customer, Helen said, "Thank you, and come back and see us real soon." She turned to Cathy. "So the United States. Big deal. Lots of immigrants have come to our United States."

"Ian was rescued from shark infested waters by a U.S. naval vessel after his mom and brother drowned in a Cuban gunboat attack that left many people dead. You don't know about any of that? Or about his being struck by lightning a few years ago, nearly killing him?"

"Really? When was that?"

"You really should read his bio, Helen. Ian has had quite a few accomplishments in his young life. I'm surprised you've given him such a hard time. You might not like his site or what he stands for, but his life's been a rollercoaster ride after losing his mom and brother in that 13-de-Marzo attack."

"Sorry dear, but us folks here don't much care about any Miami news."

"Helen, a bunch of kids drowned in that attack. Wow. I can't believe you don't know about that."

"I know Mr. Weaver jokes about your Ian being a banker once."

"I wouldn't know why. Ian was more than just a banker; he ran a bank much bigger than Diamond."

"Well, it still doesn't explain that crazy site of his. Foolish shenanigans, you ask me."

Good thing no one's asking you Helen.

"So you don't know about his videos?"

"Other than for what made the paper, something about his piling up his furniture in front of the furniture store in town, no."

Let's hope it stays that way thought Cathy as more lunchtime customers entered the lobby. And so while Helen and Cathy put on their best smiles while doing Diamond Bank business, inside Weaver's office, no smiles were forthcoming, as a war of words had commenced.

Chapter 37

"How in the hell did you get by
Helen?" Weaver was on the phone with his wife when Ian came through the door. But he stopped Ian from taking a seat. "Don't even think to sit down." To his wife, Weaver said, "Listen honey, I gotta go now. I got someone here who just showed up unexpectedly and I need to deal with them, and no, it's not your mother. We'll talk about all of what you bought today when I get home. Just don't keep buying any more of it until I get home, alright?" It was something his wife obviously didn't like hearing because she hung up on him.

Ian went to shut the door, but was rebuked there also. "Just leave my door open. You ain't staying long."

"I don't know about that, Weaver," said Ian, closing the door anyway. "I'm pretty sure you don't want anyone to hear what I came to say." This got Weaver hurrying to his feet, which wasn't such an easy feat, coming from a chair too small for his bulk. Weaver's months of worrying had gained him 40 pounds. He eventually did come from his desk though to demand Ian state what he came for.

"I got no time for any of your nonsense today, Mr. Suarez."

"Relax, Haas."

"Oh, Haas, is it?"

"I'm headed out of town, so I only have a few minutes to spend here, so relax. Besides, with the money you've gotten from me, the least I should be entitled to is a few minutes of your time, don't you think?"

"I don't think anything of the kind, and don't ever call me Haas again, you hear?"

"Fair enough. Now can I sit?"

"No." Weaver feigned impatience by looking at his watch. His mother-in-law was due at the bank at any minute, and that was bad enough for one day.

"So I'm left standing then?"

"Look Suarez, just spit out what you came to say and get out." Weaver wanted to return to his desk until suddenly remembering something. "Mr. Suarez, open your jacket."

"Open my jacket? Why?" Ian had actually expected this, but played as if offended. "Why you want my jacket open?"

"Because I want to check you for that pen camera you used on that idiot furniture manager down the street."

"I got no pen camera on me, Weaver. I'm just here to talk."

"Talk my ass. You ain't catching me like you did that idiot down there. Now open that suit of yours." Ian did as asked, while silently thanking the spy watch manufacturer for making such a well-designed and inconspicuous watch.

Weaver got so close to the watch camera that his image became blurry while checking Ian's pockets for a camera. Once satisfied that Ian had no camera, Weaver went to sit down.

"So, are we good now?" asked Ian. "Now can I sit?"

"No. And I kid you not Mr. Suarez, if you do have a recording device, you best put it on my desk right now, or feel the wrath of my lawyer later."

"Only here to talk, Weaver."

"Your antics won't fly with me, boy. Best not go there with me."

Weaver's bulk caused his chair to squeak loudly while he tried getting comfortable. "So, why is it you're here, Mr. Suarez? If it's to moan some more about your house, then . . ."

"I didn't come to moan over any house."

"Look. Whatever. Best just save your spiel. Besides, you were the one who mentioned at our meeting how time was precious, remember? And if this it about your account, then you, as an ex-banker, should know that I can't override a Revenue freeze. And did I hear you right, that you're leaving town? Is it for good? Cause if it is, I'm not surprised, what with all the trouble you've caused yourself with that site of yours."

"For a man who doesn't have time for me, you sure know a lot about me."

"I'm not one of those idiots you've mesmerized with all that shit you write about on your site. So just say what you came to say and get out."

"So, you think those who read what is written on my site are idiots, do you?"

"If the shoe fits, know what I mean?"

"So do people like the Smiths count as idiots?"

"The Smiths? Who the hell? Oh, you mean Nancy and Willard. Well, if they're keeping up with your site, then they must be."

A knock at the door got them both turning to see Cathy sticking her head through the door. "Uh, Mr. Weaver, you wanted to know when your mother-in-law pulled up. Well, she's here."

Weaver caught Cathy sneaking a wink at Ian. Both men next turned to the window to see an older woman coming from the same Jag that Ian had seen parked at 34 Starling Circle.

It was all made clear to him then.

Weaver looked at Cathy, who was still standing there, and said, "Okay, Cathy, look, just keep her busy until I finish with Mr. Suarez here," Weaver gave Ian a hard stare, "which I don't think will be but a few minutes more. And Cathy, do not let her slip by you, cause she will. Offer her coffee. Anything. Just keep her out in the lobby until I'm through here, you got it?"

"Yes. Keep her busy. Got it."

This time Weaver caught Cathy smiling at Ian. *Looks like these two know each other* thought Weaver. *I sure hope Cathy's not a federal plant.*

"Just go ahead and shut the door behind you, Cathy."

"Yes, sir." Cathy did as told and headed to the lobby to intercept Weaver's M-I-L.

Weaver caught Ian staring at his bookcase, in particular the large replica Gutenberg bible held open by ceramic prayer hands. Weaver didn't appreciate Ian's smirking when seeing his prized bible. "You have a problem with the bible, Mr. Suarez?"

"With the bible, no. With those hiding behind it, yes. You really are full of surprises, Weaver."

"You got room to talk. Look at you and your antics. And by the way, how is it that you know Cathy?"

"Well, if you must know, Cathy and I go way back."

"Really? Well it sure is a small world, eh?" said Weaver.

"Funny you should mention small world, Weaver."

"Oh? Why's that?"

"It's because of this being a small world that *your* antics have finally caught up to you."

"Caught up to me? What the hell you babbling about?"

Weaver stood and began putting on his Armani jacket. On his jacket was his lapel pin. He began straightening his tie while saying, "Please spit out what it is you came to say and be done." The sun suddenly broke through the clouds to reach Weaver's office and shone upon his diamond ring and pin. It was the sparkling of the diamonds that was caught beautifully by Ian's spy-watch camera.

"Okay, I'll spit out what I came to say. How about I start with your ring and pin."

This got Weaver's attention. "My ring?"

"And don't forget your pin." Ian had Weaver's *full* attention now.

"What's my ring got to do with any of *your* troubles?" Hearing his mother-in-law hollering out in the lobby got Weaver hurrying for the door.

"You keep forgetting your pin, Weaver. And I wouldn't quite open the door just yet."

Weaver turned from the door angry. "You've had your say. Now I want you to go." Weaver hurried back to his desk to remove something from his top drawer.

"Hold up there, Weaver. If you're thinking of pressing an alarm or something, then stop."

What Weaver had reached for was his cell phone. "Mr. Suarez, I'm not that worried about you to sound any alarm, but I will call the sheriff if you don't get out of here." Horns suddenly blowing from cars almost colliding outside distracted Weaver from stopping Ian from sitting. "I thought I told you not to get comfortable."

"I think I've earned this comfort. And if you want to call the sheriff, then by all means call, but I guarantee you that it won't be *me* going to jail. In fact, I'll probably get a reward when mentioning to certain folks about Sir Davit's ring being on *your* finger. *You* will probably need the sheriff's protection then."

"Why, you really *are* crazy! Get out of here! I told you already I don't have time for your crap today."

Ian surprised Weaver by taking from his pocket the spare key to 34 Starling Circle. The key came with a genuine 14K gold DHE keychain that had been given him as a gift from the bank. Ian tossed the key onto Weaver's desk (where it coincidentally landed on top of *his* foreclosure file, a file that was being picked up later by the local Revenue agent in town).

"You can at least give the keychain to your mother-in-law, since I'm pretty sure you've already rekeyed the house."

"Suarez, why the hell are you here?"

"I already told you. Your ring and pin brought me here."

"Why won't you get it through your thick skull that *you* getting tossed from DHE wasn't because of *me*, but was because of *you* not paying your fines? *You* chose not to follow the rules. *You* pissed residents off. That's what got you thrown out of DHE. Not me."

"I haven't mentioned DHE, Weaver. It's your ring and pin I'm mentioning now. You might sleep at night thinking you're in the clear, but you don't fool me. Your ring and pin says all there is to say about you. Now it's time for a little payback."

"Payback? Why you . . ."

Ian crossed his legs in a confident manner and said, "Hey, at least I'm giving you fair warning of what's to come, which is more than I can say for you giving me any warning before tossing me to the curb."

"There you go rambling crazy again. Please tell me you're finished now."

"Crazy is you wearing that ring and pin." Ian leaned in closer for the benefit of the camera. "And how it is you're not in prison like the rest of your buddies?" Ian suddenly snapped his fingers as if remembering something. "Oh, I get it. You probably tossed everyone under the bus, so you could stay in the clear."

The camera here caught Weaver's angry scowl. "Quit blabbering and get out. Besides, I bought this ring and pin from a guy in New York who needed money."

"Nice try, Weaver. What, you try to convince yourself with that, too?"

Weaver went from scowl to belligerent. "Don't hold against me what *your* foolish nonsense did to you. Your stupidity and your fines are what got you evicted, so quit the melodrama. Now fuck you and get out!" Weaver had gone to absentmindedly fiddling with his ring again. He did that whenever nervous.

"Trying to hide your past on a slab in Pennsylvania didn't work for you either, Weaver. Yep, I'm onto that, too. My advice? Best start swallowing that ring before those coming to talk to you see it."

"Get out!"

Both could hear Weaver's mother-in-law getting antsy out in the lobby.

"Mr. Suarez, you either walk, or leave in handcuffs. Makes no difference to me at this point." Weaver held his finger over the nine on his smartphone. His ring sparkling again in the sunlight angered Ian. "You know Weaver, it might not be a bad idea if you did call the sheriff, cause those coming to speak to *you* aren't coming for a friendly chat, I can tell you that."

Weaver let out an exasperated sigh, tossed his cell phone back on his desk, and sat back heavily in his chair. "What do you want from me, eh Mr. Suarez? You come to extort me or something?"

"Extort you? Hey, I wouldn't know the first thing about extorting anyone, so no, I'm not here to extort you, though getting my money from my account . . ."

"You know I can't override a Revenue freeze."

"The name Albert Morella mean anything to you?" Ian went in for the kill. He knew he had Weaver when seeing his face go ashen.

"Albert Morella? Uh, I don't think so."

"You're reaction has already given you away, my friend, and that man's blood is also on your hands. You and your associates did quite a number on Albert and his family. I'm sure you know about his hanging himself. Now, I don't know who's coming to see you first, his wife and her attorneys, or representatives of those you sold down the river in New York. Either way, I'd hate to be in your shoes right about now."

"Still more melodrama, I see?"

"Albert Morella's death is no melodrama, chief. You left his wife and his sons hanging on that noose, so get your house in order Haas, cause the melodrama's just beginning. Now maybe you'll see what I mean about this small world catching up to you. And you, with the audacity to still be wearing that ring and pin. Talk about crazy."

Weaver stood. Something told Ian to stand also. Violence was in Weaver's eyes when asking, "So, who else have you been talking to, eh Mr. Suarez?"

"In for a penny, in for a pound. Isn't that what your self-knighted Mr. Davit used to say? At which one of his soirées did he give you that ring and pin, huh? Was it at the one just prior to you turning state's evidence? Plus, getting both must mean you were in like Flynn, right, Weaver? So who else besides my friend Morella did you steal from?" Ian started for the door. "Never mind answering that, your world is shameful enough as it is."

Weaver was having a tough time containing himself. "Who else do you know, Suarez?" But Ian had already reached the hall. Weaver's mother-in-law saw that and came hurrying for Weaver's office. Ian turned to Weaver and said, "Forget all that now. You got plenty more to worry about coming now. But remember, the Fed doesn't much forget an $18 million rip-off. Turning state's evidence can only help you so much. Plus, I hear your associates doing time at Rikers have some tally sheets they want to show off of your Florida dealings. If that's true, then it sucks being you. Swimming in a sea of sharks will get you bit, my friend. Believe me; I know that to be true." Weaver half-heartedly greeted his mother-in-law as she pushed her way past him to get to a chair in his office. "Hurry up and get done with him. I got some complaining to do about that new bitch neighbor of mine."

Weaver instead decided to follow Ian to the lobby. "I see why they declared you mental, Suarez."

"Mental is you wearing that ring."

"Hurry up!" yelled Weaver's M-I-L from inside his office. "I got an earful for ya, you putz!"

Ian laughed at that. "Wow! A real handful in there now. Oh, and don't forget to give her the keychain."

Leaving Weaver speechless was a rare moment in the big man's life. It had cost him a fortune to keep his past a secret. Even his wife, as pryingly intuitive as she was, had never quite gotten, nor cared about the reason why they had to suddenly depart from their beautiful Manhattan digs, to move back to their $4 million Florida ranch home, a home his wife called their 'boondock home.'

Ian headed straight to Cathy with Weaver following.

Shit, I misjudged this Suarez fellow thought Weaver, while calling out for Ian to stop. *He was a banker, for crying out loud.*

Helen's eyes widened when seeing Ian being followed by her boss.

I've gotta get the hell outta here, thought Weaver while watching Ian head towards Cathy. *Soon as I can, I'm gone. Outta sight. Outta mind. Outta state. Outta country! Leave the bitches here. Gotta be some sweet pun-tang down in the islands or in the Amazon. Cost me a lot less, too.*

Money. It had always been about money with Weaver. But his ill-gotten gains is what caused him his 'duh-dumb' moment that had come back to haunt him. Of course he knew about the Morella money. He knew about all the money hidden in his bank during the HCD heydays. It's what had afforded him both the Manhattan and Florida homes. But his mother-in-law yelling at him from his office meant having to begrudgingly walk away from Ian.

As for Ian, he'd had enough of the Richard 'Dick' Weavers of the world, a lifetime of enough of people set on doing wrong instead of right. Seeing Cathy prepping to go to lunch gave Ian an idea.

"Hey Cath? How about you forget about working here and come work for me to manage my website? You're computer savvy enough to handle that for me, and I'll pay you good money. Better than what you're making here. How about it?"

"I say we start with lunch and discuss it. I don't much like working here anyway. Too much bitching about this and that." Cathy suddenly laughed. "Hey, I just used 'bitching' in a sentence; must mean I'm ready to manage Quit Your Bitching and Start the Revolution!"

"Sounds like it. So, lunch it is. Let's go. And say bye to your friend."

Cathy looked directly at Helen. "Bye, you old biddy. And I'm glad I never opened an account here." Cathy ended by sticking her tongue out at Helen. "Let's go. I'm in the mood for a revolution."

True to his word, Ian created a managerial spot for Cathy at QYB, a position she managed from her home after moving Ian in. He also introduced her to all his online friends, which included his classmates still working on Street. He even introduced her to his print shop buddy in town (after catching up on what agents had wanted to know about him). That day, after lunch, the two drove to Daytona to buy a used Chevy Corvette that Ian got at a great price. It had become night when they finally got the car on the road, and instead of driving the forest road back west, they decided to spend the night at a hotel where the margaritas were famous. It was a great place for making up for lost time. By then, 'Heartless Banker Payback' had garnered 3,000 hits and was rising. But it was an unplanned fifth video that put Ian over the top for his QYB fans.

Chapter 38

'Heartless Banker Payback' came

at a time when one in seven homes were being foreclosed upon, and one in eight Americans were on food stamps. The previous month had seen 330,000 new bankruptcy filings alone, plus another $5 trillion in losses to pension funds. What little cash people had, they hoarded.

Adding to the public's misery was the dollar becoming more devalued, which drove gas liter prices up. Ian had been right in his guesstimation of that, also. He wrote a scathing post he titled: 'How the twelve Federal Reserve Chairs are ruining this country.' This posting, too, got a lot of attention. He was viewed by his QYB fans as a modern day prophet, especially when he correctly guessed that the government would demand more Special Drawing Rights (SDR) after their quantitative easing jacked up prices on more than just oil. (*Quantitative easing, or the printing of money to supposedly *help* the economy grow, instead *ruined* the economy for years to come.) Ian's credibility grew exponentially with his postings and with his payback videos. Weaver's arrest only made Heartless Banker Payback that much harder to swallow. Most bankers began locking their doors then.

A new situation occurred over Weaver's arrest, a situation that saw 142 of his 160 manipulative pocket mortgages heading to foreclosure when no bank would take them. None of the Maes wanted to pick up any of Weaver's mortgages after his arrest, either. Once again, Ian jumped in to help. He started a new charity fund through QYB that would help keep these families in their homes. His act of faith brought an additional 300,000 new subscribers to QYB, which pushed the QYB numbers past 10 million. Cathy's savvy computer skills helped to keep the 10 million focused on Ian's latest writings, which he was doing from the comfort of her home.

Novem ber brought another cold snap that hung over North Central Florida for days. With it came rain, windy conditions, and even some hail. But it wasn't the wind or hail that woke Ian. It was the lightning that brought him fully awake from Cathy's bed.

But even lightning had to take a backseat to Ian waking up famished and wanting eggs. But wanting an omelet in a house with no eggs meant having to cross the street to get some from the supermarket.

He rose, shaved, showered, and then gave thought to driving the Vette across the street, which would be a hassle, since it meant having to drive all the way down the street, to then make a U-turn for getting into the supermarket parking lot. But by then, the storm had subsided.

Cathy was still asleep when Ian decided to go to the supermarket on foot. *Probably faster anyway* he thought, while putting on his camera watch. He'd gotten to where he liked wearing the watch because it actually looked sorta nice. The walk would also help clear his mind of some 'Jenna' stuff anyway. He threw on his coat and quietly left the duplex with Cathy still sleeping.

Hearing the front door close is what woke Cathy. She slipped out of bed, pulled back the curtains, and watched as Ian started texting while walking to the crosswalk. Cathy was puzzled over who he might be texting. The answer would come soon enough when she checked her email.

Try as he might, Ian just couldn't connect with Davis Electronics. He tried both ringing and texting and got nothing. He blamed the storm for making service terrible. His interest in speaking to Jenna was to let her know he wanted no more of her emails, especially of the type she'd been sending of late. He was worried if Cathy checked his inbox, there would be trouble. It's what he most worried about while crossing the street. He was convinced, though, that Cathy would stay asleep until he could show her the latest Jenna emails. But he was mistaken about Cathy being asleep. She was right then reading through emails.

Ian was more puzzled than happy over Jenna's latest offer of an island hookup. (Cathy was just then reading about that, too.)

Ian got so absorbed in trying to make another call to England, that he missed seeing the man hiding among the tree line behind the filling station.

Ian's other worries were over the previous night's Skype session with Mike, or rather non-Skype session, since they both had been disconnected right after signing in. More troubling had been the terrible ringing left in his ear before tearing the headset off his head. The squealing signal had been hard to take. That had him worried too, worried enough to miss hearing the steps coming up behind him.

Concentrating on keeping his shoes and pants dry is what kept Ian from hearing his shadow jumping the same puddles. His shadow wound up doing a better job of keeping *his* shoes and pants dry than Ian did. Ian's lower pant legs were wet by the time he reached the store, where his shadow stopped and did not follow him in.

Ian gave thought to just going ahead and filling a cart full of food and pushing it home, a practice residents living across the street had gotten used to. But a sudden drop in his sugar level made Ian dizzy a moment, which nixed that idea. It was just eggs, bread, and cheese after that. He grabbed his favorite trail mix on the way to the register, with Cathy's favorite popcorn the last item that he grabbed before the register. It was while paying that he decided on some cashback from his Wolfe prepaid debit card for dinner and a movie later that evening. He made his shadow most happy when he saw him pocket the five-$20 bills.

It was while walking back through the parking lot that the clouds unleashed themselves of more rain, enough to get Ian running underneath the filling station's canopy. Lightning started then also, which got him switching on his watch camera while under cover of the metal canopy. The downpour had by then created a curtain of water that poured off all four sides of the metal canopy.

More lightning crackled above, which made Ian instinctively cringe. His watch camera caught the lightning and his cringing, but not of his shadow moving in.

Ian thought of calling Cathy to come get him, but she'd been staying up late working on the site, so he decided to let her sleep. He was thinking if the rain eased, he would make a run for it. His watch camera continued recording the lightning that webbed throughout the clouds above, and the occasional boom that came with it. He tore at his trail mix bag while his watch recorded the center drain filling fast with rainwater. He then noticed the security camera above the gas pumps and waved to it. (The lone attendant was at that moment busy mopping up a milk spill.) The continuing downpour was loud enough to hide the approaching steps of Ian's shadow.

Ian had just started chewing his favorite chocolate covered raisins, which came with his trail mix, when a lone bolt of lightning drew his attention to the clouds. He was waiting for the loud boom when his attacker's box cutter tore across his chest!

Cathy was beside herself when failing to make contact with Jenna. This was after seeing Missouri Mike's latest email message, with the subject line saying: BEWARE OF JENNA. SHE IS TROUBLE. Mike's message was the darnedest message ever. But what annoyed Cathy more was that her computer savviness couldn't get her to open Mike's warning message. Cathy had already figured Jenna for trouble. *But an island hookup? Really?* Cathy was fuming over that. She still wanted to get Mike's take on Jenna (but agency scramblers were making that impossible). So, while Cathy continued trying to make contact with Jenna Davis, and while Missouri Mike tried texting Ian's old number, agency tracers got to work. Mike's sending of Jenna's URL, which would show from where her erotic pics were coming from, was the first thing zapped by agency tracers. Cathy was so wrapped up in her anger that she failed to look out her window and see Ian being attacked by the worst type of criminal 150-yards away.

Jamal Peterson was on a 10-day crack binge. The gorilla on his back wanted more crack. The cocaine had robbed him of all his senses except one . . . to rob. Proof of his losing his senses was in robbing a younger and much healthier Ian, as opposed to Jamal's usual robbery victims who were old and mostly female. Just that morning he'd robbed a 74-year-old woman who'd been feisty enough to hang on to her purse a bit too long. A hard shove to the ground had relinquished her of her purse, and her $50, which didn't amount to much crack. Now the gangly six-foot Jamal was looking to smoke up Ian's $100, a temptation just too hard to pass up by one so hooked on drugs. Jamal Peterson's addiction had driven his reasoning way off the charts when sticking Ian with his box cutter while under the eye of the station camera, and in broad daylight. A second slash at Ian meant Jamal didn't care.

Jamal was shaky but quick with his box cutter, and though it was a dull blade in his cutter, it still cut jaggedly, but cut nevertheless.

Ian almost choked on his trail mix when seeing the blade coming at him. Had it not been for his spitting out his mouthful of trail mix, he might have choked. Still his attacker kept slashing.

Ian saw some of his blood drip to the floor and mix in with the rainwater heading to the drain. The sight of that angered him, but he kept his cool, even when more thunder roared, which made his attacker jump. All was caught by his spy watch camera, including his attacker's third slash. (The camera here showed a near demonic look on his attacker's face.)

"Yo, white boy, you best start handing over your wallet."

Jamal gave the air a vicious slash to get Ian's attention. "And quit looking up at that camera. Man inside ain't gonna help you any. Now, your money or your life, make no never mind to me. But I will cut your heart out, if you don't hurry." Another vicious slash proved his attacker meant business.

Ian tried aiming his spy watch at the man, to get a good facial recognition, but was sidetracked by seeing blood from his arm dripping down his hand and hitting the floor. It slowed his reaching for his wallet, which annoyed his attacker. "You deaf, white boy?" Jamal was loud and antsy. "Money or your life, motherfucker. I ain't got all day." His next slash cut Ian's jacket and nicked his chest.

"Hurry your ass, white boy!"

Ian's watch camera here recorded the eerie sound of the wind howling all around them. The metal canopy made the wind sound even louder.

Ian felt the wind and storm only added to the surrealism of his being robbed. Having his feet frozen in place annoyed him. Having his body locked tight annoyed him more. But his fright and freeze moment was beginning to wear off, as his mind was starting to take over. But he knew to be careful while marking his time.

"I'll cut you some more, you don't hand over yo wallet."

Ian didn't doubt it for a minute. But it was his blood dripping from his cut arm that got his mind shaking off the fright and balling his fists behind his back. Squeezing tight his hand made the cut on his arm bleed even more.

Jamal never caught on to Ian balling his fists behind his back, not even with seeing him grimace as if hurting while making for his wallet.

Once again Ian got caught staring up at the surveillance camera. That brought another slash that cut his hand. "I told you before, punk, cut that shit out. Now what's taking yo sorry ass so long to hand over yo wallet?" Another slash tore open Ian's shirt. "Yo wallet, motherfucker!"

Jamal missed seeing Ian turning angry.

Ian's anger was from thinking he hadn't survived the ocean and being struck by lightning, which had stolen 4 years of his life, so that some obvious drug-crazed fiend could just cut him and rob him. Ian moved closer. His hand wasn't on his wallet anymore.

It wasn't about losing the hundred dollars per se, though Ian still hated handing over the money; it was more seeing his blood staining his clothes that got him ready to strike. He watched his attacker and bode his time carefully, closing in ever so slightly on his targeted area. He was helped by a thunderous boom after another bright flash of lightning made his attacker flinch again. Ian was right where he wanted to be.

"Looks like you don't hear so good, white boy; so I think I'm just going to cut you up some more." Suddenly, the clouds darkened as if curtains being drawn closed on a stage.

It was right then that Ian struck.

Ian hit his attacker hard and cobra-quick, hitting him solid on the trachea. But he paid the price for hitting him so hard.

Ian saw stars when striking the boney neck of his attacker. He wanted to cry out, but didn't. His attacker wanted to cry out, too, but couldn't.

Jamal swung his knife in self-defense and nicked Ian's face. This only upset Ian more, who followed up his left to the trachea with a right that connected with Jamal's Adam's apple. Ian followed that up with a left that landed solidly on Jamal's chin, though it hurt his hand terribly.

Seeing his attacker stagger, gave Ian another shot at moving in close until . . . his attacker swung wildly and sliced off a piece of his left ear.

Ian now had more blood running. But he didn't care. He was numb to pain. All he wanted was payback.

Another wild swing of Jamal's rusty blade caught Ian in the right pinkie and cut off his cuticle. But even that couldn't stop Ian from throwing one last haymaker that landed right on Jamal's nose.

Here Ian's watch camera clearly recorded Jamal howling in pain. Ian howled too, since he'd struck him with the bad pinkie hand. But it was another blow that staggered his attacker and then dropped him to a knee.

Ian had just used the same survival instinct that a mother uses when trying to free a trapped child from a car, or a firefighter uses when charging back into the flames to save another person, or a person who jumps into a raging river to save a stranger from drowning. His instinct to fight is what saved him from getting cut even more. But he received as much as he gave. It also put him on his knees, to then slide down the side of the gas pump while watching his attacker start to slowly walk away . . . and then suddenly get knocked to the ground by the hood of the Vette!

Cathy had only meant to scare off Ian's attacker, not send him crashing into the bushes. It was a good thing she hit the brakes when she did, or she just might've killed him when hitting him with the long hood of the car.

The cocaine that was still running through Jamal's system is what put him back on his feet. Moments later he was in the woods, but not before turning around and giving Cathy the middle finger. The sound of sirens got him stepping back into the woods. Jamal was left to wonder what to say to his dealer to get him to front him more dope. Distant sirens getting louder got him hurrying away.

Cathy was shocked to find Ian in such bad shape. His multiple cuts, including his ear, were bleeding profusely and his right pinky finger with its missing cuticle looked awful. But she kept her wits about her while helping Ian get to his feet. She knew the sirens approaching could mean trouble for Ian. She didn't want him healing in jail. She managed to get Ian inside the car and drive off just as the first sheriff's car pulled up.

Cathy next made one tough call when calling her ex-friend Rachel. Rachel was an RN about to become an ARNP. She was also the one who'd slept with Cathy's former boyfriend.

"Save it, Rachel. You can make it up to me now. I'm with someone new anyway. And that's why I'm calling. I need for you to fix my new boyfriend up. He got robbed and got cut up real bad and needs stitching. There's five hundred dollars in it for you if you can do him at your house, and I don't mean *do* him."

"Lucky for you it's my day off from studying," said Rachel, being still worried though. "You said he was cut? It's not a gunshot, right?"

"Knife cuts mostly."

"He isn't like near death or anything, is he?"

"No. He's coherent. He's awake and sitting beside me. But he's bleeding all over the car."

"Good thing the seats are red," kiddingly shouted Ian, though sounding like he was hurting.

"Five hundred bucks, huh?"

"In cash, soon as you're done."

"Okay, well, then come on over."

"Frank isn't there, is he?" asked Cathy.

"Frank and I were over days after . . ."

Cathy hung up.

An hour later, Ian was all stitched up and on antibiotics, thanks to Rachel. Meanwhile, back at the Super Pumper Gas Station . . .

The clerk was having a tough time explaining why he didn't know where the robbery victim went after investigators saw him on the surveillance tape. They had already found Jamal's bloody box cutter, dropped when he was hit by the Vette, and adding credence to a robbery having been in progress. "And you don't know where he went?" asked the lead investigator for the umpteenth time.

"Haven't a clue, detective. I saw him getting knifed and I called it in. Saw a car and he was gone. That's it." To the detectives, Ian was the $64,000 question. (The DNA from the box cutter would later match up with several strong-arm robberies done by Jamal Peterson in the vicinity. Jamal was later found holed up in an area shelter after having robbed yet another elderly couple). But it was the missing robbery victim that had investigators scratching their heads, more so when finding no area hospital having admitted any robbery victim with severe slash wounds. But the mystery man was about to reveal himself in a new video he would title: Attack becomes Payback! Once Ian's new video went viral, his anonymity was truly shot.

Part VI

An enemy mind goes rampant.

This grand party of misfits will end this Republic of ours the moment they learn to bribe us with our own money. That time has come.

(Posted on QYB before taken offline.)

Chapter 39

If it bleeds, it leads. That's how

it is with the media. And that's how they dealt with Ian's 'Attack Becomes Payback' video. In the video was blood, so the media itself helped Ian's video go viral. Thousands of folks wanted to blog with Ian then. Word of mouth also helped to spread his 'Attack Becomes Payback' video. Tens of thousands of daily new viewers clicked on to QYB to see Ian's Attack video. (A wheelchair bound woman in Florida credited his video for giving her the moxie to wait her time while hoodlums ransacked her home before she pulled from under her seat cushion a .38 snub-nose, which she used for blasting them away. Ian didn't have much to say on that.)

Sticker orders also came in hot and heavy, which was a blessing, since the extra income afforded Ian to invite Cathy for a week's stay at a luxury hotel in St. Augustine. They stayed at a place Ian had visited often during his golfing days. It was here where he did his best recuperating and writing.

Ian used Cathy's iPad to write on, while leaving the Jenna laptop off and using it only as a backup. At one point he even considered selling the Jenna laptop on eBay. But his conscience wouldn't let him. He did, however, remove the battery pack from the laptop for fear of leakage, which wound up angering London's agent Ferguson something fierce.

Ian was also using the latest ICP protection device, which came in a flash drive format, sold to him by Cheryl. (ICP is a device that is used primarily by pharmaceutical R&D reps needing to guard their secrets. ICP re-serializes protection codes 250 times a minute when online, similar to Lockout, making it literally impossible for hackers or snoopers to get past ICP.) The device was *the* perfect safety lock for Ian. Using a combination of SIM cards, ICP, and checking in under his Wolfe alias helped to safeguard him also.

Cathy continued to handle QYB's day-to-day business while also using ICP, though more leniently, since as managing director, she hadn't much to worry about. But Ian's continued postings were a problem. Every piece he posted dealt with a hot topic item, including his predictive posting of "Black Friday being a sales bomb this year."

That's when he first mentioned a boycott, which sent him further up Homeland's watch list.

Black Friday had already become a problem for many shoppers, as people had become more imprudent and impatient at the early startup of 5 a.m. Shoppers were sick of the stampedes caused at some malls around the country, stampedes that had caused death and destruction in some stores in the past. There was also the increase in parking lot robberies (two teens had been killed over a new Play Station the previous year). And now here was Ian mentioning a boycott to the whole thing.

But mentioning a boycott, while products like furniture, computers, and even auto sales were needing Black Friday as a lifeline, made Ian out to be an enigma to Corporate America.

Ian didn't care.

In the meantime, he continued to delete any emails from Revenue, SAC Rubio in Miami, Jenna, or any other non-pertinent emails that went counter to his start the revolution motto. He did however continue to send out heartfelt thank you's to all those wishing him a speedy recovery from his Attack wounds. He wrote the message, and Cathy generated it electronically, sending it to thousands of email addresses.

His print shop buddy continued to handle all the sticker sales, with the profits being deposited onto Ian's reloadable money card.

But while growing accustomed to their carefree moment in the sun, and as a winter chill forced them to put the top back on the Vette . . . a new warrant was issued against Ian by a California judge.

December 1st Ian posted the following:

IRSuarez@QYB.com: As I predicted, Black Friday was a bust and the rest of this holiday season doesn't look to be much better for the economy. This is what happens when too much printed money finds its way to certain hands that are not interested in 'We the People.' I believe 'We the People' have had enough of this inflationary nonsense. I mentioned a boycott before Black Friday and I'm mentioning it again. A bigger boycott. Of longer duration. But more on my boycott later. I think I've given the G eavesdroppers enough for one day. But rest assured, we will stop bitching and make changes happen.

He left many QYBers wondering about this boycott plan. They wouldn't have long to wait to find out what his plan was all about.

December 2nd . . .

Ian was getting ready to go on-air on the famous Lou Tucker Show. He and Cathy were still in St. Augustine, though having changed to a different hotel. Cathy was sitting at the table, checking facebook and posting Ian's daily blog responses, while Ian sat out on the balcony prepping his phone with a new SIM card just before going on-air. He was just a few minutes from going on when hearing Cathy holler, "Hey Ian, this Ms. Dizzy Dee's request through facebook is actually Mike!"

"Geez, Cath. I really don't have time for him right now. Just chat with him and give him my new cell number. He's probably been trying to text me at my old number. Tell him I'm sorry about that, and that I'll chat at him later." It was coming up on 2 o'clock.

"He says he definitely can't connect through email, and he's certainly not going to try Skyping again. Ah shit, he says he's certain the Feds will want to talk to me."

"So? You haven't done anything wrong. You manage my site, and that's legit. No one knows we're a couple."

"Yeah, but Jenna knows, thanks to you. And Mike's saying here you should cut all ties with her, and I agree. I say delete her from your contact list."

"But she paid fifty grand to get me out of jail."

"Which doesn't make any sense at all. I think you should do as Mike suggests and trace back her URL. See where it leads."

"How about you do that while I'm talking to Tucker. I'm calling in now. Tell Mike I'll chat at him later through *your* facebook account."

"You going to tell Lou about your boycott idea?"

"He already knows about it. Why do you think he wants me on-air? Where better to get a three day boycott started then on the Lou Tucker Show?"

Cathy, before going back to chatting with Mike, raised the volume on the room radio so she could hear Ian's on-air interview with America's #2 talk radio show. Her going back to chatting with Mike allowed federal agents to trace Mike's signal back to his cabin in the woods.

Lou Tucker started his show by reading some of Ian's latest blog postings. "Okay folks, so this is from the founder of Quit Your Bitching, Mr. Ian Red Suarez, who will be on-air in just a moment. But I did want to read this to you, so here goes . . . Ian writes . . .

'It has come time to quit our bitching and make our unity be heard. We need to start making our unity work for us. But not with violence. We'll get nowhere with any street violence, frenzied mobs, or even a simple protest. Those we think serve and protect us could care less about serving and protecting us. I have a better idea. Right after Christmas, as we wind down the year, what say 'We the People' commit to a 72-hour boycott of *all* purchases like gas and *all* household products like furniture, computers, groceries, even car purchases. I suggest as many of you who can, to also stay home for that 72-hour period starting on January 1. Stay home. Buy nothing. This will show those that are running the show, who are *really* running the show. We the People will mean to do business by doing *no* business at all. United we stand. Divided we fall, and we've been falling for too long now. Consider this boycott *your* own payback boycott, with no violence, no pepper spray, and no rubber bullets. Buy nothing from January first to the third. My QYB site awaits you to sign our petition. And *go boycott!*' Lou Tucker gave his audience a moment to let Ian's words sink in before bringing Ian on-air.

"How you doing, Ian?"

"Never better, Lou. And thanks for having me."

"My pleasure. And did you know I had your friend and author, Dr. Dana Warrick, on my show yesterday?"

"No, I didn't. But I haven't spoken to her in a few days, so I wouldn't have known."

"She talked you up a pretty good game."

Most of the 22 million listening had heard her talk Ian up.

"Well, Dr. Dana's good people," commented Ian.

"Selling lots of books of late."

"She's a good writer. Every time she writes a piece for QYB, she gets lots of readers."

Agents were having a difficult time tracing Ian's phone. (The ramifications from the Olympic Games virus debacle from a few years back {Olympic Games was a virus created to thwart the Iranian nuclear program and began from a simple flash drive}that then ran amuck throughout the World Wide Web had gotten judges to ease up on signing anymore eavesdropping orders.) The CIA and NSA eavesdropping of phone and text messages had also made judges leery to anymore eavesdropping over the right to privacy. Orders to intercept Ian's phone signal had not been signed, but SAC Rubio in Miami was still trying to find him anyway using SAT.

"**F**orget your holiday plans, agent Rubio." Last thing Rubio had wanted to hear was that. She had booked passage aboard a cruise liner months in advance for her entire family. Now her boss was telling her to put her cruise vacation on hold until dealing with the Ian issue.

"But sir, I've already got my vacation trip planned!"

"Then go out and find this guy, Rubio. Go find him and bring him in. Do whatever it takes. Get this London guy, Ferguson, to help you. But get this idiot off the internet and out of our hair, and then go take your vacation." Her boss never gave her a chance to respond.

Rubio already knew that Ian's routine was to post from area libraries because surveillance there was tough, thanks to the Central Florida county libraries updating their privacy filters for thwarting identity theft. Between that and Ian's ICP device, Ian couldn't be targeted. The descrambling feature of his ICP device made his Wi-Fi and URL signals literally ghost signals. He could write and send Cathy his post from anywhere. But that still didn't stop JennaCal412 from emailing Cathy, while Ian was still chatting with Tucker, to tell her that she'd given Cathy up to the authorities.

"So, I got Ian Red Suarez, founder of the 'Quit Your Bitching and Start the Revolution!' website here on the phone with me, and I gotta tell you folks, I really like this guy." Lou was a right-of-center, to-the-point, no-nonsense, well-informed host. He was also a big fan of QYB, and was elated to have Ian on-air.

"Thanks for that, Lou."

"So a boycott, eh Ian?"

"Yep. A boycott."

"Think your boycott's going to do anything?"

"Not just my boycott, Lou. It's everyone's boycott."

Lou was handed a note by his producer. On it was written the words 'get him to tell you where's he's holed up.'

Lou slid the note back and mouthed the word "no."

"Why shouldn't it work, Lou? I believe the American people are fed up and rightly so, so yes, it'll work. Can't make the economy any worse than it is already. Let's see what happens after January third."

Soon as they broke for their first commercial break, Ian broke out a new phone. He wasn't taking any chances. Lou knew ahead of time about Ian's phone swapping technique. His phone bank operator was ready to take Ian's call from his new phone. They were back on-air four minutes later.

"We're back with Ian of QYB." Lou was heard rustling papers while asking Ian, "So, don't you think your boycott's a tall order? I mean, it's only a few weeks before Christmas, and then New Year's right around the corner."

"Ah, don't go selling people short, Lou. You watch. We get enough people onboard with the boycott, get them to sign the petition that we'll post as evidence to people's disliking of Washington's handling of the economy, and I bet the boycott makes a difference."

"Ever the optimist. Well your numbers are certainly showing that people are getting onboard with this boycott idea."

"Growing as we speak. And can you blame people? I mean, I think I speak for a few people when saying that we're fed up with the lethargy that's taken over our elected officials. I'm astounded that civil unrest hasn't started already, what with the direction this economy has taken."

"And you think your boycott's gonna change all that?"

"It's a start. The administration of years back ran on 'hope and change', remember? 'Change we could believe in'? Well, here's something that will definitely be the start of change. At least I hope so, anyway."

Lou spoke to his audience a moment. "If you don't already know Ian's site, go punch in QYB on your browser and check out his speaking points. And don't forget to read his bio. This is the guy they found floating in the ocean after his boat was attacked by Fidel's goons. They killed his mother and brother in that attack. Then he comes here and makes a fortune in banking, gets struck by lightning, and bam, he's got QYB running! Read his bio. It's incredible."

"I don't know what to say after that, Lou."

"You deserve it, amigo. All the stuff you've been through. Confiscations and all. So anyway, how many have signed your petition?"

"At last count, we were at 16 million plus."

"Whoa. Big numbers. Maybe you should run for politics. You're getting better numbers than some we've voted for in Washington."

"I wouldn't think to turn on the people like that." Ian's tone turned somber. "But all kidding aside, it's sad to think we live in a time where people actually have lost faith in the election process."

"So, why suggest a boycott during such tough times?"

"America always rebounds during tough times, Lou. Check our history."

"But you've only got weeks to organize it, Ian. New Year's is just around the corner."

"It's when Americans are backed against the wall that they think better, Lou."

"But a three day boycott, Ian? And what about the folks who can't stay home from work those three days?"

"For those who've got to punch the clock, by all means, punch the clock, cause lord knows it wouldn't do any good having more people on the unemployment roll. But we're all one kindred spirit during the boycott; I can assure everyone listening of that." Ian needed a moment to drink from his water bottle. He stretched the kink out of his outstretched leg while sitting four floors above the hotel parking lot, and noticing Cathy had fallen asleep while listening in. Running QYB had been most difficult during these days.

"So, a boycott's the way to go, eh Ian?"

"I'm just one voice in a sea of voices, Lou. If we're united, with these numbers, then yes, the powers that be will most definitely take notice. And that's what we want, to be noticed, to see a real change that we can believe in. People coming together to make a difference. Simple as that, Lou."

"Sounds good, Ian."

"Good things, good results, Lou. Bad things, consequences. We'll see if it's good results or consequences come the fourth. But yes, boycott on!"

"And on that note, we'll take another break to pay the bills. In the meantime, you folks go check out QYB. And when we come back, Ian, I want you to tell me a little about your payback videos."

"Alright."

"Great. Sit tight and we'll be right back."

And that's when SAT radar in Miami got a ping on Ian's phone. But Rubio and her agents' elation at finding Ian was short lived as he again changed out his phone for a new one. Four minutes later . . .

"And we're back with Ian Red Suarez of the Quit Your Bitching website." Lou waited on his intro music to die out before continuing. The music took a little longer than usual to fade.

"How about your videos, Ian?"

"What about them?"

"What gave you the idea for all these payback videos of yours?"

"Situations and circumstances."

"Fair enough. And what about what you wrote last night about America having become a paycheck-to-paycheck nation?"

"That's how most Americans are living today, Lou."

Lou ruffled more paper. "Paycheck to paycheck, huh?"

"What Middle America is going through is pure class warfare. Sort of reminds me of when I was growing up in Cuba. Man, we had it bad back then. But living paycheck-to-paycheck isn't much better, and this is supposed to be the greatest nation on Earth. I hear the talking heads going on all the time about there being a light at the end of the tunnel. I just want to know *what* tunnel, so I can let the rest of you know what tunnel. Only tunnel I see is one that comes with higher rates, increased taxes, and more fees. You probably know that Congress was in session again today to find funding for food stamps. Now there's more 'light at the end of the tunnel' nonsense for you. This isn't going to end well for us, Lou. You know it. I know it. The people out there know it, too. We need to make a noise that will be heard from the greatest nation on earth, not a debtor nation, but a great nation. That's why I considered a national boycott as sort of being like our Boston Tea party moment."

"But so close to the ball dropping?"

"Heck Lou, it took the tossing of tea to get King George III to admit that America deserved its time. It was tea then. It's boycott now. Just another challenge to see Americans through. Oh, and let's be leery of the media. And I don't mean your radio media. You guys are doing a great job. But the print and television media has for years been intentionally blocking all 'moving forward' projects with their own take on things. There is no news any longer. There are agendas and ramblings. They are doing more harm than good. So, let's say yes to the boycott, turn off our babel boxes, and let's remove the blinders from our eyes." Ian drank more water before continuing. "And now more what? Gas prices on the rise again? And milk at $7 a gallon? I don't know how people are making it, especially those that have children. Lou, this economy is shot through with more holes than Swiss cheese. You think hyperinflation was bad? I don't want to see the day when it takes an American a wheel barrel full of money to buy bread. Go ask the Germans how great that felt when they had to do it after World War I. Hell Lou, it led to World War II! We'll have to soon invent a new word for what's going on here. I got one. How about super-hyper? How's that sound? Now to all you listening, remember, too many facts can hide the truth. So let's get the party started by going online and signing my petition and . . . *go boycott!*"

"Here-here," chimed in Lou, then asking, "Why so intent on this boycott of yours, Ian?"

"Lou, both my mother and brother died trying to reach this great nation of ours. I'd like to think they didn't die in vain."

"There you have it folks. We'll take a few calls while we still have Ian with us, but in the meantime, go check out his payback videos. They're a riot. And do sign his petition."

North Florida's SAT radar caught Ian's signal again. A short burst of 40k hertz terminated Ian's phone-in. He was left with a terribly loud ringing in his ear from a disruption signal meant to block him, but inadvertently blocking Lou's signal too. Radio listeners were left fiddling with their dials. The Tucker soundboard went haywire due to the disruption signal. All wireless feeds were severed.

Four stories below, the hotel parking lot began filling with police and unmarked cars. Ian didn't need to guess who they were looking for. He woke Cathy from her catnap while swapping out a new phone and tossing the old one inside the toilet reservoir. Their St. Augustine days were over.

Cathy did a quick change from old clothes to new while watching Ian hurry to pack his other six phones. Soon as they were ready, they hit the hallway. They made straight for the rear stairwell, which took them to the second floor pool deck area. Beyond the pool were steps leading to the rear parking lot. They waited for a cop car to go by before hurrying through the rear parking lot and making for the neighboring hotel where Ian had purposely parked the Vette.

And so while agents were showing Ian's photo to the hotel clerk, he and Cathy had already slipped by police and were south on A1A.

While agents stormed their fourth floor hotel room, Ian and Cathy were discussing where to have dinner.

It was at dinner where Ian surprised Cathy with wanting to bring in the New Year on Miami Beach. But it would require leaving behind the Vette for a more inconspicuous car.

Flagler County was where Ian parked the Vette and rented a nondescript four-banger that would take them south. He no longer felt safe heading back to Cathy's house. New Year's on the beach was what he knew best.

"But a whole 27 day stay, Ian? Can we afford that?" She wasn't completely against the idea, if they could afford it.

"Sure. Why not? Rick's already deposited this week's money from the stickers, and it's certainly enough to afford us a full month's stay at any motel on the Beach. I imagine Miami Beach is all booked up, so we'll try North Beach instead. Less crowded anyway."

"You're the boss, Ian."

"Alright. Then we go." North Miami Beach it was.

While driving . . . the markets continued to teeter. No longer was Street growing its numbers, now with the Dow having lost 20% of its value since right after Black Friday. It had been nearly a generation before since retail numbers had been so off. And here was Ian suggesting a boycott to ruin numbers even more.

Ian's boycott had the Federal Reserve (which is neither federal nor has anything in reserve) in a hellacious quagmire. His suggesting boycott with 18 million plus and rising petitioners led 33,000 lobbyists (this is the usual number of lobbyists who make the rounds in Washington, outnumbering 3 to 1 those tasked to taking down Ian) to cut their vacations short so they could holler for more PATRIOT involvement. News of an additional 285,000 layoffs to start the New Year, added another 285,000 sign-ins to Ian's petition. QYB had now surpassed 30 million subscribers, this all in just 7 hours of driving.

Ian chose the Sands Motel in North Miami Beach because the manager was a fan of QYB. Cathy met the man through facebook. He welcomed them by giving them a great room near the beach. The room was theirs for the remainder of the month.

But the weather turned wickedly cold and foul for Miami, leading to steaming showers for lifting the mood before each breakfast. Right after breakfast (and some fun) it was time to work. Mike continued to chat with Ian through Cathy's Ms.DizzyDee account while active sequential software, intelligent enough to distinguish right hand/left hand keystroke errors, finally discovered Ms.DizzyDee as actually being Mike. That got federal agents starting for Mike's cabin, and while he chatted with Ian, they began surrounding his cabin. Ian's Vette by then had been found also, parked near the rental agency that gave up Ian's new rental. It wasn't just Mike's noose that was tightening.

Chapter 40

Ian finally got to chat with Mike

on Cathy's facebook page. Yet no sooner had he begun to chat when the beeping in his head started again. The beeping got so loud that it slowed his typing when responding to Mike's comments about Jenna and her software business.

"What's wrong, Ian?" asked Cathy when seeing him grimace.

"Ah, nothing. Must be a headache coming on."

"What's Mike telling you?"

"Same thing he told you. Not to trust Jenna. Oh, wait, Mike's finishing his comment."

IRSuarez: But Jenna's site looks legit. She's got turn page stuff, same as my site, and it isn't cheap to webmaster those pages.

Ms.DizzyDee: I traced her URL to a security link that leads straight to Homeland in Homestead. Best watch your ass, Ian. When was Jenna's last email to you?

IRSuarez: Funny you should ask, cause it's Cathy who's been getting more of her emails than me. In fact, Cathy's waiting for me to finish with you, so she can use her iPad to send Jenna a response to an email she sent threatening us with the police. Something about a reward for me. Jenna's been sending some *weird* stuff. She even sent a Photoshopped mug shot of me. Can you believe it? And also what of this Marshall Evans guy who bailed me out in California? I can't figure him out either.

Ms.DizzyDee: Just be on your guard. I sense trouble. You've stirred up a hornet's nest with your boycott.

IRSuarez: Looks like you got your own hornet's nest stirring up your way. And what's the deal with this armory heist?

Ms.DizzyDee: I had toyed with the idea of leading a protest rally in front of this particular armory because of the NSA spying nonsense. My shop manager and his buddies ramped my protest up a level. But don't worry about me. I'll get things straightened out in time. In the meantime, I can go to ground if trouble comes looking for me. You, on the other hand, you're out in the open, so watch yourself. The Fed's going to want to put you out of commission before your boycott ever starts.

IRSuarez: And you say the cops are probably pressing charges against Cathy for being with me and not turning me in?

Ms.DizzyDee: She's part of your whole deal. Just remind her to also watch her back.

IRSuarez: So can you join us down here?

Ms.DizzyDee: I just warned you to be careful, and you go giving away your location. Eyes and ears, remember? I don't need to be a psychic to know what'll happen to you if you're found. The Feds are probably searching for you as desperately as they're searching for me.

IRSuarez: I'm up for the challenge.

Ms.DizzyDee: Not on a challenge you can't win, you're not. Just watch yourself. And before I forget, thanks for the money you sent me.

IRSuarez: What are friends for?

Ms.DizzyDee: So what happened to you on the Tucker Show? One moment you're making great points, the next you disappear off-air.

IRSuarez: I think the Feds jammed my signal. We also had to skedaddle out of our hotel after that.

Ms.DizzyDee: Why?

IRSuarez: The hotel parking lot filled with cops. And you're right; a psychic didn't need to know who they were after.

Ms.DizzyDee: Proves my point of you being wanted, and not just over missing your court dates. If it's any consolation, you laid out your boycott rather well on the Tucker Show.

IRSuarez: Thanks. I was going to wrap up with comparing my boycott to the Iwo Jima flag raising before getting knocked off air.

Ms.DizzyDee: Iwo Jima flag raising? I don't follow.

IRSuarez: America was nearly broke from the war when that flag got raised. They actually wound up losing that hill and most of the original guys that raised it, but it still sold war bonds like crazy. Everyone was on the war bandwagon then. This is kind of like me raising a similar flag and hoping people will like what they see.

Ms.DizzyDee: Don't go hanging your hat on any flag raising, my friend. People today aren't the same as back then. No one gives a crap about anything but surviving these days.

IRSuarez: You best re-think that, my friend, cause this economy is as bad as any war, if not worse.

Ms.DizzyDee: And on that note, I gotta run. My trip alarm just sounded. It could be a hog, and I'm hungry.

IRSuarez: Happy hunting. I'm out!

Mike knew he wasn't about to grill any hog when his power suddenly went out. He hadn't been just talking words when saying he could go to ground if trouble came his way; in fact, it was more like underground where Mike went, into his self-dug tunnel, built years ago as part of his survival bunker under his cabin. His tunnel ran 300-yards and ended at his woodshed near the back woods.

The agents moving in on the cabin had found the back woods too thick to walk through, so they didn't think to check for a wood shed when moving in on the cabin from the front yard. But Mike wouldn't be at all bothered by the thick woods.

A trapdoor found in the kitchen floor got him started down a wooden rung ladder that put him in his tunnel, just as the first flash-bang grenade went off above. He hit a switch that got his generator started and gave him light to see by until getting to the woodshed. He waited for a second flash-bang grenade to go off, accompanied by agents yelling for him to "give himself up!" before pushing out the metal grate that was hidden behind a stack of firewood prior to entering the shed.

While agents rushed inside Mike's cabin, Mike was already in the woods and making for his second line of escape, while hearing eyes-in-the-sky approaching.

Mike had hidden a dirt bike among some tall weeds near a stream, so he cranked it right up and rode along a thin footpath, just as agents were finding his kitchen trapdoor.

He only needed to ride but a few miles before getting to his third line of escape. Meanwhile, eyes-in-the-sky stayed hovering over his cabin, thinking agents had him trapped in his bunker. By then, Mike had ditched the bike into the stream to cut down on the heat signature and headed straight for a friend's barn a few hundred yards away. A beat up Ford station wagon was waiting for him. The wagon was topped with gas, a fake beard, wig, and glasses, stored in the glove box, would help Mike get to Iowa. Friends in Iowa would get him to Canada.

In Baltimore . . .

Agent Ferguson was part of the team that arrested Dr. Warrick at her War College office. She had just sent Ian an email when agents came charging through her door. The last thing Ferguson noticed before leaving Dr. Warrick's office was her having Ian's QYB logo as her screensaver on her laptop.

Ferguson hurried back to Miami on a redeye flight that very night. He was hurrying because he didn't want to miss Ian's takedown.

While flying, he sent angry emails to both Ian and Cathy, but neither responded. Even Photoshopping more pics of the two of them being arrested didn't get him a response. At least not yet. But the Jenna laptop wouldn't stay silent for long.

In Miami . . .

SAC Rubio was just then reading her latest text message regarding S/A London's Eye-for-an-Eye mission. She was shocked to read the kill order that came with the text.

Chapter 41

"And Jenna's *still* sending us

stuff!" Cathy was beside herself while reading Jenna's latest email.

"You would think she would stop with the emails after sending those stupid mug shot photos done with Photoshop. But nope; here she goes again with a new email." Cathy was beyond angry once finished with JennaCal412's latest email.

The cold outside had already ruined Cathy's plans at wanting to sit in the sun to write and read. The cold brought her right back to the room after just 15 minutes of sitting outside.

Cathy was feeling a little cooped up in the room, with the 'all work and no play' attitude getting to her. Ian was up to his regular trick of visiting the local library to use their computer. The local library in this case was just down the street.

Cathy harked to Ian about the latest Jenna email until . . . seeing the dollar amount Jenna was offering Cathy, if she gave up the location of where Ian was staying. She deleted that message as Ian walked past her to get to the bathroom.

"Yeah? So what's Jenna's email about this time?" Ian had to raise his voice over the shower. He was getting himself ready for an early dinner.

"Ah, same old same old nonsense from her," answered Cathy.

Ian stuck his head out of the bathroom. He was stark naked when saying, to Cathy, "Well, I sure hope you're not getting too upset about my knowing her."

"You knew her before finding me. But it's still a dumb thing having a fling with someone over the internet."

"A fling? She started as a fan of QYB."

"Whatever. You let it get too far. But forget all that. I want to talk to you about something that's come to my mind."

"Yeah? What."

"I think it might be best if we split up. At least until after the boycott."

"What! But Cath, you said yourself, it's just someone over the internet. Besides, this morning you said we were forever."

"Not splitting up in a bad way, silly. But think about it. We got less than a week before your boycott starts, and everyone we talk to says the authorities are wanting to stop us. It sure wouldn't do any good if you got found before the boycott. If I was home, I could run things from my computer. And why are you getting out that laptop? You're naked."

"I want to send Jenna an email telling her to stop sending us stuff, and you're using our iPad."

"Go shower. Forget that bitch. Just take Mike's advice and delete her from your life; and while you're at it, toss that laptop in the trash."

Cathy hurried to slam shut Ian's laptop before he had a chance to possibly check his trash file and find Jenna's latest bribe to her. "I swear I'll strangle that bitch if I ever meet her."

"Okay babe. I'll forget the email and go shower."

"I'll be right in there with you."

"So no more talk of leaving?"

"I still think that's a good idea, Ian. Think about it. It won't do us or any of your QYB fans any good if you go to jail before or during your boycott. At least from home I can continue to post and blog, so long as you keep sending me the stuff you want me to post. Your boycott's the best thing yet. You can even keep my iPad with you, so long as you toss out Jenna's laptop."

"Hell with that, Cath. I'd rather sell it to a pawnshop or something. Maybe our manager buddy here might want to buy it. But I still don't want you leaving me, though."

"Well, I'm not leaving just yet. Besides, after January third, you'll head back to me. Just grab a bus from here and I'll pick you up like in Orlando or something. We'll go see a lawyer about your court stuff after the third. Honey, if you don't mind, I don't want to see you going to jail, and my going home gives QYB a chance at success during the boycott. You've gotta admit it makes sense." Cathy made a pouty face. "Besides, I've run out of things to wear."

"I can buy you more clothes."

"Save the money. You'll be needing that for your lawyer. Now let's go before the hot water runs out." While they were making love in the shower, QYB continued to receive encouraging emails like:

InezG452: We're with you in our house, Ian. And thanks for the stickers. Boycott on!

Miner7.1: Yes to boycott/No to the government's bullying tactics. Boycott on!

E.Tinymailer1: Lost my job right before Thanksgiving. Probably would've lost it anyway, since I'm going to be staying home during your boycott. We're with you in our house. Boycott on!

MTR55WM: I'm mad as hell since losing my job to outsourcing. Gonna lose my house next. The family and I are right now packing. But we're still going to boycott.

Salmo446: Outrageous what these times have become and bound to get worse. Thanks for being real. I hate the media bullshit. Hope your boycott does something. Boycott on!

MariaR606: I'm Cuban also, and I too, remember what it was like growing up in communist Cuba. First they removed God from our lives, schools, and provinces, and then they tried removing our faith. Seems like the same thing's going on here.

Retiredforlife151: I remember the Red scare during the Cold War. Looks like we got to worry about a worse scare right here in our own backyard.

Riotstein5: I'm a retired cop. You're right to think more bullying is on the way. I see real bullets replacing rubber bullets, if folks don't start towing the line. And so long as young folks only concern themselves with RAM speed, gigabytes, and texting speed, then the bullying has already won.

More emails like this kept coming every minute while SAT radar in Miami kept searching for Ian.

Ian's new buddy at the Sands Motel gave him a bunch of discount coupons to use around town; coupons like for Vizcaya, the Seaqarium, Metro Zoo, and the Planetarium, plus discounts to all the neighboring restaurants including the Chinese restaurant down the street, which had become their favorite. It was within walking distance of the motel, which made it convenient, but not in 28° weather. (The weather in Miami prior to Ian's boycott had broken Miami's old record set on Jan. 19, 1977, where it actually snowed.)

Cathy's face was beet red from the cold when entering the restaurant and finding a booth. But her face turned even redder when hearing Ian tell her he had sent Jenna a new email while she had been dressing.

"Ian, are you out of your mind? Why would you send her another email? And this after we discussed not writing to her anymore. Plus, how could you send an email, if my iPad's charging?"

"Sent it off her laptop, babe. But hey, I don't know why you're so upset. How else am I supposed to get her to buzz off, if I don't tell her?"

"By just not contacting her anymore, that's how."

"Well, never mind that. Let's talk about you leaving me. What's the plan?"

"We've already gone over this. And I thought I told you to toss that laptop in the trash?"

"I'm not throwing away a perfectly good laptop, Cath. Besides, I'll need it. I want you to take your iPad with you, that way you can communicate with me while you're on the road. Best that way."

Twenty-one miles south, Rubio was having her agents gear up for their drive to North Miami Beach after her tech agent, Emily Lloyd, got a hit on the Jenna laptop. SAT's mainframe had done a wonderful job tracing Ian's last email signal.

Rubio had Emily Lloyd sit beside her in her SUV while Ferguson sat in back. But as soon as Lloyd pointed them north on Collins Avenue, the Jenna laptop went offline. (Ian had shut down the Jenna laptop right after sending his message.)

But they knew it was North Miami Beach nonetheless. In back, Ferguson did his part to try and get Ian back online.

Rubio eyed Ferguson through her rear view mirror. They shared a look of knowing a secret that would lead to murder, when Ferguson stared back and said, "It is what it is, agent Rubio."

Tech agent Lloyd was left wondering about that.

Now it was surveillance time.

Dinner was for discussing when Cathy would leave, which was decided would be New Year's Eve. "That leaves you a couple of days to fill your flash drive with postings, Ian. I'll need that so I can keep posting from home. Oh, and by the way, while I'm gone . . . Don't you even *think* to write Jenna any more, you hear? And I might as well tell you, I've seen her attached pics. I know you've been throwing them in your trash bin so I wouldn't see them, but I have."

"You have?"

"Yep. I went back as far as your trash bin would take me, and found she's been sending you erotic pictures of herself since October, and that's only because your bin only goes back so far. Just don't get any ideas while I'm gone."

"Come on Cath. That's insulting. You know I wouldn't even think . . ."

"*Men.* But I kid you not, Ian; you mess around on me and I swear you'll never see me again, and you know that's something I mean."

Her saying that is what sent Ian into manic mode. By the time they got to the register to pay, Ian was fidgeting and pacing.

Cathy tried calming him during their walk back to the room.

"Hey, come on, Ian. It's chilly enough already without my having to jog to keep up with you. Relax and slow down. You're like speed walking. And remember, we'll only be separated for a week or so. Right after the boycott, we'll be together again." She raced ahead of him to cut him off. His face was as beet red as hers from the cold.

"We're a team, honey. Plus, we still have two whole days for fooling around."

This did bring a slight smile to Ian's face. "I care so much about you, Cath. All that time back in school . . ."

"That was a long time ago, Ian. But just do me a favor, and no more emails to that bitch, okay? And wait until after the boycott to make contact with Mike again. He's got enough trouble without us getting involved. You just stay focused and write some good stuff that I can take back with me. Now let's hurry. This cold's killing my horniness."

"I love it when you talk dirty."

"That's not talking dirty. But let's get to the room and you'll hear dirty."

But Ian's manic mode ruined everything. It was too difficult to shake manic mode while making love when his enemy mind was taking over. It was sex and pace, sex and pace. Cathy wanted to leave right then, but she didn't want to give away her hand.

Ian's mania didn't ease much during the next two days, which then brought them to the 31ˢᵗ and the morning of Cathy's departure. Two blocks south were five agency cars parked in the Chinese restaurant parking lot and hoping this was the day Ian would eat out. There was just half a day to go before Ian's boycott was to begin, and the quicker Rubio could find him, the quicker she could be joining her family on their cruise. It was then that they spotted Ian's rental car with Cathy driving it and pulling away from the Sands Motel.

"Well, I'll be damned!" said an excited Rubio, right before slamming the shifter into drive and leading the charge into the Sands Motel.

T he Sands manager was just opening up for business when Rubio, Ferguson, and Lloyd came storming into the lobby. Rubio ordered her other agents to stay near their cars and keep their eyes on all the rooms. She also noticed Ferguson clearly eyeing the rear stairwell beyond the manager's desk as they walked in. *Looks like this fool's going to charge off without me.* But she first had the manager to contend with.

"Listen here," she was holding up Ian's license photo, "I know this man's here because I just saw his main squeeze tear out of this parking lot. Now, I need his room number."

Ferguson began heading for the stairwell.

"Hey Ferguson," Rubio's voice sounded agitated, "there's one boss here today, and it ain't you." Ferguson made as if he was deaf.

"Ferguson, don't you even think to do a door-to-door by yourself." Perfectly tone deaf.

In agent Lloyd's hands was Ferguson's laptop, which suddenly chimed with a new incoming email. This stopped Ferguson in his tracks. "Oh bloody hell! Tell me it's him."

Rubio was just as shocked when seeing it *was* Ian. "Wow! Couldn't ask for better timing. We might not need his room number after all."

"Definitely him, alright," said Lloyd. "He's looking to chat with Jenna."

Rubio noticed the manager reaching for the house phone. *Strange time to be making a call with his motel flooded with agents* thought Rubio. To Lloyd,

Rubio said, "Get him to give up his room number." Rubio looked over at Ferguson and said, "Just wait. We might not have to do a room-to-room if Lloyd gets him to give up his room number." She turned on the Sands manager and shouted, "Put down that phone right now! I need a room number and I need it now!"

Meanwhile, in room 114 . . .

Ian was just then noticing his main cell phone was missing when replying to Jenna.

IRSuarez: Why do you need my room number?

JennaCal412: Just need it. It's a surprise.

The room phone suddenly rang. Ian slammed shut the laptop, putting it in standby, while reaching for a phone that had no one at the other end.

Rubio sensed the possibility of getting on the cruise ship ASAP if getting the Ian issue done and over with. But she still needed his room number. Lloyd was having no luck, and the Sands manager was playing dumb. *No fool hangs up a phone so quickly unless doing something that ain't right.* Rubio pulled back her coat to show her badge and her gun to the manager. *Lord, I'm going to need my vacation after this extraction.*

Rubio was all about following orders. But the kill order on the son of a dead Irish bomber from years back still had her stymied. A second text message, sent right after the first, had confirmed to her how the Ian issue must end. It was still hard to swallow. *Plus the killing of an American citizen on U.S. soil's going to be a problem if it's found out.* Rubio's head was full of troubling thoughts, made worse with the manager playing dumb to knowing Ian. But thinking of her family got her to focus.

"So, suddenly you don't know this man's room number, huh?"

"Oh, the bloody hell with this!" Ferguson charged right into the stairwell and began banging on doors.

Rubio right then got a call on her radio about Cathy.

Cathy Hancock was right then adjusting her rearview mirror while driving onto the I-95 on-ramp. She still hadn't noticed the unmarked agency car following three cars behind her. A state trooper was ordered to fall back behind the agency car, for fear his markings would scare Cathy into doing something stupid. Cathy's face and tag had already been confirmed, with

Rubio also giving the orders to her takedown. "Don't take her down yet. Let's see if this Ian character tries contacting her next. Let me know if she answers her phone or makes for her iPad." Rubio got off her radio and went back to working on getting Ian's room number.

Chapter 42

Cathy was so busy gathering her

thoughts over what to say to Jenna that she failed to pick up on the agents following her since she left the motel. Thinking girl-talk is what got Cathy forgetting to keep her guard up. She scrolled through Ian's phone contacts while driving and found Jenna's contact info. Moments later she was using the phone's microphone to send Jenna a voice text. "Uh, Ms. Davis, this is Cathy Hancock. I am doing as you asked in your email from last week. Please return my call as soon as possible. I have left Ian and want my $20,000. I am not giving up his whereabouts until knowing your money's in my account." Cathy tossed the phone aside and went back to driving. She was thinking how much better her drive would be once she was in the Vette.

That's when agents lit her up.

Cathy's text also went directly to Ferguson's laptop. Lloyd caught it while in the Sands lobby, but she didn't bother to mention it to her boss while Rubio dealt with the Sands manager. Lloyd did, however, trace the SIM signal transfer from Ian's phone, but other than for the Chinese restaurant purchases that they already knew about, there was nothing to lead them to Ian's room. Rubio was working on that. Meanwhile . . .

Ian was hurrying to dress. He knew getting a phone call from his manager friend and getting no response when calling back to the front desk meant trouble.

Last thing he put on was a green satiny shamrock tie that Cathy had bought him as a gift for bringing in the New Year. It was more a gag gift than a real tie since she'd bought it across the street at the Dollar Store. But Ian liked the tie, and it went well with his long sleeved dress shirt. He next grabbed the Jenna laptop and began emailing his friend Steve in Doral. He wanted to see if he could get his friend to maybe pick him up and take him to a hotel in South Miami, and invite Steve to a nice dinner if possible, when suddenly hearing the squawk of a police radio out in the hall. Ian had no time to grab his jacket from behind the front door because the door handle was being jimmied!

Ian hurried to climb out the bathroom window that led to an alley between the Sands and the neighboring motel. Under his arm was the Jenna laptop, which was still booted up.

He caught a Wi-Fi signal from the neighboring motel, which he used for sending Steve the message with subject line reading: Need You to email me back ASAP. Ian hit send and got pinged by Lloyd. He did not notice how much faster the Union Jack icon was blinking in the taskbar. Ian's noose was tightening fast.

"So, the room number?" Rubio could read the manager's nervousness. But having Ferguson suddenly take off on her was still a distraction. She could hear him banging on doors while waiting on the manager to spill. *This Ferguson's going to be a problem* thought Rubio.

But she knew nothing of Ferguson's seven years of keeping tabs on Ian. Had she, she would've better understood his wanting closure. Ferguson missed his night out with pub friends. He missed being back home in England. Rubio signaled for two of her agents to follow Ferguson while she dealt with the manager.

"I'm not going to ask you for that room number again."

Her slight Cuban accent made the manager more nervous.

Two North Miami Beach police cruisers came into the parking lot. Rubio would rather not have had the uniformed officers there, but there was nothing she could do about the radio chatter bringing NMB officers to a North Miami Beach location.

"Sorry, ma'am," began the manager. "But I don't recognize that man in the picture."

Rubio eyed the half-filled pegboard. "Don't give me that bullshit. You got a half-filled motel and you don't know where he's at?"

"Maybe he's not here."

"We know he's here, you moron." Her kickboxing and karate skills wanted to chop him right in the mouth. "Now spare me from having to do a room-to-room. Just tell me where he is. He might've even checked in under the name Wolfe. Now that's a name I'm sure you would remember." She next showed him Cathy's license picture.

"He was with this woman here. Do you recognize her?"

"No, ma'am."

"What about deliveries? We know he's been getting Chink food from down the street. Come on now; work with me here. I still got an office party to go to, and you're wasting my time."

"We get deliveries from that restaurant all the time. You don't expect me to remember where every one of them deliveries go, do you? Besides, most of the delivery people know this place like the back of their hand. They don't need to check in with me."

Rubio motioned for one of the uniformed cops to come inside. Once inside, she told him to take out his cuffs.

"Now wait a minute," said the startled manager, "I told you I don't know where he's at."

"You're going to jail for obstructing a federal agent if you don't tell me his room number. How this plays out is on you." The cop dangled his cuffs as an emphasis to what Rubio had just said.

"But I got no Suarez or Wolfe in the books. Look for yourself."

"Then he paid in cash. You would remember cash, wouldn't you? Especially in a half-filled motel. So, which is it? Room number or jail?"

Thoughts of missing dinner with his wife and kids and then missing that night's fireworks on the beach got the manager saying, "He's in room 114."

"Took you long enough." Rubio turned to the cop and said, "Arrest him anyway."

"But wait! I gave you his room number!"

The cop made quick work of cuffing the manager.

Rubio never looked back at the man while hurrying her troops to room #114.

She saw Ferguson halfway down the hall still banging on doors.

"Quit that, Ferguson. I got the key." Rubio showed him the key to #114 while picking up her pace. "Let these people be. We got him." And that's when the cop radio went off, the radio that put Ian to running, and sent Rubio through the roof!

"What? Am I surrounded by idiots today?" Rubio pointed at the cop whose radio had squawked loudly. "They forget to teach you at the academy to lower your radio when serving a warrant? Conyo, you idiot! Now you and your partner there, you go check around back and make sure this fellow doesn't go jumping out some window or something." She could tell the man didn't take well to being reprimanded by her. *Too bad.*

Lloyd was who pointed the cops in the direction of the stairwell.

"There are windows in the alley. Best check there."

By then, Rubio was standing in front of #114.

Meanwhile . . .

Ian had to stop to empty his shoes of sand. Besides the hassle of sand-filled shoes, he was also disappointed at having just a few straggling couples to hide among while trying to distance himself from the Sands. The cold was keeping the locals indoors, and the world economy had killed the beach tourism trade that year.

Ian had never seen the beach so empty during a holiday. A small group of Norwegian tourists were the only ones taking advantage of the surf, albeit freezing cold, frolicking, and yelling while in the water as he walked by.

Ian's new worry was knowing it was going to be tough making it to the 163rd street bus bench without being seen. But he did think he was far enough away from the Sands to try and send a new SOS email to Cathy. While at it, he sent a repeat copy of his previous message to Steve. A third email he sent to Dr. Warrick, taking her up on her offer of her spare bedroom in Baltimore during his boycott.

It was tough typing and sending messages on the bulky 17.3-inch laptop while walking. He spotted an empty table at the back deck to one of the motels on the way to 163rd street, so he decided to sit and finish writing while taking a momentary break.

The cold temperature caught up to him next. Because he had left behind his tie clip, his shiny shamrock tie kept whipping him in the face. He got to walking again right after sending Dr. Warrick's message.

"I got him again, boss!" Agent Lloyd was ecstatic at having Ian back on her radar. Her enthusiasm even brought Ferguson closer. "But his signal's no longer coming from this building." Lloyd checked her screen and pointed out to the beach. "He's somewhere on the beach." It was all Ferguson had to hear. He went charging down the hall and moments later was on the beach.

Rubio let him go. She wanted to check Ian's room out anyway, but not until clearing it of agents. The only person she let enter was Lloyd and her laptop.

No sooner had Rubio started to look around the room when a new text message to her phone told her of Cathy's arrest. (Cathy had been read the riot act before being handcuffed and taken to lockup.)

Down the street . . .

Ian had the 163rd street bench in his sight, but there was no bus anywhere to be seen. He decided instead to go get coffee from the fast food restaurant across the street while waiting on the bus. He would use the restaurant to hide in until seeing the bus.

Rubio just did miss seeing Ian enter the restaurant, as she herded everyone back to their vehicles.

Rubio ordered Lloyd to patch into the overhead traffic cams. But even with a bigger eye view of Collins Avenue, they still couldn't find Ian. Rubio hated to think she'd lost him; hated even more to think what her superior's would say about her losing him. *Have my ass for sure* she thought.

Carmen Rubio had been the first in her family to graduate from law school. But she'd found the practice of law not to her liking. She decided to try out for the Bureau, where she passed with flying colors, though angering her father in doing so. That had been 26 years ago. She'd made peace with her father since. Rubio was nearing 50, but looked to be 35. She credited her kickboxing skills and her workouts for that. She had two grown sons who were on the cruise with their grandfather. Hard work, perseverance, and dedication to her job is what had earned her the position of Special Agent-in-Charge to one of the nation's busiest offices. She was determined to finish her Ian mission, though not liking the kill order involved. It was what the bosses wanted though, and she was not the type to countermand their authority, not even if it was a kill order. Her bosses wanted closure; she'd give them closure. But a kill order on a citizen gone rogue didn't make a whole lot of sense to her. Ruining her vacation was reason enough to finish. Rubio was broken of her musings by seeing Ferguson running across the street. *Now where the hell is that freak going?* Her answer came when he entered the Dollar Store. *An absolute odd duck that one.*

"Where we headed now, boss?" Lloyd had stayed beside Rubio while eyeing her laptop. So far the overhead cameras had shown nothing.

Rubio pointed to the fast food restaurant across the street. "I think I'll go get me some coffee."

Ian saw who he correctly assumed were two women agents headed his way. He waited until the two were entering the restaurant before slipping out the playground door. The raised lid of the restaurant's dumpster hid him from Rubio and Lloyd.

But not from Ferguson.

Ferguson was hurrying out of the Dollar Store with a bag in his hand when seeing Ian sneaking around the side of the restaurant. He coolly put down his bag of flags to reach inside his coat and withdraw his silenced pistol.

Rubio didn't see Ian, but she definitely saw Ferguson taking aim at someone with his silenced piece while she was waiting on her coffee. "Holy shit, Lloyd! Look out there. That idiot Ferguson's gonna take a shot at someone. Move! Move out of my way!" Rubio, in one fluid motion, rushed past Lloyd, swung open the door, and yelled for Ferguson to stop. She rushed right into his line of sight.

Ferguson was angry for having his sight blocked, but angrier still when Rubio came and pushed his gun hand down.

"Are you out of your mind or what, Ferguson?"

Hearing Rubio yelling at Ferguson got Ian turning while running alongside the 163 bus, which didn't want to stop. (The driver hadn't seen anyone sitting on the bench, so he never even slowed down.)

Rubio signaled her agents to go after Ian while she dealt with Ferguson. "You must be crazy if you think you're going to get me filling out tons of paperwork over this guy. And you with a silenced piece. Put that damn thing away before some moron with a phone takes your picture!"

Ferguson had never been spoken to like that, and certainly not by any woman. But Rubio looked the type who could back up her words, so he let it go and re-holstered his gun. Rubio then left to go deal with Ian, who was still standing in the street yelling "ASSHOLE!" to the 163.

"Freeze right where you're at," yelled one of Rubio's agents to Ian.

Ian's lone chance of escape was gone. A sudden drop in his energy level brought on by the fear of going to jail, plus a low sugar drop, brought Ian to his knees. He put his hands on top of his head and waited on the inevitable, which came seconds later. Agents next searched his pockets where his room key was found. A tall pale-skinned fellow with a British accent is who got him back to his feet and headed back to room #114.

"Well, Wolfe old boy; we finally get to meet, eh mate?"

Ian was by then surrounded by agents. "You all don't have to crowd me, you know," said Ian. "It's not like I'm going to grow wings and fly away." It was when the wind blew open Ferguson's coat and revealed his silenced piece that Ian wished he *could* grow wings and fly.

Chapter 43

Ian went from a high mania to

outright depression in seconds. He felt the worst anxiety ever when being brought roughly to his feet while handcuffed.

"You don't have to pull me so hard, agent. I promise I'm not going to run." This just got the Brit pushing Ian towards the motel.

"Oh, I know you ain't running, mate, because if you do, I'll shoot you right in the back. I don't care. Now let's just get back to your room, so we can talk." To Ian's left was tech agent Lloyd wanting to know about his passcodes, passwords, and security algorithms to the Jenna laptop. Lloyd told him she was going to tear apart the laptop soon as they were in the room and she wanted those codes so that tearing apart the laptop would be easier. But instead of answering her, Ian keyed in on his motel manager buddy sitting in the back of the squad car. He mouthed the word "sorry" while being pushed past the car.

Ian's nerves were shot. The numbing effect from the chill had left his skin clammy and cold with just the long sleeve shirt to keep him warm, which wasn't keeping him warm at all.

It seemed to take forever to get back to the motel, but they finally did get there. Once in the room, Ferguson shoved Ian hard into the one lounge chair in the room, while Lloyd went immediately to the table to begin examining the Jenna laptop. She would next start extracting the hard drive once finding nothing incriminating on the screen.

It took a few minutes for Ian to feel any warmth from the heating vent, even though it was right near him. Out in the hall, the police activity surrounding Ian's room had gotten the attention of a few of the motel guests. Rubio's agents shooed them all away.

Agent Lloyd had the hard drive in her hand when asking Ian, "What am I going to find on this thing?"

Rubio waved agents away from the door before coming to stand over Ian. "You going to answer my agent?"

Ian stayed silent.

"Oh, so you want to play silent, huh? Well, I would certainly advise against that, Mr. Suarez."

"Call me Ian."

"Okay then, Ian; so let's see if what I tell you now will get you to talk." Rubio stepped away to emphasis her delivery. "All your blogger friends, those you most chat with, are right now being visited by agents. Some are going to jail, thanks to you. What do you think of that? Oh, but that's right, you're not speaking. I guess I'll just have to have agent Lloyd here post that you and Mike St. Donovan were actually planning something far worse than just a boycott *during* your boycott."

"Is this your good cop/bad cop routine?" asked Ian. "Because if it is, it sucks."

Rubio pointed to Ferguson, who had just tossed onto the bed his bag from the Dollar Store. From the bag he took out three flags, a Cuban flag, an American flag, and an Irish flag. From a folder he had brought from Rubio's Excursion, he took out photocopies of the Declaration of Independence, the Constitution, and the Bill of Rights. Even Rubio was a little stunned by Ferguson's props.

The last thing Ian saw while the Brit was setting out his props was his holstered silenced sidepiece.

"Yes, well," continued Rubio, "this here is agent Ferguson. Ferguson came all the way from London just for you, Ian, and as you've already seen, he isn't too thrilled to be here."

An incoming text to Rubio's phone interrupted her. While she read her text, Ferguson spoke. "You can forget all about your little boycott cause it ain't happening."

"So, I say again," interrupted Lloyd, while holding out the hard drive, "what am I going to find on this thing?"

"Nothing! Nothing is what you're going to find on that hard drive," said Ian in a raised voice. "You'll find the same stuff you'll find on any store-bought hard drive . . . an operating system."

Ian turned from Lloyd to look directly at Ferguson. "So why would you come all the way from London for me?" But Ferguson, too, was suddenly distracted by an incoming text to his phone. Both messages were pertaining to Ian. Ferguson got to reading his too, just as Rubio finished reading hers.

"Say, Ferguson," said Rubio, "you mind meeting me out in the hall when you're done reading your text? There are some things we need to go over." Rubio looked at Lloyd while pointing at Ian, "You watch him until I get back." To Ian, she said, "Don't you even *think* to give my agent a hard time," as Rubio walked to the door, ". . . and tell agent Lloyd whatever it is she needs to know about your hard drive. It will go better for you if you do."

"Well then let me begin by telling you this," started Ian, "I want my lawyer before I do any more talking."

"We'll talk about that when I return," answered Rubio.

"No, let's talk about it now."

"No, Ian, it doesn't work that way." Ferguson had just finished his text, laid out his photocopies, and then followed Rubio out.

Rubio pointed two of her agents to guard the room door as she and Ferguson walked further down the hall so as not to be overheard. Their discussion would be over how Eye-for-an-Eye was to end.

Back in the room, Ian was feeling weird vibes from the flags and documents lying on the bed, this while Rubio and Ferguson were getting into a heated debate over the Ian issue.

"No, Ferguson, you're wrong. I don't have to agree with any of it."

"But it's *your* people who have us a boat already fueled and ready to go. So what's the problem?"

"The problem is I don't see why we have to kill the man."

"Well blimey hell, agent Rubio; you can't go changing the rules now. My text said you're a boat person. Who knows? Maybe that's why they picked you. But it's too late in the game to go changing your mind now. I ain't waiting any longer to do this fellow in. Seven years is enough. You know this. So let's get cracking."

"Don't patronize me, you limey fuck! We're talking about a U.S. citizen here."

"Well bugger that, eh?" They were suddenly interrupted by Lloyd, who had come hurrying from the room to find them in their heated discussion. "Uh, sorry to interrupt you, boss, but there's a problem with his hard drive."

"What problem?"

"There's some safety encryption uploaded by a friend of his in Central Florida. If I try opening more of his files, I might lose all his info. I really need to check his drive back in my office." Ferguson chanced lighting a cigarette while the two women talked. He drew deep on his fag as Rubio hurried back to #114.

"**I**an."

"Yes."

"So nice to see you wanting to be social. That's good." Rubio sat on the bed across from him. "Agent Lloyd tells me there might be a problem with your hard drive."

"First, it's not my hard drive. The thing came with the laptop."

"You aren't hiding stuff on your drive that you wouldn't want us to find out, are you? Is that maybe why you had your drive encrypted by your friend?"

"It was a security program she installed, and no, I'm not hiding anything."

"Sure you don't have any schematics or plans that you're trying to hide? Your friend Missouri Mike had stuff on his computer."

"I wouldn't know the first thing about Mike's computer."

"Come now, Ian; you run a site that calls for a revolution . . . see where I'm going with this?"

"Then you got my site all wrong."

"Whatever."

"Look agent, I only know Mike through my website. We've been meaning to meet, but we never got the chance. I know nothing about his computer, nor of him for that matter. The only thing you'll find on my drive is my writing stuff."

"So my agent's not going to find anything incriminating on your hard drive? Nothing that'll keep us working overtime, this being New Year's Eve and all?"

"Only my writing stuff. Swear."

"What about those payback videos of yours?"

"What about them?"

Ian started to get up from his chair, but got pushed right back by Rubio. "Stay seated, Ian. I just want to know if you're a homegrown terrorist or something."

"I'm not a homegrown anything. I just run a site. That's it. So now, when do I get to see my lawyer? I don't think I should be saying any more without my lawyer present."

Rubio played deaf to his request. "So there's no chemical diagrams or stuff like that on your hard drive? In one of your files, maybe?"

"Agent, you're talking to a guy who's never even been able to grow a beard!"

"Hey Ian, *you're* the one running chats with a famous microbiologist."

"Yeah, and one who sells a massive amount of books."

"My point exactly."

In through the door came Ferguson with two NMB cops following behind him. "These uniformed yanks here say they've come to transport our bloke."

Rubio came from the bed and stopped the cops from reaching for Ian. "Forget it guys. We're taking him in ourselves. We're not done questioning him."

Ferguson gave a smirk to Rubio and said, "I was kinda hoping we were."

Rubio ordered the room cleared. She granted Lloyd her request for going back to the office, plus telling Lloyd to take the troops back with her. She and Ferguson would bring in Ian themselves.

Ina felt really weird about seeing the room empty except for him, Rubio and Ferguson.

As soon as the door closed behind Lloyd, Rubio went right at Ferguson. "This Eye-for-an-Eye is bullshit!"

Ferguson was taken a little by her anger.

"Agent Rubio, please, just let me take me pictures and we're gone."

"All this man's guilty of is running a stupid website," said Rubio angrily while pointing at Ian. "Yeah, he's probably a pain in the ass, maybe, probably, sure, but we're already shutting down his site. What more do you want?"

Ferguson smiled when hearing her ask that. "There's still the thing about his old man."

"His old man? But that was his old man, not him!" Rubio still spoke angrily. "This is bullshit over his old man and you guys in London, you hear me? I say we take him before the judge and let the judge deal with him." Ian sat with mouth agape the whole time while hearing Rubio and Ferguson's exchange.

"Told you before, agent Rubio; you can't go changing the rules just because you don't like the game." Ferguson gathered up his props and moved towards Ian while speaking to Rubio. "Especially this late in the game. We got our orders. But if it's any consolation, just look at the chaos our man here has started with that website of his. I mean really, agent Rubio, throwing out furniture? Throwing a computer at the CEO of a major computer company; then crashing his car over lack of service? *Really?*"

"It's *your* people who have a thing for this man because of some Eye-for-an-Eye bullshit."

"Yeah, but it's *your* people who allowed *me* to be *here* for this bullshit, so game on. Beside, he's Wolfe's son, for crying out loud. Proof of that is in his site. Blood runs thick in these here Wolves. Now just imagine our boy here with a button in his hand. You know he's got friends who know about making buttons with vest packs."

Ian's face turned to shock when hearing that. "Hey! What the hell kind of craziness is that?"

"Rubio," continued Ferguson, as if Ian weren't even in the room, "even *your* people think this fellow here might have ties with some of those old Cuban cronies from G2." Ferguson looked to Ian for a reaction to that.

"Cronies at G2? What the hell you talking about?" Ian started up from the chair and again got pushed back down.

"I even bet this wanker knows something about them missing Iranian fuel rods. Cuba would be a perfect place to hide them. They've hidden stuff like that there before." Ferguson looked at Ian. "Yep. You being Cuban and all, you probably still have folks communicating with you from over there, don't you?"

"You're crazy."

Ferguson ran his middle finger slow across his throat. "You're as good as hung, Wolfe. You're finished."

Ian couldn't take it anymore. He went to stand, and again got shoved back in his seat.

"What the hell is this!" yelled Ian at Rubio. "A new way of scaring folks? A boat? Fuel rods? My being Cuban? I want my lawyer and I want him now!" Ian looked at Ferguson and angrily said, "The only thing I know about Cuba is that my mother and brother drowned trying to escape it! You must have missed that in your report." Ian ended with saying "moron" under his breath, to then start struggling with his handcuffs while wanting to stand again.

Ferguson took in a deep breath before shoving Ian so hard back in his chair that it almost toppled over.

"Stay seated, you fool. No one's asked you up yet." Ferguson looked at Rubio. "Can I take me pictures now? And remember, we got that thing with his site going offline at 6 o'clock and I'd like to be on a plane home by then. And you still got his Missouri Mike buddy to deal with. But we really gotta finish here."

"Finish what?" yelled Ian.

Ferguson surprised Ian with, "I bet you're a real shit, just like your old man was." (Ferguson's shit sound like *kite*. This was Ferguson's way of psyching himself up for the kill.) "All that terror *shit* that your old man was involved in; your mom and him and all their plans; some of that must have rubbed off on you. I bet you and your Missouri buddy have shared a conversation or two about wiring up vests and trucks and stuff, eh Wolfe?" Ferguson enjoyed aggravating Ian and it looked it. "Hell, if S/A hadn't put a bullet in your old man's head, I bet his rampage would still be going on. But hey, I'm just here to make sure your breed ends."

Rubio stopped the antagonizing with, "Enough already, Ferguson. Quit talking foolish. Ian here wasn't even born when his old man was doing his bombing stuff." Ian again tried to stand, and again got shoved back into his chair by Ferguson.

"Bombing stuff? His old man wasn't bombing stuff, agent Rubio. He was blowing up everyone he could, including his own father who was asleep when crazy fucking wanker Wolfe blew him to pieces! And then to wind up in Cuba sipping umbrella drinks with the bearded ones? Fuck that shit." Ferguson tapped his holster. "What I should do is just pop Wolfie boy here in the head and be done with it. One little pop that no one hears and we're through."

"Well, then I guess that's why the boat, eh? So you don't pop here."

"Fair enough, agent Rubio. Now can you at least help me take me pics?"

It had gone beyond the surreal for Ian. He looked pleadingly at Rubio and asked, "I really would like to see a lawyer right about now."

"The only one you're going to see is your maker," answered Ferguson for her.

"Why's he doing all the talking?" asked Ian of Rubio. "Why's he intentionally trying to screw with my head?"

Ferguson had meanwhile reached into his pocket to get out his handcuff keys. "You listen good, boyo," he said to Ian. "I'm going to release you of those handcuffs so you can hold up me flags and papers." Ian took in the copies of the Declaration of Independence, Bill of Rights, and Constitution.

"What the hell are all these flags and papers about, anyway? I'm not holding up anything without my lawyer being present."

"Save your breath," said Ferguson, while lifting Ian roughly to his feet. Ferguson worked off the cuffs and left Ian massaging his wrists while handing over his phone to Rubio. "Click on camera and do me the honors, will ya Rubio?"

"I'm not going to hold anything up," repeated Ian.

Ferguson grabbed Ian by the neck and gave him a hard squeeze.

"You fucking wanker; you'll hold up me flags and papers and you'll like doing it."

"What the hell is it with this nonsense? And why do you need me to hold up these documents?"

Rubio had backed away a few steps so she could get a better angle at Ian holding up Ferguson's props.

"You just stand just like that boyo, and don't move, or I'll pop you one. Swear I will. Those flags and papers are going to win me 200 quid, so fucking hold up me stuff or I'll crack your skull wide open."

But the flags, Bill of Rights, Declaration of Independence, and Constitution weren't so easy to hold with wrists sore from the tightness of the cuffs. Ian dropped two of the flags while Ferguson was getting him to hold his stuff just so. Dropping the flags angered Ferguson. "I'm going to sock ya solid, put me boot up your arse, you don't hold me things up right. I'll put them cuffs on extra tight, if you don't do me right, boyo."

"This has to be the weirdest arrest I've ever seen."

"Shut your bloody trap and stand still!" Ferguson turned to Rubio and said, "Go ahead and take his picture." But Ian right then let slip one of the photocopies from his hand.

Ferguson became enraged with that. "Bloody fool!" Ferguson grabbed Ian by the throat again. "Damn Wolfe." He let go of Ian's throat so he could pick from the floor the Bill of Rights. "Like father, like son. Can't get anything right."

That's when Ian struck.

Ian waited until Ferguson was bent over picking up the photocopied document to kick him in the ass and sent him sprawling to the floor. He thought about going for the door, but wanted to at least land one solid punch on the man causing him so much grief, until he, too, was suddenly on his knees and bleeding.

Rubio had caught Ian on the side of the head with a high side-kick with her high-heeled shoes, nailing him on the side of the head. She kicked him hard enough to cut him deep on the temple. Ian went down bleeding.

Ferguson was infuriated for getting kicked in the ass by Ian. He hurried to grab Ian by the throat and lifted him to his feet while Ian was still woozy. "You bloody fool!" Ferguson, while still holding Ian by the throat, turned to Rubio and asked, "Did you take the picture?"

"No."

Ferguson again jammed his flags and documents into Ian's hands. With blood pouring down Ian's head, he told Rubio to hurry and take the picture.

Ferguson really wanted to squeeze the life out of Ian right after Rubio took the picture, with bloody documents and all, but Rubio held him off from hurting Ian by pushing him away while on her way to the bathroom to get a towel to wipe Ian's head clean.

Ferguson slapped Ian on the head anyway when putting on the cuffs.

Ian, still a bit disoriented, said, "Why do you need the cuffs if you've beaten me this way?"

"You were the one who got yourself beat, Wolfe." Ferguson squeezed tight the cuffs, and again grabbed Ian by the throat.

"Foolish Wolfe. It's going to be my pleasure to put you out to pasture." Rubio pushed Ferguson's arm away so she could get to Ian's head wound.

"Agent Rubio, why are you wasting your time cleaning up this fool?"

"I can't wait to see what my lawyer is going to say when seeing me this way," said Ian to Rubio. "You almost cracked my head open with your shoe."

"I forgot about my high heels. But you didn't give me much choice, Ian." She kept toweling him dry, the towel becoming red with blood. "Besides, I can't have you bleeding in my car."

The beeping in Ian's head started right then, louder than ever, leading him to ask Rubio, "You hear that beeping noise?"

"No." Rubio was too wrapped up in thinking of her cruise ship to worry about any beeping. She just wanted Ian's bleeding to stop so she could get him to her SUV without anyone taking a picture of their bleeding prisoner.

Ferguson got to checking his phone and seeing the picture Rubio took of Ian. He liked what he saw. It made him smile. "My mates at the pub are going to love this, his bleeding and all." His mates at his London hangout were actually going to hate paying up.

Rubio cared little about Ferguson's bet. She cared more about asking Ian a few questions before leaving room #114.

"So tell me something I don't already know about your friend Missouri Mike," Rubio was still holding the towel to his head, which she was planning to toss into the garbage as soon as the bleeding stopped. "I've got a SITREP on my desk that says your friend might be planning something big to hinder your boycott. You got anything to say to that?"

"I don't want to answer any more questions," said Ian.

Ian thought it strange that Rubio first removed the plastic trash liner from the room trashcan before dropping in the bloody towel and then putting back the liner.

Rubio pointed to Ferguson's props on the bed. Some of the papers had left bloodstains on the bed. "That was stupid of you, Ferguson. See if you can wash off some of that blood to break up some of the DNA trace. I don't want anything pointing to us being here." Ferguson begrudgingly did as asked.

"I thought tactics like these went out with the Nazis," said Ian, while being jostled to his feet by Rubio. But another incoming text stopped Rubio from getting Ian to the door.

This time it was Revenue's OJI Terrence from Atlanta wanting to know more about Ian's arrest. He had been checking through some of Homeland's revenue requisitions on future takedowns and noticed Ian's name on the list.

A call to Homeland's Miami office told him of Ian having been found. OJI Terrence was wanting to know if any money had been found with Ian.

Rubio thought Terrence's LocEmAllUp.gov domain name was rather crazy. "Uh, Ian . . ."

"You can go back to calling me Mr. Suarez. I don't particularly like a person who bashes my head open and thinks we're on a first name basis."

"Enough with the pity party. That was your fault that I had to . . ."

"Pity party?"

"Look, I got some Revenue guy wanting to know if you've got money stashed here. You should best fess up if you do, cause you know if housekeeping finds it, they'll keep it."

Rubio noticed Ian's cut had begun to bleed again.

"Only money I have, I gave to my girlfriend, who, by the way, I'm pretty sure is wondering why I haven't contacted her yet."

Rubio pointed him to the door. "You don't have to worry about your girlfriend Cathy." Ferguson was done trying to clean the blood marks on the bed. He more smudged than cleaned the blood. Rubio just made a face when pointing everyone to the door while also texting Atlanta's OJI.

"Why do you say I shouldn't have to worry about Cathy, agent Rubio?" Ian sounded genuinely worried.

"Because we arrested your girlfriend earlier. She's on her way to lockup as we speak." Rubio heard Ian breath a deep sigh of misery while being pushed to the door by Ferguson while she was still texting. "Hey Ferguson; no more rough stuff with the man, okay? Just get him to my truck."

"Yeah. Sure." Ferguson pushed Ian out into the hall anyway.

Rubio waited until they were gone before sending her text.

From: SAC Rubio/Miami

To: LocEmAllUp.gov/OJI Terrence.

Subject: Ian Red Suarez

Mr. Suarez accidentally drowned while attempting to escape. A DHS report will be forwarded to your office tomorrow. We are still trying to recover the body. No money or valuables were found in his possession.

Rubio next put her phone in silent mode. She didn't want to be bothered anymore by someone who would use LocEmAllUp.gov as a domain name.

Chapter 44

Riding in Rubio's Excursion was

like the ride from hell. Her recently reconditioned leather seats was part of the problem. Her driving was another. Not having put a seatbelt on Ian is what had him sliding all over the backseat. Her erratic swerving in and out of traffic only made his sliding more painful. Through it all, the beeping in his head got louder, which just made the ride even worse.

"Damn it, agent Rubio; either slow down or strap me in. You're killing me back here, and these cuffs are cutting off my circulation."

"Fuck your circulation, Wolfe," said Ferguson, still miffed over being kicked in the ass.

Rubio blew through another red light.

"You're going to kill us, agent." Thankfully, Rubio's blue dash bubble was continuing to do what it was meant to do, get traffic out of the way. Another sudden lane change got Ian sliding again.

Rubio eyed him through her rear view mirror. "Those payback videos of yours are quite something," she said.

Ferguson interjected with, "And would you believe *all* the idiots he's got watching that stuff?"

Ian chanced getting closer to them as Ferguson talked.

"You want to tell me what was with me holding those flags and stuff?" Ian was tasting blood in his mouth just as Ferguson shoved him back in his seat. "Stay back there, Wolfe. I don't want no wolf bite from you." Ferguson smiled at his silly joke. "And you holding those flags and papers just won me 200 quid."

"Making money off my misery? I don't get it."

"You wanted a revolution, right? You're all about payback? Well, me pub mates thought if you refused to hold those bloody freedom documents, they would make their money back. Sort of their own payback, if you will. So thanks for bagging me that 200 quid, Wolfe."

Rubio's two-way radio crackled to life. "Lord, not another interruption."

It was tech agent Lloyd again. Rubio picked up her handset and hit receive. "Go ahead, Megan."

"I'm pretty sure you want the latest Intel on Dr. Warrick."

"What you got, Megan?"

"Dr. Warrick's a very sick woman, boss."

"Sick? How so?"

The call caught Ian's attention.

"Terminally ill, boss. Cancer, specifically. The woman's in stage four and rejecting remission. Doesn't look like she's gonna be around much longer, boss."

"Well, damn shame that. Might be a reason why she's so involved with our Ian here."

"What you mean, boss?"

"You know, like nothing-to-lose, let's write books about how bad it can get."

"That's quite an imagination you have, agent Rubio," said Ian, from the back seat.

"Well, thanks for the update, Megan. Now let the troops know I'll be seeing them all later at the party, but I'll be indisposed until then. Got it?"

"You got it, boss."

"If you need me, text me. But try not to need me."

"Roger that, boss." Rubio was done with fellow agents for a while.

Ferguson took from his pocket a device that looked similar to a voice recorder. But it wasn't a voice recorder. Ian knew he was sunk when seeing the 'Davis Electronics' logo stamped on the side of the device that Ferguson put to his mouth.

"So, Ian my love, we finally meet." Ferguson let out a loud laugh that sounded shrill and high-pitched when going through the pricey pitch vocalizer used for pitch-setting vocals in recording studios.

"Oh, Ian," Ferguson continued to speak through the Davis device, "and this whole time you never once mentioned me. What a scoundrel you are, my love. And if you're wondering where I got the name Jenna from," Ferguson removed his mouth from the device and said in his own voice, "from me mum, stupid!"

Ian hadn't much to say on that. Ian hadn't much to say on anything anymore. The beeping in his head was driving him crazy, and the laughter coming from the shrill device was making him even crazier.

"Look, Rubio. Look at our Wolfe." Ferguson again removed his mouth from the device to talk to Rubio. "Our Wolfe's at a loss for words. Can you believe that?" He put his mouth back to the device, turned to Ian, and said, "All's fair in love and war, me love. Now how 'bout a kiss, eh?"

The shrill laughter even grated on Rubio.

It was seeing Ian's defeated look in her mirror that got Rubio saying, "Enough already, Ferguson. Stop it. You've had your fun."

Her flashing dash light continued getting cars to move.

Her next erratic lane change got them onto the Julia Tuttle Causeway. With tires squealing and her horn blaring she managed to squeeze from the onramp into the emergency lane and all the way to the left lane, the speed lane, although not much speeding was being done because traffic was so heavy. Soon as she could though, she stepped on the gas and got roaring again.

To his left, Ian could see a long line of cruise ships at the Port of Miami waiting to load and unload passengers.

"I was supposed to be on one of those cruise ships," said Rubio, while angling her mirror for a better look at Ian. "But thanks to you, I'm stuck here. Hell, now I'm not feeling so bad for hitting you."

Ian broke eye contact with her and spoke while seeing the Herald building coming into view. "I just want to see my lawyer, that's all."

Rubio looked at Ferguson and said, "Fire up my iPad and see what's going on with his site." Ferguson took her iPad from under the seat and next showed Ian that his website was already offline.

"Offline for good, mate." Ferguson smiled big for Ian when saying that.

"Why this treatment, huh?" Ian was doing everything he could to keep it together, especially when seeing the last exit to the federal lockup go by. "Hey, agent Rubio, wasn't that the exit?"

"You asked why this treatment? Well, your payback videos and boycott is why, Ian," said Rubio.

"So, we're back to Ian now." Ian tried scooting closer to Rubio, but got pushed back by Ferguson. "Let the lady drive, Wolfe."

"Your site's the reason for this treatment, Ian."

"Hey, so Wolfe," Ferguson was back to badgering him again, "what you think of my little vocal device, eh, pende . . . pende . . ." Ferguson looked to Rubio to help him with his Spanish. "What was it you said he was when we arrested him?"

"Pendejo. It means like idiot or asshole."

"Oh yeah, Wolfe; you're a pendejo, alright." Ferguson looked right at Ian and said, "One *big* pendejo."

"Quit talking to me. And quit calling me Wolfe. My name's Suarez. S-u-a-r . . ."

"Shut the fuck up, Wolfe. You're a Wolfe through and through, and don't go forgetting it, either."

Rubio roared down the Key Biscayne exit and ended up idling impatiently on the US1 light. Soon as the light changed, she roared into the Key Biscayne toll plaza.

Her direction definitely had Ian's attention.

She showed her badge to the toll booth operator who waved her through.

"So, what do you and your friend Dr. Warrick usually talk about when *not* online?" Rubio surprised Ian with her question.

"Why in the hell are we all the way out here, agent Rubio? I don't know of any court building being way out here."

"I'll ask again; what do you and Dr. Warrick talk about . . ."

"I'm pretty sure you know what we talk about." Ian had his angry tone again.

"Hey, don't get mad with me. *You're* the one breaking the law."

"What law have I broken?"

"Several so far."

"Several? I write and post my writings on *my* website. Dr. Warrick, she writes and posts *her* writings in *her* books. She does a little blogging on my site, but so what. Nothing we do is against our constitutional right to do. Or have we lost the right to free speech in America?"

"Sounds more like his daddy when he speaks," added Ferguson.

"So, what about my lawyer?" Ian ignored Ferguson's comment. "My lawyer doesn't live on Key Biscayne." Ian was starting to sound desperate.

"You know that on paper you and your friends, like Dr. Warrick and this Missouri Mike fellow, all are ideal candidates for wanting to start big trouble in America. But you probably already know that." Rubio was hurrying to get to the docks.

"What big trouble would we want to cause?" Ian was back to fidgeting with his cuffs again.

"You really need me to spell it out for you, Ian?"

"Yeah, spell it out for me, agent Rubio."

"Let's start with you being fined $20 million dollars back in the day. And what about all that government confiscation? Who better to carry a grudge than you?"

"And forget your girlfriend, mate. She sold you down the river already," added Ferguson.

"Let that go, Ferguson," said Rubio, back to looking at Ian in the rearview. "He's got plenty to worry about without his precious Cathy. I still want to know why the revolution."

"Chip off the old block is why," answered Ferguson for Ian.

Ian made as if looking behind him. "You all talking to me?"

Rubio's response was to cut her wheel and send Ian slamming into the right side door.

"Ouch!"

"That's for being a smart ass."

And that's also when the Homeland boat came into view.

Ian saw Ferguson go for his vocal device again.

"Oh lookie there, Ian. It's boat ride time."

"You're a psycho, you know that?" But Ian was cringing inside at seeing such a large speedboat. His thinking was that they might take him to Guantanamo or something similar.

Ferguson noticed Ian struggling with the cuffs again. "Quit messing with those, Wolfe. You're having those on even when you board the boat, hear me?"

Ian was about to say something to Ferguson when seeing Rubio make for her own voice recorder after shutting down her truck.

"Oh great," said Ian when seeing her holding her device to her mouth. "What does yours do?"

"Not to worry, Ian. I got no games to play. This is just a straight up voice recorder."

"And what's with the boat? Part of this psychobabble treatment?"

"What about your friend, Missouri Mike?"

"I thought you were finished asking me about Mike."

"Do you know where he's hiding?"

"No."

"You can get me to slow this process down if you start giving me something on your buddy, Mike St. Donovan. Or any other buddy you think I need to know about."

"You've been eavesdropping on me long enough to know all my buddies."

"What about those Northern Blue characters who got into that shootout with police up in Northern Missouri? Do you know any of them? Or those who helped Mike escape from his cabin?"

"He probably did that on his own, and no, I know no one. Look agent Rubio, I'm done talking, alright?" The beeping in his head had grown so loud that he could barely hear Rubio.

Ferguson had gotten out of the truck and made for Ian's door.

"You really need to tell agent Rubio whatever is it she wants to know, mate. After all, where you're going, you won't be needing any information."

"My friend Mike's hiding for the same reason I was hiding, so why would I want to give him up?"

"And what was the reason for your hiding? Remind me again?" asked Rubio, as she got out of the truck.

"I was hiding to protect my right to free speech, which you are apparently denying me anyway."

Rubio paused her recorder. "I might as well save my batteries, if that's what you're going to tell me. Now, you need to get out of my vehicle." Ferguson made a grab for Ian's legs, just as his cell phone rang.

Ian's fears grew exponentially when hearing Ferguson say into his phone, "Oh yeah, it's junior Wolfe alright. Oh yeah, got him right here. No, you just get my money ready for when I get back. Yeah, we got him cuffed. Uh-hmm . . . as we speak. Bollocks to that! You already got my pic. Read 'em and weep. Now get together me money, and because you're such good blokes, first round's on me." It was at that moment that the file bearing Ian Red Wolfe/Suarez's name was being deleted from multiple computers at multiple agencies.

Ian tried finding his quiet place. But Ferguson brought him back with a slap to the leg. "Come on, Wolfe. We need you to get out."

Rubio had turned her recorder back on before getting to Ian.

"So, what about your microbiologist friend? Cancer means she's another with nothing to lose, so have you two only been chatting, or planning?"

Ian slid away from her, which made him an easy grab for Ferguson. "Got you! Now let's go, mate."

He pulled out of Ferguson's grasp and then got grabbed by Rubio, who still wanted to talk. "My SITREP says you and Warrick might even be talking in code. Is that true?"

"What now, agent Rubio? More psychobabble? Now you think I'm a spy? *Really?*" Rubio held Ferguson off from grabbing Ian, as she wanted him to continue. "Agent Rubio, if you've read my site, then you know I'm an open book to everybody. I've got nothing to hide from anybody. Well, maybe from Revenue, but that's only because they're such a pain in the ass." Hearing Ferguson moving in made Ian turn around and kick Ferguson squarely in the chest. But that still didn't stop Ferguson from grabbing at his legs and still pulling him out.

"This psychobabble's gotta stop, agent Rubio! Now get me to a lawyer, a judge, anybody, but stop this crap!"

While getting pulled from the truck, Ian slammed his head on the running board. It made him bite his tongue and caused him a new bruise on his head, to add to his cut temple, swollen eye, and hands gone numb from cuffs that were too tight. He was on the ground and looking up at Ferguson when hearing Ferguson say, "End of the line for you, mate."

Beyond Ferguson's feet bobbed the 51-foot confiscated drug runner Donzi boat with the word HOMELAND on the side.

Ian gave Rubio a pleading look. "Why am I here? This can't be because of my site." Suddenly Ian began to yell, "HELP ME! SOMEBODY HELP ME!" His yelling was cut short by Ferguson putting his shoe over his mouth.

The cuffs made it easy to lift Ian back to his feet.

Ferguson's manhandling of Ian made it impossible for Ian to run, while Rubio continued deaf to his torment. Her focus was on taking advantage of there being no witnesses to see them leave with Ian on the boat.

Ian managed one last kick at Ferguson, but it wasn't enough to stop Ferguson from tossing him in the speedboat.

"Quit kicking me, you arse. Ain't no one out here gonna help you."

"So help me, if I get a hold of you . . ."

"You ain't gonna get a hold of me Wolfe, so keep still while I go untie this boat."

"Kiss my . . ." Rubio grabbed him from behind to hold him in place while Ferguson untied the million and a half dollar boat.

The cuffs won out in the end.

Rubio found the boat keys right where her text told her to find them, underneath the dash in a magnetic key box. She had the triple 850's fired up and ready to go by the time Ferguson jumped in once pushing Ian into the middle seat of the triple seat cockpit.

"Here's where your revolution ends, Wolfe," Ferguson said mockingly.

Rubio expertly pulled the speedboat away from the dock.

They were headed to the no wake zone when Ferguson asked Rubio, "Why don't you ask him something about his father's connections in Cuba? More specifically, I'd like to hear stuff about when he was a kid, growing up with a bomber father in the house." Ferguson turned to Ian and punched him in the shoulder. "You know; like stuff about Operation Tiburón? Or about those missing fuel rods? Come on Wolfe, talk. You see Rubio's about ready to shove this boat to full throttle. Best say something, mate."

"You really are an ass, you know that Ferguson? I was 14 when my mother got me out of Cuba. What 14-year-old kid do you know's a spy, huh? You must be on some hallucinogenics or something." This angered Ferguson enough to grind his knuckles into the cut on Ian's temple. Ferguson got it to bleed again, but try as he might, he still couldn't get Ian to cry out. Ian held his tongue while seeing stars from the pain, and fighting a wave of nausea that came from Ferguson's grinding knuckles.

"Soviets train sleepers younger than 14, Wolfe. You don't fool me." Ferguson wiped his bloody knuckles off on Ian's shirt.

"Take these cuffs off me and we'll see who's going to be fooling who." Ian was determined to fight even with handcuffs on, so long as it slowed his nightmare down. "I dare you to take these cuffs off me; see if you hit me again." But Rubio's throttling up the triple engines and slamming them into their seats made fighting a moot point. Ahead was nothing but ocean.

Rubio kept the triple engines roaring at 70 knots for 45 minutes before deciding to throttle down. By then, they were in 2,000 feet of water, which was where she wanted them to be. There wasn't another boat or ship in sight.

Ian waited for the engines to quiet so he could speak. "You know lots of folks are probably wondering where I'm at." He tried putting some bravado in his voice, but it was hard. He saw Rubio go for her recorder again while putting the boat in idle. "So again with the recorder, eh agent Rubio? What do you want me to say now?"

This time, the recorder wasn't for him.

"This is special agent-in-charge Carmen Rubio of the Miami district 6 field office. Today is 31 December and the time is 1420. I've been charged with notification order A3/grade 7 on one Ian Red Suarez. Ian is the founder of the website: Quit Your Bitching and Start the Revolution. Ian is also the son of the late eighties bomber, Ian Red Wolfe. My transport orders are covered under the same A3/grade 7 order. Onboard with me today on KB Homeland boat 11/11 is London's S/A rep, agent Landers Ferguson. Agent Ferguson has been assigned the completion order to this Eye-for-an-Eye mission." Ian knew right then that his end had come when seeing Rubio hand over her recorder so she could get voice recognition on Ferguson.

Chapter 45

While the boat idled, it was slapped hard by waves. They had to wait for the 51-foot boat to stop rocking so they could get Ian from his seat and onto his feet.

Rubio noticed him eying her gun. "Now really Ian, how are you going to manage that with your hands cuffed, huh?" Seeing Ferguson removing his wristwatch got more of Ian's attention.

"And does the name 'el Magico' mean anything to you, Ian?" Ian was still eyeing Ferguson and didn't get the gist of Rubio's question.

"Huh? El Magico? Who's that?"

"Your mom's first husband."

"You mean Col. Morales? Oh, please don't tell me I'm out here because of him, too?"

"Your mom sure knew how to pick 'em."

"That was a long time ago, agent Rubio. And regardless of what you think about my mother . . ." Ian pointed with his head to the ocean beyond, ". . . she's still buried somewhere out here, for trying to escape a system that doesn't seem much different than the one you're working for."

"Spare me."

Ferguson grabbed Ian and lifted him from behind. Ferguson was strong enough to lift Ian clear over the rear rail, to which Ian surprisingly didn't struggle. "So this is how it ends? You two armed thugs tossing me in the ocean?" Ian gave Rubio one last pleading look. "Well, at least tell Cathy that I love her."

"Why would you love a girl who sold you out?" Ferguson's barb wasn't necessary, but that's how Ferguson liked to play.

"What will happen to Cathy, agent Rubio?" asked Ian.

"We're keeping her on ice until she sees the error of her ways."

"Whatever that means. Well go ahead and dunk me then. I've been here before. No biggie. But remember, I still go out the winner, since it took the two of you busting me up and then handcuffing . . ." the rest of his words were drowned by saltwater.

He couldn't believe he was right back in the ocean again. Upon surfacing, he saw Ferguson reaching for his gun. He worked miraculously hard to get himself back underwater and kicking away from the boat. Ian managed to swim dozens of yards away from the Homeland boat before needing air. It was impossible to control his buoyancy with his hands still cuffed, while hating to think what it would feel like being shot, what the pain from a bullet would feel like, or how quickly the blood would attract the big ocean predators. He'd seen them before. He didn't want to see them again.

But no shot ever came.

He popped his head out of the water and watched instead Rubio rev the boat before pulling away. But she wasn't leaving. She had just thought of a better way of getting rid of him.

Ian caught the wake of the retreating speedboat full in the face as Rubio went to lining him up for a high speed rundown. With his one good eye, he saw Rubio turn the boat around and slam the throttle hard forward. The power of the triple engines lifted the craft way in the air before settling back in the water and then aiming right at him.

A hundred yards separated the hull from his head. But instead of panicking or trying to swim underwater, Ian kicked up with his legs to show himself while yelling, "COME ON! BRING IT!"

"I think that pendejo's challenging you to run him over," said Ferguson, a bit surprised by Ian's actions.

That's when the sun did a funny thing. Something most unusual. The sun lit up the immediate area with a surreally bright light that resembled spotlights on a stage. The area of the ocean where Ian had been dumped in was the only area visited with such bright sunlight. Even the tops of the waves were filled with light. The roar of the triple engines was what ruined the beautiful moment.

Ian got to kicking again, taunting them to hit him . . . when suddenly bumped by something in his back. He turned and saw a dead body appear from the water and go floating past him. A second body popped from the water right in front of him. A third bloated body bumped him on the side as it, too, floated by, a half face staring at him. Ian was horrified to see the ocean releasing itself of those from within the two halves of the 13-de-Marzo tugboat. This ruined his martyrdom moment.

Ferguson was thinking a few extra quid when aiming his cameraphone back at Ian (while Rubio was just then thinking how best to word her promotional demands after their kill order was complete) . . . when they both saw Ian go under.

The last thing Ian saw, before letting himself be taken home, was the word HOMELAND go roaring overhead. His last thought, before giving in to the hands that he'd known since birth, was to think how easy it would have been to fill his last Mind journal with this, his final event. Ian surrendered to the joy of knowing that he was being taken home by his mother and brother.

Except . . .

Epilogue

The beeping is what woke him.

But it wasn't in his head. The beeping was all around him.

He hadn't a clue where he was. He thought he was alone, but he felt like he wasn't.

Through the haze, he saw a face staring down at him, and as the haze cleared, he saw it was the face of a young woman, a woman he didn't know, looking quite worried. Then he noticed the EMS uniform. This did not bode well with him, as the beeping continued in the background.

Kendra was celebrating her first full month with EMS team #1019. But the excitement of her first month was cut short when Ian was brought in from the golf course. Lying on the gurney before her was her biggest challenge yet. His burns alone made for an uphill battle to keep him alive. Traffic due to the storm was also making it tough to reach the JMH/Trauma Center, where a team of care specialists were waiting on Ian. The objective was to get him there in time.

Kendra was extremely cautious at cutting away the clothes and avoiding the melded skin of his upper body. But there was melded skin to deal with that was blocking his airway, also. She cut away at that, which did at least get him to stop wheezing. She called for help from her team leader, Ray, who was riding up front and radioing in Ian's vitals. Kendra needed help to do a tracheotomy, but Ray was still busy with the vitals. Kendra cut into his trachea and began shoving in the breathing tube. She still needed Ray's help, who finally hurried to help her. Ray first squeezed his nose shut to block out the stench of burnt flesh before helping with the tube.

Yet no sooner had Kendra gotten the lungs to clear, then the heart began to slow . . . slower . . . slower still until . . . flat lining again.

Third time in 12-minutes.

Kendra re-jelled her paddles and reset the charge for a higher voltage from the cardiac defibrillator machine.

ZAPPPPPPPPPP! Nothing.

She dialed up more juice.

ZAAAAAAAAPPPPPPPPPP!

Her face washed over with relief when seeing the monitors all start to beep again.

What she hadn't expected was for Ian's eyes to pop open!

His eyes suddenly popping open caused her to drop her jell-smeared paddles onto her new scrubs. But she was at least happy to see his eyes open, until her penlight confirmed there was no life behind the blank stare. She had little time for pondering, as Ian's heart began to slow again.

"Ray, I'm losing him again. I'm going to up the juice some more."

"Forget it, Kendra. You've already shocked him three times. That's enough."

"Then I'll hit him with adrenaline." Kendra didn't wait to get an okay when hurrying to open the pre-packaged syringe that resembled a small bike pump, which she then stuck right into Ian's heart.

She got the intended result. She got his chest heaving and his heart starting again. The machines were back to beeping loudly and steady again. Kendra replaced her frown with a smile.

Outside the truck, thunder boomed. Rain pelted the top of EMS truck #1019 while in route to JMH/Trauma. The noise of the storm hid from Kendra the first sign of Ian's breathing getting shallower, his heart beginning to fade again, the beeping growing fainter, until flat-lining again.

It was Ray who reached over and stopped Kendra from getting the paddles ready. "I'm calling it."

"But Ray, I can bring him back!"

"No, you can't, Kendra. He's a goner. Can't you see that? I'm calling it." Ray looked at his watch. "You've had him for thirteen minutes and nothing. I'm definitely calling it."

But I'm right here! Don't give up on me!

Besides his melded airway and damaged heart, the lightning had also caused Ian severe nerve damage. He had nerves fused together along his spine, which had numbed most of his neuron receptors, which was a good thing, since the pain would've been too hard to handle. But he could still see.

He tried wiggling his toes. Nothing.

He tried moving his fingers. Nothing.

He tried sitting up. Nothing.

Tried speaking. Out of the question.

All he could do was stare at the pretty young redhead trying fiercely to save him. That's when Ian caught a whiff of himself, the worst thing he'd ever smelled. *This must be what death smells like.* He heard the truck's siren get louder when coming under the JMH portico. The rain that poured off the portico splashed loudly atop the truck, muffling the sound of the rear doors opening.

Ian couldn't hear what Ray was saying. But he could read lips. What he read on Ray's lips wasn't good.

But I'm right here, damn it! Can't you see that?

"I'm writing this up as one heck of an effort on your part, Kendra."

"But Ray, his eyes!"

Yeah Ray. My eyes!

It was Ray who reached over and turned off the generator that powered the monitors, defibrillator, and the ventilator. That's when the beeping finally stopped, a beeping that had been following Ian for what seemed to him seven years.

But wait . . . . years? But if I'm here, then how long . . . and where's Cathy? She could explain this to me. Unless of course, this has all . . . **Oh no!**

Ian's enemy mind had finally revealed its true intent.

"You can't save them all, Kendra."

Tears started to well up in Kendra's eyes when seeing Ian being prepped for cold storage.

"But his eyes, Ray."

"You know that's a reaction to all the juice you gave him. This poor guy's had enough juice running through him to light up that course he was on." Trauma members had started to jump in back until stopped by Ray. "Slow it up, people. We got a goner here. We had him, but lost him. Kendra here's got the T.O.D. Looks like it's next of kin now."

What next of kin? I've got nobody. Ian's last moments on Earth was watching Ray pull the sheet over his face.

At that precise moment, while Ian was being wheeled to cold storage, the storm that struck him down and scared people to believing a tornado was about to descend from the clouds, suddenly began to ease. The clouds, once so thick that it had made the day look like night, were now allowing the first bits of sunlight to shine down upon the city and to shine down upon Ian's sheeted body right before being wheeled into the darkened halls of cold storage. Now the sun was making everything right-as-rain again.

"Ian was wrong to think he'd cheated me. I'd given him his chance when younger, much as many of you have gotten your chances. But you need to remember, that when I come a-knocking, it's time to go. Whether it's Ian, or whether it's you. Don't any of you go thinking you can cheat me now, you hear?"